THE

* A young woman discovers her boyfriend's fatal attraction to a lover who is perfect, cold, and dead.

* Trapped inside an asylum, a man prepares a chilling Last Supper.

* On the streets of Manhattan a chic club caters to the kinky tastes of the dead and beautiful.

*A suicidal writer recalls his experiences of war, women, bullfighting . . . and the living dead.

*At a rural bingo hall the newly risen assemble for rousing games twenty-four hours a day.

Plus fourteen other terrifying tales.

STILL DEAD
BOOK OF THE DEAD II

MORT CASTLE * CHAN McCONNELL * NANCY A. COLLINS * K. W. JETER * GLEN VASEY * JOHN SKIPP and CRAIG SPECTOR * DAN SIMMONS * SIMON McCAFFERY * ELIZABETH MASSIE * GAHAN WILSON * KATHE KOJA * GREGORY NICOLL * DOUG MORNINGSTAR and MAXWELL HART * POPPY Z. BRITE * ROBERTA LANNES * J. S. RUSSELL * BROOKS CARUTHERS * NANCY HOLDER * DOUGLAS E. WINTER

OTHER BANTAM TITLES
BY JOHN SKIPP AND CRAIG SPECTOR

THE LIGHT AT THE END
THE SCREAM
THE BRIDGE

EDITED BY JOHN SKIPP AND CRAIG SPECTOR

BOOK OF THE DEAD

STILL DEAD

BOOK OF THE DEAD II

Edited by John Skipp
and Craig Spector

BANTAM BOOKS
NEW YORK · TORONTO · LONDON · SYDNEY · AUCKLAND

STILL DEAD
A Bantam Falcon Book/August 1992

FALCON and the portrayal of a boxed "f" are trademarks of Bantam Books, a division of Bantam Doubleday Dell Publishing Group, Inc.

ISBN 0-553-29839-9

Published simultaneously in the United States and Canada

Bantam Books are published by Bantam Books, a division of Bantam Doubleday Dell Publishing Group, Inc. Its trademark, consisting of the words "Bantam Books" and the portrayal of a rooster, is Registered in U.S. Patent and Trademark Office and in other countries. Marca Registrada. Bantam Books, 666 Fifth Avenue, New York, NY 10103.

PRINTED IN THE UNITED STATES OF AMERICA

RAD   0 9 8 7 6 5 4 3 2 1

to
Ronald Gordon Spector
1924–1991

an end to pain,
then peace . . .

ACKNOWLEDGMENTS

The editors would like to thank Richard, Adele, Sandy, Shirley, Lou, Janna, Marianne, Lisa W., Melanie & Mikey, Pat, Poppy, Linda, Gary, Dori, Dino, Buddy & Holly & Damien, Matt & Alli, Cathy & Jesus, Mary & Steve, Ervin & Elizabeth, Barbara, Michael, Charley, Gram, Joan, the Walter Bros., Kim, Kim, Rusty, Randy, Beth, Paul, Doug, Judy, Judy, Dave, Jane, Jane & Michael, Brian, Scott, Leslie & Adam, Axel & Dona; John & Everett of Optic Nerve; Greg, Bob, and Howard at KNB; Spanky, Igor, Jo, Robert, Dee, Tony, Clive, Harlan & Susan, Mick & Cynthia, R. C. & Marie, Dangerous Visions and Forbidden Planet, the Bohemian Illuminati, Hollywood (in all its glory), Wacko's, *La Luz de Jesus*, Barney's Beanery, the Cat & Fiddle, the cities of Pasadena, New Yawk, and El Lay, the state of Pee Aye; all the folks at our going-away; all the people who helped us move; all the people from the first *Book o' the Dead*; plus undying admiration and gratitude for Tom, Mort, Davey, Nancy, K. W., Glen, Dan, Simon, Beth, Gahan, Kathe, Greg, Doug (again), Poppy (again), Roberta, Russ, Brooks, Nancy, Doug, Mark Zeising, and (of course, again) George.

Regrets to Mark, John, Pat, Wayne, Ivan, and the others

for whom it didn't work out this time. Sincere apologies to Melissa, and the others who waited forever. No thanks whatsoever to the tiny hell-people, who know exactly who they are. Love and smooches to the rest of the tribe, who know not only *who* they are, but which way is up as well.

And a final expression of *uber*-love to our loyal, discerning, incredibly brilliant (and stunningly attractive) readership. On behalf of all dead peoples, everywhere, we thank you.

CONTENTS

TOM SAVINI
FAST FOREWORD
xiii

INTRODUCTION:

JOHN SKIPP & CRAIG SPECTOR
NINETEEN NEW WAYS TO KICK DEAD ASS
1

PROLOGUE:
LONG BEFORE THE FALL

MORT CASTLE
THE OLD MAN AND THE DEAD
9

PART ONE:
WHERE WERE YOU
WHEN THE LIGHTS
WENT OUT?

CHAN McCONNELL
DONt/WALK
37

NANCY A. COLLINS
NECROPHILE
49

K.W. JETER
RISE UP AND WALK
64

GLEN VASEY
ONE STEP AT A TIME
72

JOHN SKIPP & CRAIG SPECTOR
THE ONES YOU LOVE
98

PART TWO:
COPING WITH THE DEAD

DAN SIMMONS
THIS YEAR'S CLASS PICTURE
109

SIMON McCAFFERY
NIGHT OF THE LIVING DEAD BINGO WOMEN
136

ELIZABETH MASSIE
ABED
141

GAHAN WILSON
COME ONE, COME ALL
152

KATHE KOJA
THE PRINCE OF NOX
171

GREGORY NICOLL
BEER RUN
183

DOUGLAS MORNINGSTAR & MAXWELL HART
PRAYER
187

POPPY Z. BRITE
CALCUTTA, LORD OF NERVES
190

PART THREE:
END GAMES

ROBERTA LANNES
I WALK ALONE
207

J.S. RUSSELL
UNDISCOVERED COUNTRIES
226

BROOKS CARUTHERS
MOON TOWERS
239

NANCY HOLDER
PASSION PLAY
265

DOUGLAS E. WINTER
BRIGHT LIGHTS, BIG ZOMBIE
279

FAST FOREWORD
by
TOM SAVINI

"To die ...... to be really dead ...... that must be glorious."

Or, as Bela Lugosi put it, "glohhhhhhrius ...... "

Glorious? I don't know, man. I can see Dracula wanting to be really dead but personally, I don't like to think about it ...... the possibilities are too disturbing ...... I mean, will I come back as a spider or some other repulsive crawling thing? Will I come back to a hideous future, or be forced to relive someone's horrible past? Will I come back as a zombie? WILL I COME BACK?

Ah! That's the question, though, isn't it? WILL I COME BACK? Or will eternity proceed, while I experience permanently what my mind briefly touches in sleep? Is it like being unconscious under anesthesia while the world drifts through infinity without me? That's the scary thing. The unknown zone.

When I die, what I REALLY want is to time travel. To go wherever I want throughout history and experience the things I've only read about. To stand in an ancient street and watch Jesus pass by, or hang out at that grassy knoll in November of '63 ...... to sit with Lincoln, or watch Michelangelo ...... to visit Lon Chaney on the set of the original Phantom. If I can't do that, then to hell with it. I AIN'T DYIN'*!!! I refuse. And that's final.*

Given how I feel about the subject, I guess it's kind of ironic that I spend so much of my time surrounded by the dead. But there you go. Over the years, I have made an awful lot of people (and other animals) DEAD......... *in the movies, anyway. I have killed so many people that I've often felt like a hired assassin. Some producer would call me up, and the next thing I knew, I'd be winging my way across the country to blow somebody's head off......... or chop somebody's head off............ or* CHEW *somebody's head off......... the list goes on and on. I started to add them up one day but just gave up. Way too much movie blood on my hands.*

And, one way or another, it always comes back to those pesky old Living Dead. Not just in the three major Dead films I did with George Romero, mind you, but straight across the board: from my first movie, Deathdream, *all the way through* Two Evil Eyes *and beyond. (Not to mention bringing that ultimate diehard, Jason Voorhees, back to life ...... and then killing him,* TWICE...... *in* Friday the 13th *parts I and IV).*

And in every case ...... from the scenes of total mayhem I'm most proud of, down to those lowly hack-and-slash gigs I'd honestly prefer to forget ...... my job on the shoot has been perfectly clear.

1) MAKE 'EM LOOK THEIR BEST. *It may well be the only dignity there* IS *in dying. Whether raisin' 'em up or knockin' 'em down, you* ALWAYS *try to make your dead folks look their best.*

2) ALWAYS GIVE THE AUDIENCE SOMETHING NEW TO CHEW ON. *Or, in other words (and for God's sake* PLEEEEEEZE!!!*), show them something that's never been seen before. From my experience, people go* NUTS *over just a little touch of magic in their lives, which is what monster*

*effects are all about. And they will thank you forever if
.... JUST FOR ONE SECOND .... you take the time
and care to take them somewhere no one else has ever
been.*

*And I guess that finally gets me around to introducing
this incredible book of Living Dead stories. They're all
set in a world that I helped create, which is kind of a
major rush for me. When you've spent as much time
around dead folks as I have, you start to believe you've
seen it all.*

*Well, I hadn't, dear reader, and neither have you. There
are tales in here that will fry your brain, shoot hot grease out
through the holes in your scalp, and make you beg for more
...... scenes that I'd give my left nut to have written ......
images that are a fucking FX artist's dream.*

*Let me go off on a tangent here for a second ...... like
this whole thing hasn't been* ONE BIG TANGENT, *right?
Anyway. One of the beauties of working with George Romero on the* Dead *films ...... aside from the fact that we were
in the midst of creating a truly original series, and we all
knew it ...... was that we had the freedom to go completely
over-the-top with our gags ("gags" in this case meaning
violent set-pieces, for those of you cinema-illiterate types).
There was always plenty to chew on ...... you'll pardon
the expression .... in* Dawn of the Dead, Day of the
Dead, *and both versions of* Night of the Living Dead.

*And that's the most amazing thing, to me, about the
two* Dead *books my pals Skipp and Spector have put together. Like George's screenplays, these stories are obviously the work of intelligent, thoughtful creative artists,
who are putting 100% more into their craft than one would
expect from a bunch of zombie stories. On top of that,
though ...... just as in George's work ...... is an element
that's almost always missing from so-called "serious" art:
a sense of fun and a sense of danger, hooked up with un-
bridled imagination and the guts to go all the way.*

*There are two stories in this book, for example ....
"Moon Towers" and "Undiscovered Countries" ......
both of them, by the way, written by new guys who*

nobody'd ever even heard of before),...... anyway, these stories have visual descriptions I would KILL *to capture on film. (No, I'm not the kind of clown that would blow a story's golden moment, just to make a point...... I see someone like that, I want them dragged out and* SHOT ...... *so you'll have to take my word for it. And when you get to those scenes, think of me, okay? I bet you'll know which ones I mean.)*

One top of all that visual coolness, however, is the fact that there are stories in there that honest-to-god MOVED *me...... which makes them one whole hell of a lot tougher and stranger than your average run-of-the-mill zombie yarn. When it comes to this book, it's like the old saying goes: I laughed, I cried, it became a part of me.*

Plus, on more than one occasion, it scared my ass off. Which...... as you could probably guess......... is not the easiest thing in the world to do.

The punch line on all this psychotic rambling is that Skipp and Spector know what's good, and they truly LOVE *this stuff...... which means that if* YOU *love this stuff, you should really pay attention. What they've done is to round up a bunch of tomorrow's most talented horror stars...... names like Simmons and Brite and Winter and Collins and Koja and more more* MORE ...... *all of whom are now lurking within these pages. Untold nightmares and wonders await you...... There is madness and magic afoot.*

So what are you waiting for? A written invitation? In that case, consider it done. It may be too late for poor old Bela, God rest his soul. But if you want some hard answers about what's on the Other Side...... if you want a serious taste of the best new horror on the market today...... if you want to know the TRUE *meaning of "glorious," friends, then please: allow me to welcome you inside.*

TOM SAVINI

INTRODUCTION:
NINETEEN NEW WAYS TO
KICK DEAD ASS
OR
RESISTING THE URGE TO DECAY

"This better not become some god-awful End Times Porn for those who can only get off on fear and laughter."

—Rev. Ivan Stang

"Lennon and McCartney were right: all you need is love. As long as you keep the gators fed."

—Stephen King

To make a long story short ...

Q. SO WHY DOES THE WORLD NEED ANOTHER BOOK OF ZOMBIE STORIES?

A. BECAUSE THEY'RE GOOD FOR YOU.

(Would that introductions could be quite so easy. Ah, well ...)

To make a short story long ...

Once upon a time—in '89, to be precise—we released an anthology called *Book of the Dead*. It was designed as a manic, high-octane compendium of all-new, original Living Dead stories, inspired by the legendary zombie films of George A. Romero. It had taken us three long years to pull it all together.

And boy *howdy*, was it ever fun to do.

From the outset, we knew that simply stealing his moves—*recapitulating his epiphanies*, as it were—would not even begin to do the trick. All we needed to underscore *that* truth was a little trip down Video Lane. There— splayed out, shameless, for all to see—were the acres upon acres of worthless zombie ripoffs that had sprung up in the wake of *Night of the Living Dead*: z-grade intestinal chomp-a-thons, woefully derivitive and cheesily executed, echoing the zombie form without a trace of Romero's guiding substance or skill.

It was painfully clear that what the world *didn't* need was the literary equivalent of a hairball like *Spookies:* one more cranially-impacted disposable gorefest, clogging the aisles of an already oversaturated and desensitized culture.

Which was perfectly fine with us. We hadn't come just to cop his licks.

It was, after all, his *mythology* we were after.

Because what Romero had done, in the course of his *Dead* trilogy, was to construct a richly-detailed apocalyptic landscape, built firmly on the wreckage of the world we knew. By the simple act of raising the dead next door— and bequeathing upon them a taste for the living—he had instantly created *a brand-spanking-new mythos* for the mid-to-late twentieth century: at once muscular and poignant, judicious and crazed; by turns deftly satirical and sledge-hammer savage.

Yes, they were among the most brutal films ever made. And *yes*, they had retained their power to shock so well that the MPAA *still* was unable to rate them. But the bottom line on Romero was this: he wasn't just stacking shocks. He was stacking revelations. These were not movies of mindless atrocity. They were films of *ideas*.

Romero's undead world was a place where hope and courage collided head-on with hopelessness and despair; where the fundamental human need for renewal waged a desperate, daily struggle against overwhelming decay. It was a world in which the lines between good and evil, right and wrong often blurred, sometimes disappearing completely.

Until the only questions left were *will we survive?*

And, if so, *at what cost?*

In short, it was a lot like the real world. And therein

lied its considerable strengths. They were brought to bear—
with real muscle and brilliance—by the authors of the sixteen stories from the first *Book of the Dead*. Cutting-edge
kickass dynamos like David J. Schow and Joe R. Lansdale
went toe-to-toe with the top of the list: Stephen King, Ram-
sey Campbell, and Robert R. McCammon. A couple of new
guys got a chance to show their stuff, to enormously nasty
effect. A couple of old pros got down 'n' dirty, impressing
the hell out of everyone. And, by and large, everybody
transcended themselves, turning out some of the finest,
most innovative work of their careers.

But the most amazing thing about *Book of the Dead*
was the fact that it had taken Romero's original filmic/
mythic landscape and literally, dramatically *expanded* upon
it: redefining his whole concept of Hell on Earth in unprecedented, perilous directions; translating it into real fiction (as opposed to novelization) for the very first time;
and, in the process, creating an entire new body of dangerous literature, with Romero's own New Breed of shambling monstrosities at its core.

Now there are some who will scoff at the whole idea
that *any* kind of fiction—much less horror fiction—is actually "dangerous" in *any* way. And, of course, they have
a point. To confuse fictive terrors with the grisly ins-and-
outs of real life is to harbor a seriously misplaced sense of
priorities; and one more zombie story, no matter how well
written or vividly imagined, is not apt to alter the course
of Western Civilization.

But . . .

Humans *need* their fairy tales. They are an essential part
of our inner lives, both personal and cultural. You don't
best send your six-year-olds off to dreamland by poleaxing
them with the headlines of *The New York Times*. You give
them something to work with. You give them *Green Eggs
and Ham*. From the earliest scribblings on the Lascaux
Caves to the latest in high-tech, 70-millimeter Sensurround
wizardry, myths have been the kindling that the fires of
imagination feed upon. We need that cultural context. We
need those fairy tales.

Many have argued that this is why horror is dangerous:

because it gives people *weird ideas;* because it densensi-
tizes them to the true horrors of the world; because it glo-
rifies death and suffering and causes anti-social behavior.
That it is in effect tantamount to a kind of *snuff literature*,
a blood-soaked bastard pornography that differs only in its
manner of penetration: beating its penises into plowshares,
then impaling people upon them.

But cultures are always blaming their artists for causing
the insanities they merely depict. It's always a terrible, stupid mistake, murdering the messenger for the bad news that
he bears. The simple fact is that *sociopaths are sociopaths.*
They don't *need* to take their cues from the world of art;
they'll take 'em anywhere they can find them, or make
them up themselves. All David Berkowitz needed was the
barking of his next-door neighbor's dog to set *him* off. And
the secret recipe for making Ted Bundys has a lot more to
do with sadistic childcare techniques than with how many
jerkoff mags he keeps stashed under his grownup bed at
night.

On the other side of the fence, many have counter-
argued that horror *isn't* dangerous, can't really even *be* dangerous. That it is, *by its very nature*, an ultra-conservative
form, where Good battles Evil for the ultimate preservation
of the Status Quo. But *Good and Evil are not political
parties*, like Republicans and Democrats or Christians and
Muslims (although a great many of all of the above might
tend to disagree.) Good ol' Good and Evil—like their mutant cousins Right and Wrong—are fundamental aspects of
the human condition. Different for everyone. Present *in*
everyone. As intertwined and immutable as life and death.

And once you strip away the pithy politicalese, the Status Quo itself is nothing more than the difference between
what was happening *before* the crisis hit, and what will be
left to survive in its wake. It's a cultural balancing act: a
way of assessing the price by which our precious survival
was purchased.

Right now, as the planet steers a course into Millennium, it's only natural that we should have a taste for apocalypse myths. They help us address our fears for the
imminent future, by staging earnest survivalist games in our

heads. They help us prepare, on the inner plane, for the impending Historical Crisis . . . in *whatever* form it might ultimately choose to take.

Because whatever it is, it's in the air, and a lot of us can taste it. *Something is about to happen.* We don't know what, but we know it's there, and a lot of us are bracing ourselves. The turning of a century is always greeted with religious hysteria, political upheaval, the rumblings of unprecedented change. This one will be no exception.

And guess what? It's almost here.

So for those of you who seriously asked the question, *that's* why we need another book of zombie stories. To enrich the pool of apocalyptic visions, the range and scope of our ability to dream it clearly. To expand upon the myth first posed by George A. Romero, because it is not only a powerful one, but a useful one as well.

In other words—and at long last—BECAUSE THEY'RE GOOD FOR YOU.

Which brings us, finally, to the book at hand.

This is a companion volume to the first *Book of the Dead*. It's not a retread of the first one's attitudes, stylistic devices, or gross-out greatest hits. In it, you'll find nineteen *more* of the freshest, finest, most imaginative and all-around *goddamndest* zombie stories ever written.

If the wild horror frontier looks a little different this time, it's because we have—with three esteemed exceptions—a whole new set of trailblazers leading the way. From Mort Castle's heartbreaking Hemingway *hommage* (''The Old Man and the Dead'') to Douglas E. Winter's incendiary Jay McInerny *pastiche* (''Bright Lights, Big Zombie''), you gotta know that this is no ordinary, meat-on-the-table horror anthology.

We've got a potent piece on lower education from Dan Simmons (''This Year's Class Picture''). Two sets of harrowing deathers-in-heat from Nancy A. Collins (''Necrophile'') and Roberta Lannes (''I Walk Alone''). Radical takes on Dat Ol' Time Religion from Nancy Holder (''Passion Play'') and K. W. Jeter (''Rise Up and Walk'').

But that ain't all. We've got bikers, beer runs, and bingo gals; death in the family, and the death *of* the family; profound mutations; dead punks on dope; *post*-pedestrian panic; and shiny nodules on the brain. Cartoon hero Gahan Wilson supplies a charming scam for rotting rubes (''Come One, Come All''); and we editor-types even throw in, for ballast, a little zombie love poem of our own.

And *way* out there—at the New Horror's coolest, cruelest cutting edge—it doesn't *get* more caustic, wry, and brilliant than Kathe Koja's ''The Prince of Nox''; more gloriously, hypnotically sensation-packed than Poppy Z. Brite's ''Calcutta, Lord of Nerves''; or more uncompromisingly, matter-of-factly shocking than Elizabeth Massie's ''Abed.''

Welcome to the second *Book of the Dead*. It took another three whole years to get here. We think it was worth the wait. You hold in your hands a thoughtful, subversive, kaleidoscopic expansion of the universe first posited by George A. Romero. You can feel his films—and the first *Book of the Dead*—reverberating through the sagas you're about to read.

But what's even more exciting, to us, is that these stories *resonate back*. Once you've read them, going back to the films or the first book isn't quite the same.

It's even better.

Have fun, and take care.

SKIPP & SPECTOR
LOS ANGELES, 1992

PROLOGUE

LONG BEFORE THE FALL

THE OLD MAN AND THE DEAD

MORT CASTLE

I

In our time there was a man who wrote as well and truly as anyone ever did. He wrote about courage and endurance and sadness and war and bullfighting and boxing and men in love and men without women. He wrote about scars and wounds that never heal.

Often, he wrote about death. He had seen much death. He had killed. Often, he wrote well and truly about death. Sometimes. Not always.

Sometimes he could not.

II

MAY 1961
MAYO CLINIC
ROCHESTER, MINNESOTA

"Are you a Stein? Are you a Berg?" he asked.

"Are you an anti-Semite?" the psychiatrist asked.

"No." He thought. "Maybe. I don't know. I used to be, I think. It was in fashion. It was all right until that son of a bitch Hitler."

"Why did you ask that?" the psychiatrist asked.

The old man took off his glasses. He was not really an old man, only 61, but often he thought of himself as an old man and truly, he looked like an old man, although his blood pressure was in control and his diabetes remained borderline. His face had scars. His eyes were sad. He looked like an old man who had been in wars.

He pinched his nose above the bridge. He wondered if he were doing it to look tired and worn. It was hard to know now when he was being himself and when he was being what the world expected him to be. That was how it was when all the world knew you and all the world knows you if you have been in *Life* and *Esquire*.

"It's I don't think a Jew would understand. Maybe a Jew couldn't."

The old man laughed then but it had nothing funny to it. He sounded like he had been socked a good one. "*Nu?* Is that what a Jew would say? *Nu?* No, not a Jew. Not a communist. Nor an empiricist. I'll tell you who else. The existentialists. Those wise guys sons of bitches. Oh, they get ink these days, don't they? Sit in the cafés and drink the good wine and the good dark coffee and smoke the bad cigarettes and think they've discovered it all. Nothingness. That is what they think they've discovered. How do you like it now, Gentlemen?

"They are wrong. Yes. They are wrong."

"How so?"

"There is something. It's not pretty. It's not nice. You

have to be drunk to talk about it, drunk or shell-shocked, and then you usually can't talk about it. But there is something.''

III

The poet Bill Wantling wrote of him: ''He explored the *pues y nada* and the *pues y nada*.'' So then so. What do you know of it Mr. Poet Wantling? What do you know of it?

F——you all. I obscenity in the face of the collective wisdom. I obscenity in the face of the collective wisdoms. I obscenity in the mother's milk that suckled the collective wisdoms. I obscenity in the too easy mythos of all the collective wisdoms and in the face of my young, ignorant, unknowing self that led me to proclaim my personal mantra of ignorance, the *pues y nada y pues y nada y pues y nada pues y nada*. . . . In the face of Buddha. In the face of Mohammed. In the face of the God of Abraham, Issac, and Jacob.

In the face of that poor skinny dreamer who died on the cross. Really, when it came down to it, he had some good moves in there. He didn't go out bad. He was tough. Give him that. Tough like Stan Ketchel, but he had no counter-moves. Just this sweet, simple, sad ass faith. Sad ass because, what little he understood, no, from what I have seen, he had it bass-ackwards.

How do you like it now, Gentlemen? How do you like it now? Is it time for a prayer? Very well then, Gentlemen.

Let us pray.

Baa-baa-baa, listen to the lambs bleat,

Baa-baa-baa, listen to the lambs bleat.

Truly, world without end.

Truly.

Not Amen.

I can not will not just cannot no cannot bless nor sanctify nor affirm the obscenity the horror.

Can you, Mr. Poet Bill Wantling? Can you, Gentlemen? How do you like it now?

In Hell and in a time of hell, a man's got no bloody

chance, F——you as we have been F——ed. All of us. All of us.

There is your prayer.

Amen.

IV

"Ern——"

"No. Don't call me that. That's not who I want to be."

"That is your name."

"Goddamn it. F——you. F——you twice. I've won the big one. The goddamn Nobel. I'm the one. The heavyweight champ, no middleweight. I *can* be *who* I want to be. I've earned that."

"Who is it you want to be?"

"*Mr. Papa.* I'm damned good for that. Mr. Papa. That is how I call myself. That is how Mary calls me. They call me 'Mr. Papa' in Idaho and Cuba and *Paris Review.* The little girls whose tight dancer bottoms I pinch, the little girls I call 'daughter,' the lovely little girls, and A. E. and Carlos and Coop and Marlene, Papa or Mr. Papa, that's how they call me.

"Even Fidel. I'm Mr. Papa to Fidel. I call him Señor Beisbol. Do you know, he's got a hell of a slider, Fidel. How do you like it now, Mr. Doctor? *Mr.* Papa."

"*Mr. Papa?* No, I don't like it. I don't like the word games you play with me, nor do I think your 'Mr. Papa' role belongs in this office. You're here so we can *help* you."

"Help me? That is nice. That is just so goddamn pretty."

"We need the truth."

"That's all Pilate wanted. Not so much. And wasn't he one swell guy?"

"Who are you?" persisted the psychiatrist.

"Who's on first?"

"What?"

"*What's* on second! Who's on first. I like them, you know. Abbott and Costello. They could teach that sissy

Capote a thing or two about word dance. Who's on first? How do you like it now, Gentlemen? Oh, yes, they could teach Mr. James Jones a little. Thinks he's Captain Steel Balls now. Thinks he's ready to go against the champ. Mailer, the loud mouth Hebe. Uris, even *Uris,* for God's sake, the original Hollywood piss-ant. Before they take me on, any of them, let them do a prelim with Abbott and Costello. Who's on first? That is good.''

"What's not good is that you're avoiding. Simple question.'' The psychiatrist was silent, then he said, sternly, "Who are you?''

The old man said nothing. His mouth worked. He looked frail then. Finally he said, "Who am I truly?''

"Truly.''

"Verdad?''

"Sí. Verdad.''

"Call me *Adam.* . . .''

"Adam? Oh, *Mr. Papa, Mr. Nobel Prize,* that is just too pretty. How do *you* like it now, thrown right back at you? You see, I can talk your talk. Let us have a pretension contest. Call me 'Ishmael.' Now do we wait for God to call you his beloved son in whom he is well pleased?''

The old man sighed. He looked very sad, as though he wanted to kill himself. He had put himself on his honor to his personal physician and his wife that he would not kill himself, and honor was very important to him, but he looked like he wanted to kill himself.

The old man said, "No. Adam. Adam Nichols. That was the one who was truly me in the stories.''

"I thought it was Nick Adams in—''

"Those were the stories I let them publish. There were other stories I wrote about me when I used to be Adam Nichols. Some of those stories no one would have published. Believe me. Maybe *Weird Tales.* Some magazine for boys who don't yet know about f——ing.

"Those stories, they were the real stories.''

V

A DANCE WITH A NUN

Adam Nichols had the bed next to his friend Rinelli in the attic of the villa that had been taken over for a hospital and with the war so far off they usually could not even hear it it was not too bad. It was a small room, the only one for patients all the way up there, and so just the two of them had the room. When you opened the window, there was usually a pleasant breeze that cleared away the smell of dead flesh.

Adam would have been hurting plenty but every time the pain came they gave him morphine and so it wasn't so bad. He had been shot in the calf and the hip and near to the spine and the doctor had to do a lot of cutting. The doctor told him he would be fine. Maybe he wouldn't be able to telemark when he skied, but he would be all right, without even a limp.

The doctor told him about a concert violinist who'd lost his left hand. He told him about a gallery painter who'd been blinded in both eyes. He told him about an ordinary fellow who'd lost both testicles. The doctor said Adam had reason to count his blessings. He was trying to cheer Adam up. Hell, the doctor said, trying to show he was a regular guy who would swear, there were lots had it worse, plenty worse.

Rinelli had it worse. You didn't have to be a doctor to know that. A machine gun got Rinelli in the stomach and in the legs and in between. The machine gun really hemstitched him. They changed his bandages every hour or so but there was always a thick wetness coming right through the blanket.

Adam Nichols thought Rinelli was going to die because Rinelli said he didn't feel badly at all and they weren't giving him morphine or anything much else really. Another thing was Rinelli laughed and joked a great deal. Frequently, Rinelli said he was feeling "swell"; that was an

American word Adam had taught him and Rinelli liked it a lot.

Rinelli joked plenty with Sister Katherine, one of the nurses. He teased hell out of her. She was an American nun and very young and very pretty with sweet blue eyes that made Adam think of the girls with Dutch bobs and round collars who wore silly hats who you saw in the Coca-Cola advertisements. When he first saw her, Rinelli said to Adam Nichols in Italian, "What a waste. What a shame. Isn't she a great girl? Just swell."

There was also a much older nun there called Sister Anne. She was a chief nurse and this was not her first war. Nobody joked with her even if he was going to die. What Rinelli said about her was that when she was a child she decided to be a bitch and because she wasn't British, the only thing left was for her to be a nun. Sister Anne had a profile as flat as the blade of a shovel. Adam told Rinelli he'd put his money on Sister Anne in a twenty-rounder with Jack Johnson. She had to have a harder coconut than any nigger.

Frequently, it was Sister Katherine who gave Adam his morphine shot. With her help, he had to roll onto his side so she could jab the hypodermic into his buttock. That was usually when Rinelli would start teasing.

"Sister Katherine," Rinelli might say, "when you are finished looking at Corporal Nichol's backside, would you be interested in seeing mine?"

"No, no thank you," Sister Katherine would say.

"It needs your attention, Sister. It is broken, I am afraid. It is cracked right down the middle."

"Please, Sergeant Rinelli—"

"Then if you don't want to see my backside, could I perhaps interest you in my front side?"

Sister Katherine would blush very nicely then and do something so young and sweet with her mouth that it was all you could do not to just squeeze her. But then Rinelli would get to laughing and you'd see the bubbles in the puddle on the blanket over his belly, and that wasn't any too nice.

One afternoon, Rinelli casually asked Sister Katherine,

"Am I going to live?" Adam Nichols knew Rinelli was not joking then.

Sister Katherine nodded. "Yes," she said. "You are going to get well and then you will go back home."

"No," Rinelli said, still sounding casual, "Pardon me, I really don't want to contradict, but no, I do not think so."

Adam Nichols did not think so, either, and he had been watching Sister Katherine's face so he thought she did not think so as well.

Sister Katherine said rather loudly, "Oh, yes, Sergeant Rinelli. I have talked with the doctors. Yes, I have. Soon you will begin to be better. It will be a gradual thing, you will see. Your strength will come back. Then you can be invalided home."

With his head turned, Adam Nichols saw Rinelli smile.

"Good," Rinelli said. "That is very fine. So, Sister Katherine, as soon as I am better and my strength comes back to me, but before I am sent home, I have a favor to ask of you."

"What is that, Sergeant Rinelli?"

"I want you to dance with me."

Sister Katherine looked youngest when she was trying to be deeply serious. "No, no," she said, emphatically. "No, it is not permitted. Nuns cannot dance."

"It will be a secret dance. I will not tell Sister Anne, have no fear. But I do so want to dance with you."

"Rest now, Sergeant Rinelli. Rest, Corporal Nichols. Soon everything will be fine."

"Oh, yes," Rinelli said, "soon everything will be just swell."

What Adam Nichols liked about morphine was that it was better than getting drunk because you could slip from what was real to what was not real and not know and not care one way or the other. Right now in his mind, he was up in Michigan. He was walking through the woods, following the trail. Ahead, it came into sight, the trout pool, and his eyes took it all in, and he was seeking the words so he could write this moment truly.

> *Beyond this trail*
> *a stream lies*
> *faintly marked by rising mist.*
>
> *Twisting and tumbling*
> *around barriers,*
> *it flows*
> *into a shimmering pool,*
>
> *black with beauty*
> *and*
> *full of fighting trout.*

Adam Nichols had not told many people about this writing thing, how he believed he would discover a way to make words present reality so it was not just reality but more real than reality. He wanted writing to jump into what he called the fifth dimension. But until he learned to do it, and for now, writing was a secret for him.

The war was over. Sometimes he tried to write about it but he usually could not. Too often when he would try to write about it, he would find himself writing about what other men had seen and done and not what he himself had seen and done and had to give it up as a bad job.

Adam Nichols put down his tackle and rod and sat down by the pool and lit a cigarette. It tasted good. There is a clean, clear and sharp smell when you light a cigarette outdoors. He was not surprised to find Rinelli sitting alongside him even though Rinelli was dead. Rinelli was smoking, too.

"Isn't this fine? Isn't this everything I said it would be?" Adam Nichols asked.

"It's grand, it sure is. It's just swell," Rinelli answered.

"Tonight, we'll drink some whiskey with really cold water. And we'll have one hell of a meal," Adam Nichols said. "Trout. I've got my old man's recipe." He drew reflectively on his cigarette. "My old man, he was the one *who taught me to hunt and fish. He was the one taught me to cook outdoors.''*

''You haven't introduced me to your father,'' Rinelli said.

''Well, he's dead, you see. He was a doctor and he killed himself. He put his gun to his head and he killed himself.''

''What do you figure, then? Figure he's in hell now?''

''I don't know. Tell you, Rinelli, I don't really think there's anything like that. Hell. Not really.''

Rinelli looked sad and that's when Adam Nichols saw how dead Rinelli's eyes were and remembered all over again that Rinelli was dead.

''Well, Adam, you know me, I don't like to argue, but I tell you, there is, too, a hell. And I sure as hell wish I were there right now.''

Rinelli snapped the last half inch of his cigarette into the trout pool. A small fish bubbled at it as the trout pool turned into blood.

A few days later Rinelli was pretty bad off. Sometimes he tried to joke with Adam but he didn't make any sense and sometimes he talked in Italian to people who weren't there. He looked gray, like a dirty sheet. When he fell asleep, there was a heavy, wet rattle in his throat and his mouth stayed open.

Adam Nichols wasn't feeling any too swell himself. It was funny, how when you were getting better, you hurt lots worse. Sister Katherine jabbed a lot of morphine into him. It helped, but he still hurt and he knew he wasn't always thinking straight.

There were times he thought he was probably crazy because of the pain and the morphine. That didn't bother him really. It was just that he couldn't trust anything he saw.

At dusk, Adam Nichols opened his eyes. He saw Sister Katherine by Rinelli's bed. She had her crucifix and she was praying hard and quiet with her lips moving prettily and her eyes almost closed.

"That's good," Rinelli said. "Thank you. That is real nice." His voice sounded strong and casual and vaguely bored.

Sister Katherine kept on praying.

"That's just swell," Rinelli said. He coughed and he died.

Sister Katherine pulled the sheets up over Rinelli's face. She went to Adam. "He's gone."

"Well, I guess so."

"We will not be able to move him for a while. We do not have enough people, and there's no room. . . ." Sister Katherine looked like she had something unpleasant in her mouth. "There is no room in the room we're using for the morgue."

"That's okay," Adam Nichols said. "He can stay here. He's not bothering me."

"All right then," Sister Katherine said. "All right. Do you need another shot of morphine?"

"Yes," Adam said, "I think so. I think I do."

Sister Katherine gave him the injection, and later there was another, and then, he thought, perhaps another one or even two. He knew he had had a lot of morphine because what he saw later was really crazy and couldn't have actually happened.

It was dark and Sister Katherine came in with her little light. Rinelli sat up in bed then. That had to be the morphine, Adam Nichols told himself. Rinelli was dead as a post. But there he was, sitting up in bed, with dead eyes, and he was stretching out his arms and then it all happened quick just like in a dream but Rinelli was out of bed and he was hugging Sister Katherine like he was drunk and silly.

He's dancing with her, that's what he's doing, Adam Nichols thought, and he figured he was thinking that because of all the morphine. Sure, he said he was going to dance with Sister Katherine before he went home. "Hey, Rinelli," Adam Nichols said. "Quit fooling around, why don't you?"

Sister Katherine was yelling pretty loud and then she wasn't yelling all that loud because it looked like Rinelli was kissing her, but then you saw that wasn't it. Rinelli was biting her nose real hard, not like kidding around, and she was bleeding pretty much and she twisted and pushed real hard on Rinelli.

Rinelli staggered back. With blood on his dead lips. With something white and red and pulpy getting chewed by his white teeth. With a thin bit of pink gristle by the corner of his mouth.

Sister Katherine was up against the wall. The middle of her face was a black and red gushing hole. Her eyes were real big and popping. She was yelling without making a sound. She kind of looked like a comic strip.

It was a bad dream and the morphine, Adam Nichols thought, a real bad dream, and he wished he'd wake up.

Then Sister Anne came running in. Then she ran out. Then she ran back in. Now she had a Colt .45. She knocked back the slide like she really meant business. Rinelli went for her. She held her arm straight out. The gun was just a few inches from Rinelli's forehead when Sister Anne let him have it. Rinelli's head blew up wetly in a lot of noise. A lot of the noise was shattering bone. It went all over the place.

That was all Adam Nichols could remember the next morning. It wasn't like something real you remember. It was a lot more like a dream. He told himself it had to be the morphine. He told himself that a number of times. The windows were open and the breeze was nice but the small room smelled of strong disinfectant. There was no one in the other bed.

When Sister Anne came in to bring his breakfast and give him morphine, Adam Nichols asked about Rinelli.

"Well, he's dead," Sister Anne said. "I thought you knew."

Adam Nichols asked about Sister Katherine.

"She's no longer here," the old nun said, tersely.

"I thought something happened last night. I thought I saw something awful."

"It's better you don't think about it," Sister Anne said. "It's war and everybody sees a lot of awful things. Just don't think about it."

VI

"Let's talk about your suicidal feelings."

"There are times I want to kill myself. How's that?"

"You know what I mean."

"Who's on first?"

"You pride yourself on being a brave man."

"I am. Buck Lanham called me the bravest man he's ever known."

"Hooray. I'll see you get a medal."

"Maybe I deserve a medal. I've pissed in the face of death." The old man winked then. That and what he had just said made him look ridiculous. It made him look ancient and crazy. "I have killed, after all."

"I know. You are a very famous killer. You have antlers and tusks and rhino horns. You've shot cape buffalo and geese and bears and wild goats. That makes you extremely brave. You deserve medals."

"Who are you to deride me?" The old man was furious. He looked threatening and silly. "Who are you to hold me in contempt? I have killed men!"

VII

The time is a drunken blur in his memory. It is the "rat race" summer and fall of 1944, and he is intensely alive. A "war correspondent," that is what he is supposed to be, but that is not all he can allow himself to be.

He has to go up against Death every time. With what he knows, oh, yes, he has to meet the flat gaze of Mr. Death, has to breathe Mr. Death's hyena breath, he has to.

That is part of it.

He calls himself a soldier. He wouldn't have it any other way. This is a war. He appoints himself an intelligence officer. He carries a weapon, a .32 caliber Colt revolver.

And don't the kids love him, though? God, he sure

loves them. They are just so goddamned beautiful, the doomed ones and the fortunate, the reluctant warriors and those who've come to know they love it. They are beautiful men as only men can be beautiful.

You see, women, well, women are women, and it is the biological thing, the trap by which we are snared, the old peg and awl, the old belly-rub and sigh and there you have it, and so a real man does need a woman, must have a woman so he does not do heinous things, but it is in the company of men that men find themselves and each other.

These kid warriors, these glorious snot-noses like he used to be, they know he is tough. He is the legit goods. He can outshoot them, rifle or pistol, even the Two-Gun Pecos Pete from Arizona. Want to play cards, he'll stay up the night, drinking and joking. He puts on the gloves and boxes with them. He'll take one to give one and he always gives as good as he gets.

He has a wind-up phonograph and good records: Harry James and the Boswells and Hot Lips Paige. He has Fletcher Henderson and Basie and Ellington. The Andrews Sisters, they can swing it, and Russ Colombo. Sinatra, he'll be fine once they let him stop doing the sappy stuff. There are nights of music and drinking and in the following days there are the moments burned into his mind, the moments that become the stories. Old man?

Well, he can drink the kids blind-eyed and to hell and gone. He stays with them, drink for drink. The hell with most of the kiss-ass officers. They don't know how foolish they are. They don't know they are clichés. The enlisted men, John Q. Public, Mr. O. K. Joe American, Johnny Gone for a Soldier, it's the enlisted man who's going to save the world from that Nazi bastard. It's the enlisted men he honest to God loves.

The enlisted men call him "Papa."

How do you like it now, Gentlemen?

The kraut prisoner was no enlisted man. He was an officer. Stiff necked son of a bitch. *Deutschland über alles.* Arrogant pup. *Ubermensch.*

No, the German will not reveal anything. He will answer none of their questions. They can all go to hell. That's what the German officer says. They can all get f———.

Papa shakes a fist in the kraut's face. Papa says, "You're going to talk and tell us every damned thing we want to know or I'll kill you, you Nazi son of a bitch."

The German officer does not change expression. He looks bored. What he says is: "You are not going to kill me, old man. You do not have the courage. You are hindered by a decadent morality and ethical code. You come from a race of mongrelized degenerates and cowards. You abide by the foolishness of the Geneva Convention. I am an unarmed prisoner of war. You will do nothing to me."

Later, he would boastfully write about this incident to the soft-spoken, courtly gentlemen who published his books. He said to the German officer, "What a mistake you made, brother."

And then I shot that smug prick. I just shot him before anyone could tell me I shouldn't. I let him have three in the belly, just like that, real quick, from maybe a foot away. Say what you want, maybe they were no supermen, but they weren't any panty-waists, either. Three in the belly, Pow-Pow-Pow, and he's still standing there, and damned if he isn't dead but doesn't know it, but he is pretty surprised and serves him right, too.

Then everyone else, all the Americans and a Brit or two are yelling and pissing around like they don't know whether to shit, go blind, or order breakfast, and here's this dead kraut swaying on his feet, and maybe I'm even thinking I'm in a kettle of bad soup, but the hell with it. But have to do it right, you know, arrogant krautkopf or not. So I put the gun to his head and I let him have it, bang! and his brains come squirting right out his nose, gray and pink, and, you know, it looks pretty funny, so someone yells, "Gesundheit!" and that's it, brother. That's all she wrote and we've got us one guaranteed dead Nazi.

VIII

A rose is a rose is a rose
The dead are the dead are the dead except when
they aren't and how do you like it
let's talk and
Who is on first
I know what I know and I am afraid and I am
afraid

IX

HOMAGE TO SPAIN

1. AN OLD MAN'S LUCK

The dusty old man sat on the river bank. He wore steel rimmed spectacles. He had already traveled 12 kilometers and he was very tired. He thought it would be a while before he could go on.

That is what he told Adam Nichols.

Adam Nichols told him he had to cross the pontoon bridge. He really must and soon. When the shelling came, this would not be a good place to stay. The old man in the steel rimmed spectacles thanked Adam Nichols for his concern. He was a very polite old man. The reason he had stayed behind was to take care of the animals in his village. He smiled because saying "his village" made him feel good. There were three goats, two cats, and six doves. When he had no other choice and really had to leave, he opened the door to the doves' cage and let them fly. He was not too worried about the cats, really, the old man told Adam Nichols; cats are always all right. Cats had luck. Goats were another thing. Goats were a little stupid and sweet and so they had not much luck.

It was just too bad about the goats, the old man said. It was a sad thing.

Adam agreed. But the old man had to move along. He really should.

The old man said thank you. He was grateful for the concern. But he did not think he could go on just yet. He was very tired and he was 76 years old.

He asked a question. Did Adam truly think the cats would be all right?

Yes, Adam said, we both know cats have luck.

Adam thought they had a lot more luck than sweet and stupid goats and 76-year-old men who can go no farther than 12 kilometers when there is going to be shelling.

2. HUNTERS IN THE MORNING FOG

Miguel woke him. They used to call him Miguelito but the older Miguel had been shot right through the heart, a very clean shot, and so now this one was Miguel. The sun had just come up and there was fog with cold puff-like clouds near to the ground. "Your rifle," Miguel said. "We are going hunting."

"Hey," Adam Nichols said, "what the hell?" He wanted coffee or to go back to sleep.

"Just come," Miguel said.

There were five of them, Pilar, who was as tough as any man, and Antonio, and Jordan, the American college professor, and Miguel, who used to be Miguelito, and Adam Nichols. They went out to the field. Yesterday it was a battlefield. The day before that it had just been a green, flat field. Some of the dead lay here and there. Not all of the dead were still. Some were already up and some were now rising, though most lay properly still and dead. Those who were up mostly staggered about like drunks. Some had their arms out in front of them like Boris Karloff in the *Frankenstein* movie. They did not look frightening. They looked stupid. But they were frightening even if they did not look frightening because they were supposed to be dead.

"Say, what the hell?" Adam Nichols asked. His mouth was dry.

"It happens sometimes," Pilar said. "That is what I

have heard. It appears to be so, though this is the first time I personally have seen it.''

Pilar shrugged. ''The dead do not always stay dead. They come back sometimes. What they do then is quite sickening. It is revolting and disgusting. When they come back, they are cannibals. They wish to eat living people. And if they bite you, they cause a sickness, and then you die, and then after that, you become like them and you wish to eat living people. We have to shoot them. A bullet in the head, that is what stops them. It's not so bad, you know. It's not like they are really alive.''

''I don't go for this,'' Adam said.

''Don't talk so much,'' Pilar said. ''I like you very much, *Americano,* but don't talk so much.''

She put her rifle to her shoulder. It was an old '03 Springfield. It had plenty of stopping power. Pilar was a good shot. She fired and one of the living dead went down with the middle of his face punched in.

''Come on,'' Pilar said, commanding. ''We stay together. We don't let any of these things get too close. That is what they are. Things. They aren't strong, but if there are too many, then it can be trouble.''

''I don't think I like this,'' Adam Nichols said. ''I don't think I like it at all.''

''I am sorry, but what you like and what you dislike is not all that important, if you will forgive my saying so,'' Miguel said. ''What does matter is that you are a good shot. You are one of our best shots. So, if you please, shoot some of these unfortunate dead people.''

Antonio and Pilar and Jordan and Miguel and Adam Nichols shot the living dead as the hunting party walked through the puffy clouds of fog that lay on the field. Adam felt like his brain was the flywheel in a clock about to go out of control. He remembered shooting black squirrels when he was a boy. Sometimes you shot a black squirrel and it fell down and then when you went to pick it up it tried to bite you and you had to shoot it again or smash its head with a rock or the stock of your rifle. He tried to make himself think this was just like shooting black squirrels. He tried to make himself think it was even easier, really, because dead people moved a lot slower than black squirrels. It was hard to shoot a squirrel skittering up a tree. It was not so hard to shoot a dead man walking like a tired drunk toward you.

Then Adam saw the old man who had sat by the pontoon bridge the other day. The old man's steel rimmed spectacles hung from one ear. They were unshattered. He looked quite silly, like something in a Chaplin film. Much of his chest had been torn open and bones stuck out at crazy angles. There were wettish tubular like things wrapped about the protruding bones of his chest.

He was coming at Adam Nichols like a trusting drunk who finds a friend and knows the friend will see him home.

"Get that one," said Jordan, the American college professor. "That one is yours."

Yes, Adam Nichols thought, the old man is mine. We have talked about goats and cats and doves.

Adam Nichols sighted. He took in a breath and held it. He waited.

The old man stumbled toward him.

Come, old man, Adam Nichols thought. *Come with your chest burst apart and your terrible appetite. Come with the mindless brute insistence that makes you continue. Come to the bullet that will give you at least the lie of a dignified ending. Come unto me, old man. Come unto me.*

"You let him draw too close," Miguel said. "Shoot him now."

Come, old man, Adam Nichols thought. *Come, because I am your luck. Come because I am all the luck you are ever going to have.*

Adam pulled the trigger. It was a fine shot. It took off the top of the old man's head. His glasses flew up and he flew back and lay on the fog-heavy ground.

"Good shot," Jordan said.

"No," Adam said, "just good luck."

3. IN A HOLE IN THE MOUNTAIN

It is not true that every man in Spain is named Paco, but it is true that if you call "Paco!" on the street of any city in Spain, you will have many more than one *"Qué?"* in response.

It was with a Paco that Adam Nichols found himself hiding from the fascist patrols. Paco's advanced age and formidable mustache made him look *Gitano*. Paco was a good fighter, and a good Spaniard, but not such a good communist. He said he was too old to have politics, but not too old to kill fascists.

Adam Nichols was now a communist because of some papers he had signed. Now he blew up things. For three months, he had been to a special school in Russia to learn demolitions. Adam Nichols was old enough now to know his talents. He was good at teaching young people to speak Spanish, and so for a while he had been a bored and boring high school teacher of Spanish in Oak Park, Illinois. Blowing up things and killing fascists was much more interesting, so he had gone to Spain.

There were other reasons, too. He seldom let himself ponder these.

The previous day, Adam Nichols had blown up a railroad trestle that certain military leaders had agreed was important, and, except for old Paco, the comrades who had made possible this act of demolition were all dead. The fascists were seeking the man who had destroyed the trestle. But Paco knew how to hide.

Where Paco and Adam were hiding was too small to be a cave. It was just a hole in a mountain side. It was hard to spot unless you knew just what you were looking for.

It was dark in the hole. Paco and Adam could not build a fire. But it was safe to talk if you talked in the same low embarrassed way you did in the confessional. Because they were so close, there were times when Adam could almost feel that Paco was breathing for him and that he was breathing for Paco. A moment came to Adam Nichols that made him think, *This is very much like being lovers,* but then he decided it was not so. He would never be as close with a lover as he was now with Paco.

After many hours of being with Paco in the close dark, Adam said, "Paco, there is something I wish to ask thee."

Adam Nichols spoke in the most formal Spanish. It was what was needed.

Gravely, though he was not a serious man, Paco said, "Then ask, but remember, Comrade, I am an aged man, and do not mistake age for wisdom." Paco chuckled. He was pleased he had remembered to say "comrade." Sometimes he forgot. It was hard to be a good communist.

"I need to speak of what I have seen. Of abomination. Of horror. Of impossibility."

"Art thou speaking of war?"

"*Sí.*"

"Then dost thou speak of courage, too?" Paco asked. "Of decency? Or self-sacrifice?"

"No, *Viejo*," Adam Nichols said. "Of these things, much has been said and much written. Courage, decency, self-sacrifice are to be found in peace or war. Stupidity, greed, arrogance are to be found in peace or war. But I wish to speak with thee of that which I have seen only during time of war. It is madness. It is what cannot be."

Paco said, "What wouldst thou ask of me?"

"Paco," Adam Nichols said, "do the dead walk?"

"Hast thou seen this?"

"*Verdad.* I have seen this. No. I think I have seen this. Years ago, a long time back, in that which was my first war, I thought I saw it. It was in that war, Paco *Viejo*, that I think I became a little crazy. And now I think I have seen it in this war. There were others with me when we went to kill the dead. They would not talk of it, after. After, we all got drunk and made loud toasts which were vows of silence." Adam Nichols was silent for a time. Then he said again, "Do the dead walk?"

"Thou hast good eyes, Comrade Adam. Thou shootest well. Together we have been in battle. Thou dost not become crazy. What thou hast seen, thou hast seen truly."

Adam Nichols was quiet. He remembered when he was a young man and his heart was broken by a love gone wrong and the loss of well-holding arms and a smile that was for no one else but him. He felt worse now, filled with sorrow and fear both, and with his realizing the world was such a serious place. He said, "It is a horrible thing when the dead walk."

"*Verdad.*"

"Dost thou understand what happens?"

"Perhaps."

"Then perhaps you can tell me."

"Perhaps." Paco sighed. His sigh seemed to move the darkness in waves. "Years ago, I knew a priest. He was not a fascist priest. He was a nice man. The money in his plate did not go to buy candlesticks. He built a motion picture theater for his village. He knew that you need to laugh on Saturdays more than you need stained glass windows. The movies he showed were very good movies. Buster Keaton. Harold Lloyd. Joe Bonomo. John Gilbert. KoKo the Klown and Betty Boop cartoons. This priest did not give a damn for politics, he told me. He gave a damn about people. And that is the reason, I believe, that he stopped being a priest. He had some money. He had three women who loved him and were content to share him. I think he was all right, this priest.

"It was he who told me of the living dead."

"And canst thou tell me?"

"Well, yes, I believe I can. There is no reason not to. I have sworn no oaths."

"What is it, then? Why do the dead rise? Why do they seek the flesh of the living?"

"This man who had been a priest was not certain about Heaven, but he was most definite about Hell. Yes, Hell was the Truth. Hell was for the dead.

"But when we turn this Earth of ours into Hell, there is no need for the dead to go below.

"Why should they bother?

"And canst thou doubt that much of this ball of mud upon which we dwell is today hell, Comrade? With each new war and each new and better way of making war, there is more and more hell and so we have more and more inhabitants of hell with us.

"And of course, no surprise, they have their hungers. They are demons. At least that is what some might call them, though I myself seldom think to call them anything.

And the food of demons is human flesh. It is a simple thing, really.''

"Paco . . ."

"*Sí?*"

"This is not rational."

"And art thou a rational man?"

"Yes. No."

"So?"

" 'The Living Dead,' maybe that's what somebody would call them. Well, hell, don't you think that would make some newspaperman just ecstatic? It would be bigger than 'Lindy in Paris!' Bigger than——''

"And thou dost believe such a newspaper story could be printed? And perhaps the *Book of the Living Dead* could be written?And perhaps a motion picture of the Living Dead as well, with Buster Keaton, perhaps? Comrade Adam, such revelation would topple the world order.

"Perhaps someday the world will be ready for such awful knowledge, Comrade Adam.

"For now, it is more than enough that those of us who know of it must know of it, thank you very kindly.

"And with drink and with women and with war and with whatever gives us comfort, we must try not to think over much about what it is we know."

"Paco," Adam Nichols said in the dark, "I think I want to scream. I think I want to scream now."

"No, Comrade. Be quiet now. Breathe deep. Breathe with me and deep. Let me breathe for you. Be quiet."

"All right," Adam said after a time. "It is all right now."

A day later, Paco thought it would be safe to leave the hole in the side of the mountain. They were spotted by an armored car full of fascists. A bullet passed through Paco's lung. It was a mortal shot.

"Bad luck, Paco," Adam Nichols said. He put a bullet into the old man's brain and went on alone.

X

"You're really not helping me. You know that."

"Bad on me. I thought I was here for you to help me. My foolishness. Damn the luck."

"I've decided, then, we'll go the way we did before, with electro-convulsive therapy. We'll—"

I am for god's sake 61 years old and I am going to die because of occluded arteries or because of a cirrhotic liver or because of an aneurysm in brain or belly waiting to go pop, or because of some some damn thing—and when I die I wish to be dead to be dead and that is all.

"—a series of 12. We've often had good results—"

and, believe me, I am not asking for Jesus to make me a sunbeam, I am not asking for heaven in any way, shape, or form. Gentlemen, when I die I wish to be dead.

"—particularly with depression. There are several factors, of course—"

I'm looking for dead, that's D-E-A-D, and I don't want to be a goddamn carnival freak show act and man is just a little lower than the angels and pues y nada and you get older and you get confused and you become afraid.

"We'll begin tomorrow—"

no bloody chance because now the world is hell and if you doubt it, then you don't know the facts, Gentlemen. No bloody chance. We ended the war by dropping hell on Nagasaki and on Hiroshima, and we opened up Germany and discovered all those hells, and during the siege of Stalingrad, the living ate the dead, and ta-ta, Gentlemen, turnabout is fair play, and we're just starting to know the hells that good old Papa Joe put together no bloody chance and we're not blameless, oh, no, ask that poor nigger hanging burning from the tree, ask the Rosenbergs who got cooked up nice and brown, ask—Welcome to hell, and how do you like it now, Gentlemen?

When the world is hell, the dead walk.

XI

When they returned to Ketchum, Idaho on June 30, the old man was happy. Anyone who saw him will tell you. He was not supposed to drink because of his anti-depressant medication, but he did drink. It did not affect him badly. He sang several songs. One was "*La Quince Brigada*," from the Spanish Civil War. He sang loudly and off-key; he made a joyful racket. He said one of the great regrets of his life was that he had never learned to play the banjo.

Later, he had his wife, Mary, put on a Burl Ives record on the Webcor phonograph. It was a 78, "The Riddle Song." He listened to it several times.

> *How can there be a cherry*
> *that has no stone?*
>
> *How can there be a chicken*
> *that has no bone?*
>
> *How can there be a baby*
> *with no crying?"*

Mary asked if the record made him sad.

No, he said, he was not sad at all. The record was beautiful. If there are riddles, there are also answers to riddles.

So, so then, I have not done badly. Some good stories, some good books. I have written well and truly. I have sometimes failed, but I have tried. I have sometimes been a foolish man, and even a small-minded or mean-spirited one, but I have always been a man, and I will end as a man.

It was early and he was the only one up. The morning of Sunday, July 2, was beautiful. There were no clouds. There was sunshine.

He went to the front foyer. He liked the way the light struck the oak-paneled walls and the floor. It was like being in a museum or in a church. It was a well-lighted place and it felt clean and airy.

Carefully, he lowered the butt of the Boss shotgun to the floor. He leaned forward. The twin barrels were cold circles in the scarred tissue just above his eyebrows.

He tripped both triggers.

PART ONE

WHERE WERE YOU
WHEN THE LIGHTS
WENT OUT?

DON'T/WALK

CHAN McCONNELL

Evan took two involuntary backward steps, thinking, *jesus, that guy looks DEAD*.

He was waiting for the pedestrian signal at Fifty-seventh and Central Park South. Which was stupid, because in the city only tourists did what lights told them. Evan had a map of Manhattan in his briefcase; squassation would have been preferable to actually unfolding it to consult in public, exposing himself to the sneers of the wavetide of walkers who didn't *need* maps.

He tried to keep his eyes dead ahead, radar pricked for bums and impediments. Simple hindbrain programming had caused him to stop for the light. Veteran New Yorkers dashed between slushing taxis; it was elegant, balletic in its way. Old ladies kept to the curb and waited on the light. Sidewalk loons. Street people who resented intrusion onto *their* corner.

Evan looked east and saw a whitehaired, toadish man squatting in an outhouse-sized newsstand shake his head in disdain. People were such idiots. This guy has seen everything the wandering world could offer to offend him. Morons, imbeciles, walking wounded.

The worst are the non-natives, like that monkey dick on the corner with the fag briefcase. See him? Lo-Cal simp. Tofu commie. Brain-dead ballbag.

Evan was pretending not to squirm under the news vendor's scorn when he was bumped forward. The NYC crowd teemed and backswelled like lemmings to shove this stranger out into the traffic. They elbowed past and made tracks like they knew where they were going.

Piker. Newcomer. OUT OF TOWNER. Want us to draw you a fuggin MAP?

Evan actually turned to see who had bumped him, and that was when he stepped backward. Two steps was as far as he could recoil before he collided *en passant* with somebody else. He wasn't just a domino, he was an *amateur* domino.

Evan bumped. Recoiled. Made a face.

The guy swayed. The flies that cut loose from his head resettled. His mouth hung, deformed by brown teeth in decayed stubs. A stringer of cloudy saliva roped his chin to his chest. Fetid rags and the stink of seawater. His unshod feet were totally black, besooted, scabbed and missing a few toes. His flesh was the tint of a blown fluorescent tube; blood had nothing to do with his color. His greasy hair was weirdly chopped, angular, alive with insects.

Evan held. He had seen bums, protected his spare change, and smelled odors meant for biological warfare.

The absolute worst had been in this city, two days ago. Guy asleep—or dead—on a bench in the middle of Upper Broadway, pants down. The crack of his ass was mortared shut with impacted feces. Flies laid eggs and fed. Evan thought he could withstand any assault; this one tightened his throat, and he put it behind him as fast as he could. A northbound D train thundered beneath the street. Evan thought it was an incoming earthquake. No one around him minded. The oily upblast of air from the tunnel grate ruffled his clothes and stirred the flies on the bum.

Flies then, flies now.

The derelict stared through Evan. He weaved as though hypnotized or drugged. Gravity toyed with him. He waited for the crosswalk signal. Some people bleated in disgust. Some made room. But not too much room, not even for this creature.

Evan timed the next taxi gap and bolted, boldly, into the street. The cab highballed past without even a horn toot, close enough to whipcrack his shirt. He felt baptized.

He made distance toward what locals called the Deuce and hung a right, not wanting to be stuck on the same trajectory as that chunk of human garbage, that guy who looked dead.

No way for anyone here to know that Evan was more than just another human ant blindly tracking food scent. He had justification, a *reason* to be here.

Three interlocking reasons, not to get highfalutin' about it.

The status bump afforded by his recent promotion in the law firm had brought with it certain responsibilities that involved travel at a moment's notice, one. He needed to drown the acrimonious split with Marie and work challenges engaged different glands, two. Full office, nameplate, better letterhead bond, keener toys, three. Feeding time in the pit of legal chickenhawks. Evan was learning to enjoy smugness.

As he proceeded west on Forty-second assorted individuals with whom Evan was not acquainted solicited handouts or offered him a good time, whatever that meant. They seemed to speak *past* him, to the city at large, with no eye contact. Evan noticed all the cinemas were playing sequels. Movies derived from other movies, an endless replication of Roman numerals that was somehow comforting in its consistency. *Buttered Clam II* PLUS *Return of the Anal Avenger*.

Here, you had to be more of a sidewalk daredevil, weaving and looping and doing every damn thing save going airborne to dodge the panhandlers, duck the come-ons, avert hazards and stay locked on course. Another crosswalk, another crowd surging ever forward.

Somewhere in this city, Evan thought, there's a man or woman who is in front. Walking with nobody ahead of them, moving fast and efficiently enough to keep from being intimidated or bullied from behind. Someone out there is strolling point on this cattle drive.

Maybe that dead guy he'd just encountered.

First were street people. Then beggars, then winos, then addicts, then derelicts. Then. Like derma or strata, scratch through enough layers and you'll hit red paydirt. Shopping carters. Bag ladies. Subway sentinels, grimed but for the whites of their lunatic eyes. Presumably you hit rock bottom with the subhuman tunnel dwellers of myth. Reptile eyes, stumps for limbs, skin chancred with phosphorescent infections, radiating a soft, venomous green.

Like that dead guy's skin.

Evan glanced back. It was a move of studied nonchalance. *Something detoured my educated and tasteful urban eye. No, I wasn't frightened or anything. Just checking, thanks.* Bums could fixate on you. If you met their blank, mad gaze, they might follow you.

Don't feed 'em and they won't follow you home.

Nobody new was tailing Evan, merely the pedestrians who were not as far ahead as he was. Keep going.

He had decided to walk back to his hotel because the novelty of New York cabbies had quickly palled, and he had not yet mustered the nerve to risk the trains without a native guide. The island was so small you could walk across it in half an hour, if you weren't a sofa spud. He gnawed a loose cuticle and bit free a nubbin of dead skin. Evan's fingertips were callused from nailbiting.

He spat out the dead skin. His own flesh, rendered unto the city as microscopic litter. Biodegradable. It was okay to abandon this tiny chunk of himself.

His hotel was in what they called Midtown. Its rooms let for a price that once could have adequately covered Evan's monthly rent. Evan was an up-and-coming junior legal partner, and his assignment to take depositions from people in Manhattan had been completed as of this afternoon, leaving him a spare day to fritter. Cosmic flux had conspired to keep him ignorant of New York City for thirty years. That could end now. Adventure trilled within him; he would return unscathed from this jungle of concrete and steel. Evan triumphant. Evan had grown up in Whiting, Indiana, with Chicago as his idea of a city. Chicago was not New York, and had prepared him poorly. This was just as humid, just as ugly, as brutal, but here it didn't matter— this was New York, New York, for godsake. An emotional Disneyland for the spiritually underprivileged, the provincially hidebound, and all the cripples of personality that America could grind forth. New York was where all things new and noteworthy happened first. . . .

The red stopped him at another crosswalk, on Broadway. To his left, a welling surf of northbound foot traffic was coming up fast. Crutching along, bottlenecking the press of bodies, was a woman with half a face.

Evan's sign changed. WALK. He was propelled forward. The woman was swallowed by the press of pedestrians. It was a flyby illusion, that she'd lacked half a face. One blink of eyes stung with smog. She hadn't *really* been missing half her face; Evan's visual crumb would never stand erect in court. Could he *prove* he'd just seen a woman with half a face? That the front of her dress was stained with what *might have* been the other half?

Evan peeked fast. The citizens headed in the opposite direction all looked alike from behind. No proof. A big-city hallucinatory joke. History already. The current carried him away, in his chosen direction, away from the pocket mystery. Forget it, move on, easy as falling asleep at the wheel of a slot car.

Evan saw his next dead person sitting at a bus stop. It appeared to be an elderly man who had begun to sag into the interstices of the bench planks. He was idly masticating a gob of meat, shiny-slick with a sweat of stale blood. Flies lit on it. Flies crawled on his face. Flies walked into his mouth. Well-fed flies walked out.

The man on the bench had no eyes. Just flies.

Evan let Broadway pull him south. Wasn't his hotel near Penn Station, Thirty-fourth or Thirty-third? Northeast or southwest corner? He resisted the urge to consult his map, trusting that he would recognize a landmark.

Don't let them know you don't belong. The city will get you there.

He peeled a sliver of nail from his index finger.

Gotcha.

His hotel boasted a liveried doorman. He was normal. He smiled at Evan. Evan passed and watched. The doorman's smile evaporated. He kept his attention on the street. For a fleeting second, Evan had merited notice. Only just. Not now.

People lingered over late lunches in the coffee shop. People in the lobby perused newspapers with disinterest, impatient for the late editions to hit. The young lady working registration informed Evan that there were no messages. She smiled, as a close to their exchange. And Evan no longer existed for her, either.

The elevator disgorged a Keystone Kops gaggle of foreigners wearing identical shoes, sunk into themselves and their shopping plans. They ignored Evan, who boarded in the company of three other guests.

None of them looked at Evan on the way up. None smiled.

In his room, Evan dry-swallowed four Excedrin and washed them down with an overpriced club soda from the room's mini-bar fridge. The TV was still on, sound down. He'd left it that way this morning. It was nondemanding companionship. Angrily he yanked the fastidious Windsor knot in his tie to half-mast. Bad for the tie.

Forget it; it was the heat, the swamp humidity. The dirty air had gifted him with a cluster headache. He needed to acclimate to this more fervid and demanding environment. Yes.

Onscreen, a too-earnest yuppie newsreader jabbered soundlessly. A chroma-keyed box superimposed behind him displayed a computer graphic of a satellite plunging back from Earth orbit.

Another malfunctioning piece of NASA garbage, thought Evan. Millions to put the damned thing aloft so it could change its batty microchip brain, and now it's gonna crash through some hayseed's barn in Wisconsin.

He nibbled a fingernail. His headache was slamming in now; body-blows.

The luridly colored screamer at the bottom of the features graphic read VIRUS FROM SPACE?

Crap. Useless minutiæ detailing why indifferently manufactured hi-tech junk didn't work worth a rat fart. Who cared? *News*—what a tragicomedy. Burning buildings and car wrecks and the nitty on the latest poverty case to spin out and smack the wall. Irrelevant noise clogging the airwaves; as if larding on scoop after scoop of non-information could possibly do anyone any good.

Why couldn't they devote a slice of prime time to why material success was a means, not an end? Why couldn't they explore how little real love there was in the world? Why not discuss how the best mounted and most carefully ordered lives could collapse into despair?

Why wouldn't one of these assholes take the time to investigate how an educated man who made all the right moves and was upward bound in his chosen field could make it to age thirty without ever connecting with another human being in any meaningful fashion?

Evan's family was dispersed—parental divorce, plus a smattering of funerals he had not attended. His relationships with suitable women were all closed files. They were confluences of income level and wardrobe and sexual programming. Evan's habit was to disengage if a liaison grew enough fibrin to start binding.

Hotel cable was a riot. On 2 was a school's-out summer sci-fi blockbuster; steroidal dudes firing thousands of rounds from automatic weapons and never hitting anything significant . . . save two or three hundred goo-filled aliens.

On 3 was a knifekill horror ragout. The body count stood at twelve.

On 4 was a suspense-action nightmare starring a puckish lead who quipped one-liners while firing thousands of rounds from automatic weapons and never . . .

On 5—the Adult Entertainment Channel—Evan saw a woman who had been fucked by a man. Then she had been fucked by two women with sex tools galore. Presently she was being fucked by three men.

He flipped back to the news channel and did not extinguish the TV. The headache finally drove him to bed, clothes on, just for a moment.

He awoke at 8:45 P.M. He briefly considered ordering from room service and gave up when he could not get an answer from the kitchen.

He straightened his seams and took the fire stairs down to the lobby. Still too hot for a jacket. He did not like riding in the elevator.

He wanted to venture into the New York night and feel it seethe. To walk around. The city had things to tell him.

Heat leached up from the sidewalk slabs. Evan slipped past the doorman, who was scanning the side street for cabs. Absurdly easy; the doorman never spotted him.

Evan's map was folded double and parked in his back pocket, just in case, you understand. The air smelled like industrial lubricant.

The stoplights, the urban neon, the billboards and crosswalk signs shone much brighter at night. They pulsed with warm electric messages, they shimmered and glared with undeniable power. Evan found them oddly romantic. Hell, what *was* New York, if not one big monument to the juice of advertising and the imparting of information? Just by drifting around, you could accumulate volumes.

There were a lot more dead people walking around, seeing the sights, absorbing the useless electronic messages. Evan noted them as surreptitiously as possible.

Evan fell in behind a couple—normal—strolling between dinner and dessert, seeking cappuccino. They had, he observed, learned the trick of walking in step despite the difference in their heights. He saw them cut a wide berth for the dead person walking in the opposite direction, toward Evan.

The dead person had the same skin hue Evan had noticed on his first sighting. A pulped and rotten nose. Gashes and gores tracked up one side of its head, as though it had been sideswiped by a garbage truck doing about thirty. It dragged one lame leg but made fair time. It did not hold up the crowd.

It did not see Evan at all. They were on different trajectories. Actually, the couple was more interesting to Evan for what the woman did.

As the dead person passed, Evan saw her glance back. She had seen this corpse on the hoof, too, and thought it as weird as Evan had earlier. Her expression was skittish and tentative; she not only *wanted* to look, she wanted to stare, and tell others, and make a scene—Evan could read all this in the instant he saw her face. But she did not want anyone, including her boyfriend, to know that she had sneaked that forbidden peek. She needed to verify to herself that she had just seen something too unearthly to exist on such an otherwise pleasant evening. The act of permitting it to pass them was an acknowledgment of its existence, but not of its existence as a *dead thing*. The strangeness of bums and beggars could excuse a lot, to a rationalizing mind, but what Evan saw in the woman's look-back was *I just saw a for-christ-sake dead thing!*

And when she had looked back, her eyes had transected Evan's. And in that moment, *he* knew that *she* knew. He bit loose a shred of callus and spat.

The woman turned back, still strolling. She rested her head on her date's shoulder. He pointed out something in a store window and they both laughed. They kept on walking.

Evan did not look behind after the dead person passed him. He hit the corner and waited on the light. He did not want to follow the couple anymore.

People stacked up behind him, raindrift in a grate. The impatient ones leaked into the street. Evan watched them pinball without moving his head. He could feel the excitement of their risk-taking, by proxy. They zigged, they zagged, they made it to the other side and beat the light. The pell-mell onrush of taxis never saw any of them.

A man stepped off the curb near Evan, weighing whether to rely on the light or go for it. He was older, midsixties, wearing a Mets cap, bifocals, and a hearing aid with a braided wire that trailed into his hip pocket. Evan wondered whether the man's audiovisual gear could be trusted in terms of the unforgiving traffic.

A dead person nudged between Evan and the older man. Evan's spine locked. He kept eyes front and tried to make sense of his peripheral vision.

If the previous ambulatory corpse had been kissed by a truck, this one had been pasted flat by an express train. A splintered jut of shoulder bone pointed right at Evan's ear, through the shreds of a green windbreaker stiff and black with dried blood. Broken rib struts stuck out on tatters of sinew. The leg nearest Evan terminated in a gangrenous stump, swollen and reeking thickly. Its skull had been pushed out of shape by some tremendous impact; hydrostatic pressure had popped free one eye. It hung by nerves and a string of ligament, the sclera gone the color of urine.

"Hey, quit pushin', dammit." The older man had spoken before he actually turned to see who was pushing. Evan could perceive the man, from the corner of his eye, better than the dead thing between them.

It stank of bile and maggots.

The older man's eyes opened up wide.

The dead thing grabbed him by the hair and chewed a raw, crimson mouthful right out of his neck. It bit the cord of the hearing aid in two. The baseball cap fell. Whatever the man might have used to holler in alarm was torn free and swallowed. The thing ate his ear and cheek with its next bite.

The sign blinked. WALK. Everyone behind Evan swept forward, jostling him as though to dislodge him. Clear the clog and keep on moving.

The older man crumpled facedown to the rusted iron of a runoff grille. The pedestrians stepped over him. By dawn he would be sufficiently stomped, chomped, and stripped down to rinse away, into the sewers.

It was easier for Evan to press on to the next light. En route he began to take note of more people, littering the curbs and subway entrances like sniper victims, leaking, sundered, or deathly still, like the bum on the bench, two days ago.

A woman in a shit-stained housecoat tried to hold her

smashed head stable as she stood up. She was dead. Big bites were missing from her breasts and legs, through ragged holes in the housecoat. She wobbled. Too much meat had been taken, especially from her neck. Her head tore loose and hit the pavement with an overripe *splut,* rolling once. Her nose stopped it like a little stabilizer. The headless body sat down hard, limbs sprawling, and remained propped against a litter basket.

The flies moved in. WALK.

Having your dick bitten off was nothing, thought Evan. Having your tits chowed or your brain gulped in hunks was no strain, compared with being an outsider. If the dead people knew . . . if Evan gave himself away by the slightest gesture, as the older man just had . . . then the dead people would make Evan a non-person. The glow-in-the-dark subterraneans would puzzle over bits of him, afloat in other people's excretions and flushings.

It was dragging on late, and Evan had no idea where he was. He dared not pull his map. He stopped at the next crosswalk.

He wondered if any of the tumbling, high-ticket space junk would fall toward New York. Maybe Manhattan. Friction might not incinerate it completely. It could hit the center of the city. Perhaps even the crosswalk in which he was standing, waiting.

WALK.

It startled him. He bit too hard on his fingernail and drew blood.

Dead people crowded up to the rear. The stench of their bacterially polluted fluids and decomposing viscera wafted at him. The coolness of their flesh buffeted from behind to ice his marrow.

All he had to do was keep *not* looking at them. He already knew what was there to be seen. He did not *have* to look.

So far, so good.

Evan stared straight ahead. A very expensive billboard huckstered an international megaconglom's most popular soft drink, original formula. As he watched, the display blew a fuse or something, lost power. The colorful visual attack ceased in a second. Now the board was a black void in the middle of miles of shouting light. In a peculiar way, the dark, blank square was more noticeable. It was as though nighttime had reclaimed a slice while Evan had borne witness.

A normal person would be terrified, thought Evan. A lone Us engirded by an army of Thems. But he was dealing, maintaining, and was surprised to feel nothing at all, especially not fear.

He could ride this predicament. The loser always has an excuse; the winner always has a program.

He was first to the next curb. First to move when the light changed. He must, therefore, have become the Guy in Front. Perhaps all those that followed him did so because they thought he was going somewhere.

Or maybe they were just hungry.

Vapor lamps make everybody look cadaverous. Bums could be pretty gross. And the city generally stinks of tons of garbage every day. No strain.

Evan waited for the next light.

NECROPHILE

NANCY A. COLLINS

I knew Mouli from my days as a strychnine junkie.

He first came to my attention at the midnight grind-house that screened gore epics like *I Eat Your Brains with a Spoon*. The Tri-State was an acquired taste, with its gummy floors and reeking draperies, and the handful of hardcore fans that frequented it came to recognize one another. I was even more conspicuous, being the only female in the group. Mouli was one of my fellow daredevils.

It wasn't hard to spot him. Even then he affected the oversized black duster, faded khaki trousers, and army-surplus boots. His thin, intense features were accentuated by the short, spiky yellow growth that covered his skull like porcupine quills. Although he wasn't very tall, he was muscled like a dancer. You'd think twice about fucking with Mouli.

We developed a nodding acquaintance at the theater's

candy counter, but we never actually spoke to one another. Then one night I was taken to the Well, a live venue with the same kind of reputation as the Tri-State, to see a local band called the Sex Ghouls. There, amongst the punkers, punkettes, skinheads, mods, metalheads, and artfags, was Mouli, still in his black duster and combat boots. My friend grabbed me by the elbow.

"Hey, Sam! There's that guy I was tellin' you about!"

I couldn't recall being told about any "guy." I was towed across the dance floor, past wildly flailing dancers, and brought before Mouli.

"Hey, Mouli! I'd like you to say hello to a friend of mine! Samantha Reed, Charlie Moulson. Charlie Moulson; Samantha Reed."

He smiled quietly, extending a long-fingered hand with large knuckles. The sleeve on his duster rode up, exposing the permanent grin of a death's-head tattooed on his pulse point. "Mouli. The Tri-State, right? Mexican Hats and a large Coke?"

I laughed, impressed. "Yeah. Call me Sam."

Mouli smiled that tight, quiet smile and fished an un-filtered Camel out of his breast pocket. "Buy you a drink, Sam?"

We spent the rest of the set huddled around a wobbly table in the back of the bar, bellowing over the amplified furor. Mouli was magnetic. He wasn't macho or domineer-ing; but there was something about the quiet, sure way he handled himself that attracted me. It was in his voice, in the way he tilted his head when he spoke. Even in the way he moved his hands. Mouli was tapped into something pri-mal. Mouli was Cool.

We had finished discussing the merits of Bottin over Savini when the band finished and one of the Sex Ghouls— a dangerously thin youth without a strand of chest hair— made his way to our table. The Sex Ghoul was stripped to the waist, his head shaved clean except for a braided for-elock. He looked like a tubercular Yul Brynner from *The Ten Commandments*.

"Hey, Mouli! Drinks on th' house. Bring th' lady if she's cool."

Mouli nodded and stabbed out his Camel with a twist of his wrist. "Okay. You interested?" This he addressed to me.

"Sure." I shrugged nonchalantly, hoping I was presenting the proper aura of world-weary ambivalence.

I followed them into the tiny "dressing room" off the bar's storeroom, where the bands prepped for their bouts on stage. A greasy mirror ran the length of one wall and below it a cheap Formica countertop. Both were cracked and smeared with graffiti. A janitor's sink occupied the far back corner, stinking of sour mops and urine.

The Sex Ghouls and their groupies and roadies and other flotsam were crowded into the narrow room, all talking at the top of their lungs. When Mouli made his appearance, one of the crowd yowled; "Awright! The Death Man's here! Now the party can start!"

There was hooting and whistling and banging of fists on cheap Formica. The forelocked Sex Ghoul produced a smoking lump of something wrapped in canvas from a portable cooler under the sink. A collection of wasp-waist beer glasses lined the countertop and two Sex Ghouls were busy decanting portions of alcohol and dry ice into each. No one paid them the slightest attention. All eyes were on Mouli. With the efficiency of a surgeon, Mouli shrugged out of his raincoat. He wore a white muscle-shirt that exposed arms alive with intertwining roses, thorns, serpents, deathsheads, and crossed knives from shoulders to wrists. In one hand he held a small brown bottle. Silence fell as they watched him withdraw the squeeze-bulb dropper in one fluid motion. He then dispensed minuscule drops of liquid into the roiling, steaming glasses. He moved with machine precision, endowed with a grace that belied his bulky shoes and raw knuckles. Once finished, he replaced the stopper in the bottle and lifted two of the glasses. He handed one of the ominously smoking drinks to me. It was cold to the touch.

"What is it?" I tried not to sound too worried.

"Witches' Brew." He sipped off the top of his drink, his eyes never leaving mine. I noticed for the first time that they were of a blue too painful to look at.

I drank, my eyes meeting and holding his gaze for the

briefest exchange. The alcohol was cold, like Stoly straight from the freezer. The fumes from the dry ice made me dizzy.

"What's in it?" I asked after I'd drained half the glass. My brain was full of fire and ice. Frost was forming on my frontal lobes.

"Strychnine." He exposed the brown bottle still cradled in his palm. I could see the white label with its grinning skull and crossed thigh bones.

For an eternal second my heart did not beat, my blood did not circulate, my lungs did not draw breath, my brain did not function. I felt the room's narrow confines draw away, and for one delicious, terrifying second I was on the edge of a precipice, staring into a fathomless void.

"Strange stuff, strychnine . . ." I was back in the room. Mouli was talking. There was something shining in his eyes. My blood surged back into my veins. My heart began beating like an angry fist. ". . . in just the right dosage, it's an incredible stimulant. Lots of labs use it to cut their speed and acid. But if you use a microgram too much, you end up with horrible, painful spasms."

"Is that so?" My words came from far away. I found myself taking another swallow of Brew. I was still on the edge of the chasm, but the exhilaration was dimming. The strychnine was already taking effect . . . my scalp was crawling, making my hair bristle. I could feel my pupils dilate. I realized Mouli was still talking to me.

"If we take a cab, we can still make the Tri-State in time for the midnight flick. They're screening *Dawn of the Dead*."

We left the Sex Ghouls and the sweaty confines of the Well for the dark belly of the Tri-State. We screwed like minks in the balcony. The warped, over-amplified screams pouring from the sound system masked our cries as we thrashed in the back row. The poison in our veins pushed us to double-jointed ecstasies.

To appreciate Life at its fullest one must be constantly aware of Death. Death is everywhere. It could be a car driven by a little old lady tripped out on Valium. It could be in an alleyway, slate-eyed and eager for a fix. It could be lurking in a stranger with the face of a choirboy and the brain of a reptile. It could be in the air you breathe, the food you eat, the water you drink. It could be roiling in the saliva of a baby's kiss. You never know. But *we* knew. As we wrapped ourselves around each other, we knew exactly where Death was. Our knowledge produced an iron-bar/ smelter rush that threatened to fuse our spines.

When the film ended and the houselights came up, we decamped to Mouli's place. I was not surprised that it was within walking distance of the Tri-State.

Nor was I surprised to find his tiny apartment papered with movie posters. Everywhere I looked there were reminders of our shared passion. I had not, however, expected the black-and-white eight-by-tens that covered every open space the posters didn't. It was then I began to grasp the extent of Mouli's fascination with Death.

Most of the photos were of disinterments. Some of the corpses were fairly fresh, their individuality not yet eradicated by rot. Most were beyond identification; little more than a collection of brittle bones wrapped in desiccated parchment. After the Technicolor splatters I grew up with, this was anticlimactic. There was a morbid interest on my part, but no disgust or horror. All I felt was the strychnine giving me slight stomach cramps. Nothing serious. The poison burned bright in my veins, giving exhausted flesh another spur.

Mouli was undressing. Despite a solid hour of sex, I had yet to see him naked. He skinned off his muscle shirt, and for the first time I saw the tattoo.

It takes a special breed of human to endure a full body tattoo. It's an incredibly painful procedure, as befits bodily mutilation. The Orientals—the Japanese *yakuza* in particular—consider the full body tattoo a sign of honor and manhood. To bear one is a testimony to one's determination and personal stamina. It is the mark of a fanatic.

Across Mouli's back was tattooed—to scale—a copy of Kubin's *The Ghost at the Ball*. A desiccated skeleton dressed in the moldering remains of formal evening wear and a beaver hat, its jaws agape in silent laughter, carried in its broomstick arms the naked body of a young girl. Was she dead? Asleep? Succumbed to a swoon of erotic abandon?

It was then I recognized Mouli for what he was; a flame. I knew he would burn me. The game was to see how long I could avoid the searing. If I was lucky, I would escape with only my wings singed. If I wasn't careful, he would char my bones to ash.

We fucked the rest of the night away on the old mattress that served as his bed. My hands grew chill as they ran across the tattoo on his back. I blamed it on the strychnine.

Mouli's hobby was photographing open graves.

He had long ago learned the names of the sextons at the local cemeteries, plying them with free liquor and shop-talk. They were eager to talk to anyone who'd listen. Few people outside of their profession had any interest in grave-yards. In turn, they'd call him whenever there was a dis-interment. Mouli would be there at the graveside as the earth was spooned up.

He had a quaint little hand-held Brownie that he used on these outings. Somehow high-speed photography just didn't seem appropriate. He developed most of his film in the cramped confines of his bathroom, sometimes locking himself in there for so long I was forced to walk to a nearby gas station.

Mouli's digs were too small for me to move into on a full-time basis, so I continued to pay the rent on my apartment in order to have a place for my things. Most of my nights were spent on Mouli's mattress. I lost weight. I saw little of my former friends. Although I kept my job at the library, I was having more and more trouble functioning at work.

The strychnine was the ultimate kick. The ultimate high. Mouli had taken me to the mountaintop and shown me the vast, black chaos of the Last Kingdom. I had caught only the briefest of glimpses, but the memory of it haunted my waking hours. How could I take such trivialities as rent, social responsibilities, and personal hygiene seriously once

I had seen Beyond? All things outside of Mouli, the Brew, and Death were inconsequential.

The sex was fire inside a diamond; cold, hot, perfect. My life became a blurred succession of work hours, feverish thrashing, damp sheets, strychnine binges, and midnight screenings at the Tri-State.

One night, after a particularly intense bout of sex, Mouli propped himself against the wall. The knobs of his vertebrae pressed against the lobby poster for *I Was a Teenage Frankenstein.* He automatically reached for his postcoital cigarette. The match hissed and sulfur wafted from his cupped palm. Even in the permanent gloom of the apartment I could tell he was watching me. I always felt his gaze, even in my sleep. It made me uneasy.

"What do you see?"

I had not expected a question. Mouli tended to be uncommunicative after sex. I moved uneasily against the sheets. They smelled faintly of mildew. Those eyes. Blue as a Maxfield Parrish sky. When he had the Brew in him, they were the eyes of a god on earth.

"You know. What do you see when you take the Brew?"

I thought of the cold dark and the spiked mixture of fear and excitement that followed. "I don't know how to describe it."

"Do you see anyone? A woman, maybe?"

I was genuinely surprised. "You see a *woman*?"

Mouli looked uncomfortable. He had said too much. His features flickered in the glow of his cigarette. "Sometimes."

I felt a tug of jealousy amid the curiosity. "What does she look like?"

He shifted uneasily, the tattoos rippling like living things in the half-light. "She's the most beautiful woman I've ever seen."

I realized then I was only a proxy. A stand-in for his unattainable fatal beauty. There had never been any pretense of Love between us. Our relationship was held together by the cement of mutual obsession and sex. Yet something went cold in me. Mouli stubbed out his cigarette and rolled back onto his hip. He was sporting another one of his tireless erections. But it wasn't for me. It was She who inspired him to rigidity. I was merely the altar on which he made his offerings.

It was around that time that Mouli got his job at the morgue.

Is it perverse for a music lover to work in a record shop? For a bibliophile to work in a bookstore? Mouli loved Death in all its forms and had spent most of his adult life surrounding himself with artifacts of that grand passion. Becoming a morgue attendant was the realization of one of his fondest dreams—like a small boy becoming a fireman. I was happy for him.

The disinterment photos were replaced, one by one, by photographs of the occupants of the city morgue. These were far more disturbing than the others because the subjects still looked *human,* despite the occasional shotgun blast to the head. The floaters were the worst. I stopped looking at the walls. There was no poetry to the Death in those pictures; the romanticism of my morbid fantasies curdled in the face of reality.

I was drifting away from Mouli. Perhaps it was a mutual disengagement. He worked the midnight shift, while I still had my day job. I slept in my own apartment more often than not. We still slept together on our days off, we attended the Tri-State, and I was still on the Brew. Our sex life was still hot enough to smelt iron, but it was the strychnine Mouli had access to and dispensed with a pharmacist's precision that kept us together. As the Sex Ghouls had said: Mouli was the Death Man. The party couldn't start without him.

Then, in the midst of Death, I produced Life.

He slumped at the card table, one of the three pieces of furniture in the apartment. We were sitting on the other two. He did not look at me, keeping his eyes on the 8×10s fanned across the tacky leatherette tabletop. Faces stared up at me; faces ruined by close-range firearms, high-speed automobiles, the nibbling mouths of fish, the bloat of cellular decay. I looked away. After a long silence he flicked at one of the roaches creeping along the edge of the table, sending it across the room like a tiny football.

"So . . . you wanna keep it?"

"No." I had to fight to keep from adding, *you gotta be kidding*.

"How much?"

"Two hundred and fifty. I've already made arrangements with the women's clinic downtown. All I need is the money."

"I'll handle it." He still hadn't looked up from those damn pictures. "I know what has to be done." The kettle shrieked. He got up and I heard the rattle of crockery—his two chipped coffee cups—in the kitchenette.

"You're not mad, are you? I mean, it's a lot of money. . . ." I felt my own fear and apprehension boiling inside me, threatening to release itself in a torrent of emotional babble. I was relieved to have the coffee to preoccupy me.

"No, I'm not angry." His voice was a flat line. "Drink your coffee."

The spasms hit me shortly after I'd finished my coffee. A sharp pain knifed my gut and I gasped aloud. Mouli looked up from his EC comic book, a mild wrinkle of interest creasing his brow.

By then the muscles were twitching on their own, participating in a painful ghost dance. My eyes were wide with panic. Although I could not see my face, I knew my lips had taken on the bluish-purple of strychnine poisoning. My hands were white as bleached paper, and the galvanic spasming of my fingers hooked them into useless claws. The abdominal spasms hit again, thrusting a gush of air out through my diaphragm and up my throat. I heard a wild, animal bleat of pain and fear.

I toppled from the kitchen chair, striking the linoleum like a piece of meat. The impact sent excruciating seizures throughout my body. It felt like invisible fists were pounding my gut, trying to stuff it up my throat.

The rigor hit my jaws, and my teeth came together with the click of jarred porcelain. I narrowly missed my tongue. The constriction in my chest and neck was unbearable. My mind fuzzed, hoping for the oblivion of a faint. With a conscious effort, I forced it back. I was all too aware of what was happening to me. The lockjaw had begun. If I fainted, the vomiting would begin, and in seconds I would drown in my own puke. The shadowy realm of my strychnine highs beckoned once more, but now I was unwilling to look. I did not want to see any more.

Two minutes had elapsed.

Mouli was there, kneeling over me. I could barely hear him for the blood in my ears and the wheezing as I struggled to breathe with the rigid muscles constricting my chest. He held something in one hand. It looked like a piece of sterile gauze.

The chloroform filled my nostrils and mouth and was drawn into my laboring lungs. The effects were instantaneous; corded muscles unraveled. Piano wire became jelly. My skull cracked the floor as rigid muscles uncurled. The blackness pushed harder at the corners of my eyeballs and things went gray around the edges. Then the sour sting of bile filled my mouth.

Mouli dragged me to my feet and somehow got me into the bathroom. I was dead meat and erratically twitching nerve-endings, incapable of supporting my own weight and flailing about as the strychnine fired my muscles. Mouli propped me against the cold porcelain of the john, his fingers wrapped in my hair to keep me from either cracking my skull open on the rim or drowning in the bowl. The vomit came up easily at first, and I was dimly aware of feeling somewhat better. Then my bruised abdominal muscles kicked in and I was dry-heaving in pain. It felt like someone was using a fishhook to pull my guts out of my mouth.

I was sliding into unconsciousness. This time I didn't fight it. Some primal core deep in my brain knew I had passed the danger zone. I was not going to die. Just as I slipped into the black, I noticed two things: that I was covered in blood from the waist down; and that Mouli was scanning my face intently, searching for some telltale mark visible only to him. I knew what he was looking for. And I knew who. I had disappointed him once again.

I came to, a mass of bruises, pinched nerves, and pulled ligaments. I felt like I had survived being beaten with a baseball bat. Movement was sheer torture, but I could move. Mindless of the agony, I packed what few belongings I still had at Mouli's apartment and left.

I told no one what happened. They would have insisted that I press charges. But I knew why Mouli had poisoned me. And I knew he'd had no intention of killing me. I walked away, free of Mouli and the Brew. They had been burned out of me. Or so I hoped.

My life returned to its familiar rhythms prior to Mouli's entrance, save that I skirted the Tri-State. I began to date again. The sex—like everything else after Mouli—was a pale copy of what I had experienced before. But I didn't care. I counted myself lucky that I had escaped at all. I'd read a brief squib in the paper recounting the death by poisoning of one of the Sex Ghouls. The one with the hairless chest and braided forelock. Seems he attempted to mix his own Brew. No mention was made of Mouli.

A year passed.

"You've got some fuckin' nerve, buddy, calling me like this!" It was the first time I'd talked to him since he'd given me the coffee laced with strychnine.

"You got every right to hate me, Sam. I wouldn't blame you if you hung up on me right now. But don't. Please. I need your help."

I looked at the receiver as if I could see Mouli's face in the earpiece. Maybe it was the connection, but there was something strange about his voice. There was emotion in it. I'd never heard it before from Mouli. Against my better judgment, I went ahead.

"Okay. I'm listening. What is it?"

"I need you to bring me your camera. You've still got it, don't you?"

"Yeah, I've still got a camera. What's wrong with yours?" It didn't make any sense. Why would he call me in the middle of the night, asking to borrow my pocket Instamatic? When we'd been together, he constantly ridiculed my camera as a cheapjack piece of shit.

"It's in the shop getting its shutter fixed." He sounded irritable. I'd asked a Stupid Question.

"It's got color film in it."

"That can't be helped. Look, can you bring it to me?"

"*Now?* Fuckin' Christ, Mouli, it's after midnight!"

"I know! I know! Look, I wouldn't ask if it wasn't important."

"Right. Where are you?"

"At work."

"At *work*? You want me to go to the fuckin' *morgue* in the middle of the *night*?!?"

"I've found Her, Sam. You gotta see it."

"No, Mouli. I *don't* have to see it. Not anymore."

"Come see." It was as if he hadn't heard me.

I listened to the dial tone for a few seconds, wondering what in the name of hell I thought I was doing.

The city morgue occupied the sublevel of the Criminal District Court Building and its only after-hours access was through the underground garage. It smelled of motor oil and exhaust. I was expecting to see Mouli waiting for me on the loading dock, dressed in his rumpled lab coat with its laminated ID dangling from his lapel, but there was no one in sight.

"Mouli? Mouli, are you here, man?"

My voice echoed in the parking garage, but there was no answer. After deliberating with myself for a couple of minutes, I decided to venture into the morgue, aware I was walking a very thin line. This was his place, even more than the balcony of the Tri-State. Mouli's charisma was strong, fed by the twin dynamos of Sex and Death, and I could feel the familiar tug of his will. It was seductive. But I had to know if my immunity was total. At least that's what I told myself.

The morgue was built during the thirties and the stainless-steel cabinets had become dulled and pitted with use. The ceramic tile that covered every surface that wasn't stainless steel was discolored with age, and several squares had disappeared completely, leaving a corrugated pattern of antique epoxy. It smelled strongly of institutional disinfectant. It disguised, but could not hide, the other smell.

''Mouli?'' I could hear someone moving around in the room beyond the large swinging door that separated the receiving area from the rest of the morgue. I pushed one of the doors open, unsure if I wanted to see what might be happening on the other side.

Mouli lay sprawled on the scuffed linoleum floor, his arms and legs splayed like a child frozen in the act of making snow angels. His stomach was ripped open, the intestines hanging out like party streamers. I was surprised at how unconvincing it looked. Hardly up to Savini's usual standards.

Mouli's dream-girl paused in her feeding. She had been a young woman in her early twenties, her hair bible black and arranged in stunning disarray. Except for the bullet hole between her breasts, she didn't look dead. Her beauty was compromised, somewhat, by the blood dripping from her chin. She stared at me with dull, unfocused eyes and returned to munching Mouli's liver.

It was only then that I heard the moaning. It seemed to be coming from all around me. It was a horrible sound; a wordless cry that conveyed emptiness and longing. It was coming from the walls. I stared as the door to the cooler-unit closest to me began to rattle as if its occupant wanted out.

I jerked my attention back to Mouli's corpse. When he opened his eyes, I tried to scream, but nothing came out. He struggled to sit up, pulling a slippery length of bowel out of his killer's hands. Mouli's sapphire-blue eyes were now clouded pearls, and he moved like a clockwork toy with an action that has wound down, but when he saw me, he *smiled*.

He got to his feet, moving like one of the arthritic old winos he used to mock whenever we went to the Tri-State. I backed away as Mouli moved toward me, oblivious to the intestines that dangled from his slit belly. It wasn't like the movies at all; there was no soundtrack, and the lighting was all wrong, and the place *smelled* of blood, bile, and things much, much worse. One thing *was* like the movies, though; they were pretty slow, so I managed to escape. I guess you could say I'm lucky.

I've been holed up in my apartment for over a week. There are thirty-seven stations on my cable box, all of them broadcasting snow. The radio stations disappeared from the airwaves after the third day. The electricity failed two days ago, and what little food I had left in my fridge has started to smell.

I've kept the door locked and bolted, with my grandmother's chifforobe in front of it, since the night I escaped the morgue, not that it will do any good. If they want me, they'll get me. It's only a matter of time.

There can't be many live ones left, judging by the yells. The first few days, the screams from the street were constant. They went on day and night; male and female, young and old. The children were the worst. That's when I stopped looking out the window.

I dreamed about Mouli last night. He was sitting in the balcony at the Tri-State with his new girlfriend. They were seated in the dark, watching the ghosts of double-features past. He looked pretty happy, for a dead guy. Happier than I'd ever seen him alive. When I woke up, all I could hear was the moaning coming from the street and the sound of someone screaming.

I still have Mouli's little brown bottle: the one with the strychnine. I took it when I left his apartment in hopes of reminding myself *why* I left him if my resolve ever weakened. It's sitting in front of me as I write this. It does not offer easy death, but it's infinitely cleaner than being devoured alive.

I've figured everything out and I understand things a

lot better now. I said it's not like the movies, but I was wrong. The reason I couldn't understand is because I'm on the wrong side of the screen. It's like trying to watch a film from backstage; everything is distorted and the perspective is all wrong. If you want to see the movie and be able to understand what's going on, you have to be dead. I've got my ticket sitting right here. All I have to do is decide if I want to go to the show.

I hope Mouli saved me a seat.

RISE UP AND WALK

K. W. JETER

The scornful had departed. For which he was, to his secret shame, grateful; they had long been a cruel burden to him. In this, his time among men, come round again. But he had borne that weight, submitted his bent back to the lash and goad of the mockers, that burden only part of the great task appointed to him by his Father.

He took another Oreo from the package in his lap and chewed it thoughtfully, meditatively, the sugar and grease and dark crumbs sliding down his throat to nourish the rags and hollow sticks of his corporeal form. The kitchen had been ransacked, the fifty-pound sacks of flour and rice and dry beans, and the cartons of institutional-size canned goods, peach halves in heavy syrup, beets, peeled tomatoes, yams, everything, all piled into the buses and trucks inside the gates. In his hiding place, dark with the wet smell of the mops and the sharp ammonia tang inside the galvanized buckets, he had been able to hear the shouting and clamor, the frantic haste of his keepers' departure. The moaning and crying of the others, their confused murmurs and sudden shrieks of fear, as they had been shepherded out of the wards—he had heard that as well, the voices of believers and disbelievers alike falling away from him.

''Where's the Big J?'' That had been the chief of the keepers, in a starched white uniform—he had been able to picture the man, standing with a clipboard in the middle of the fury down in the ground-floor lobby. ''Goddamn it, where is that stupid motherfucker?''

''Come on, forget him,'' the other keepers had shouted. ''Let's get the fuck *out* of here.''

The voices and the running footsteps had faded away, beyond the building's walls. Outside, under the bare-branched trees that lined the gravelled drive, the buses and trucks had coughed and roared, grey exhaust spilling out in the stinging autumn air. He had crept out of the hiding place, down the corridors of the now-silent building, and to one of the barred windows. He'd peered out, keeping his head down so they wouldn't see him. The last bus was already heading for the gate, and through the steamed-up glass had been visible the face of one of the faithful, an obese schizophrenic who'd always carried a tattered bald doll through the wards, that she told everyone was her baby, the one the doctors had lied about and said was dead. Her pudgy hands had scrabbled at the misted glass, her swaddled eyes beseeching toward him, connecting for a split-second, yearning for the salvation from which they were abducting her.

The Big J—they'd called him that for so long that it'd become his true name—ate another Oreo and blessed the woman, his follower gone with the others into the wilds of exile. The package was almost half-empty now, and black crumbs were scattered across the front of the loose, faded green pajamas. There were other garments he would wear someday, a gown of white samite, radiant in its glory . . . but not yet. He brushed the crumbs away and wondered what he should do now. Perhaps—and it was hard to keep his heart from sinking into ashes inside him—perhaps even now his waiting wasn't finished.

That had always been the hardest part: the years of waiting. Waiting for that which the Big J knew was true to be revealed to all the sons of man. That he had returned among them, and the millennia of their own waiting were at an end, the days of prophecy, the last days, commenced at last.

For weeks before this, the portents had been written in the sky, and inscribed in the hubbub of voices swirling around him. He had not listened to the actual words, the exclamations of dismay from the keepers clustered around the television in the staff lounge; the lashing of raw emotion in their shouts and cries, the fear of the disbelievers caught in their unrepentant state, had told him what he already knew. The wheel of time had ceased its turning. All was to be made, by him, new again.

The terror in the hearts of the wicked and unredeemed—his great, all-encompassing pity swelled inside him, as another Oreo crumbled in his mouth. Perhaps he should forgive them all, intercede in their behalf; he'd have to think about that. Even the worst of his tormentors, the chief of the keepers on the evening shift . . . the one with a laughing white smile in a coffee-black face, who'd always palmed the bicolored capsules of the Big J's medication into the pockets of a starched white uniform (*he* had never minded about that, as going without the bedtime doses had let him walk in the glory of his Father all through the night's deep hours) . . . the one who'd smiled into his face and said, "I don't know where they get that shit, in cartoons and shit like that, 'bout people like you thinking they're Napoleon, you know, walking 'round with their hands inside their PJ's? 'Cause I've had twenty or so, right here in this ward, who all thought they was *you*, Big J; they *all* thought they was Jesus Christ—how 'bout that for bein' nuts?" Smiling and smiling, and laughing when the other keepers behind had laughed, all of them savoring their mirth.

And there had been a crueler jest, one time in the hydrotherapy room, when the chief of the keepers had been elevated with strong wine or the medications he and the others kept back from the more docile inmates. "Come on, Big J! You can do it!" The keeper had shouted in his red-eyed merriment. Clouds of steam had rolled up from the water, collecting in beads on the green-streaked walls. The spastics floating pink-skinned in their harnesses had gaped and trembled; even the heavy-faced depressives had lifted their eyes and watched. The other keepers had taken up the chant. "Come on, Big J! *Walk* across that water! You can do it, you can *do* it! You're the *Man*!" And he had felt the power swelling in his breast, the glory, the knowledge of his anointing, and before that, the prophecies of his return. So long ago, when the sea had calmed beneath his feet, and he'd strode out to the amazed fisherman . . . His head had sung, the smell of chlorine and steam instead of cold salt filling his breath. The mockers had stopped laughing for a second as he stepped out onto the pool's surface; his bare foot had touched the lapping water, and then he had plunged into its depths. The chief of the keepers had hauled him out, gasping and sputtering for breath, and their laughter had battered against the damp tiles.

It hadn't been his time yet. *How much longer, O Lord?* he'd wept and prayed through the crawl of bitter days. The Oreo between his teeth turned to ashes as he remembered. Perhaps he wouldn't forgive his chief tormentor; justice, the great weighing of souls in the final days, had to be done. And it was unlikely that the man had repented, even as he fled from the wrath foretold in the sky's burning letters. The Big J chewed and swallowed, nodding his head in recognition of his Father's wisdom.

He pulled the thin wool blanket closer around his shoulders. The grey winds outside had invaded the building, seeping in through the broken windows behind the bars. In the last hours of panic, those of clouded mind had run through the corridors, shrieking and smashing all that had fallen to their hands. They had reminded him of the Gadarene swine. But these demon-possessed unfortunates had not fallen over a cliff edge, but had been rounded up by the keepers, then bound in canvas restraints or sedated by injections and loaded into the buses and trucks. A great peace had fallen upon the building, a silence like the desert in which he had found solitude before, so long ago.

Was it his time yet? Even now—how would he know? *Give me a sign, O Lord.* He closed his eyes and prayed as he ate another Oreo.

Another time, in secret . . . when all his mockers and tormentors had been downstairs in the staff lounge . . . in the murmuring night of the dormitory beds . . . he'd gotten out of his, laying the covers back, and had gone to the last one, at the end of the row. He'd known, before anyone else, that the old man there was dead. The rasping breath and fluttering heartbeat had stilled at last. The moon had thrown luminous blue stripes across the floor as he'd stood at the side of the deathbed, feeling the glory blossom inside himself. *Now, O Lord?* The Big J had laid his hand on the old man's brow. *Rise up, Lazarus.* His head had sung with light. *I command thee—rise up and walk.*

The bitterness of wormwood. One of the keepers had come on his rounds, flashlight shining from bed to bed. And had found the Big J standing beside the dead, unmoving form, weeping with silent tears.

How much longer, O Lord?

The package of Oreos was nearly empty. He had found the small cache of food, a cupboard in the staff lounge, when he had come down from his hiding place above. There were other things in there as well—it would be enough. He knew that his Father would provide.

From outside the building, sudden noise battered through the silence. A screech of tires, then the impact of metal against stone.

He was deep in his meditations, and only looked up from the hands clasped over the cellophane package in his lap several minutes after the silence had sealed 'round the building again.

The corners of the blanket trailed after him as he climbed the stairs. From the second-story window that gave the best view, he looked out to the courtyard.

A double black line had been incised through the wet leaves covering the circular driveway. The crumpled shape of a car, rain drizzling over the distorted angles, lay piled against the high cement rampart that marked off the building's steps. A wisp of steam drifted from the radiator.

There were other broken shapes. One, a woman or a man—the Big J couldn't tell, looking down at the car—hung halfway through the windshield's sharp fragments, face-down against the bent metal of the hood. The rain diluted the blood, washing a pink lace across the right fender.

Another had been thrown clear. Glass bits sparkled in the body's hands and the ribbon wounds of its face. The small drops of rain shimmered the red puddle widening from the back of the head.

He could see one more inside the car, twisted on the backseat, a white face gazing blankly upward, a thick red rag welling in the open mouth.

He looked upon the dead without anguish. The flesh was transitory, a tattered robe for the spirit. How foolish of these to have fled, when there were no more hiding places to be found, not in all the crevices of the earth. Had they, in their flight, seen the building from the road beyond the trees and thought it could be their refuge? And, in their haste, run to meet their demise? Foolish, foolish—no sanctuary in the last days. He closed his eyes, forehead against the window bars; his lips moved with prayer.

The last days . . . the coming of the great time . . . his time . . . The faint high note sang inside his head, as when he'd stood beside the old man's deathbed, in the long night desert of his shame and doubt. The light that banished darkness blossomed from his heart. Perfect knowledge and power and truth—

He stuck his hand out between the bars, rain spattering across the knuckles and ridged tendons. Palm raised, he blessed the dead and called to them.

Something stirred below. He heard it, and a fierce wild joy broke inside him.

The Big J opened his eyes and saw the face lifting from the crumpled hood of the car. There was enough left untorn to show that it was a woman. The body slowly rolled onto its side, the arm straightening against the metal. A searching, avid gaze, from the one eye left intact in the face, met his.

A muffled pounding came from inside the car. The one inside scrabbled at the pieces of the side window as it fought to extricate itself from the narrow space. A spear of chrome gouged its ribs, peeling back the flesh into a banner of red stigmata. It didn't notice, but struggled harder, its openmouthed gaze also locked upon the face of its savior above, the voice that had called to them from the building's window.

The broken form on the driveway staggered to its feet. The head turned on the twisted neck, the rain washing the blood from the eyes, so it could see the face of its redeemer as well.

He stood back from the bars, glory flooding his breast. His time had come at last. Now all the world would know.

Below, the resurrected moved haltingly toward the building. The woman slid off the car's hood and joined her brother in an awkward, reverent progress toward the voice that had raised them. The third Lazarus fought clear of the car and tumbled out onto the ground, then pushed itself upright and followed after.

The Big J hurried down the stairs. These were the first: his first miracle, the first to see his presence among men again. The ritual of communion was needed now, to bind them all in grace.

The bars over the ground floor entrance were locked in position; they had clanged shut when the last of the keepers had fled. Through the iron, he saw the believers approaching. He would have to hurry. The strength of their faith was written in their yearning eyes.

He came back from the staff lounge with a box of Nabisco Vanilla Wafers clutched to his chest. The Oreos, black and with their cryptic symbols engraved on each side, hadn't seemed appropriate. But these would do fine. He quickly sanctified the contents of the box as he ran.

They were already coming up the steps outside. He tore open the box and rooted inside. He held one of the sacred host out through the bars.

"This is my flesh," he said, the wafer held by the tips of his fingers. "Take of it, and eat."

The first was the man who'd lain on the driveway, the woman a few steps behind. With a clumsy blow, the man knocked the wafer into a red-streaked puddle. The cold fingers gripped the Big J's hand, and pulled it to the mouth stretching open, grey lips drawing back from the broken teeth. The woman jostled beside, grabbing hold of his forearm, bringing her own face down to the soft flesh below his wrist.

Inside his head, the high singing note dizzied him. Light and joy broke free, blinding him. But he could still see—the third communicant had joined the others. The hands clutched in their fervor at his arm.

Their mouths were filled with a wine that steamed in the cold air, the red abundance trickling from the corners and down their throats.

"Yes . . ." He nodded, blessing them. "This is my blood. Take of it, and drink."

A hand reached through, grasping him behind the neck. He did not resist, but brought his face up against the bars. Iron touched the sides of his brow.

The faces of the blessed came toward his, seeking the kiss of peace. The peace that passeth understanding.

ONE STEP AT A TIME

GLEN VASEY

I

Hospital corridors. Stainless steel air. Uniformed personnel alone (smiling somberly at visitors) or in groups (gaggling at the workplace, wholly unself-conscious). My mother walking in front, needing to show that she's in charge, that she knows the way, that she *is not* lost. Kate and I following her, attempting heart-lightening dialogue with our sons Barry and Jordan. Barry and Jordan are ten and eight years old, they have been to this place only once before. When my father was still in a coma. They are afraid for him and a little afraid of him. They love him as fiercely as he loves them, and with good reason.

We shared the spacious elevator with a couple of technicians transporting a rack of incomprehensible equipment. Everyone knew their roles. Just another day on the job to them, jiving back and forth about some title fight due that night or just completed. We were on a pilgrimage, silent, respectful, watching the floor indicator with an intensity it really didn't deserve.

All of my senses, all of my emotions were intensified, magnified, clarified, almost too pure. Like a mild dose of very clean LSD. Everything seemed slightly too real. Every third thing seemed like something I wouldn't have noticed, or that wouldn't have made such an impact if I'd been in a more standard state of mind. I'd been living with these sensations, more on than off, for close to two months. Somewhere within me there was a dam bulging under the pressure of it all. Ready to burst. No cracks yet.

Off the elevator. Down a short corridor like all the other corridors. Around a corner into a more spacious corridor, immensely long, wide enough to drive a car through.

One hundred feet away my father was sitting in a big, green, vinyl-upholstered chair outside his room. That in itself was progress. Three weeks before (the last time Kate and I had been able to get down) he had still been wholly bedridden. Head downcast, he was playing with the ties of his hospital gown with the mute absorption of a child, half-fascinated, half-annoyed by them.

When we were fifty feet away, his head came up and his eyes focused on my mother. No reaction. He looked past her, saw Kate and me, and smiled broadly. When he looked past us and saw the boys, his smile became a beacon of pleasure. Indifference, expression of joy, announcement of Beatitude. All as it should be. The final and illuminating smile was a gift that the boys had granted him after all. Uninhibited, it was a smile I hadn't known him capable of in my own youth. Blessed are the Grandfathers. . . .

FIVE YEARS AGO

"Duane." A nervous flutter of the hands, a downward glance; characteristic of a man unused to speaking his emotions. Rare bravery against a lifelong conditioning. We

are, of course, alone. "When I see how you are with the boys, it makes me wish that I had been more patient, that I'd treated something spilled in the car like something spilled in the car and not some crime."

Meaning exactly what he says, and a million other things that are much too difficult to say.

When he allows his eyes to come up to meet mine, mine are ready. Through a wonderful array of friendships and loves, I have known since my teens the lesson that my children are just teaching him in his sixties: communication of intense emotion is to be sought, the touching of eyes is at the center of this.

I smile. "Dad, you came around. I came around. Our tempers were problems for both of us at times, but I never doubted your love, or that you'd be there for me when I needed you. No matter what I'd done or how inconsiderate I'd been."

"Well, I just wish I'd been more patient. I'd have enjoyed your childhood so much more."

I can see him pull up short of saying that I would have enjoyed my childhood more. From his perspective that is a too-selfish wish.

As we drew up to where he sat I smiled back at my father, feeling my heart contract in volume even as it increased in mass. Ours had always been an odd sort of storybook father-son love. Not the fairy-tale double-good-guy sort, nor yet the wise father permitting the rebellious son to make sufficient mistakes and come back to the fold. It was deeper and more complex than either of those scenarios. A long time coming, and so more cherished for knowing the difference between its presence and absence. Only through mutual error, mutual recognition, and mutual repentance is such intensity possible. Where there is such intensity, anything at all is possible.

So I believe.

So I must believe.

FIVE YEARS AGO

My parents left hours ago. Are certainly home by now. The boys are asleep. Kate and I are in bed, talking. She wants to know what it is like to have a father that loves you. One that stays around, remains active in your life for more than eleven years.

"It's odd," I say. "When I was a kid I always knew he loved me, but he never showed it. Sometimes he'd holler at me over something that made no sense; I'd be frightened, puzzled. Then he'd smile and I'd realize that he was pulling my leg, that fooling me like that was some sort of crazy camaraderie. Other times he'd talk sternly to me and I'd think it was the same sort of joke. I'd laugh and he'd back-hand me quick as lightning. One time he hit me so hard, so fast, that his twist-o-flex watch went flying off his arm. Somehow as it came off it took a big chunk of skin from the back of his wrist with it. Must've cut a vein back there 'cause he bled a lot. I don't remember pain from the blow. What I remember is worrying whether my dad's wrist hurt, whether he'd be okay."

The bunk beds in the next room creak. One of the boys repositioning himself. Kate and I listen until silence returns. There is something very comforting about such interruptions.

I smile, continue, "It's funny how differently my sister and I reacted to him. We didn't know it at the time, but we've talked about it a lot since we both got out of the house.

"One time—Deb must've been ten, I would've been six or seven—we were bickering in the back of the car, fighting over something too obscure for either of us to remember. Mom kept telling us to cut it out, but we kept it up. All of a sudden the Hand of God comes lightning-bolting over the front seat, smacking us both silly, left and right. Father was giving us his undivided attention while the car he's driving is roaring along the turnpike at seventy-plus. All I could think of was how wrong I had acted, how I shouldn't have made him angry. Meanwhile, all Debbie can see are head-

lines blaring FAMILY OF FOUR DIES IN FREAK HIWAY CRASH; *subhead: Father's Rage Dooms Kin.*

"She told me once she would lie awake nights hoping that someone would show up in the morning to take her away to the Good Parents. I used to lie awake afraid of just the opposite."

My father's head bobbed excitedly. He tossed a hand clumsily in the direction of my sons and spoke: "Noum boyrear doway pixta." His throat was phlegmy, his vocal coordination was slow, his false teeth were absent. Enunciation was nearly impossible for him, but he smiled when he was done.

I tilted my head, returned the smile, and confessed that I hadn't quite understood what he was saying.

My mother, who had moved into a position behind his chair as if she were protecting him from us, started speaking over him, telling us that we shouldn't expect to understand him.

I ignored her and concentrated hard on my father's voice and movements. I knelt beside his chair in an attempt to draw closer to him, to exclude everything that was not he and I.

"Noum boysrear dorway pixtas," hands wagging back and forth over his lap then flashing outward as if dismissing something, all a ghost of his former agility. I still didn't get it. Incomprehension as physical pain.

"No one can really understand what he's saying," my mother droned on as if my father wasn't present at all. "Sometimes the nurses pretend to, but I don't see how that's going to help him any. The doctor says he doesn't even *know* most of the words for things he used to know, so how can you expect him to say them. . . ." She spoke as if his current condition was not miracle enough, was not an incredibly encouraging improvement. As if he couldn't possibly be hurt by anything she was saying.

TWO MONTHS AGO

"He was without oxygen to the brain for between five and ten minutes. Our best guess is eight minutes. Anything under five leaves a path open to complete recovery. Anything over ten virtually precludes any chances for any sort of recovery at his age. Eight minutes puts him in a grey area."

"What's his prognosis?" I ask.

"May I be very blunt?"

"I'd appreciate it."

"We haven't done an EEG yet, so we can't estimate the amount of brain damage he has suffered. He's in a coma now. All his vital signs are healthy: heart rate, blood pressure, his kidneys and other organs are processing the way they should. There seems to be no organic damage at all. All of these are very good signs ... at this point. But he is on a respirator. Without it he would cease breathing. His lungs aren't getting the necessary messages from his brain. If he is going to make any recovery at all, the first sign will be when he resumes breathing on his own. If that doesn't happen, he can't come off the respirator. If he doesn't come off the respirator soon, he is unlikely to ever come off. In that case we're looking at him remaining in a vegetative state and maybe wishing that he weren't so damn healthy, maybe hoping that something like kidney failure or pneumonia might crop up to force our hand."

Father, grandfather, fisher, hiker, canoeist, gardener, individualist: a crystallization of the worst possible fate. No Living Will. Options diminished. I am thinking immediately of Jerry, one of the longest and strongest of my many friendships. One of the deepest. Not far from where I now stand, he lies in a bed in his aunt's house, weakened and rail-thin from AIDS. Jerry would understand. Jerry would give up a syringe of his blood if I needed it. If it was the only escape available.

If I had to take that risk, I would.

For my father.

I ignored my mother and asked my father to repeat himself once more, fearful that I would miss it again, disappoint and frustrate his attempt at conversation, fail him. He did repeat. The results were no clearer to me. My mother droned on.

When Dad saw my confusion, he shrugged, waved his hands, and looked away. Hurt. Disappointed and frustrated. I had failed him and no amount of regret would ever compensate for that failure.

TWO MONTHS AGO

My mother and I enter a room filled with electronic gadgetry, hanging plastic bags, and tubes of every dimension. All are attached to my father. This is my first visit since the heart attack, my mother's third. She has told me what to expect.

"He won't even know you are there. It won't matter to him one way or the other." I don't want to hear it. Won't believe it.

My father's mouth is filled with the tube from the respirator; it goes deep and stretches the dimensions of his throat. His hands are strapped to the bed to prevent him from reflexively yanking the damn thing out.

His eyes are closed. Have been closed for fourteen hours now.

I move to the side of the bed. To his good ear.

"Hi, Dad."

His eyes open, fix on mine with an intensity of feeling, a depth of intimacy that the most passionate moments of romantic love could only hope to mimic. Suddenly we are together, fishing, caught unexpectedly in a violent downpour. We race back to the car for our raingear. Rummaging through the trunk, we pause to look at one another. We are drenched already. Laughing, we toss the rainsuits back into the trunk and march off to resume our fishing.

I smile into his pain-wracked eyes, "I love you, Dad. I know you must feel confused right now, frightened, but

*you're going to be okay." I am not whistling in the dark,
I know this to be true; as surely as I know that he is looking
at me, seeing me, recognizing me. I can see, feel, taste, and
breathe the essence of this truth.*

I tell him how it will have to be.

*"The first thing you have to do is start breathing for
yourself. The machine is helping you now, but you have to
remember how to do it yourself. Relearn it. That's the first
step. There's a long way to go after that, but you can't
worry about that now. One step at a time. I know it's hard,
but try to breathe on your own. Then we can get that
damned uncomfortable thing out of your throat."*

His eyes drift away from mine, then shut.

I allow myself tears.

*For the two days that I am able to stay, he opens his
eyes only to the sound of my voice. I don't believe my
mother will ever forgive me that.*

*She tells me that it isn't really recognition, that it is an
involuntary stimulus-response to the deeper register of my
voice. I tune her out.*

*When I speak to him of Barry and Jordan, he tries to
smile around that damn contraption.*

"It's the pain," she says. "He's grimacing."

A jovial nurse came over to join us, "Hi, Pete."

My father smiled, waved from the wrist.

She turned to us. "I can't believe the improvement I
see in him daily. Did you tell them what you had for breakfast, Pete?"

My father shook his head.

"A whole bowl of oatmeal and some juice, and Sue
brought in some doughnuts and I dunked them in milk and
fed them to him bite by bite. He ate two of 'em! He's a
hungry guy, and no wonder. He's put on five pounds in the
last few days." She was beaming with pride in him. He
glanced shyly away.

Until a few days ago he'd been unable to swallow without aspirating. His time on the respirator had short-circuited

his gag reflex so badly that they'd had to feed him through a tube that went directly into his stomach. Eating solid food was another giant step, one the doctor had only recently warned us against hoping for. But I'd had a talk with my dad about that, too. He listens to me.

"And we took a walk today, didn't we, Pete?"

My father nodded.

"Down to the end of the hall, that big window there." She pointed. "He put his hand up against that window and said, 'It's colder than I thought,' just as clear as day. Isn't that right, Pete?"

Another nod, shyly smiling.

"And he went to the bathroom today by himself, first time. Looked at me and said, 'I can do it,' so I waited outside and he did just fine. Later today we're going to get him into the bathtub. Won't that be nice, Pete?"

My wife leaned over and whispered conspiratorially to my father, "What kind of bath do you want? A bubble bath?"

Dad fixed her with a sidelong glance and his most impish mischievous grin. "Watch it!" he warned her, enunciating perfectly.

My father's humor had always run toward dry, so he did his best to contain his mirth. Kate and I laughed profoundly. The nurse joined us. Barry and Jordan still found the strangeness of the situation stifling and my mother just looked scared, as if she were losing rather than regaining him. There was, however, sufficient laughter to make my father very proud.

ONE YEAR AGO

My father is driving his Chrysler New Yorker, a car he has worked damn hard to earn and one with as many bells and whistles as a NASA space shuttle. He is surprised when he glances down and sees the digital speedometer reading "100." He knows he isn't traveling that fast.

Soon he figures out that he had inadvertently pressed a button that switched his readings from mph to kph. He rubs his dry palms together in anticipation, grinning eagerly as he tells his wife, "Can't wait till the next time we get the boys in the car. Now that I know how to do that, I can have a little fun with them. Won't even have to draw their attention to it. Barry and Jordan are sharp, they don't miss a thing."

He will prove to be right, of course. Their reactions to his little trick will be wonderful.

My father suddenly stamped his left foot while his left hand made a grab for Jordan's leg. The eight-year-old danced back, giggling nervously, uncertain how to accept my father's clowning gesture in these circumstances.

I was elated. I'd seen my father pull that very stunt on the boys a million times. I'd heard him snap off amusing quips like he had just done with Kate a million more. The doctor had warned us steadily to expect personality changes. He claimed they were the most common permanent effect of brain trauma. It has been said that the mind is the best part of a man. I would add that a sense of humor is the best part of a mind. My father's sense of humor was intact, which boded well, as far as I was concerned, for his full recovery.

FIVE YEARS AGO

"The real change came the year before I moved out." Kate was drifting off to sleep now, but I kept talking. "One Saturday he took me shopping for fishing gear. We'd never gone fishing, together or separately, hadn't ever even discussed the possibility. We needed everything and he bought it all at once, all top-flight equipment, too. Two months later he went and sunk a couple hundred into a canoe and a small outboard. Every pleasant weekend from there on out we went fishing together; even after I'd moved out, I'd cancel plans with friends at the drop of a hat if he asked me to go with him. We hardly spoke at all during those trips, but we were together. Maybe he saw it as a last

chance. Debbie was already gone, I would be soon. It was something. It was important to us both.''

I leaned over and hugged him. ''I'm really proud of you, Dad.'' The feeling of his arms coming around my back to embrace me was a wonderful thing. I leaned back a bit so I could meet his eyes. ''You know, you've surprised everyone by coming back this far, this fast, but you've done it. You're ornery and you're stubborn, and you've done what the doctors said we had no right to expect. *You've* done it. I suspect you've got a few more surprises in store for us, too, huh, Dad? You can keep on improving. There's no limit to how far you can come back if you just keep taking it step-by-step.''

My father hung his head and wept, every muscle in his face, neck, and shoulders suddenly clenching in an attempt to keep the tears inside. He trembled.

''I know it's gotta be scary, Dad. There's still such a long way to go. It must seem endless to you. If you could only see how much progress you've made already, you'd feel confident that you could make it all the way. You *will* make it. We'll help in every way that we can, but it's your job to keep putting one foot in front of the other.''

Not long after that he was taking this advice quite literally. I held my dad's right hand and my youngest son held his left as we headed toward the window at the end of the hall. One hundred and fifty feet of hospital chrome and white, relieved by occasional full-sized prints of Matisse and the open doors of other people's high-rent high anxieties.

We took it a step at a time, my father pausing to examine every one of the Matisse prints.

''They are beautiful,'' I said.

My father nodded.

''Would you like some big prints like these to hang in your room?''

He nodded and wept, loving the beauty, hating the admission of the continuing siege.

We came to a double set of swinging doors with head-level windows. He stared hard at these and steered us in their direction. The small, square windows looked out into a stairwell.

"Reconnoitering?" I asked. "Plotting your escape?"

He nodded absently, then caught my eye and nodded grimly.

"When you're ready, you call me. I'll drop what I'm doing and come 'round to pick you up."

He nodded again and humor crystallized into mutual promise.

I tugged on his hand, led him over to the large windows that overlooked the parking lot. "Can you see the cars out there, Dad?"

My father nodded.

"See the maroon mini-van way the hell at the end of the lot, over on the left?"

No response. Staring.

"That's our new car. The old car was dying. We couldn't trust it to get us here and back. That's why we couldn't come down last week or the week before. That's the car we always wanted, just like you always wanted the New Yorker. But we really got it for you, Dad. We got it so we could come to see you. And that's the getaway car we'll use for your escape."

SEVEN WEEKS AGO

I grab my mother's arm and forcibly steer her out of the room. She has been dressing me down and waxing pessimistic, arguing over every point of conversation even though we are ostensibly here to visit my father. His eyes are open more often now. They call it a light coma. They say there's no knowing how much he's taking in. But there are times when I know I see recognition in his eyes. When my mother starts bickering like this, his eyes drift shut.

"Listen, Mom, you've got to stop talking like that in front of Dad. It's making him withdraw. We want him to come back out."

"I just don't know why you're in there telling him about his finances and his garden and things like that. Talking to him about fishing trips you went on, making plans for fishing trips when he gets out. He can't understand anything you're saying to him, and he's never going to be going on any more fishing trips."

My fists clench tightly, I try to keep my voice level, calm. "If he can understand me, then they are things he'd like to know, things he'd like to remember, like to hope for. If he can't understand me, then they are soothing, reassuring sounds in a familiar voice. When I speak about these things he looks at me. When you start bickering he goes away."

She turns away from me.

"Listen, Mom, I know you're upset. I know how awful you feel. I feel awful, too."

"You can't possibly have any idea how awful I feel!"

"He's my father...."

"I've known him longer than you! Besides, I don't know why you even pretend to care, after the way he treated you when you were little, after the way you treated him!"

My clenched fists begin to move, but I spin myself around and leave the room before they have a chance to strike her. I want to stay. I want to scream in her face that that shit is long gone, it's done, it's over. That he's more than made up for it. But the threat of my fists won't let me. I leave the room. Leave the floor. Leave the hospital.

Abandoning my father to her.

"I think I know what your father was trying to say when we first got there."

We were halfway through the long night-drive home. The boys were asleep in the back of the van. I glanced over at Kate to show that I had heard, that I was interested, then looked back to the road. The lights of the oncoming cars seemed far too bright. The mile markers and green highway signs seemed to flash by too swiftly. But we seemed to have been driving for an eternity already, with forever still to go.

"Remember those pictures of the boys we brought with us last month?" she asked.

FIVE WEEKS AGO

It is the first time that we have seen my father since they moved him out of the ICU. In the waiting room a nurse informs my wife and I that Dad is making some valid attempts at speech now, though much of what he says is unintelligible. My mother hadn't mentioned this to us. He's been off the respirator for a week but he cannot swallow, stand or even sit up on his own.

Kate and I have an opportunity to visit him alone, as the nurse takes pity and keeps my mother occupied.

Kate and I talk. My father smiles and nods a lot. A bouncy nod that doesn't seem to mean anything at all. Somehow he seems more distant than he had when he was in the light coma, less reachable. The doctor has told us that he has plateaued: that we can expect no more leaps in his recovery. Just steps. Small steps. Steps that might falter and cease at any point. He may or may not learn to swallow. He may or may not learn to stand, to walk, to make conversation. It may be months, or years of slow, painful, nearly invisible advances. This may be it.

It is the most difficult visit yet.

I stand on my father's right, the side of his good ear. Kate stands across the bed from me. We talk. He smiles, nods. We could be anybody. There is no real contact.

Kate pulls two photos from her purse, school pictures of Barry and Jordan. She holds them in front of him. He stares and puzzles for a long while.

"Do you know who these two boys are?" she asks him.

He looks at her suspiciously, then back to the photos. He smiles and nods. The gesture means nothing. The look preceding it had said it all: "Is this a trick question? Are you trying to fool me by showing me pictures of people I don't know?"

We talk about the boys for a while, things they've done recently, things they will do soon, the wishes they have sent.

Then Kate turns away from him and hangs the pictures on the wall where he will be able to see them. While her back is turned he stares harder at the pictures. By the time she turns around to face him again his face has brightened, his eyes are dancing, he is pointing a shaking finger first at the pictures, then at her. He is trying to sit up in his excitement.

"Kasherin," he says. "Kate!" He is nodding vehemently now, still pointing a quaking finger at her.

Kate beams, steps closer to him, touches her chest. "That's right, I'm Kate."

He clutches one of her hands in his trembling one, reaches his other hand out to grasp mine and brings our two hands together above his chest. Clasping our hands there, he squeezes with all of his strength, then closes his eyes in gratitude.

A connection made and blessed in a single action.

Later Kate expressed the belief that a visit from Barry and Jordan might inspire my father to some surprising leaps of improvement.

My mother's analyses was simpler still: "He hasn't said my name yet!"

"He was saying," Kate went on, " 'Now that the boys are here we can throw away the pictures.' It was a joke. The hand motions were a pantomime of tearing-up and throwing-away."

"Jesus, you're right. I wish I had caught it at the time. I wish I hadn't frustrated him."

"Well, if your mother would've just shut up for two seconds . . ."

"Yeah, I know. She's been pissing me off all along. If my dad had ever signed over power of attorney to me, I think I'd probably file for divorce in his behalf, then get a restraining order against her. I couldn't believe it when the nurse was telling us how well he'd done the other day signing his name, how she just couldn't wait for the nurse to wander off so she could tell us he really hadn't done that well, that it was really indecipherable, all as if he wasn't even there or his pride couldn't ever be hurt.''

Kate nodded. ''He really needs someone who'll spend some time building him up, not tearing him down.''

''I wish I could spend four hours a day with him.''

And that was the beginning of our plan.

By the time we got home all we needed to do was shift it into action. I arranged an emergency leave of absence from work, called my friend Jerry at his aunt's house—she had taken him in almost as soon as he'd been diagnosed—and arranged to stay with him for as long as several weeks, called the social worker at my dad's hospital and arranged for extended visitation, and called his therapist and discussed modifications of the plans that Kate and I had come up with. That done, I called my father's doctor and insisted that he talk to my mother about lessening her visits to twice a week.

Two days later I left feeling terribly self-indulgent. I was getting to march off in the role of consoling hero while Kate was stuck at home with no car and no help for the everyday stuff, besides coping with a severely tightened budget and increased expenses.

She kissed me at the door and offered some words of encouragement. Neither of us knew at the time that that was the night the corpses started rising.

II

The ensuing two weeks were insane for just about everyone on the globe. I was aware of this peripherally, but have to admit that I was pretty well absorbed by and can only fairly report my own slice of insanity.

ONE AND A HALF WEEKS AGO

The setting is dim. Night. A single electric bulb, augmented only by the ghost lights of a small tv, illuminates a large and deeply cluttered room.

Jerry's World. A world of imported sensations. Jerry, who, when I first met him and for many years after, had been a wholesale exporter of sensations; an intruder in people's living rooms via the magic of phosphor dots, his Castro beard and beautiful long hair making him a natural target of the cameras at the anti-war and gay rights rallies where he had waxed eloquent from any number of makeshift podiums. Jerry, who had opened up my mind and heart, giving me many opportunities to think about and feel things that I hadn't even known existed.

I am sitting at the foot of his bed, next to the tv. I have taken this position as much to obstruct my view of the television as to give myself an unobstructed view of my friend. Jerry divides his attention evenly between the tv and me, occasionally interrupting the flow of our conversation to use his remote control to increase the volume or to activate the VCR with which he is recording what he calls "the highlights of the World Catastrophe."

He tells me that two months ago he had a vision that informed him that he had one hundred days left on this planet. "I keep thinking I should have a going-away party, but it has to have a theme." He smiles, then is shaken for a full minute by a racking series of coughs.

When the coughing passes, he smiles again. Never a large man, the disease has eaten forty pounds from his frame, but his smile—always far more contagious than the illness that has wasted his immune system—has lost nothing of its old charm.

"You've always read more science fiction than I have," he continues. "How does Alpha Centauri sound? I don't know why it came to mind, but I want to be sure to pick someplace where I won't wind up with some queen at my party screaming: 'You don't want to go there, Sister!'"

Before I could respond, the tv has caught his attention. His fingers set the machinery whirring to catch the latest clip. I glance over involuntarily and immediately remember why I have avoided doing so. The ghouls have an illness-wasted look to them. Like Jerry. Like my father. Their movements are awkward and uncoordinated. Like Jerry

*making the difficult journey to the bathroom on nearly mus-
cleless legs. Like my father learning to walk again.*

I look away. I look at nothing.

*"The Powers That Be can't possibly make this fiasco
as antiseptic as the Gulf War. It's too widespread, too random, too variable. Make no mistake, though, it's worse than
they're letting on. Much worse."*

*Adding, a moment later, "And the graphics aren't even
as pretty."*

*In the twenty years that I have known him, Jerry has
always been the most reliable of my sources on both fronts,
the political and the aesthetic. I have no choice now but to
believe him.*

*I am silent now. Thinking of Kate and the kids, alone.
Thinking of my father, who in a few days has already displayed significant progress. Thinking of Jerry, who has
chosen one hell of a time to die.*

*"I've got to go to bed," I say. "I have to be at the
hospital pretty early."*

*Jerry nods. I leave the room, feeling guilty about so
many things.*

My days consisted of rigidly ordered chaos. I arrived at the
hospital each morning at nine. My father and I would put
together puzzles, color in coloring books, build things with
Tinkertoys and Legos. I would read to him, teach him simple songs on my sons' Casio keyboard, show him picture
books. Anything to restore the lines of communication between his hands and eyes, his mind and body. We exer-
cised. Took walks down to the end of the hall where there
was a window, a stairwell and a pay phone. There was no
phone in his room. They said there was no point to it. I
gave my father a handful of quarters and taught him to dial
Jerry's number, in remembrance of our mutual promise.

I never left the hospital before 9:00 P.M. When I'd get
back to Jerry's, his aunt always had a meal prepared for
me to take up to him. He'd sit up in his bed, watch the
tube, tell me of the day's newsworthy events and his current
theories regarding them, and pick at his food. I'd listen

intently and eat ravenously, all of my plate and whatever Jerry couldn't finish. At 10:30 I'd excuse myself and use a phone downstairs to call Kate. By eleven I'd be back in Jerry's room, where we'd smoke pot, drink Coca-Cola, and talk until I couldn't stay awake a minute more.

I'd catch a couple of hours' sleep, then start the whole grueling process over again.

The hospital became a crazy-place as the "zombie plague"—as some were calling it—increased. As it became more understaffed and more overworked, the remaining personnel grew happier to have me there. I was cooperative and readily assumed many of the chores they no longer had time for. I didn't mind giving my father baths, feeding him, or changing his linens, but I resented the time it took away from our planned therapies.

I spent those two weeks watching my father gradually improve and Jerry steadily worsen. I spent that time feeling glad that I could be present for them in their times of need, and feeling tremendously guilty about leaving Kate and the boys alone in a world gone utterly insane.

THIS EVENING, LATE

"Oh God, Kate, it's all-at-fucking-once, isn't it? Shit. I could cope with a best friend slipping away before my very eyes, I could cope with the devastating loss and excruciating gains my father's situation presents, I could cope with my asshole, greedy-needy mother and all her nonstop shit, I could even cope with any one of them and the separation from you and the boys. But all at once? Damn! I'm so fucking stressed-out. I don't sleep anymore. Then God goes and throws this fucking nightmare on the world just to make things all-the-fucking-jollier. Shit! And now I'm dumping on you. Just-the-fuck what you need." I am poised on the brink between rage and tears.

"You don't have to apologize for that," she tells me. A stab. A twist of the knife. She doesn't mean it that way. If she did, it wouldn't have half the effect.

"Christ! I've abandoned you and look what's happen-

ing to the world. When have you guys needed me more than this?"

She doesn't answer. Can't.

I go on, *"Every day I see Dad improve as a direct result of my presence here. Every day he's more eager, more able. It's a fucking role reversal, the child teaching the father to walk, to talk, to make some sense of the world. I get to be my mother's parent, too, teaching her not to throw tantrums, not to be rude, the difference between acceptable and unacceptable behavior. Christ! Barry and Jordan never took half this much effort from you and I combined, not in their eighteen aggregate years!"*

I pause, move the phone to my other ear, wipe a sweaty palm on my pants leg, sigh, and try to reassert control, direction. *"I had him working on arithmetic today. Simple stuff, but stuff they said he'd never do again. Even so it'll be months, maybe years before he's come back as far as he can, before he's really Dad again. I can't do it. The more I give, the less I have to give. If I push myself too far, I won't be any benefit at all to anyone.*

"Every night I leave the hospital thinking that I should come home to you and the boys. At least for awhile. Till this crazy plague is over. I get back to Jerry's ready to tell him that I'm leaving the next day and I see him wasting away faster than my father is improving. He's a fucking skeleton, and he thinks he's got pneumonia again. He doesn't eat unless I encourage him, he forgets his medication until I remind him. I find myself wondering if going home is really running away. Is my desire to do right by you guys really stronger than my desire to be rid of all of this constant responsibility? Do I have the right to abandon them just to relieve myself?

"I feel so torn. I can't stand it, Kate."

"Oh Duane, when I think of what Jerry and your father are going through, what you're going through, it makes me feel guilty for wanting you home so badly."

"Don't," I tell her. Her sympathy only deepens my sense of guilt. Then impulsively: *"I'm coming home tomorrow. I'll have to go by the hospital in the morning. I told my dad I'd be there and he's come along enough that*

he would know the difference. I'll have to stay long enough to teach him our phone number, but I think he'll pick it up a lot quicker than he did Jerry's. I'll tell him why I'm going and that I'll be back when I can.''

There is a long pause. ''Oh God, Duane. I want you home, I really do, but . . .''

''Tomorrow afternoon or evening.''

''If you're sure.''

''I am. It's really what my dad would want me to do. If he could grasp the situation, he'd tell me that my place right now is by your side. Yours and the boys'.''

No sooner had I hung up than the phone rang.

''Hello?''

''Now!''

A single, anguished syllable, then scuffling and voices in the background and a dead line.

I made the thirty-minute drive in under twenty. The hospital was even crazier than it had been that afternoon. The emergency room had spilled cots out into the lobby. Uniformed personnel were scarce and complaints were loud. Jerry was right, things were deteriorating a lot faster than anyone wanted us to believe. I didn't have time to pursue such thoughts.

Upstairs I was stopped by a nurse who told me my father was asleep.

''He had packed all his things like he was getting ready to leave. When we tried to get him back to bed, he became combative. We had to give him a sedative.''

I pressed past her and on to his room.

The very air of his room stopped me cold. Everything in the room was incredibly still, demanding stillness in response. There was nothing. Nothing at all. Large as the universe, smaller than a molecule of hope. My father was not sleeping. I would have known that without looking, without seeing the awkward angle of head and neck, without seeing the exposed gums in his gaping mouth, without seeing his motionless chest.

If, for two months and more, I had been in a mildly hallucinogenic state regarding sensations, perceptions, awareness of things seen and unseen, now I had unexpectedly mainlined an outrageous quantity of something truly righteous. In that moment I could hear/feel/sense feminine fingers gliding over a computer keyboard at the nurses' station some fifty feet behind me; the collective moanings and whimperings of untold ER patients four floors below me; the metallic whirring of Jerry's VCR as he copped another segment of what he had recently been calling "all the last news unfit to print" fifteen miles away; and, most forlornly and tellingly, the gentle creaking of Barry and Jordan's bunk beds as they shifted in the night ninety miles from where I stood.

But from my father's body, five feet away, there was nothing at all.

I turned to step back into the hall to shout for help.

I stopped myself.

How long had it been this time? Less than five minutes? More than ten? What could they possibly do for him? Bring him back to a coma, a respirator, the long, slow process in front of him again? Was even *that* too much to hope for? Would I find myself in a week's time finally asking Jerry for a sampling of his blood to induce organic failures? Would Jerry still be there to ask?

NINE YEARS AGO

"Duane." My father is speaking as he drives, my mother is sitting beside him, I am in the backseat. "I want you to do me a favor."

I know what he is going to ask. We had spoken of it recently during a fishing trip and I had told him that a request of this nature required witnesses at least, and should also be included in the will that he had not yet made.

"When I pass away, I want to be cremated, then I'd like for you to take the ashes and scatter them around some scenic trails and trout streams in upstate New York or in

*the Pennsylvania mountains. Someplace that you know I
would have liked to be.'' His voice is easy and comfortable,
as if he is looking forward to the event.*

It is my firm belief that few of us can come to terms
with our own mortality without first coming to terms with
the mortality of our parents. Though he and I had discussed
this before, it is only now that I feel myself experiencing
this moment of epiphany. Tears well up.

My mother bites into the moment with unrestrained anger. ''Oh yeah, I can hear your family now: 'She went and
burned *him!*' ''

My father dons his serious face and gently soothes,
''Oh Dorrie, I'm sure that some of them will see it in a
more charitable light than that. At least one of them will
stand up for you and say: 'At least she waited till he was
dead!' ''

I laugh as I cry.

My father smirks with satisfaction.

My mother crosses her arms and stares angrily out the
window.

ONE WEEK AGO

Jerry is saying, ''And everyone is sidestepping the topic of
how they are disposing of the dead. I'm sure the crema-
toriums can't handle the flow fast enough. Maybe they're
using trash incinerators or digging mass graves and top-
ping them off with quick-drying cement. I'm convinced that
they're avoiding the issue because they're afraid the pop-
ulace will be reminded of Auschwitz. The last thing they
need is people making a fuss over the only functional means
of disposal they've come up with.''

Getting my father out of the hospital was easier than I had
anticipated. I had the advantage of being a familiar face to
some and had picked up enough scuttlebutt to know which

doctors' names, when barked officiously, would ward off interference from the others.

Getting him off the gurney and into the middle seat of my mini-van, our pre-ordained getaway car, was a considerably more difficult chore. My father had been gaining weight as rapidly as Jerry had been losing it and was nearly back to his former one eighty-five.

I finally did get him settled and got his seat belt securely fastened. He slumped awkwardly to his left, but there wasn't a hell of a lot I could do about that. I walked around to the driver's side and climbed in.

By then my adrenaline was running so high I left souvenirs of my tires on the hospital's parking lot, though there had been no sign of any sort of pursuit.

An hour into the two-hour drive, I heard the first stirrings behind me. I eased down to seventy and rearranged my rearview mirror so that I'd know as soon as he'd come around enough to sit up. When he did, I eased down the rest of the way and pulled over onto the shoulder. I cut the headlights and the parking lights, switched on the dome light and turned to face him.

He was sitting nearly upright, every muscle in his body tensing and relaxing in nonsequential spasms. His head was rocking back and forth, as if vehemently denying something. His eyes were closed, his mouth open. Saliva dribbled over his exposed gums.

"Dad," I said softly. Nothing.

"Dad," louder this time and his eyes snapped open. Those eyes were deep pools of sorrow, pain and confusion. They locked on mine imploringly, searchingly, like a lover beseeching help beyond hope.

"I love you, Dad. I know you must feel confused right now, frightened, but I'm going to take care of you."

He reached his arms out toward me, fingers twitching spasmodically. He strained against the seat belt. He wanted to embrace me, but I couldn't let him. That hurt.

I watched his chest. Listened. Still no sign of respiration.

"The first thing you have to do is start breathing, Dad.

You've got to teach yourself how to breathe again. I know that sounds impossibly difficult, but you can do it. That's just the first step. You've got a long way to go, I know, but you're stubborn and ornery and I know that you can handle it. We'll just take it one step at a time.''

His eyes were full of tears. I knew that he was recognizing me, that he wanted to please me. His strainings against the seat belt subtly changed. I could see that he was using the pressure against his diaphragm to try to force himself to breathe. I smiled bravely and my smile gave him heart. I could see it.

Several strands of hair, grown long for lack of recent barbering, had fallen over his forehead into his left eye. It didn't seem to bother him. He didn't blink. But seeing it set off a sympathetic irritation in my own eye. Without thinking, I reached over to brush the hair away.

That was when everything changed so violently, so rapidly and unexpectedly. Frantically he clutched at my forearm, his grip so fierce, so strong that pain shot up my arm and exploded in my brain. I tried to pull my arm back, but couldn't. In a moment he had my hand hoisted to his mouth and was biting down on it with all of his savage strength. I felt and heard the breakage of a dozen tiny bones and immediately knew that only his lack of teeth was preventing a far more serious injury.

I went blind, dead, then exploded into awareness. I could see my free arm swinging toward him in a wide arc, throwing off tracers like some time-lapse photo. I could see/hear/feel the impact of my palm on the side of his head, spasming his jaw, dislodging my other hand. Swinging back after the follow-through, I caught his nose and mouth with the back of my hand. Palm, backhand. Palm, backhand. Connecting each time with greater force, my voice a screaming, wordless cadence.

Ten times or more I struck him before I could stop myself. When I did stop, I stopped abruptly, suddenly fearful in some way that I could never have anticipated, in some way that I could never explain. I stared at the hand I had been hitting him with as though it belonged to someone else, as though it *should* have belonged to someone else.

Then I looked up at my father. His face was bruised and lacerated, his nose was broken and there was blood already dancing in the white of his left eye. He too was staring at one of my hands, but not the one I had hit him with. He was staring at the bleeding hand, the one that he had tried to eat. There was no defiance in him. No anger. He had no concern for his own hurt or the terrors of his own circumstance. He was watching me bleed. Anxious for my welfare. I could tell that he regretted what he'd done.

I turned away, switched the lights back on and pulled back onto the highway.

Night. Crisp and silent. Rushing past me. Me sliding through it. Me and my father. Going home.

The meal I had shared with Jerry only hours ago worked its way up into the back of my mouth. I tried to swallow, choked and coughed, splattering the dashboard in front of me, some even reaching the windshield. I smiled.

I stared at my hands, one gripping the wheel so fiercely it looked white in the tantalizing shadowplay of highway night, the other laying dead atop the wheel, unable to grip, bloody and spattered with mucus and bile.

They were the hands of a man, not a child now. They had become my father's hands. Quick, large, strong. Instruments of justice. I smiled and smiled.

My father was quiet now. Thinking about how he had behaved, how he would behave in the future. I was very proud of him. He'd come such a long, long way. He'd made such great strides already. Kate would be happy to see him. And the boys, the boys would be overjoyed. I couldn't wait to show him off.

They would be proud of him, too. They'd welcome him, of course. With open arms.

I smiled and smiled and smiled.

THE ONES YOU LOVE

JOHN SKIPP AND CRAIG SPECTOR

In the dream
we are fighting again
as only wife and husband can
the same old cul-de-sacs of unreason
flooded in the backwash of ancient resentments
disappointment born of unrealistic expectations
trust carelessly laid out and
even more carelessly
violated

in the dream
we are no longer in love
and your eyes are black with dead romance
black and cold as an unlit hell
black and madly raging as the eye of a hurricane at night
no hickory and olive underlying the angry flash of them
no mollifying color at all

in the dream
your eyes are black like mine
above your cruel and lovely lips
lips forming words
that were meant to maim and disfigure but
most of all stop *my* words from coming
coming at you like poison darts
to stun you into silence
this is how we fight
tearing into each other's souls
with tongues like teeth and nails

in my dream, there is no rest
and the night goes on forever

Our bed stands
in the middle of the room
like a shrine to a dead god
offering sacrifices nightly
on the altar of indifference

Our bodies never touch
but your heart still thrums
like the drums of some hostile tribe
echoing through the halls
of our barren and beautiful house
etched in plaster
absorbed by brick and wood
a chiaroscuro of hurt
where love once stood

I clutch
like a shipwreck survivor
grasping at hope
floating like driftwood
your silhouette a distant shore
a million miles away
on the other side of the bed

I drift
through nights made of hours
made of minutes made of moments
each marked by the beating
of my black and bleeding heart
battered by waves of regret
deafened by your
siren-song

I lose
my grip
wondering how much longer
the beating can go on
I sink
into blackness
cold as any unlit hell
until at last
the beating
can go no longer

until at last
the beating
stops

When the pain comes
suddenly
like a fist
twisting in my chest
the dream smears like a watercolor
and our voices smear as well
twin shrieks across the soundscape
blotting out the pounding of my hemorrhaging heart
wound too tight and exploding now
erasing me in my sleep
without a prayer
without a sound

in the pain
you no longer exist
and the dream-shards disperse

like atoms

when the blackness comes
it is deeper than your eyes
and lasts forever

no

the darkness peels back, like a layer of skin, and all at
once without warning i am back in the world. there
are soft sheets clenched tight between my fingers,
thick in my grip as my hand comes up to touch my
lips. and it feels like when i was just a baby, and the
whole wide world was new, and the only emotions
were love and fear.

only now i am not afraid.

the universe floods
with sound
taste
sensation
and the light
in our quiet bedroom
is like no light i've ever known

i roll over
and there you are
and i find that the anger is gone like the dream
and i find that when i close my eyes
you're gone as well
but when i open them again
it all comes back
with you

i thank you for that
and i find that i still love you
—yes—
never more so than now
here and sleeping beside me

astoundingly warm
i love you now
i love you intensely
because i remember
everything
and because you are here
to remind me

it is love
for the sweet heart-shaped ass
accidentally pressed against me
love for the long sloping small of your back
love of your heartbeat
the *feel* of your heartbeat
the feel of your lungs' sweet breathing song
it is love
for the mind
that concocted the brain
love
for the blood that concocted the vein
it is love for every part of you
that propels my body
closer

your head is buried
under the pillow, as usual
the better to hide your dreams away
the pillow is soft and smells of your skin
it muffles the sound of my clumsy advance
but the mattress responds to my shifting weight
and you stir in your sleep
annoyed
unsuspecting
body unconsciously shifting away from me
keeping the requisite distance
between us

but i am in love with you now

my body, stupid and slow, fumble-falls upon you. it's
the smell of your sweat that i love, the sleepwalker
dance of musk and languid motion beneath the t-shirt
that locks in your soft belly warmth. my idiot hands,
blunt flesh mittens, paw at your shoulder blades,
holding you back as you crawl up from slumber.
beneath the pillow, you begin to lift your head. i fall
upon you, awkwardly pin you facedown. my lips trail
across the back of your neck. and there are no words.

now.

my face goes wet and blind and all at once my mouth
is full of gristleflesh that spurts and tears and grinds
between my teeth. there are no words from beneath
the pillow, no arguments now, just muffled screams
and a desperate bucking motion. i close my eyes,
seeing black, continuing to feed in the hot and dark.
my teeth scrape bone as i wade in. bestial. slick with
red. you will not stop kicking. you will not stop
kicking.

this is how i love you.

I love
the way you open to me
from behind
i love the scarlet lapping
as you soak into my skin
and i burrow
i nestle
i make my home inside you
as you are displaced
one violent mouthful at a time
teeth and tongue
pressing insistently
peeling fascia from membrane
crushed blood vessel from screaming nerve
feasting on pharynx and gullet as i dig deep and find
your ever-hidden heart

suddenly revealed
exposed
mine

i climb
inside your jaws
gnawing through muscle and mucous and fiber
dragging your tongue down from within
i know no deeper love than this
as i coil around you
spasming bucking
you trembling in kind
and then finally
you stop

i come up for air
that i no longer need
and my face smears on the sodden pillow
that falls away as i roll you over
and look into your eyes

i stare into the blackness
unfolding there
in those
deep wide
circular pits of night
staring blindly, seeing
a darkness twice as cold and deep
as any unlit hell
but all the anger
is gone
we are one

it is delicious
like oysters from a shell
i dine on you in this way
for an hour

and then i hear the sound

 i half rise—slow, witless, unsteady—and my gaze
drags toward the door. beneath me, you stir: the first
weak tremor. responding, perhaps, as well. it doesn't
matter. the sound comes again. i struggle to my feet
and lurch toward the corridor, throw open the door
into light. scum-clotted fingertips lovingly trace the
wallpaper patterns, the infinitesimal hairline cracks in
the plaster. they are familiar. i remember everything.

 it is love alone that propels me.

she awakens
from the terrible dream
that mommy and daddy are fighting again
she is still crying as i enter the room
holding wide her sweet three-year-old arms for me
not awake enough yet to register the change
inviting me to hold her please
knowing that i would never
ever violate
that trust

she loves her daddy
and i love my little girl

PART TWO

COPING WITH THE DEAD

THIS YEAR'S CLASS PICTURE

DAN SIMMONS

Ms. Geiss watched her new student coming across the first-graders' playground from her vantage point on the balcony of the old school's belfry. She lowered the barrel of the Remington .30-.06 until the child was centered in the crosshairs of the telescopic sight. The image was quite clear in the early-morning light. It was a boy, not one she knew, and he looked to have been about nine or ten when he died. His green Teenage Mutant Ninja Turtles t-shirt had been slashed down the center and there was a spattering of dried blood along the ragged cleft. Ms. Geiss could see the white gleam of an exposed rib.

She hesitated, lifting her eye from the sight to watch the small figure lurch and stumble his way through the swing sets and around the jungle gym. His age was right, but she already had twenty-two students. More than that, she knew, and the class became difficult to manage. And today was class picture day and she did not need the extra aggravation. Plus, the child's appearance was on the borderline of what she would accept in her fourth grade ... especially on class picture day.

You never had that luxury before *the Tribulations*, she chided herself. She put her eye back against the plastic sunhood of the sight and grimaced slightly as she thought of the children who had been "mainstreamed" into her elementary classes over the years: deaf children, blind children, borderline autistic children, children suffering from epilepsy and Down's syndrome and hyperactivity and sexual abuse and abandonment and dyslexia and petit mal seizures ... children dying of cancer and children dying of AIDS. . . .

The dead child had crossed the shallow moat and was approaching the razor-wire barriers that Ms. Geiss had strung around the school just where the first-graders' gravel playground adjoined the fourth-graders' paved basketball and four-square courts. She knew that the boy would keep coming and negotiate the wire no matter how many slices of flesh were torn from his body.

Sighing, already feeling tired even before the school day had formally begun, Ms. Geiss lowered the Remington, clicked on the safety, and started down the belfry ladder to go and greet her new student.

She peered in her classroom door on the way to the supply closet on the second floor. The class was restless, daylight and hunger stirring them to tug against the chains and iron collars. Little Samantha Stewart, technically too young for fourth grade, had torn her dress almost off in her nighttime struggles. Sara and Sarah J. were tangled in each other's chains. Todd, the biggest of the bunch and the former class bully, had chewed away the rubber lining of his collar again. Ms. Geiss could see flecks of black rubber around Todd's white lips and knew that the metal collar had worn away the flesh of his neck almost to the bone. She would have to make a decision about Todd soon.

On the long bulletin board behind her desk, she could

see the thirty-eight class pictures she had mounted there. Thirty-eight years. Thirty-eight class pictures, all taken in this school. Starting with the thirty-second year, the photographs became much smaller as they had gone from the large format cameras the photo studio had used to the school Polaroid that Ms. Geiss had rigged to continue the tradition. The classes were also smaller. In her thirty-fifth year there had been only five students in her fourth grade. Sarah J. and Todd had been in that class—alive, pink-skinned, thin and frightened looking, but healthy. In the thirty-sixth year there were no living children ... but seven students. In the next-to-last photograph, there were sixteen faces. This year, today, she would have to set the camera to get all twenty-two children in the frame. *No*, she thought, *twenty-three with the new boy*.

Ms. Geiss shook her head and walked on to the supply closet. She had fifteen minutes before the school bell was programmed to ring.

Carrying the capture pole, pliers, police handcuffs, heavy gloves, and the rubber apron from the supply closet, Ms. Geiss hurried down the broad stairway to the first floor. At the front door she checked the video monitors to make sure that the outer courtyard, walkway, and fourth-grade playground were empty except for the new boy, tied on the apron, slung the Remington over her shoulder, pulled on the gloves, unbolted the steel-reinforced door, made sure the pliers and handcuffs were reachable in the big apron pocket, lifted the capture pole, and stepped out to meet her new student.

The boy's t-shirt and jeans had been slashed even more by the razor wire. Tatters of bloodless flesh hung from his forearms. As Ms. Geiss moved out into the sunlight, he raised his dead face and dulled eyes in her direction. His teeth were yellow.

Ms. Geiss held her breath as the boy lurched and scrabbled in her direction. It was not because of his smell; she was used to the roadkill scent of the children. This new boy was a bit worse than most of her students, not quite as bad as Todd. His trousers were soaked with gasoline from wading the moat at the edge of the schoolground and the gasoline smell drove away some of his stench. She found herself holding her breath because even after all these months . . . *years,* she realized . . . there was still a certain tension in meeting a new student.

The boy lurched the last fifteen feet toward her across the courtyard cement. Ms. Geiss steadied herself and raised the capture pole.

At one time the capture pole had been a seven-foot wood-and-brass rod for raising and lowering the tall upper windows in the old school. Ms. Geiss had modified it by mounting a heavy fishing reel wound about with heavy-duty baling wire, adding eyelets to guide the wire, and jury-rigging a device on the end to lock off the double-thick loop. She'd gotten the idea from watching old videos of *Mutual of Omaha's Wild Kingdom.* Whatshisname, the big, handsome fellow who'd done all of the work . . . Jim . . . had used a similar device to catch rattlesnakes.

This poor child is more deadly than any rattlesnake, thought Ms. Geiss. And then she concentrated totally on the capture.

There were no problems. The child lunged. Ms. Geiss dropped the double loop of wire over his head, released the catch to tighten the noose, and locked it in. The wire sank deep into the boy's throat but was too thick to slice flesh. If he had been breathing, the noose would have strangled him, but that was no longer a concern.

Ms. Geiss took a step forward and the boy lurched, staggered, swung his arms, and went over backward, his head striking concrete with a sickening, soft-melon sound. The teacher checked over her shoulder to make sure the courtyard and playground were still clear, and then she pinned the flailing child, first with the extended capture pole, and then with her foot. The boy's fingernails scrabbled against the thick leather of her high boot.

With a practiced motion, Ms. Geiss dropped the pole, secured the child's wrists with one gloved hand, handcuffed him with her free hand, and sat on his chest, tucking her print dress in as she did so. Ms. Geiss weighed one hundred and ninety-five pounds, and there was no question of the child escaping. With a critical eye she assessed his wounds:

the chest wound had been the fatal one, and it looked as if it had been administered by a meat cleaver or long knife; the other gashes, tears, bites, and a single bullet wound high on the child's shoulder had all been added after he was dead.

Ms. Geiss nodded as if satisfied, pried back the wriggling child's lips as if inspecting a horse, and pulled his teeth with the pair of pliers. The boy made no outcry. She noticed that flies had lain eggs in the corner of his eyes and she made a mental note to take care of that during cleanup.

Shifting her weight only slightly, the teacher reversed position on the boy's chest, lifted his bound wrists, and efficiently pulled his fingernails off with the pliers. The only blood was in the dried and matted substance under his nails.

The child was snapping at her like an angry turtle, but his gums would never have penetrated skin, much less Ms. Geiss's rubber Wellingtons and the corduroy trousers she wore under the dress.

She glanced over her shoulder again. Months ago she had been surprised by five of them—all adults—who had come soundlessly through the wire while she had been watching the children at recess, and there had been only six cartridges in the Remington. One of the head shots had been a near miss; she had corrected her aim when the lurching man was only four feet from her, and the adrenaline of that encounter kept her vigilant.

The playground was empty. Ms. Geiss grunted, pulled the new boy to his feet with the wire noose, opened the door with one hand, and shoved him in ahead of her with the pole. There would be just enough time for cleanup before the first bell rang.

The first thing on the morning's agenda was writing the schedule on the chalkboard. Ms. Geiss had always done that to show the children what they would be doing and learning that day.

The first thing on the written schedule was the Pledge of Allegiance. Ms. Geiss decided that she would go ahead with that and introduce the new boy after it. He sat now in the third from the last desk in the row closest to the windows. Ms. Geiss had taken the handcuffs off, clipped on the leg manacles that were bolted to the floor, run the waist chain around him, attached it to the long chain that ran the length of the desks, and set his iron collar in place. The boy had flailed at her, his dead eyes glimmering for a second with something that might have been hunger, but a child's arms were simply too short to do damage to an adult.

Even before the Tribulations, Ms. Geiss had smiled when she watched movies or television shows where children used judo or karate to flip adults around the room. From her many years' experience, she knew that simple laws of mechanics meant that a child's punch was usually harmless. They simply didn't have the mass, arm length, and leverage to do much damage. With the new boy's teeth and claws pulled, Ms. Geiss could handle him without the capture pole or chains if she wished.

She did not so wish. She treated the children with the distance and respect for contamination she had shown her one HIV-positive child back before the Tribulations.

Pledge of Allegiance time. She looked at her class of twenty-three children. A few were standing and straining toward her, clanking their chains, but most were sprawled across the desks or leaning from their seats as if they could escape by crawling across the floor. Ms. Geiss shook her head and threw the large switch on her desk. The six twelve-volt batteries were arranged in series, their cable leads connected to the gang chain which ran from desk to desk. She actually saw sparks and smelled the ozone.

The electricity did not hurt them, of course. Nothing could hurt these children. But something in the voltage did galvanize them, much as Galvani's original experiments had activated frog legs into kicking even though the legs were separated from the frogs' bodies.

The students spasmed, twitched, and lurched upright with a great clanking of chains. They rose to their toes as if trying to rise above the voltage flowing into their lower bodies. Their hands splayed and curled spasmodically in front of their chests. Some opened their mouths as if screaming silently.

Ms. Geiss put her hand over her heart and faced the flag above the doorway. "I pledge allegiance to the flag," she began, "of the United States of America. . . ."

She introduced the new boy as Michael. He had no identification on him, of course, and Ms. Geiss was sure that he had not attended the school before the Tribulations, but there were no other Michaels in the class and the boy looked as if he might have been a Michael. The class paid no attention to the introduction. Neither did Michael.

Mathematics was the first class after the Pledge. Ms. Geiss left the class alone long enough to go downstairs, check the row of video monitors, and get the learning rewards from the long row of open freezers in the downstairs hall. She had scavenged the freezers from the Safeway last year. Donnie had helped. Ms. Geiss blinked twice when she thought of Donnie, her friend and the former custodian. Donnie had helped with so many things . . . without him she could never have managed the work of processing the learning rewards out at the chicken nugget plant on the edge of town . . . or wiring the Radio Shack video cameras and monitors. If only Donnie hadn't stopped to help that truck filled with refugees that had broken down just off the Interstate . . .

Ms. Geiss shook off her reverie, adjusted the sling of the Remington, and carried the box of learning rewards to the teachers' lounge. She set the microwave for three minutes.

The smell of the heated nuggets set the students into clanking, lurching agitation when she entered the classroom. Ms. Geiss set the reward box on the table near her desk and went to the chalkboard to start the math lesson.

Thank God Donnie knew how to handle the chicken-nugget-processing equipment out at the plant, she thought as she wrote numerals from 0 to 10.

The children, of course, would not have eaten chicken

nuggets. The children, as with all of those who had returned during the Tribulations, had a taste for only one thing.

Ms. Geiss glanced at the tray of heated nuggets. Against her will, the smell made her own mouth water. Somewhere in one of those freezer boxes, she knew, were the deep-fried and nugget-processed remains of Mister Delmonico, the former principal, as well as at least half the former staff of the elementary school. It had been Donnie who had realized that the spate of suicides in the small town should not go to waste; it had been Donnie who remembered the chicken-nugget plant and the large freezers there. It had been Donnie who had seen how useful it would be to have some nuggets with one when encountering a wandering pack of the hungry undead. Donnie had said that it was like the way burglars brought a rare steak along to distract guard dogs.

But it had been Ms. Geiss who saw the potential of the nuggets as learning rewards. And in her humble opinion, the overbearing Mr. Delmonico and the other lazy staff members had never served the cause of education as well as they were doing now.

"One," said Ms. Geiss, pointing to the large numeral she had drawn on the board. She raised one finger. "Say 'one.'"

Todd chewed at the new rubber ring Ms. Geiss had set in his collar. Kirsten tripped over her chain and went face-down on the desk. Little Samantha clawed at her own clothes. Justin, still chubby ten months after his death, gummed the plastic back of the seat in front of him. Megan lurched against the chains. Michael had twisted himself around until he was staring at the back of the room.

"One," repeated Ms. Geiss, still pointing to the numeral on the chalkboard. "If you can't say it, hold up *one* hand. One. One."

John snapped his toothless gums in a wet, regular rhythm. Behind him, Abigail sat entirely motionless except for the slow in-and-out of her dry tongue. David batted his face over and over against the lid of his desk. Sara chewed on the white tips of bones protruding from her fingers while behind her, Sarah J. suddenly thrust her hand up, one finger striking her eye and staying there.

Ms. Geiss did not hesitate. "Very *good, Sarah*," she said and hurried down the row between groping hands and smacking mouths. She popped the nugget in Sarah J.'s slack mouth and stepped back quickly.

"One!" said Ms. Geiss. "Sarah raised *one* finger."

All the students were straining toward the nugget tray. Sarah J.'s finger was still embedded in her eye.

Ms. Geiss stepped back to the chalkboard. In her heart she knew that the child's spasmodic reaction had been random. It did not matter, she told herself. Given enough time and positive reinforcement, the connections will be made. Look at Helen Keller and her teacher, Annie Sullivan. And that was with a totally blind and deaf child who had had only a few months of language before the darkness descended on her. That one baby word—*wa-wa*—had allowed Helen, years later, to learn everything.

And these children had possessed *years* of language and thought before . . .

Before they died, completed Ms. Geiss. *Before their minds and memories and personalities unraveled like a skein of rotten thread.*

Ms. Geiss sighed and touched the next numeral. "Two," she said cheerily. "Anyone show me . . . show me any way you can . . . show me *two*."

After her own lunch and while the students were resting after their feeding time, Ms. Geiss continued with the bulldozing of houses.

At first she thought that isolating the school grounds with the moat and razorwire, lighting it with the searchlights at night, and installing the video monitors had been enough. But *they* still got through.

Luckily, the town was small—fewer than three thousand—and it was almost forty miles to a real city. Now that the Tribulations had separated the quick and the dead, there were almost none of the former and few of the latter left in the area. A few cars filled with terrified living refugees roared through town, but most never left the Inter-state and in recent months the sound of passing vehicles had all but stopped. A few of *them* filtered in—from the countryside, from the distant city, from their graves—and they were drawn to the generator-powered searchlights like moths to a flame, but the school's thick walls, steel-mesh screens, and warning devices always kept them out until morning. And in the morning, the Remington solved the problem.

Still, Ms. Geiss wanted a clearer field of fire—what Donnie had once called an "uncompromised killing zone." She had reminded Donnie that the term "killing zone" was a misnomer, since they were not killing anything, merely returning the things to their natural state.

And so Ms. Geiss had driven out to the line shack near the unfinished section of the Interstate and come back with the dynamite, blasting caps, detonators, priming cord, and a Caterpillar D-7 bulldozer. Ms. Geiss had never driven a bulldozer, never exploded dynamite, but there were man-uals at the line shack, and books in the Carnegie Library. Ms. Geiss had always been amazed at people's ignorance of how much knowledge and useful information there was in books.

Now, with a half hour left in her lunch break, she en-tered the bulldozer's open-sided shelter, climbed up onto the wide seat of the D-7, disengaged the clutch lever, set the speed selector to neutral, pushed the governor control to the firewall, stood on the right steering wheel and locked it in position with a clamp, made sure that the gears were in neutral, and reached for the starter controls. She paused to make sure that the Remington .30-.06 was secure in the clamp that had once held a fire extinguisher near her right hand. Visibility was better with the houses in a three-block radius of the school blown apart this way, but there were still too many foundations and heaps of rubble that the things could hide behind. She could see nothing moving.

Ms. Geiss set the transmission and compression levers to their correct settings, pushed the starting-engine clutch in, opened a fuel valve, set the choke, dropped the idling latch, clicked on the ignition switch, and pulled the lever that engaged the electric starter.

The D-7 roared into life, black diesel smoke blowing from the vertical exhaust pipe. Ms. Geiss adjusted the throttle, let the clutch out, and gave traction to just the right tread so that the massive 'dozer spun to its left and headed for the largest pile of rubble.

An adult corpse scrabbled out of a collapsed basement on her right and clawed across bricks toward her. The thing's hair was matted back with white dust, its teeth broken but sharp. One eye was gone. Ms. Geiss thought that she recognized it as Todd's stepfather—the drunkard who used to beat the boy every Friday night.

It raised its arms and came at her.

Ms. Geiss glanced at the Remington, decided against it. She gave traction to the left treads, swung the bulldozer smartly to the right, and lowered the big blade just as she opened the throttle up. The lower edge of the blade caught the staggering corpse just above its beltline. Ms. Geiss dropped the blade once, twice, stopping the third time only when the corpse was cut in half. The legs spasmed uselessly, but fingers clawed at steel and began pulling the upper half of the thing onto the blade.

Ms. Geiss pulled levers, got the machine in reverse, put it back in low gear, lowered the blade, and bulldozed half a ton of rubble over both halves of the twitching corpse as she shoved the mass of debris back into the basement. It took less than a minute to move another ton of rubble over the hole. Then she backed up, checked to make sure that no other things were around, and began filling in the basement in earnest.

When she was done, she stepped down and walked across the area; it was as flat and smooth as a gravel parking lot. Todd's stepfather might still be twitching and clawing down there, at least his upper half, but with twelve tons of rubble packed and compacted over him, he wasn't going anywhere.

Ms. Geiss only wished that she could have done this to all the drunk and abusive fathers and stepfathers she'd known over the decades.

She mopped her face with a handkerchief and checked her watch. Three minutes until reading class began. Ms. Geiss surveyed the flattened city blocks, interrupted by only a few remaining piles of rubble or collapsed foundations. Another week and her field of fire would be uninterrupted. Stopping to catch her breath, feeling her sixty-plus years in the arthritic creak of her joints, Ms. Geiss climbed back aboard the D-7 to fire it up and park it in its shelter for the night.

Ms. Geiss read aloud to her class. Each afternoon in the lull after her lunch and the students' feeding time, she read from books she knew that they had either read in their short lifetimes or had had read to them. She read from *Goodnight Moon, Pat the Bunny, Gorilla, Heidi, Bunnicula, Superfudge, Black Beauty, Richard Scary's ABC Book, Green Eggs and Ham, Tom Sawyer, Animal Sounds, Harold and the Purple Crayon, Peter Rabbit, Polar Express, Where the Wild Things Are,* and *Tales of a Fourth Grade Nothing.* And while Ms. Geiss read she watched for the slightest flicker of recognition, of interest . . . of *life* in those dead eyes.

And saw nothing.

As the weeks and months passed Ms. Geiss read from the children's favorite series: *Curious George* books, and *Madeleine* books, and the *Black Stallion* series, *Ramona* books, the *Berenstain Bears,* and *Clifford* books, and—despite the fact that priggish, politically correct librarians had tried to remove them from the children's public library shelves not long before the Tribulations began—*The Bobbsey Twins* and *The Hardy Boys* and *Nancy Drew.*

And the students did not respond.

On rainy days, days when the clouds hung low and Ms. Geiss's spirits hung lower, she would sometimes read to them from the Bible, or from her favorite Shakespeare plays—usually the comedies but occasionally *Romeo and Juliet* or *Hamlet*—and sometimes she would read from her favorite poet, John Keats. But after the dance of words, after the last echo of beauty had faded, Ms. Geiss would look up and no intelligent gaze would be looking back. There would be only the dead eyes, the slack faces, the open mouths, the aimless, mindless stirrings, and the soft stench of rank flesh.

It was not too dissimilar from her years of teaching live children.

This afternoon Ms. Geiss read what she always thought of as their favorite, *Goodnight Moon,* enjoying as she went the lilt and litany of the small ceremony of the young rabbit's endless goodnights to everything in his room as he attempted to put off the inevitable moment of sleep. Ms. Geiss finished the little book and looked up quickly, trying, as always, to catch the flicker in the eye, the animation in the muscles around mouth or eye.

Slackness. Vacuity. They had ears but did not hear.

Ms. Geiss sighed softly. "We'll do geography before recess," she said.

The projected slides were brilliant in the darkened room. The Capitol dome in Washington. The St. Louis Arch. The Space Needle in Seattle. The World Trade Center.

"Hold up your hand when you see a city you know," said Ms. Geiss over the whirring of the projector's fan. "Make a motion when you see something familiar."

The Chicago Lakefront. Denver with mountains rising in the background. Bourbon Street at Mardi Gras time. The Golden Gate Bridge.

The slides clicked past in Kodachrome splendor. The children stirred sluggishly, just beginning to respond to the first stirrings of renewed hunger. No one raised a hand. No one seemed to notice the bright image of the Brooklyn Bridge on the screen.

New York, thought Ms. Geiss, remembering the September day twenty-seven years earlier when she had taken the photograph. The first invigorating breezes of autumn had made them wear sweaters as she and Mr. Farnham, the science coordinator she had met at the NEA convention, had walked across the pedestrian deck of the Brooklyn Bridge. They had gone to the Metropolitan Museum of Art and then walked in Central Park. The rustle of every leaf had seemed audible and separate to Ms. Geiss's heightened senses on that perfect afternoon. They had almost kissed when he dropped her at the Hotel Barbizon that evening after dinner at the River Café. He had promised to call her. It was only months later that Ms. Geiss had heard from a teacher friend from Connecticut that Mr. Farnham was married, had been married for twenty years.

The children rustled their chains.

"Raise an arm if you recognize New York City from the pictures," said Ms. Geiss tiredly. No arm was raised into the bright beam of the projection lamp. Ms. Geiss tried to imagine New York City now, years after the onset of the Tribulations. Any survivors there would be food for the hundreds of thousands, the *millions* of flesh-hungry, un-clean creatures that had inherited those filthy streets. . . .

Ms. Geiss advanced rapidly through the remaining slides: San Diego, the Statue of Liberty, a bright curve of Hawaiian beach, Monhegan Island in the morning fog, Las Vegas at night . . . all places she had seen in her wonderful summers, all places she would never see again.

"That's all the geography for today," said Ms. Geiss and switched off the projector. The students seemed agi-tated in the darkness. "Recess time," said their teacher.

Ms. Geiss knew that they did not need exercise. Their dead muscles would not atrophy if they were not used. The bril-liant spring daylight only made the children seem more obscene in their various stages of decomposition.

But Ms. Geiss could not imagine keeping fourth graders in class all day without a recess.

She led them outside, still attached to their four gang chains, and secured the ends of the chains to the iron rods she had driven into the gravel and asphalt playgrounds. The children lurched this way and that, finally coming to a stop, straining at the end of their tethers like small, scabrous, child-shaped balloons waiting for the Macy's parade to be-gin. No child paid attention to another. A few leaned in Ms. Geiss's direction, toothless gums smacking as if in anticipation, but the sight and sound of that was so common that Ms. Geiss felt neither threat nor alarm.

She wandered farther out across the fourth-graders' playground, threaded her way through the winding exit maze she had left in the razor wire, crossed the gravel expanse of the first-graders' playground, and stopped only when she reached the moat she had dug around the small city block the old school and its playgrounds occupied. Ms. Geiss called it a moat; the military-engineering manuals she had found in the stacks of the Carnegie Library called it a tank trap. But the specifications for a tank trap called for a ditch at least eight feet deep and thirty feet wide, with berms rising at an angle of 45 degrees. Ms. Geiss had used the D-7 to dig a moat half that deep and wide, with the slowly eroding banks no greater than twenty degrees. However the dead would come at her, she thought, it was improbable that they would be driving tanks.

The gasoline was a touch she garnered from an old article on Iraqi defenses during the Gulf War. Finding the gasoline was no problem—Donnie had commandeered a large tanker truck to borrow gas from the underground Texaco tanks to power the generator he and she had set up in the school—but keeping the fuel in the moat from soaking into the soil had been a puzzler until Ms. Geiss had thought of the huge sheets of black poly left out at the highway department depot.

She looked down at the tepid moat of gasoline now, thinking how silly this self-defense measure had been ... like the spotlights on the school, or the video cameras.

But it had kept her busy.

Like pretending to teach these poor lost souls? Ms. Geiss shook away the thought and walked back to the playground, raising her whistle to her lips to signify the end of recess. None of the students reacted to the whistle, but Ms. Geiss blew it anyway. It was tradition.

She took them to the art room to shoot the picture. She did not know why the studio used to take the pictures there— the color would have been infinitely better if they had posed the children outside—but the photo had been taken in the art room for as long as anyone could remember, the students lined up—shortest in the front rows even though the front rows were kneeling—everyone posed under the huge ceramic map of the United States, each state made of fired, brown clay and set in place by some art class half a century or more ago. The corners of the ceramic states had curled up and out of alignment as if some seismic event was tearing the nation apart. Texas had fallen out eight or nine years ago and the pieces were glued in without great care, making the state look like a federation of smaller states.

Ms. Geiss had never liked Texas. She had been a girl when President Kennedy was killed in Texas, and in her opinion things had gone to hell in the country ever since then.

She led the children in by rows, slipped the end of their gang chains over the radiator, set a warmed pan of learning rewards on the floor between the camera and the class, checked to make sure the film pack she had put in that morning was advanced properly, set the timer, moved quickly to stand next to Todd—straining, as the other students were straining, to get at the nuggets—and tried to smile as the timer hissed and the shutter clicked.

She shot two more Polaroid pictures and only glanced at them before setting them in the pocket of her apron. Most of the children were facing front. That was good enough.

There were ten minutes left in the school day by the time she had the class tethered in their seats again, but Ms. Geiss could not bring herself to do a spelling list or to read aloud again or even to force crayons in their hands and set the butcher paper out. She sat and stared at them, feeling the fatigue and sense of uselessness as a heavy weight on her shoulders.

The students stared in her direction ... or at least in the direction of the pan of cooling nuggets.

At three P.M. the dismissal bell rang, Ms. Geiss went up the wide aisles tossing nuggets to the children, and then she turned out the lights, bolted the door shut, and left the classroom for the day.

• • •

It is morning and there is a richness of light Ms. Geiss has not noticed for years. As she moves to the chalkboard to write the class's assignments next to schedule chalked there, she notices that she is much younger. She is wearing the dress she had worn the morning she and Mr. Farnham walked across the Brooklyn Bridge.

"Please get your reading books out," she says softly. "Green Salad Seasons group, bring your books and comprehension quiz sheets up front. Mystery Sneaker, I'll take a look at your vocabulary words when we're finished here. Sprint, please copy the Skillsbook assignment and be ready to come up front at ten-fifteen to answer questions. Anyone who finishes early may get a Challenge Pack from the interest center."

The children scatter quietly to their assigned tasks. The group at the front table read with Ms. Geiss and answer questions quietly while the other children work with that soft, almost subliminal hum that is the universal background noise of a good classroom.

While the Green Salad Seasons group writes answers to questions at the end of the story, Ms. Geiss walks among the other children.

Sara wears a kerchief in the form of a cap. The knots protrude like tiny rabbit ears. Normally Ms. Geiss does not allow caps or kerchiefs to be worn in the classroom, but Sara has undergone chemotherapy and has lost her hair. The class does not tease her about it, not even Todd.

Now Sara leans over her Skillsbook and squints at the questions there. Occasionally she chews at the eraser on the end of her pencil. She is nine years old. Her eyes are blue and her complexion is as milkily translucent as a shard of expensive porcelain. Her cheeks seem touched with a healthy blush, and it is only upon closer inspection that one can see that this is a soft pass of makeup that her mother has applied, that Sara is still pale and wan from her illness.

Ms. Geiss stops by the child's desk. "Problem, Sara?"

"I don't understand this." Sara stabs a finger at a line

of instructions. Her fingernails are as chewed as the eraser on her pencil.

"It says to find the proper prefix and put it before the word," whispers Ms. Geiss. Up front, Kirsten is sharpening a pencil with a loud grinding. The class looks up as Kirsten blows shavings off into the waste basket, carefully inspects the point, and begins the grinding again.

"What's a prefix?" Sara whispers back.

Ms. Geiss leans closer. The two are temporarily joined in a bond of conspiracy produced by their proximity and the hypnotic background hum of classroom activity. Ms. Geiss can feel the warmth from the girl's cheek near hers.

"You remember what a prefix is," says Ms. Geiss and proceeds to show the girl.

She returns to the front table just as Green Salad Seasons, her top group, leaves for their desks and Sprint, her small remedial group, comes forward. There are only six students in Sprint and four of them are boys.

"David," she says, "can you tell me how the dolphin both helped and hurt the boy?"

David frowns as if in deep thought and chews on the wood of his pencil. His Skillsbook page is blank.

"Todd," says Ms. Geiss, "can you tell us?"

Todd turns fierce eyes in her direction. The boy always seems distracted, involved in some angry internal argument. "Tell you what?"

"Tell us how the dolphin both helped and hurt the boy?"

Todd begins to shrug but avoids the motion at the last moment. Ms. Geiss has broken him of that habit by patient and positive reinforcement—praise, extra classroom duties if he can get through the day without shrugging, a Good Scholar Certificate to take home at the end of the week. "It saved him," says Todd.

"Very good," says Ms. Geiss with a smile. "Saved him from what?"

"From the shark," says Todd. His hair is uncombed and unwashed, his neck grubby, but his eyes are bright blue and angrily alive.

"And how did it almost hurt the boy?" asks Ms. Geiss,

looking around the small group to see who should participate next.

"They're coming, Ms. Geiss," Todd says loudly.

She glances back at her biggest student, preparing to warn him about interrupting, but what she sees freezes her before she can speak.

Todd's eyes are suddenly vacuous, sunken, and clouded white. His skin has become the color and texture of a dead fish's belly. His teeth are gone and his gums are a desiccated blue. Todd opens his mouth wider and suddenly it is not a mouth at all, but just a hole excavated into a dead thing's face. The voice that emerges rises out of the thing's belly like a tinny recording echoing in some obscene doll.

"Quick, Ms. Geiss, they're coming to hurt us. Wake up!"

Ms. Geiss sat up in bed, heart racing, gasping for breath. She found her glasses on her nightstand, set them in place, and peered around the room.

Everything was in order. Bright light from the external spotlights came through the blinds in the tall window and painted white rectangles on the floor of the upstairs classroom she had modified as her bed- and living room. Ms. Geiss listened hard over the pounding of her pulse but heard nothing unusual from the classroom below her. There were no noises from outside. The silent row of video monitors near her couch showed the empty hallways, the light-bathed courtyard, the empty playgrounds. The closest monitor showed the dark classroom: the students stood or sprawled or leaned or strained at chains. They were all accounted for.

Just a dream, Ms. Geiss told herself. *Go back to sleep.*

Instead she rose, pulled her quilted robe on over her flannel nightgown, tied her rubber apron on over that, stepped into her boots, lifted the Remington, found the bulky pair of night-vision goggles that Donnie had brought from the city surplus store, and went out to climb the wide ladder to the belfry.

Ms. Geiss stepped out onto the narrow platform that

ran around the belfry. She could see in all four directions and only a bit of the east yard of the school was blocked by the front gable. The spotlights reached across the playgrounds and moat and illuminated the first rows of bulldozed rubble where surrounding houses had been. Nothing moved.

The teacher yawned and shook her head. The night air was chill; she could see her breath. *I'm getting too old to spook myself like this. There's more threat from the bands of refugees than from the adult dead things.*

She turned to go down the ladder, but at the last second paused by the junction box she and Donnie had rigged there. Sighing softly, she threw the switch that doused the spotlights and then fumbled with the night vision goggles. They were bulky, clumsy to fit on her head, and she could not wear her glasses under them. Also, she always felt like she looked like an idiot with the things on her head. Still, Donnie had risked a trip to the city to get them. She moved her glasses up on her forehead and tugged the goggles down.

She turned and froze. Things moved to the west, just beyond where the blaze of spotlights had reached. Pale blobs moved through the rubble there, rising out of basements and spider holes in the rubble-strewn lots. Ms. Geiss could tell that they were dead by the way they stumbled and rose again, faltering at obstacles but never failing to come on again. There were twenty . . . no, at least thirty tall forms moving toward the school.

She turned to the north. Another thirty or more figures moving there, almost to the street. To the east, more figures moving, already within a stone's throw of the moat. Still more to the south.

There were more than a hundred of the dead approaching the school.

Ms. Geiss tugged off the goggles and sat on the edge of the ladder, lowering her head almost to her knees so that the black spots in her vision receded and she could breathe again.

They're never organized like this. Never come all at once.

She felt her heart lurch, shudder, and then commence pounding again.

I didn't think there were that many of the things left around here. How . . .

Part of her mind was screaming at her to quit theorizing and do something. *They're coming for the children!*

It made no sense. The dead ate only living flesh . . . or the flesh of things recently living. It should be *her* they were after. But the terrible conviction remained: *They want the children.*

Ms. Geiss had protected her children for thirty-eight years. She had protected them from the worst of life's sharp edges, allowing them to have the safest and most productive year she could provide. She had protected her children from each other, from the bullies and mean-spirited amongst themselves; she had protected them from callous, stupid teachers and brainless administrators; she had shielded them from the vagaries of ill-formed curriculum and faddish district philosophies. Ms. Geiss had, as well as she was able, protected her fourth graders from the tyrannies of too-early adulthood and the vulgarities of a society all too content with the vulgar.

She had protected them—with all her faculties and force of will—from being beaten, kidnapped, emotionally abused or sexually molested by the monsters who had hidden in the form of parents, step-parents, uncles, and friendly strangers.

And now these dead things were coming for her children.

Ms. Geiss went down the ladder with her apron and quilted robe flapping.

Ms. Geiss did not have any idea why there had been a flare pistol in the highway storage depot in the room next to where she had found the blasting caps, but she had appropriated the pistol. There had been only three flares, heavy things that looked like oversized shotgun shells. She had never fired one.

Now she hurried back to the belfry with the flare pistol

in her hand and the three flares in her apron pocket. She had also grabbed four boxes of .30-.06 cartridges.

Some of the dead things were still a hundred yards away from the playground, but others were already wading the moat.

Ms. Geiss extracted a flare from her apron, opened the pistol, and fumbled to set the cartridge in. She forced herself to stop and take a breath. The night goggles were hanging around her neck, heavy as an albatross. *Where are my glasses? What did I do with my glasses?*

She reached up into her hair, pulled her bifocals down, took another breath, and dropped the flare cartridge into the pistol. She clicked the breech shut and threw the spotlight switch, flooding the playgrounds with white light.

A dozen or more of the things were across the moat. Scores more were almost to the street on each side.

Ms. Geiss raised the flare gun in both hands, shut her eyes, and squeezed the trigger. The flare arched too high and fell a dozen yards short of the moat. It burned redly on gravel. A naked corpse with exposed shinbones gleaming stepped over the flare and continued lurching toward the school. Ms. Geiss reloaded, lowered her aim, and fired toward the west.

This time the flare struck the banked mud on the far side of the moat and dropped out of sight. The red glare sizzled for a second and then faded. A dozen more pale forms waded the shallow barrier.

Ms. Geiss loaded the final flare. Suddenly there was a *wooosh* like a wind from nowhere and a stretch of the western moat went up in flames. There was a lull and then the flames leaped north and south, turning the corner like a clever display of falling dominoes. Ms. Geiss moved to the east side of the belfry catwalk and watched as the fire leaped along the moat until the school was in the center of a giant rectangle of thirty-foot flames. Even from fifty yards away she could feel the heat against her face. She dropped the flare gun into her large apron pocket.

The two dozen or so figures that had already crossed the moat lumbered across the playground. Several went down in the razor wire, but then ripped their way free and continued on.

Ms. Geiss looked at her hands. They were no longer shaking. Carefully she loaded the Remington until the magazine was full. Then she rigged the rifle's sling the way the books had shown, set her elbows firmly on the railing, took a deep breath, and set her eye to the telescopic sight. With the flames still burning, she would not have needed the searchlights. She found the first moving figure, set the crosshairs on its temple, and slowly squeezed the trigger. Then she moved her aim to the next form.

At the edge of the playground, the other things were crossing the moat despite the flames. It appeared that none had turned back. Incredibly, a few came through charred but intact; most emerged burning like fuel-primed torches, the flames shimmering around their forms in parallel waves of orange and black. They continued forward long after rotted clothes and rotted flesh had burned away almost to the bone. Even half-deafened by the report of the Remington, Ms. Geiss could hear the distant pops as cerebral fluid, superheated into steam by the burning corpse beneath it, exploded skulls like fragmentation grenades. Then the figure collapsed and added its pyre to the illumination.

Ms. Geiss shifted her aim, fired, checked over the sight to make sure the thing had gone down and stayed down, found another target, aimed, and fired again. After three shots she would shift along the balcony to a different quadrant, brace herself, and choose her targets. She reloaded five times.

When she was finished, there were over a hundred forms lying on the playground. Some were still burning. All were still.

But she could hear the crashing and rattling of steel mesh where more of the things had gotten through, especially on the east side of the school. The gable there had blocked her line of fire. Thirty or more of the things had gotten to the school and were tearing at window screens and the reinforced doors.

Ms. Geiss raised the collar of her robe and wiped her face. There was soot there from the smoke and she was surprised to see that her eyes were watering. Slinging the Remington, Ms. Geiss went down the ladder and went to her room. Donnie's 9mm Browning automatic pistol was in the drawer where she had put it on the day she had cremated him. It was loaded. There were two additional magazines and a yellow box of additional cartridges in the drawer.

Ms. Geiss put the box and magazines in her apron pocket, hefted the pistol, and went down the wide stairway to the first floor.

In the end, it was exhaustion that almost killed her.

She had fired all three of the magazines, reloaded once, and was sure that none of the things were left when she sat down on the front walk to rest.

The last corpse had been a tall man with a long beard. She had aimed the Browning from five feet away and put the last round through the thing's left eye. The thing had gone down as if its strings had been cut. Ms. Geiss collapsed herself, sitting heavily on the sidewalk, too exhausted and disgusted even to go back through the front door.

The flames in the moat had burned down below ground level. Smaller heaps added their smoke and glow to air already filled with a dark haze. A score of sprawled forms littered the front steps and sidewalk. Ms. Geiss wanted to weep but was too tired to do anything but lower her head and take deep, slow breaths, trying to filter out the stench of cooked carrion.

The bearded corpse in front of her lunged up and scrabbled across the six feet of sidewalk to her, fingers clawing.

Ms. Geiss had time to think *The bullet struck bone, missed the brain* and the thing had batted away the Browning and forced her backward, pinning the slung rifle under her. Her glasses were knocked off her face as the thing's cold fingers ripped at her. Its mouth began to descend, as if offering her a lipless, open-mouthed kiss.

Ms. Geiss's right hand was pinned but her left was free; she scrabbled in her apron pocket, scattering loose bullets, finding and discarding the pliers, finally emerging with something heavy in her grip.

The dead thing lunged to bite off her face, to chew its way through to her brain. Ms. Geiss set the cartoon-wide muzzle of the flare pistol in its maw, thumbed the hammer back, and squeezed the trigger.

Most of the fires were out by sunrise, but the air smelled of smoke and corruption. Ms. Geiss shuffled her way down the hall, unbolted the classroom, and stood looking at the class.

The students were uncharacteristically quiet, as if they had somehow been aware of the night's events.

Ms. Geiss did not notice. Feeling exhaustion breaking over her like a wave, she fumbled with clasps, undid their neck and waist restraints, and led them outside by the gang chains. She pulled them through the gaps in the razorwire as if she were walking a pack of blind and awkward dogs.

At the edge of the playground she unlocked their iron collars, unclasped them from the gang chains, and dropped the chains in the gravel. The small forms stumbled about as if seeking the balance of the end of their tethers.

"School is out," Ms. Geiss said tiredly. The rising sun threw long shadows and hurt her eyes. "Go away," she whispered. "Go home."

She did not look back as she trudged through the wire and into the school.

For what seemed like a long while the teacher sat at her desk, too tired to move, too tired to go upstairs to sleep. The classroom seemed empty in a way that only empty classrooms could.

After a while, when the sunlight had crawled across the varnished wood floors almost to her desk, Ms. Geiss started to rise but her bulky apron got in her way. She took off the apron and emptied the pockets onto her desktop: pliers, a yellow cartridge box, the 9mm Browning she had re-trieved, the handcuffs she had taken off Michael yesterday, more loose bullets, three Polaroid snapshots. Ms. Geiss glanced at the first snapshot and then sat down suddenly.

She raised the photograph into the light, inspected it carefully, and then did the same with the next two.

Todd was smiling at the camera. There was no doubt. It was not a grimace or a spasm or a random twitch of dead lips. Todd was staring right at the camera and smiling— showing only gums, it was true—but smiling.

Ms. Geiss looked more carefully and realized that Sara was also looking at the camera. In the first snapshot she had been looking at the food nuggets, but in the second photograph . . .

There was a sliding, scraping sound in the hallway.

My God, I forgot to close the west door. Ms. Geiss carefully set the photographs down and lifted the Browning. The magazine was loaded, a round was racked in the chamber.

The scraping and sliding continued. Ms. Geiss set the pistol on her lap and waited.

Todd entered first. His face was as slack as ever, but his eyes held . . . something. Sara came in next. Kirsten and David came through a second later. One after the other, they shuffled into the room.

Ms. Geiss felt too tired to lift her arms. She knew that despite her musings on the ineffectuality of children's hands and arms as weapons, twenty-three of them would simply overwhelm her like an incoming tide. She did not have twenty-three cartridges left.

It did not matter. Ms. Geiss knew that she would never hurt these children. She set the pistol on the desk.

The children continued to struggle into the room. Sarah J. came through after Justin. Michael brought up the rear. All twenty-three were here. They milled and stumbled and jostled. There were no chains.

Ms. Geiss waited.

Todd found his seat first. He collapsed into it, then pulled himself upright. Other children tripped and bumped against one another, but eventually found their places. Their eyes rolled, their gazes wandered, but all of them were looking approximately forward, more or less at Ms. Geiss.

Their teacher sat there for another long moment, saying nothing, thinking nothing, daring barely to breathe lest she shatter the moment and find it all illusion.

The moment did not shatter, but the morning bell did ring, echoing down the long halls of the school. The last teacher sat there one moment longer, gathering her strength and resisting the urge to cry.

Then Ms. Geiss rose, walked to the chalkboard, and in her best cursive script, began writing the schedule to show them what they would be doing and learning in the day ahead.

NIGHT OF THE LIVING DEAD BINGO WOMEN

SIMON McCAFFERY

Even on her bad days, Edna Mae Brewer was invincible. She'd won five games straight since arriving at noon, excitedly calling out ''Bingo!'' after marking the last winning square on her playing sheets. The third time she fairly shrieked it in excitement, though her fellow contestants in the hall paid her not the slightest heed. The woman sitting directly across from Edna stared vacantly ahead like a wax figure, streaks of colored ink smeared across her face like a Maori mask. On Edna's left, an elderly black man in a soiled, ripped turtleneck gazed up at the high ceiling while his outstretched hands groped blindly about on the wide table. He swept his ink dauber and stack of playing cards onto the floor and made no effort to retrieve them.

In a remote way this total disinterest in her good fortune

rankled Edna, who was competitive by nature. In the old days, when a player's numbers came in, folks had not just sat there like stones. Most cheered as the caller checked off the winning numbers. Others groaned and everyone applauded like disinterested businessmen at a luncheon. Some even glared at the winner with genuine hatred, muttering under their breath as they discarded their losing sheets.

This was no way for a Christian to behave, Edna knew, but she could commiserate; she herself had sat near a big winner on occasion and felt resentment glow in the pit of her stomach like a hot lump of coal.

Tonight, however, Edna felt just fine, thank you. This was largely due to the fact that she had won every game of the session so far, from the Early Bird up through the Bonus Blackout round. Some of the wins had taken longer than others, but she'd kept at it; hunched over her game sheets, concentrating fiercely while marking off numbers.

A tiny voice inside Edna's head pointed out that though she was undeniably a skilled and seasoned bingo player, the fact that all of her opponents were dead might have something to do with her long string of successes. This nasty little voice, which sounded not unlike her nagging (and thankfully deceased) husband, Frank, irritated Edna. Winning was winning and fair was fair. Was it her fault zombies weren't cut out for the fast-paced competitiveness of high-stakes bingo?

The next game got underway. The caller, once a handsome young Creek Indian named Joe, began plucking numbered Ping-Pong balls from the big, Plexiglas hopper on the green-carpeted dais. Joe still wore the tattered remains of his cheap tuxedolike outfit, though it was badly discolored and seemed to disappear in and out of his flesh in places. Joe's gray face was beginning to look unsightly, Edna noted—like an ice-cream novelty left unattended in the sun—and he was having difficulty calling the numbers in an intelligible fashion. Some sounded as if he was speaking through a veil of rotted seaweed. To make matters worse, he also ate some of the Ping-Pong balls.

Edna had prepared for this, however, positioning herself at a table close to the calling booth. Numbers garbled beyond recognition could usually be eyeballed before the little white spheres disappeared back into the hopper or Joe's mouth.

In an orderly row before her were the tools of the trade: ink daubers and paper playing sheets. Not long after the Reawakening, Edna had helped herself to several new ink daubers behind the now-deserted concession stand. The daubers were larger, gaily colored, and more expensive than those she had once played with. Her old dauber was squat and plain, and she had refilled it with tap water dyed with food coloring because Frank had strictly limited her playing money. The new daubers, used to mark pink, red, and purple circles on the throwaway paper sheets, were scented to smell like strawberries, cherries, and grapes. Edna didn't mind when, hunched over the table, the sickly-sweet smell of the colored ink filled her nostrils; it almost blocked out the odor of her nearby opponents, who sat in dazed rows and shambled blindly along the aisles.

Edna continued marking her sheets in a businesslike fashion, never missing a single number—the secret of winning (*Besides playing against zombies,* the Frank-voice reminded). Toward four o'clock, her stomach began rumbling. How she wished she could hail a uniformed runner and order a burrito with the works and a large Pepsi! In the old days, during a typical eight-hour session, Edna might consume three burritos with hot sauce and sour cream, a cheeseburger, several bags of chips, a small dish of soft ice cream (chocolate and vanilla swirled together), and a legion of soft drinks.

Now, with the food in the snack bar trampled and spoiled, she was forced to bring her own munchies: vacuum packs of beef jerky, vacuum-sealed cans of cheese curls, and scores of candy bars that wouldn't go over—thanks to BTA and TBHQ, whatever they were—until October 1996. There was a sprawling Alpha-Beta supermarket three blocks from the bingo hall, and until its shattered roof finished falling in, it served as Edna's super-snack bar. Digging through her canvas tote bag, she extracted a Slim Jim and tore into it with her teeth. The taste was salty and greasy and wonderful, though not as satisfying as a deep-fried jumbo burrito with everything crammed inside.

During the next pattern game in which the winner was required to form a kitelike pattern, a zombie caromed off the back of Edna's chair, causing her marker to smear across the sheet.

There! That had ruined it! And she had been three numbers away from completing the tail of the kite and winning five thousand dollars. The big tradeoff with zombies, she fumed, was that though they were a cinch to beat at bingo (or any game, for that matter), they possessed the manners of . . . wild pigs. They might slump in quiet, swaying rows for hours, uttering hardly a moan, or they might knock about like mummies, overturning tables and making a general racket without so much as an apology if they disrupted a game! It was enough to heat the collar of the most patient, God-fearing soul, especially a dyed-in-the-wool bingo fanatic like Edna.

After winning two more games—the "Round Robin" and "Crazy T"—in quick succession, Edna noticed twilight was stealing its way inside the huge hall. She immediately set down her dauber and reached below her chair.

This time the tote bag produced a large silver flashlight. The light had been scavenged from the shattered hulk of the bingo security guard's station wagon, a Ford Futura, which now rested upside down in the hall parking lot. The long-necked light held six fat, D-size batteries in its gut and was heavy enough to use as a club if the need arose. Its beam was strong and steady, like a prison searchlight.

Now, with shadows forming like fathomless pools inside the hall, Edna clicked it on and positioned it so she could read her cards and keep an eye on Joe. With nightfall the interior of the hall would quickly sink into an absolute blackness. Edna would need the light to continue playing and, at midnight, to make her way to an exit. Without its shepherding beam, she knew from experience, one might bump around for an eternity searching for the door.

In the first weeks after the dead had decided to walk again (and feast on live people and play bingo), Edna had found the hall too unsettling to remain in after sundown.

Just the zoolike sounds of zombies shuffling about like blind men had sent icy splinters of terror through her heart. But the light made a considerable difference and didn't attract them.

Nothing seemed particularly to gain their attention, not even Edna, who might be considered, through the dead orbs of a zombie, to be the biggest deluxe burrito around. Like everyone else Edna had kept her distance from them (and, more importantly, their *teeth*) after they had clawed their way out of the cold ground, but none had ever attacked her. This was, she was now certain, due to years of chemical cancer treatment she had suffered at the hands of young doctors who thought themselves little Gods. The zombies smelled her, yes, but the meat was . . . no good.

Edna found this situation immensely agreeable. The best part was that zombies wiping out civilization didn't mean she had to quit the only activity that had ever brought her joy. In a way (and He definitely worked in mysterious ones—one look at the hundreds of zombies roaming the interior of the Riverside Avenue Bingo Hall confirmed that!), it was an enormous blessing; a miracle. Edna now enjoyed bingo each and every day, and never paid so much as a penny to play. The coins and bills choking the legion of abandoned cash registers in the city meant nothing. There were none of the worries, setbacks, and anxieties of her previous life. There was no Frank (she definitely had them to thank for that) to complain about bills and starchy meals. The troubles of that dead life had sloughed off as quick and easy as Joe's face. Not even her ponderous weight mattered anymore. None of it mattered. There was only her love of the game.

And now, like never before, Edna was an undeniable winner; the unbeaten empress of all-day, all-night bingo.

Clasping an ink dauber in her plump right hand and hefting the flashlight in her left, she aimed the beam at the silhouetted figure on the dais. Joe, issuing gobbling sounds that might have been numbers, started a new game.

ABED

ELIZABETH MASSIE

Meggie's a-line dress is yellow, bright like a new dandelion in the side yard and as soft as the throats of the tiny toads Meggie used to find in the woods that surround the farm. There aren't many stains on the dress, just some spots on the hem. Mama Randolph, Quint's mother and Meggie's mother-in-law, ironed the dress this morning, then gave it to Meggie with a patient and expectant smile before locking the bedroom door once more. Meggie knows that Mama likes the dress because it isn't quite as much a reminder of the bad situation as are the other blotted and bloodied outfits in Meggie's footed wardrobe.

From the open window, a benign breeze passes through the screen, stirring the curtains. But the breeze dies in the middle of the floor because there are no other windows in the room to allow it to leave. The summer heat, however, is quite at home in the room, and has settled for a long stay.

There has been no rain for the past fourteen days. Meggie has been marking the days off on the Shenandoah Dairy calendar she keeps under her bed. Mama has not talked about a grandchild in almost a month now; Meggie keeps the calendar marked for that, as well. Mama Randolph's smile and the freshly ironed dress lets Meggie know that the cycle has come 'round again.

Meggie moves from the bed to the window to the bed again. There is a chair in the corner by the door, but the cushion smells bad and so she doesn't like to sit on it. The mattress on the bed smells worse than the chair, but there is a clean corner that she uses when she is tired. She paces about, feeling the soft swing of her hair about her shoulders as she rocks her head back and forth, remembering the feel of Quint's own warm hair in the sunlight of past Julys and the softness of the dark curls that made a sweet pillow of his chest.

At the window, Meggie glances out through the screen, down to the chain-linked yard below. The weeds there are wild and tall and tangled like briars in the forest. The fence is covered with honeysuckle. There is the remainder of the sandbox Quint used as a child. It is nearly returned to the soil now, and black-eyed Susans have found themselves a home. Mama says it will be a fine thing when there is a child to enjoy the yard once again. She says when the child comes, she and Meggie will clean up the yard and make it into a playground that any other child in Norton County will envy.

Mama had slapped Meggie when Meggie said she didn't know if there would ever be any more children in the county.

On the nightstand beside Meggie's bed is a chipped vase with a bouquet of Queen Anne's lace, sweet peas, red clover, and chicory. Mama said it was a gift from Quint, but Meggie knows Quint is long past picking gifts of wildflowers. Beside the vase is a picture of Meggie and Quint on their wedding day three years ago. Meggie wears a white floor-length dress and clutches a single white carnation.

Quint grins shyly at the camera, the new beard Meggie had loved just a dark shadow across his lower face. It would be four months before the beard was full enough to satisfy him, although it never satisfied his mother.

"You live in my house, you do as I say, you hear me?" she had told Quint. And although Meggie believed in the premise of that command, and managed to follow the rules, Quint always had a way of getting by with what he wanted by joking and cajoling his mother. And in the dark privacy of night, while cuddling with Meggie in bed, he would promise that it wouldn't be long before he had saved enough money to build them their own small house on the back acre Mama had given him by the river.

But that was back when Quint worked the farm for his mother and held an evening job at the Joy Food Mart and Gas Station out on Route 146. Back when they had a savings account in the Farmers' Bank in Henford and Meggie happily collected her mother-in-law's cast-off dishes to use as her own when the house by the river was built.

And then came the change. Things in Norton County flipped ass over tea kettle. Old dead Mrs. Lowry had sat up in her coffin at the funeral home, grunting and snarling, her eyes washed white with the preserving chemicals but her mouth chattering for something hot and living to eat. Then Mr. Conrad, Quint's boss down at the Joy Food Mart and Gas Station, had keeled over while changing a tire and died on the spot of a heart attack. Before Quint could finish dialing the number of the Norton volunteer rescue squad, Conrad was up again and licking his newly dead lips, his hands racked with spasms but his teeth keen for a taste of some Quint-neck. Quint hosed him down with unleaded and tossed in his Bic lighter and then cried when it was over because he couldn't believe what had happened.

They all believe now, alrighty.

The dead wander the gravel roads and eat what they may, and everyone in Norton County knows it is no joke because they've all seen one or two of the dead or know someone they trust who has seen one or two. The newspapers say it's a problem all over now; the big cities like Richmond and D.C. and Chicago got dead coming out of their ears. There is a constant battle in the cities because there are so many. In Norton County it is a problem, and a couple people have been eaten, but mostly the walking dead get burned with gasoline or get avoided by the careful.

A thud in the downstairs hallway causes Meggie to jump and clasp her hands to the bodice of her yellow dress. The permanent chicken bone of fear which resides in her chest makes a painful turn. She presses her fists deep into the pain. She waits. Sweat beads on her arms and between her breasts. Mama Randolph does not come yet.

Meggie turns away from the wedding portrait on the nightstand and tries to remember the songs she sang in church before the church closed down. But all she can remember are some psalms. She walks to the clean spot on the bed and sits. She looks at the window, at the footed wardrobe, at the stained chair near the locked door. Above the chair is a Jesus picture. If there was some way to know what Jesus thought of the change, Meggie thinks she could bear it. If Meggie truly believed that Jesus had a handle on the walking dead, and that it was just a matter of time before He put a stop to it all, then Meggie would live out her confinement with more faith. But the picture shows a happy, smiling Jesus, holding a little white lamb with other white lambs gathered at His feet. He does not look like He has any comprehension of the horror that walks the world today. If He did, shouldn't He be crashing from the sky in a wailing river of fire to throw the dead back into their graves until the rapture?

Meggie slips from the bed and kneels before the picture. Jesus' smiling face moves her and His detachment haunts her. Her hands fold into a sweaty attitude of prayer, and in a gritty voice, she repeats, "The Lord is my shepherd, I shall not want. . . ."

The crash in the hall just outside the door hurls Meggie to her feet. Her hands are still folded but she raises them like a club. The sound was that of a food tray being carelessly plopped onto the bare hall floor, and of dishes rattling with the impact. Mama Randolph brings Meggie her breakfast, lunch, and dinner every day, but today Mama is early.

Meggie looks at the screened window and wishes she

could throw herself to the ground below without risking everlasting damnation from suicide. There is no clock in the room, but Meggie knows Mama is early. The sun on the floor is not yet. straddling the stain on the carpet, and so it is still a ways from noon. But Meggie knows that Mama has something on her mind today besides food. Mama's excitement has interrupted the schedule. Mama has been marking a calendar as well. Today, Mama is thinking about grandchildren.

Meggie holds the club of fingers before her. It will do no good, she knows. She could not strike Mama Randolph. Maybe Jesus will think it is a prayer and come to help her.

The door opens, and Mama Randolph comes in with a swish of old apron and a flourish of cloth napkin. The tray and its contents are visible behind her in the hall, but the meal is the last of Mama's concerns. When business is tended, the meal will be remembered.

"Meggie," says Mama. "What a pretty sight you are there in that dress. Makes me think of a little yellow kitten." The cloth napkin is dropped onto the back of the stinking chair, and Mama straightens to take appraisal of her daughter-in-law. There is something in Mama's apron pocket that clinks faintly.

"Well, you gonna stand there or do you have a 'good morning'?"

Meggie looks toward the window. Two stories is not enough to die. And if she died, she would only become one of the walking dead. She looks back at Mama.

"Good morning," she whispers.

"And to you," Mama says cheerily. "Can you believe the heat? I pity the farmers this year. Corn is just cooking on the stalks. You look to the right out that window and just over the trees and you can see a bit of John Johnson's crop. Pitiful thing, all burned and brown." Mama tips her head and smiles. The apron clinks.

Neither says anything for a minute. Mama's eyes sparkle in the heavy, hot air. The dead folks' eyes sparkle when they walk about, but Meggie knows Mama is not dead. The older woman is very much alive, with all manner of plans for her family.

Then Mama says, "Sit down."

Meggie sits on the clean spot on the mattress.

Mama touches her dry lips. She says, "You know a home ain't a home without the singing of little children."

Oh, dear Jesus, thinks Meggie.

"When Quint was born, I was complete. I was a woman then. I was whole; I'd done what I was made to do. A woman with no children can't understand that till she's been through it herself."

Meggie feels a large drop of sweat fall and lodge above her navel. She looks at the floor and remembers what Quint's shoes looked like there, beside hers in the night after they'd climbed beneath the covers. Precious shoes, farmer's shoes, with the sides worn down and the dark coating of earth on the toes. Shoes that bore the weight of hard work and love. Shoes Quint swore he would throw away when he'd earned enough money to build the new house. Shoes that Meggie was going to keep in her cedar chest as a memory of the early days.

Quint doesn't wear shoes anymore.

"You know in my concern for you and Quint, I would do anything to make you happy." Mama nods slowly. "And if I've got it figured right, you're in your time again. I know it ain't worked the last couple months, but it took me near'n to a year and a half before I was with Quint."

Mama steps over to Meggie, and leans in close. Her breath smells of ginger and soured milk. "A baby is what'll help make some of the bad things right again, Meggie. It's a different world now. And we've got to cope. But a baby will bring joy back."

"A baby," echoes Meggie. "Mama, please, I can't—"

"Hush, now," barks Mama. The smile disappears as quickly as the picture from a turned-off television set. She is all business now. Family-making is a serious matter. "Get abed."

The word stings Meggie's gut.

"Abed!" commands Mama Randolph, and slowly, obediently, Meggie slides along the mattress until her head is even with the pillow.

Mama purses her mouth in approval. "Now let's check

and see if our timing is right." Meggie closes her eyes and one hand moves to the spotted hem of the yellow dress. In her chest, the bone of pain swells, hard and suffocating. She cannot swallow around it. Her breath hitches. She pulls the hem up. She is naked beneath. Mama Randolph has not allowed undergarments.

"Roll over." Meggie rolls over. She hears the clinking as Mama reaches into her pocket. Meggie gropes for the edge of the pillow and holds to it like a drowning child to a life preserver. Her face presses into the stinking white pillowcase.

The thermometer goes in deeply. Mama makes a tisking sound and moves it about until it is wedged to her satisfaction. Meggie's bowels contract; her gut lurches with disgust. She does not move.

"Just a minute here and we'll know what we need to know," crows Mama. "Do you know that I thought Quint was going to be a girl and I bought all sorts of little pink things before he was born? Was cute, but I couldn't rightly put such a little man into them pale, frilly clothes. I always thought a little girl would be a nice addition. Wouldn't a little girl just be the icing on the cake?"

Jesus help me, prays Meggie.

"Here, now," says Mama. The thermometer comes out and Meggie draws her legs up beneath the hem of the dress. She does not want to hear the reading.

"Bless me, looks like we done hit it on the head!" Mama is almost laughing. "Up nearly a whole degree. Time is right. My little calendar book keeps me thinking straight, now don't it? I'll go get Quint."

Mama goes out into the hall. Meggie watches her go. Then she falls from the bed and crawls on her knees to the Jesus picture. "Oh dear blessed Lord you are my shepherd, I shall not want I shall not want I shall not want." Jesus watches the lambs and does not see Meggie.

Meggie runs to the window and looks out at the flowers and the dead sandbox and the burned cornfield over the top of the woods. It was those woods that killed Quint. One second of carelessness that crushed Quint's skull beneath John Johnson's felled tree. Quint had gone to help the neighbor clear a little more land for crops. John and Quint had been best buddies since school, and they were always trading favors. But when Quint went down under the tree trunk, brains and blood spraying, and he died, and when he rose up again, he was through trading favors. He wanted a lot more of John than he'd ever wanted before. And he got it. There wasn't enough of John left to rise with the other dead folks, just some chunks of spine and some chewed-up feet.

Mama Randolph found Quint after this meal and he showed no immediate urge to eat her as well, so she brought him home and found he was just as happy eating raw goats and the squealing pigs he had tended as a live man.

Mama is in the doorway again. Behind her is Quint. He is dressed in only a pair of trousers that are gathered to his bony waist with a brown, toothmarked leather belt.

"Abed!" says Mama. "Let's have this done."

Meggie goes back to the bed. She lies down. She knows what Mama will do next. It is the worst to come.

Quint is directed to stand in front of the old chair. Meggie cannot see Jesus anymore but that is a good thing. What is to happen is not for anyone's eyes, especially the Savior's. Meggie looks at her husband. His hair is gone, as is the flesh of his mouth and the bulk of his nose. There is a tongue, but it is slimy and gray like an old rotted trout. The left side of his head is flattened, with the exposed brain now blackened and shimmering, reminding Meggie of a mushroom she tried to save once in a sandwich bag. The eye on the left is missing, but the right eye is wide and wet. The skin of Quint's abdomen is swollen and it ripples like maggots have gotten inside. One hand has no fingers, but the other has three, and they grope awkwardly for the zipper of his trousers. Quint somehow knows why he has been brought upstairs.

Mama Randolph moves beside Meggie and motions for her to hoist up her dress. Meggie flinches, hesitating, and Mama slaps her. Meggie does not hesitate again.

Mama then rolls up her sleeves. She says, "Quint needs

extra stimulation to do what he has to do. Watching helps him. You know that. So be still and let me do my job.''

With the perfunctory movements of someone changing a fouled diaper, Mama coaxes the younger woman's legs open, and parts the private folds so Quint can have a better view. Then she begins to rub Meggie's clitoris slowly, while stroking the sensitive skin of Meggie's inner thighs with the other hand. Meggie will not watch. She digs her fingernails into her sides until the pain sings with the rush of blood to her genitals.

''Quint, do you remember? Do you see Meggie? Her pretty dress?'' says Mama. ''Look, Quint, now isn't this lovely?'' She leans her face into Meggie's crotch and licks the whole length of slit. The breath from her nose is warm; the wetness of her saliva is cool. Meggie groans. Shame boils her mind and soul. Pleasure teases her body.

''Mama, Quint, Jesus, no! I shall not want I shall not want!''

Quint grunts. Meggie bucks her head and shoulders and glances at him. He has opened his fly and has found his penis. It is yellowed and decaying, like a bloated fish on a riverbank. As he pulls, it rises slightly. The pre-cum is purpled.

Mama sucks gently and then with a fury. Meggie's body arcs reflexively. Bile rushes a burning path up her throat and dribbles from the corners of her mouth. When Mama's lips move away for a second, Meggie crashes back to the mattress. The acid rockets upward once more and Meggie gags. Mama brings her tongue to Meggie's spot again, and then thrusts her thumb into the opening. Meggie feels the walls of her vagina gush, betraying her in her ultimate moment of revulsion and horror.

''I shall not oh dear God Jesus I shall not!''

''Good girl,'' Mama says matter-of-factly. ''This is fine. Just a minute now and you'll be ready.''

Meggie writhes on the bed, enraged tears spilling from her eyes and soaking the mattress. Mama holds her firmly, finishing her work. Then Mama stands up.

Quint has a line of moisture on what is left of his upper

lip. One side of his mouth twitches as if it would try to grin.

Mama gestures to her son. "Come now, Quint, Meggie can't wait for you." Quint stares, grunts, then stumbles forward. As he passes his mother, she says, "I'd really love a granddaughter."

Meggie turns her face away. She closes her eyes and tries to remember last summer. Days of light and shadows and swimming and play, days of work and trials and promises of forever. But all she can do is smell the creature climbing onto her. All she can do is feel the slopping of the trout-tongue on her cheek and taste the running, blackened brain matter as it drips to the edge of her lips. He burrows clumsily; his body wriggles as his knees work between her knees, and his sore-covered penis reaches like a dazed, half-dead snake for her center. Meggie bites her tongue until it bleeds to keep from feeling the cold explosion of semen from the putrid organ. And as if in some insane answer to it all, her vaginal walls contract suddenly in a horrific, humiliating orgasm.

It is all over quickly. Mama pulls Quint off, then gives Meggie a kiss on the forehead and tells her to stay abed for at least an hour to give the seed time to find the soil.

Alone, with the door locked and the lunch tray balanced on the smelly chair seat, Meggie lies still, her dress still hunched up. She holds her left hand in her right, pretending the right one is that of a living, breathing Quint. She puts the hand to her face and feels the tender stroking. And then she lowers the hand to her abdomen, and presses firmly. There will be a new human in there soon, if Mama has her way. There could be one already. This could be Mama's magic moment. Meggie wishes she could know. It is not knowing if or when that brings her mind to the edge of twisting inside out.

She looks at the window. There is no breeze now, only the persistent heat. The edge of sunlight stands on the carpet stain.

" 'S different," Mama Randolph had said. "Different world now. Just 'justin' to cold water is all. Might not wanta do it, but sometimes just can't be helped. Gotta survive, after all.''

Meggie holds herself and closes her eyes. She wonders about the different world. She wonders if there will be a baby to grow and use the playground outside her room. And she wonders if the baby, when it comes, will be cuddly and bouncy and take after his mother. Or if it will be stillborn, and take after its father.

COME ONE, COME ALL

GAHAN WILSON

Professor Marvello tightened two guy ropes with an expert twist of his strong, pudgy little hands in order to make the poles holding the big canvas sign spread out above the platform stand a little taller, then he squinted upwards at it with a slightly grim, lopsided smile of satisfaction.

The sign read

* MARVELLO'S * MIRACULOUS * MIDWAY *

in ornate, gold-encrusted letters four and a half feet high—exactly the height of Professor Marvello himself, by his personal instructions—and a multitude of spotlights helped each letter glitter proudly out at the silent, surrounding darkness.

Marvello regarded the effect with satisfaction as he

carefully and neatly made the ropes' ends fast around their shared cleat, then he meticulously brushed a speck of Kansas dust off the lapel of his red and white checkered coat and adjusted the bright yellow plastic carnation in its button hole.

"A nice night," he murmured to himself softly, sweeping the horizon with a benign if slightly wary gaze, and taking a long, fond sniff of the warm, wheat-smelling night air blowing in from the dark fields all around. Professor Marvello had been plain Homer Muggins of Missouri in his youth and he still admired simple, farmy scents. "A hellavuh nice night."

Then, adjusting his straw boater, he turned to business, flicking his bright little blue eyes down to see if the light was glowing on the solar battery like it ought to be, jabbing back a switch to start the circus music whooping, and plucking the microphone from its metal perch on the banner-bedecked rostrum. That done, Marvello squared his small but sturdy shoulders, softly cleared his throat, and spoke.

"LADIES AND GENTLE—"

Too loud. You didn't need it that loud because there was no competition. No competition at all. He stooped with a slight grunt, bending to turn the knob down on the speaker system, then straightened his rotund little body so that it stood proudly erect as before and spoke again.

"Ladies and gentlemen, boys and girls," he said, and the nasal drone of his voice swirled out from a baker's dozen of speakers and rolled over the midnight landscape of flat, dimly-furrowed earth, sparse trees and long-deserted farmhouses. "Come on, come on, come on. Welcome to the fabulous, most wonderful, undeniably and by far greatest show left in the world. Come and see and be astounded by the one, the only Marvello's Miraculous Midway—the sole remaining sideshow in the world."

He paused, hacked, and spat over the edge of the platform onto the dusty ground. He gazed at the dust, at its dryness, half-reached for the flask of whiskey in his hip pocket, but then decided against it. Not yet. Later.

Did he hear a shuffle? His eyes guardedly darted this

way and that. Not sure. Sometimes they stayed hidden just out of sight, watching you put up the show, standing on one foot and then the other, no idea what to do with their hands, hardly able to wait. Like kids, he thought, like kids.

"Don't miss it, don't miss it, don't miss it," he intoned. "Come one, come all, and bring your friends and loved ones so that everyone in this lovely area, in this beautiful county of this remarkable state, can be fortunate enough to experience the entertainment thrill of their lifetime, so to speak. So to speak."

Yes, yes indeed, there was a shuffle. He avoided looking in its direction, plucked a large polka-dotted handkerchief from his other hip pocket, the one not containing the flask, and wiped his brow in order to conceal his covert peering.

There it was, just by the popcorn stand. Raggedy, forlorn, and skeletal. It was dressed in torn blue denim overalls and the tattered remains of a wide-brimmed straw hat. There was no shirt, there were no shoes. It stared at him, mouth agape, and he could just make out the dull last remnant of a glint in its eyes and a vague glistening in its mouth.

"Good evening, sir," Professor Marvello said, giving it a formal little bow, an encouragingly toothy grin. "I observe you possess the percipiency to have been attracted by the sounds and sights of our outstanding exhibition. May I be so bold as to congratulate you on your good taste and encourage you to step a little closer?"

It swayed, obviously undecided. Professor Marvello increased the wattage of his grin and, producing a bamboo cane from inside the rostrum, employed it to point at an enormous depiction of a huge-breasted Hawaiian hula dancer painted in classic circus poster style on a bellying rectangle of canvas.

"Miss La Frenza Hoo Pah Loo Hah," he announced proudly, and leaning forward towards the wary watcher, winked confidentially and continued in a lower tone as one man of the world speaking to another, his S shaped smile taking on a new chumminess and his voice growing increasingly husky and intimate.

"I am sure, my dear sir, that a man of your obvious sophistication and, if I may say it, *je ne sais quoi,* is well aware of the extraordinary sensual jollies which may be produced by the skilled locomotion of swaying hips and other anatomical accessories on the part of a well-trained and imaginative practitioner of the art of hula dancing. Permit me to assure you that the lovely Miss Hoo Pah Loo Hah is *extremely* knowledgeable in these matters and will not fail to delight the sensibilities of a bon vivant such as yourself. Come a little closer, there, my good man, don't be shy."

The figure swayed, its dark green, stiff arms lolling, and then one large, bony foot pushed forward, stirring up a little puff of dust.

"That's the way, that's the way," said Marvello in an encouraging tone. "There's the brave fellow. Excellent. You're doing just fine. I trust, in passing, you've observed how plump the lovely Miss La Frenza Hoo Pah Loo Hah is, my dear fellow: how fat her hips, how round and fulsome her breasts, how meaty she is in all respects. I trust you've not let those aspects of our lovely dancer get by you, my good sir."

The overalled figure paused as if to study the poster with increased intensity, or perhaps it was only getting its balance. There was a kind of gathering, a moment of staggering confusion, then it lurched itself forward with a series of crablike waddles until it had worked its way well into the brightly lit area before Professor Marvello's platform. This one had semi-mummified, its skin had dried more than rotted, and the dark green-brown of its bony, beaky head and face bore more than a slight resemblance to an Egyptian pharaoh's.

"Over here, over here, my wizened chum," said Professor Marvello with encouraging enthusiasm, indicating the tent's entrance with a wave of his bamboo cane. "Keep heading towards that welcoming aperture before you, spur yourself on with rapt contemplation of the sexual gyrative wonders the lovely Hoo Pah Loo Hah will perform before you as envisioned in your most private dreams, and of course never forget nor neglect the generous pulchritude of her charms, which is to say the amazingly large amount of tender flesh which bedecks her frame.''

When the mummy farmer paused at the entrance, Professor Marvello raised the tent flap invitingly with the tip of his cane.

''No need to pay, my good man,'' he intoned, though the thing had not made the slightest attempt to reach into its pockets. ''The Marvello Miraculous Midway is a rare phenomenon indeed in this hard world, my dear sir, being gratis, entirely free of charge. A generous, altruistic effort to brighten the, ah, lives of such unfortunates as yourself. Go right on in, do go right on in.''

A few prompting prods from the tip of Marvello's cane between the separating vertebrae of its narrow, bony back, and the overalled entity finally committed itself and lurched on into the tent to be greeted by the soft throbbings of Hawaiian music, the heady scents of tropic flowers.

''Almost looked happy for a moment there,'' murmured Professor Marvello thoughtfully, nudging the tent flap so that it fell softly back into place as the music and the scent of flowers ceased abruptly.

Nearly at once there was another timid shuffling, this from the far left, hard by the ring toss stand, and two figures edged sidewise into view. What was left of a mother and daughter.

They were dressed in faded, flowered frocks which were frayed and torn and flecked with a multitude of dark, dry stains. The girl was missing her scalp on one side of her head, but a glistening gold braid with a large pink bow on its end grew from the other. Her mother held her hand tightly but mechanically, a habit that had somehow survived the loss of everything else.

''Fun for the entire family,'' Professor Marvello cooed into his microphone, essaying a fatherly wink which somehow slipped over into the lewd. ''Let me assure you, Madame, and your precious little princess standing so trustingly by your side, that the Marvello Miraculous Midway fully satisfies both young and old. Both of you may positively and without reservation enjoy it to the full, as we unhesitatingly guarantee to completely and entirely please folks from eight to eighty. Do come up, do come up.''

He turned and waved his cane at the flapping portrait of a man whose mighty body bulged everywhere with layer upon layer of huge, rippling muscles, but whose calm, heroically mustachioed face radiated an almost saintly kindliness. With serene calm the man was carefully lifting a school bus packed full of laughing children high above a torrent of swirling water.

"Observe a true wonder of the world—Hugo, the Gentle Giant. He has the strength of a lion, but within his huge chest softly beats the heart of a doting lambkin. Here we are privileged to witness him depicted performing his daring, legendary rescue of a group of innocent children from the raging waters of the Jamestown flood. That's right, dears, come a little closer. That's right. My, what a sweet little girl. You must be very proud, Mother.''

They swayed closer and Marvello noticed the girl's sharp, tiny teeth were constantly snapping, chewing on the air she walked through. He gave her an especially intimate grin.

"I'll wager Hugo has a lollipop or some other sweet edible possibly more to your taste, little missy," he confided. "Something chewy, something wet, something juicy, something nice! The gentle giant has never been able to resist the tender implorements of hungry little children, dear.''

The child's eyes lost some of their glaze as she neared, tugging at her mother now. Marvello could hear her teeth clacking dryly. He reflected that it was a remarkably nasty little sound and gently prodded the tent flap up invitingly as he touched a hidden button which caused a deep, kindly voice to boom out from inside the tent amidst the excited chirpings of happy children.

"It sounds like everyone's having a fine old time," Marvello observed, leaning over his rostrum and smiling gently down. "A fine old time. Why don't you go join them, darlings?''

He paused, furtively turned a dial, and then appeared to listen in happy surprise as the children's voices coming from inside the tent were suddenly amplified in a burst of avid glee and enthusiastic crunchings and slobberings and gulpings became increasingly audible.

"Harken," hissed Marvello excitedly, holding his hand cupped dramatically behind an ear. "Harken at that, will you? It's my guess dear old Hugo has just now given his little chums inside some particularly tasty morsels—he has a whole tub full of them, you know—something ripe and gooey, something positively *dripping,* just the way I know you sweet things like 'em, eh? *Eh?*"

He leaned lower over his rostrum and leered openly at the two of them.

"Take a friendly tip from me, from your dear old Uncle Professor Marvello," he whispered, *"and hurry on in before it's all et up!"*

The girl's feverish pulling increased into a desperate frenzy of haulings and jerkings, and the two of them were halfway into the tent when the mother balked stubbornly, her filmy eyes bulging up at Professor Marvello with slowly increasing interest, staring up at the smooth pink skin of his neat little double chin in particular.

"No, mother, no," said the professor with a dry, friendly chuckle, firmly pointing at the entrance with his bamboo cane. "No, *non, nyet, nein* . . . the food's in there, sweetness. Inside the tent with dear old Hugo."

The mother's cracked lips writhed back, the lower one splitting slightly with the effort, and this brought her teeth entirely into view for the first time. They had been longer than the ordinary run of teeth in life to the point of deformity, but now, because of the shrinkage of her gums, they were of an appalling size and curvature. When she fully opened her mouth wide in Marvello's direction, it looked like a mantrap fitted out with yellowed boar's tusks. Quietly, without fuss, he placed the tip of his cane on the side of her shoulder, on the meatiest part so it would get a good purchase, then he shoved it with an efficient and expert brutality, timing his nudge with the haulings of her still-tugging daughter, and sent the two of them tumbling clumsily into the tent's opening.

"Get inside there, inside with you, you grinning, rotting

cunt," Marvello drawled softly, nudging the flap so that it rolled down smartly and pushing another button which caused the sounds of Hugo and the happy children to cease forthwith.

There was a faint sparking noise from within the tent and a wisp of acrid burning wafted outwards. Marvello frowned slightly at this and consulted a series of dials set into the rear of the rostrum just to make sure all the readings were correct. It would never do to have a mechanical failure during a performance. It would never do at all.

He paused to give his face another wipe with his polka-dot hanky and to reponder the advisability of a sip from the flask. It was dry work; neither man nor beast could deny that it was dry work. He had allowed himself to pull the flask a third of the way out of his pocket when he froze at the sound of a persistent and complicated growling coming from the darkness to his left. He let the flask slip back into its hiding place and peered carefully in the direction of the growling, his hand screening his eyes from the spotlights overhead.

At first he saw nothing, but then he became aware of activity in the darkness outside the midway, an ominous black milling highlit with small metallic gleams. It stirred closer, then suddenly boiled out into the lighted area to reveal itself as a group of fifteen to twenty very large ones moving together as a unit.

They were a shaggy, snarling army of the night. Huge, all of them, built like bears and almost as hairy, and they all favored black leather outfits with bones and flames painted on them and lots of stainless steel rivets pounded in along the hems. Some wore visored caps, others Nazi helmets, the rest went bareheaded to show off bizarre shavings and haircuts, and a few had lost their scalps entirely. One of these last had a crude swastika hacked crudely into the top of his skull.

They were a group of bikers who had somehow, almost touchingly, managed to stay together after death. The gaudily-terrifying tattoos on their skin may have faded or dimmed with mildew when they had not sloughed off altogether, and some of their bulging muscles and beer bellies might be lying exposed and rotting in swaying hammocks of flesh gone to leather, but their sense of being a group had survived into their new condition beyond a doubt. They all still glared balefully out at the world from a common center.

"Come this way, my dear gentlemen, do, for your pleasure's sake, come this way," Marvello intoned into the mike, upping the bass dial slightly to give his voice a little more authority. "I perceive without difficulty that you have wandered long and far—both in life and in your present status, from the looks of you—and it is my considered professional opinion that you all are tired, very tired, very, *very* tired, yes, every one of you without exception, yes, and that you could all do with a little relaxation. Relaxation."

First they gaped vaguely around at the show in general, staring at the bright lights and flapping pictures and glittering words, but one by one their eyes began shifting in the same direction during Marvello's spiel until they had all zeroed in on the professor himself, the only living human in sight. Their stomachs began to rumble audibly and then they started to whine and bark, first one by one and then in a pack, like wandering wolves instinctively organizing at the sight of a lost and lonely child.

"Relaxation..." Marvello murmured the word thoughtfully once more, seeming to be blissfully unaware that any harm might befall him from his visitors. "And you have come to the right place for it, gentlemen, you couldn't have come to a better, because we have here on the premises of Marvello's Miraculous Midway one of the all-time expert practitioners of producing that enviable condition."

He turned and pointed with his bamboo cane at a large canvas rectangle bearing the painting of a thin, brown man wearing a turban and a loin cloth, staring intensely with his large, dark eyes, and holding his hands poised weirdly out before him with all his fingertips pointed directly at the viewer.

"Allow me to direct your attention to this depiction of one of my most valued and trusted associates, the Swami Pootcha Ahsleep," intoned Marvello, beaming down at his guests in a friendly fashion, a man anxious to share a boon. "Pootcha Ahsleep."

The bikers steadily continued their sinister, shuffling approach and Marvello noticed that their odors preceded them and was interested to smell that the peculiar stench of tanned leather gone mouldy had at last managed to completely dominate their other mingled stenches of decay.

"The Swami and myself," he continued, "both studied the occult arts at the very same Tibetan monastery during our childhood, but I am not ashamed to freely admit that Ahsleep, my old-time pal and fellow scholar, far exceeded me in a number of the difficult arts there imparted, particularly outshining me in the little-understood and seldom-mastered skills of *hypnotism*!"

As he uttered this last word with great emphasis, his hand moved smoothly under his rostrum and the Swami's eyes painted on the poster suddenly began to lighten and darken in a slow, even pulsing as the sound of a snake charmer's horn began to wail eerily from the tent's interior. For the first time the bikers paused in their meaningful progress toward the professor and shifted their large, jack-booted feet with the beginnings of indecision as they stared up with steadily-increasing interest at the poster's throbbing eyes.

"I see you have noticed the irresistible fascination which the Swami's eyes inevitably hold for any intelligent observer," pointed out Marvello, lowering the bass even further and emphasizing the singsong quality which he had allowed to creep into his voice, allowing it to move in and out of the melody of the Hindu flute. "It is very hard to take one's eyes from their deep, hypnotic gaze, very hard. I'm willing to hazard you gentlemen even now are finding it increasingly difficult to look away even as I speak to you, that you are starting to discover that it is, in fact, impossible. Impossible. That you cannot look away. You cannot look away."

One particularly huge biker at the rear had rather worried Marvello from the start, since for most of his hulking approach his head had been held at an odd, low angle and the professor had been unable to determine if the man actually had any eyes left with which to see the Swami's flashing gaze, but now, at the professor's last words, the biker's head had lifted with a painful-looking, sudden twist of his inflated, purple neck, and Marvello was greatly relieved to observe that it seemed he did have one eye left, after all. Not much of it, true, but enough for the purpose.

Gently, making as little fuss about it as possible, Marvello teased the tent flap open. The snake charmer music subtly increased in volume, grew more complicated, and the professor timed his commands to match its cadence.

"Walk into the tent, gentlemen," he intoned softly, intimately, close to the microphone. "Walk into the tent for peace at last, lovely, soothing peace. It's waiting in the tent, my wandering friends, my little lost sheep. All you need to do is stumble in any which way you can and take it for your own. Walk into the tent for peace. For peace."

With their various shuffles, staggers and lurches in almost perfect rhythm, they began moving toward the opening with their gaze fixed dutifully on the throbbing eyes of Pootcha Ahsleep. They had almost gotten there when the large biker Marvello had noticed in particular, the cyclops with the faulty eye, hesitated and then halted entirely. He twisted his head this way and that in a mounting panic, and then he began to howl monotonously, to push and flail at his companions desperately in a sort of clumsy fit.

"Damn," murmured Marvello under his breath, for he saw that the fellow's piss yellow, distended staring eye had chosen this unfortunate moment to explode altogether and that its slimy juices were even now slithering smoothly down from his freshly-emptied socket, down along the rough stubble of his cheek.

Now that he was totally blind he could no longer see Pootcha Ahsleep's hypnotic gaze, and since his retention span was almost nonexistent if not entirely so, he had forgotten that gaze completely and was no longer under the Swami's spell. As his pointless, panicky struggles and flailings increased, he began to seriously impede the steady, tentward drift of his companions.

"*All* of you must go into the tent, dear follows," Marvello commanded, rising to the challenge. "*Every one* of you, with no exceptions, that's what the Swami wants. Recall that you are an organization of sorts, and press together proudly as you did when you thundered down the highway on your mighty machines, your fine black hogs. Keep the herd entire, keep the pack complete. That's the way, boys, that's the way.''

The others had now crowded firmly around their blind companion, heaving a surrounding wall of hairy flesh up against him until they had actually lifted him, so that the black toes of his boots scuffed the ground uselessly and he was as helpless as a small child hauled through a mall by its mother.

''Good lads,'' drawled Marvello, watching the bikers shuffle into the tent, carrying the struggling rebel along in the center of the group with the pressure of their rotting shoulders and bellies. ''Good lads.''

He lifted his cane, holding it at the ready, and when the last of the bikers had finally stumbled into the tent, he darted its tip at the flap with the speed and accuracy of a striking cobra, closing the opening instantly.

''That had a distinct and genuine potential of becoming downright unpleasant,'' he mused into the darkness, turning off the Hindu music abruptly.

Without bothering to enter into any further debate with himself, he plucked the flask from his hip pocket, unscrewed its cap with dispatch, and gratefully swallowed a good full inch of its contents. Perhaps he should altogether abandon this little hobby he'd developed of buck and winging the first stages of the scooping. Those damn bikers could have done him in. He replaced the cap on the flask and slid the flask back into his pocket, then took up the microphone.

''I believe,'' he said, smiling benignly around at the empty midway, ''I believe the time has come for the Grand Finale.''

What had happened up to now was, as Marvello would have freely admitted, a mere frivolity, a bit of harmless self-indulgence, a catering to his sense of whimsy. Now the evening was wearing on and he had his quota to meet and it was time for sterner stuff, it was time to really crank the Midway up full blast, it was time to let her rip.

He bent to his rostrum with a faint sigh of resignation and began a major readjustment of the control board built into its rear, and as he pushed its buttons and turned its knobs and slid its levers along their slots, a vast alteration began taking place along the abbreviated midway.

First the lights dimmed almost to darkness, so that the towering silhouettes of the signs and tent peaks seemed a sort of Stonehenge; then, after a significant pause, the lights began to glow again, but changed from their former bright, bodacious white to sinister variations on the color red, ranging from burning crimsons to ominous scarlets, which were all of them so splashed and spattered with bright gouts of orange and rust that the whole place seemed to be suddenly soaked in gore.

Following that, the crudely painted, innocent carny posters of freaks and fire-eaters and rounded women in spangled tights rolled out of sight while their places were smoothly taken by huge blank screens which rolled smoothly into view in order to receive the projections of three-dimensional, violently colored, moving pictures showing freshly ripped-out bowels quivering in random loops, still-beating hearts exposed in chests newly torn open, and many such other anatomical wonders.

At the same time the entire area was suddenly infused with the overpowering odor of fresh-spilled blood and the air was rent with a ghastly din of screams and shrieks mixed with the sounds of flesh being hacked and sawed amid the gurglings and splashes of spouting arteries and spilling guts.

"Very well, very well," murmured Professor Marvello softly, giving the ghastly effect his labors had created a steady, professional appraisal, carefully and critically observing all its grisly nuances.

"Not bad, not bad at all," he finally opined. "Perhaps a few more sobbing women, a little upping of the stench of newly-opened innards."

He bent to turn a dial, then brightened and smiled as awful feminine gaspings and groanings joined the cacophony sounding about him and a new, tangy reek invaded his nostrils.

"Just the needed touch," he said to himself, adjusting his boater and bow tie contentedly.

He took up his microphone and spoke into it loudly and clearly so that his voice rang out resoundingly through the sea of darkness all around.

"Ladies and gentlemen, boys and girls. This is it, this is it. What you've been shambling around trying to find out there in those used-up fields and little bitty no-account towns, what you've been yearning for, hungering for, and likely starting to doubt to believe could possibly exist."

He pulled a lever and a thick, vomitous, charnel stench blew enthusiastically out of the four outlets of a tall pipe overhead, gouting forth its ripe, rich odors into each cardinal direction simultaneously.

"It's here, it's here, in Marvello's Miraculous Midway, my good friends, right here on this very spot where you hear the sound of my voice inviting you one and all. Inviting you all. Forget those friends and loved ones you've sucked dry so long ago, dear hearts, leave off trying to content yourselves with the wandering, shriveled cows and dogs and cats you run across less and less these days, and come on in, come on in!"

Marvello heard a faint, choking meep and turned to see a tiny shape crawling into the gory light of the Midway. It was the corpse of a baby dressed in a long lacy dress that trailed along behind it as it hauled itself determinedly through the Kansas dust with what was left of its tiny, rotting fingers.

"Not much, but you're a start," said Marvello, observing the little creature with interest as it struggled toward the entrance. "If I'd have known the likes of you was out there, I'd have lured you in during the preamble with Wally Mysto and his Edible Animal Puppets. Land's sake, I do declare this little nipper must have drowned in its baptismal font. Yes, I'd have sworn the likes of you would have shown up for one of the earlier shows, sweetness, yes I would, but there's no accounting for taste."

He made no move to close the flap as the baby cleared

the entrance and entered the tent. He'd only done it with his earlier visitors because he liked the effect, the truth be told. A vague electrical sputtering, a curl of smoke, and perhaps the faintest hint of a tiny, cut-off wail were ignored completely by Marvello because a surrounding murmur of activity had taken his full attention. He straightened and stared into the surrounding darkness.

There were so many of them, but then there were always so many of them. The first few rows now emerging into the ruddy light were distinct, you could read their separate forms, see their individual bodies, observe that one was little more than bones and shreds of leather, another was so ballooned with gas it could not bend its limbs but only totter, and that a third had the steel sutures the surgeons had clipped onto its arteries still dangling from its opened chest, but once you got past the first few rows of them, they all started to merge into one heaving thing moving at you. Steadily. Hungrily. Endlessly.

"Come one, come all," said Marvello softly, staring out at them. "Come one, come all."

He took a pull at the flask, replaced it, and leaned into the microphone, standing firmly on the balls of his little feet.

"Juicy, juicy, juicy," he crooned, watching the front curve of them filling in the midway. "Lots of blood, lots of blood, lots of blood. Lots of fresh, chewy flesh, too, friends, *lots* of it. Sweet, sweet flesh like you haven't had between your teeth since God alone knows how long. Yummy, yummy, yummy."

He reached down to push a button and a soft red coiling of light began making its way 'round and 'round the opening of the tent, pulsing like a newly opened, still bleeding wound. They saw it, of course, they always saw it, and they headed for it just like flies heading for shit, as they were meant to.

He'd often noticed those among them that reminded him of people he'd known and he'd wonder *was* that old Charlie Carter he just saw stumble in there? *Was* that what-sisname who used to sell papers at that newsstand on the corner of Dearborn and Washington? Was that *Clara*? She had a great laugh, did Clara. He could remember just how it felt when he held her shoulders. He'd sure as hell hoped that thing hadn't been Clara.

They started cramming themselves into the entrance. Somehow or other they always managed it. There were snarls and struggles and so on, but in the end they always somehow managed it.

"That's right, dear hearts," he said, smiling down at them, but he knew there weren't any of them listening to him now, not after he'd turned on the doorway lights. "Have a fine old time, enjoy yourselves to the fullest."

At this stage of the game he could sing old sweet songs if it struck his fancy, and he sometimes did, just for the hell of it, or because he was feeling mellow. From here on in the Midway did all the work. From here on in it was purely automatic. But the old habits die hard.

"Let that one-legged gentleman through, folks," he said after he'd observed a hopping fragment get pushed aside by the eager multitude for the fourth or fifth time. "There may not be all that much left of him, but I absolutely guarantee that what there is is just as hungry as the most complete among you. I absolutely guarantee it."

He smiled quietly and took another pull from his flask. What the hell, he thought, what the hell, the night's work was drawing softly and successfully to its close, so what the hell.

The damndest thing was that once he actually *had* seen someone he knew go into the tent, really and truly had, no doubt about it, but the whole thing had given him a real hoot, a genuine kick in the ass, praise be, because it'd been a man he'd truly hated, Mr. Homer Garner, onetime proprietor of the Garner Hardware Company of Joplin, a real revolving son of a bitch who'd done him dirty back when he was just a kid and really needed the money, didn't know any better way to get hold of it. It had given Marvello undiluted joy to observe the even-uglier-than-usual, pus-leaking remnants of Mr. Homer Garner shamble helplessly into the tent.

He was glad, you might even say genuinely grateful, that he'd never seen anybody he liked go in there, since he was certain sure he would not have enjoyed that in the least. Of course the danger of such a thing happening had diminished considerably through the years. He didn't suppose there were all that many left in either category, those he'd hated or those he'd liked, when you came right down to it. He supposed most of them were dead by now, *really* dead, not just shuffling-around dead. Dead and buried dead, the good, old fashioned way.

Marvello leaned over the rostrum, proping himself on spread fingertips, and sized up the Midway. The crowd was down to the final stragglers now, the really timid ones, wandering in at last from wherever they'd been shyly hiding their bones. It wouldn't be long at all now. The show was almost over.

He glanced down at the glowing readout, watching how the number was growing at a slower and slower pace now that the big rush was over. They kind of relaxed when there weren't so many of them around. They almost sort of strolled in when you got down to the last little trickle.

The readout showed a good score, of course. It was always a good score.

"You don't want to miss it," he called out softly to the final, staggering arrivals, then he took another pull, washing the booze around his teeth before he swallowed it. "Nossir, you don't want to miss it."

One left, now, just one. Standing out there in a cockeyed stance, swaying, looking around with its dim eyes, pawing the air with its shriveled little hands. A tough one to turn, this baby. A real hard sell.

"All your friends and loved ones are in there, my handsome fellow," he said, smiling out at the solitary figure.

On an impulse, he turned off the lights moving around the doorway, the lights that pulled them in no matter what. He felt like bringing this one in himself.

"Why be lonely?" he called out, cooing, first waving his cane in the air to get the thing's attention, and then, when he'd caught its eye, pointing it at the entrance and giving its tip a tiny, emphasizing twirl. "Come, come, your solitude serves no purpose, and it's self-inflicted to boot. Cut it short, old chum, cut it short. All those near and dear are but a few short steps away, a mere totter or two. They are all eagerly awaiting your august presence inside. They're all inside.''

It looked up at Marvello, aware of him for the first time. Rags of skin swung from its forearms, blowing slightly in the night breeze. It took a step or two forward. It lifted its head and sucked the odors coming from the tent through its nose hole.

"Smells even better *in* the tent, friend,'' he said. "Say, don't be a spoil sport, don't be a party pooper. You only lived once.''

It wavered idiotically for another half minute and then, its jaws starting to work, starting to wetten, it began to shuffle steadily ahead. Marvello nodded down at it, finishing off his flask as it passed by him and stepped into the darkness of the entrance. There was a final electrical crackling, a last wisp of smoke.

Marvello carefully slipped the flask back into its pocket, threw a series of switches, then hopped gracefully off the platform just a moment before it began to pull itself smoothly back into a slot which had opened at the bottom of the tent.

The showman stood on the hot, dry, dusty ground, his hands in his pockets, and watched, interested as always, while the entire Midway slowly started to fold in on itself. Marvello never failed to enjoy this moment. Sometimes he felt it was, in a way, the best part of the whole show.

First the poles shortened, smoothly telescoping, then the wires and ropes rolled back in perfect synchronization onto hidden spools as the fabric of the main and smaller tents sucked inward, beginning with large tucks, then working down to smaller and smaller ones, all of them tidy, all of them precise, and soon the whole thing had reduced itself to a neat rectangular block which confined and sculpted itself still further, until, when it had neatly resolved itself unmistakably into the shape of a huge truck, highly polished panels rose from all around its base to form the truck's sides and top and wheel guards, and shiny bits of chrome and glass rotated into view to make up its grille and headlights and trim.

There on the side of the truck, in proud, tall letters of glistening gold, a bold sign read:

* MARVELLO'S * MIRACULOUS * MEATPIES *

Marvello regarded the truck with satisfaction for a long moment before he walked to its side, opened its door, and made himself comfortable in the driver's seat. He turned the waiting ignition key, and when the engine instantly began a strong, steady purring, he reached forward to the glove compartment, extracted the full bottle of whiskey waiting there, pulled its cork, and took two long, slow, deeply satisfactory swallows.

He rolled down the window, looked out in a friendly fashion at the empty space which had been the Midway just a little while before, and gave it a friendly wave. He drove smoothly across the soft bumpiness of the field until he reached the straight, flat Kansas highway, and there he turned northward, following the beams of his headlights onto his next gig.

THE PRINCE OF NOX

KATHE KOJA

The Prince of Nox upon a table, pinned by plastic, praying for death.

The lights were recessed blue above him; his sky. Punishing medicinal smell, reek of plasma and clean gore. Directly beneath him, the smooth gurney landscape; they would not waste a real bed on him. His restraints, ignored because ubiquitous, specially made to bind the strong and mobile dead: hurried fruit of a terrible specialization but not a growth industry, no, or at least not anymore; what had the drivers of the plague wagons done with their vehicles when the crisis was over? Slimly constructed gauntlets of some heavy material, not precisely cloth nor precisely plastic, the dull metal fasteners like nickel scabs on the pale false flesh pinning forehead, chest, arms, legs, abdomen. They were smart enough, here, to be very careful.

He stretched, a little, the hemisphere of his restraints.

To his left was the unwindowed wall, to his right the door
bristling its redundancy of locks. He had a call button—
perhaps the ultimate grotesquerie—and a long-empty saline
drip. From a small metal tree hung his chart, a monstrous
thing with a definite life of its own. His name was written
in fading blue capitals, alongside it and underlined (twice),
his date of death.

He remembered everything.

His name was Death; the yang to birth's yin and he had
gone through it heedless as a tramp, stunned by plain sensation when he should have been most aware. Still, how
was he to guess that that first metamorphosis was itself the
gate to a grander change, how could he have foretold? The
nervous parking lot of a Piggly Wiggly, one of the few
stores still open at night, the assault a surprise more dread-
ful than death would be: grabbed from behind by hands
missing fingers, teeth on his body like porcelain chips and
his own blood spraying stupid across the windshield of his
Chevette, brown-bagged milk, cigarettes, lunchmeat smashing to a pulpy goulash on the blacktop. Lunchmeat. That's
what it all came down to, the gift of life. Kiss of life. Lust
for life. Crouched and dying against the hood of his car,
his assailant's brute heedless attention now bestowed on the
man trying for the car next to his, a big grey late model
Ford like an elaborate moving sarcophagus, the man struggling with those stubborn jaws on his throat as if they were
the hinges on the gates of hell. Good luck.

The hood of his own car still warm, his temples and
bowels one swimming migraine; disorientation; the plunging loss of control, horrible, *horrible*. And then: resuscitat-
ing agony, tissues lurching not back to life but back to
service. All the smells. His own shit. His own blood. Meat,
somewhere, very ripe. Hiding behind the store, its back
door open—the clerks were all dead, all two of them, he
had watched them die—he hunched sideways in the pour
of fluorescence, staring at his hands, unable to believe they
could now reduce a human body to chunks and shreds.

Until he did it. Murder; but he was starving, the meat
smell was *everywhere*: so absolute it reduced to the status
of whim the greedy threshold quest for orgasm, until then

the strongest physical emotion he could imagine. To this hospital moment he still did not consciously remember whom he had killed, how, recalled only the sense of vomit-fullness before he lay where he was to sleep, less than half a mile from the parking lot where he had achieved zombiehood, Piggly Wiggly everlasting.

His sleep was not as it had been, less dreams than random firings of misdirected neurons, cessation but no rest. He woke like an appliance turning on, itchy with dried blood, the yellowish gravel of broken patio blocks stubbling his cheek, the backs of his hands. He lay in the driveway of a house, fake brick, fake farmhouse mailbox and lurching gutters, the whole carelessly abandoned like a bad idea: there were still toys in the overgrown yard, a garden hose half-coiled, gritty chunks of charcoal in a rusting grill. When he stood up he was very dizzy; it was almost impossible to keep an even gait. So, he thought, remembered thinking (remembering now in the slow radiation of blue above him, the heinous scent of meat he could smell but not touch), that's why they walk so funny.

Inside the house through the open back door, cereal box still on the kitchen counter, more toys underfoot. Newspapers in the living room, he could not read them, he could not properly focus his eyes. In the bathroom, a small dog recently dead behind the toilet. More toys in the tub, a duckie, a pair of red flat-bottomed boats that fit, moored, in the palms of his cold hands. He did not realize he was crying until he smelled his own tears.

He put everything back the way it had been and left the house, doors locked this time; it seemed important that the house stay undefiled. It was easier to keep to the sidewalk, less chance of stumbling. He walked back to the main road, careful to keep away from the infrequent cars until he realized there was no longer a reason to care.

The Piggly Wiggly had been looted, but was empty now, broken windows shivered lightly by the building wind. There was a car in the parking lot, a blue Toyota slewed defensively diagonal before the phone stand. It was empty as well.

How much time had passed, for him, for the world? Had everyone died? And if they had, where were they now?

Inside the store there was a radio, cheap and forgotten under the counter. He turned it on, sat atop the counter to listen while sorting through the contents of his wallet; he could not read any of the various identification, but he recognized himself on the driver's license.

Apparently the plague, the infestation, had finally reached downstate; they had all said it could not happen, that the Army, the National Guard had the outbreaks contained to the heavily populated metro areas, that if you stayed away from the big cities you would be okay. The usual smug rural paranoia, glaringly reinforced by daily newscast scares, closer and closer until there were sightings, here and there, more and more but no actual deaths. Stay out of the cities, they said. Lock your doors. Of course now they had been proved completely wrong, but then again they probably no longer cared. The only question left half-worth wonder was Who; who finally brought the death, who rode the pale horse; and did it matter?

No. Of course not.

He killed and ate a pregnant teenager that afternoon; her bones snapped in his hands like fragile clasps of cheap jewelry. Soon afterward he walked in front of a truck, a quarter-ton pickup driven by two women whose vast and rolling eyes were almost blinded by outrage and terror, and found what it was like to fly.

It was possible to walk a long way without feeding. He tried to go as long as he could, and as far. He was moderately successful.

He had forgotten that his name was Peter, that he was a cost accountant, that he had no close friends and a wife who did not particularly like him.

He thought he might live forever.

Did you use alcohol? Did you use prescription drugs? Stimulants or antidepressants of any kind? How about non-prescription drugs? Cocaine? Amphetamines?

No.

Were you ever diagnosed as having hypertension? Diabetes? AIDS? MS? CP? Huntington's? Hodgkin's? All the brain diseases, finally, which at least made some sense if not enough: no, he told them. I was perfectly healthy. I didn't even smoke cigarettes regularly.

Senses: enhanced olfactory, to a level of sophistication comparable only to the most advanced carnivores. Enhanced night vision. Auditory unchanged. Tactile senses deteriorated to a large degree. They never asked about his sense of taste.

Angry eyes. Notations. Without adequate medical records, without a formal autopsy they were reduced to that old fallback standby, asking questions. They asked the same questions a lot. He wondered if they knew that.

They smelled so good.

Irony: having died once, stupid and fast and too dumbfounded for real awareness as he crossed the line from life to hyperlife, now all he wanted was to die again, passing this time into the fullness of erasure; to unbecome. Irony once more, but one infinitely warmer: in his first life he was not much, in fact he was nothing and no one, *no one,* his problems, the sorrows of his emptiness less than cliché and his heart too dull to even notice the rolling time sucked from him by cold attrition; but now in death, the answer.

The vessel must be emptied before it can be filled.

He had not been transformed, as if from frog to royalty, all in a moment, in fact it took him the better part of a season, warm to cold, to realize that he had changed. Again. In his dark vagabond travels, street to street to highway and death after death after death, he assumed of the others he saw, the ones he watched without joining, an aimlessness informed by innocence and more than equal to his own. At last, shy and stealthy, he followed and then joined a trio met outside what had been a parochial school, standing blanched and faintly steaming in blind yellow streetlight circles.

He told them, haltingly in their silence, of his theories—he had a lot of theories then, many of them to prove subsequently untrue, one or two in the next few minutes— and spoke of his ideas, his belief that there must be a different way to live, that this course of wandering, of empty killing, was wrong. Death is *good*, he told them earnestly; it should not be randomly bestowed, there should be a *purpose*, a reason behind it. Kill and eat, yes, it had to be done and was in its way perhaps not so bad, perhaps not even as bad as the old way which was the same thing, really, wasn't it? Hadn't it been? Just disguised. It had still been eater and eaten, but without blood, and maybe this new way was better. Cleaner, because everyone *gained*, wasn't it so?

Wasn't it?

It was like talking to the light poles. No answering. No talking.

No thinking.

No nothing.

He remembered trying again, simpler words, louder in his frustration, louder until he was screaming at them, right there in the parking lot, they were *nothing*, less than animals, stupid eating machines; in the bland reflection of their eyes was his first serious consideration of suicide. The last immortal man on earth. What a joke. He left them there and promised himself he would live—and die if he had to—alone, he would never come near any of them again, he was *different*.

He stayed different.

He became lonely.

Eventually, after nights in the snow, curled like a sad surly insect in a bitter cocoon, he realized what was happening, had been, what he had truly become. Was it a coincidence that he alone retained the gift of awareness, of a consciousness more severely tempered and refined than even those who had never died? Was it a coincidence that he alone understood what a *gift* it all was?

No. It was not. There *is* more in heaven and earth, more than the dead and the living: there was a place inside him that death did not hamper nor life release, that had blossomed now in this terrible half-life to make of it, and him, something new.

And there was work to do.

He cried then, he was so happy.

We transcend death, we *are* death, we are the afterlife. His message, preached to a herd begun as worse than cows, grisly cud and slack stares. Quite the congregation, clustered together like flies around a sore, wandering away, then back to stand as stupid as before. But they had listened, he knew they had. Because even those eyes could widen, even there was the echo of the place inside him: emptiness filled calling to the guttering void of others: here is what you need. Be filled. And eventually, through reservoirs of patience and demand, they learned. Not much, even after all his efforts, but enough to rise at least a step or two above the level of simple slaughtering machines, dumb animals feeding at the living trough of the ever-lessening pool of victims—because of course the others, the ones left alive, were learning too, after a shockingly long period of numb terror that decimated them through its fostering of stupid theories, ruinously reckless modes of action; that vaccine, for example, what a disaster that had turned out to be.

Not for him, though, or his people. For them it was not apocalypse but transformation, a changed order of being. Fruit of his relentless teachings, as slow as they, finally he had guided them in choice of their victims—who in deepest fact were truly victims no longer: choose not the healthy but the ill, the old, the sleepers on benches, the hiders in crevices too small for living eyes to find: take from them the sorrows life has forced upon them; empower them all. They are empty: fill them. And painlessly, it must be done painlessly: no ugliness, no slobbering feast, just a seamless entrance to the infinite. And his people, relieved now of the burden of total senselessness, restored in some distant way to the habit of order, had responded with tenacity collective, a dark unconscious charity that absolved, rather than bestowed, pain. They had given all that was left for them to give, they had given of *themselves,* not taking but making, no longer the heedless gobble it had been—although unfortunately that continued, there were still some he could not reach, usually the ones gone so far for so long that nothing but a well-placed bullet could get their attention—now the process had become more than a process, it had evolved into nothing less than the sacramental.

But in the end what difference had it made? They all died again at last, painfully, in clumps and lowing droves; he had never taught them a way to save themselves; it had not seemed necessary. Why fear death when death is what you are? His own survival had been almost a comic fluke, found as he was pinned beneath an unused refrigerator in the basement of an abandoned community center, their summer's hive, lair, church; he had tried to block the door, found his strength distracted until it was too late, and lay there stunned as an idiot bug, unable to escape the grim combat faces in their hypersterile suits, saved only—irony again—by his sudden terrified cries of Please. Over and over: Please, please. Ask nice, his mother used to say. The inability to do so had killed his people, sent them en masse to crematoria, their bewildered cries of hunger and unease unmarked by him, incarcerated as he was in this monolithic facility, unable to hear or help.

Still he had loved them, in a way, and needed them certainly, and certainly they needed him. God help us if they ever get smart—if he had heard it once in the days before his own sloppy exit, he had heard it a million times, and twice that afterward. Well, he was smart, and more than mere intelligence: he was aware. By his being he brought epiphany; from emptiness, the first intelligence of what it meant to be full. He had enough brains for all of them.

And now he *was* all of them, all by himself.

•   •   •

How long had it been, they wanted to know, since he had eaten real food? As opposed, he supposed, to the synthetic humanity they fed him, the hideous fake flesh. God. Real food. Don't make me laugh, he said. That *was* the real food. Realer than dead animals and dead fish. You drink blood too, you just call it gravy.

They hadn't liked those answers, liked others even less, liked least of all his answers incomplete, his silences that fed their frustration, boiling to a shout, We have to *know*! We have to find out.

Why do you ask me? Yelling now himself. Why me.

Because you're the only one whose brain didn't turn to neuron puree, you're the only one who still has an IQ. Because there isn't another one like you.

Slowly, there in his prison, he came to new theories, black knowledge seeping as cruel and inevitable as infection through the blood. The zombie epidemic, the reign of the rapturous dead, was effectively over. What few shambling wanderers remained—none of them *his,* he was sure— were walking a very short line thanks to the Army's new improved assembly line techniques, practice evidently having finally made perfect.

So. Why then were the doctors, the NIH bullies, so greedy to find out what differed in his post-death physiology, what possible difference could it make at this late date? And why do it with such idiotic Twenty Questions sloth, for God's sake? Why not just perform a lengthy slice and dice, study each cell individually if that was what it took to get where they wanted to go?

Where did they want to go?

He had a theory for that, too, and the more he pondered it the more correct he knew himself to be. They wanted to make themselves like him. Immortal. But without struggle, or pain. Or work, real work, his work, the plumb and scorch of the heart, the soul. No. They were doctors, they didn't believe in souls. Just find out what he has so we can get it too, synthesize it, something. We have the greatest concentration of experts in the history of medicine, for fuck's sake, we ought to be able to do *something*. He's just a zombie. He's just a zombie.

Stropping his wrists against the restraints, a slow and antique care, trying to slough to the bone. No, he told them. I won't cooperate with you anymore. There is nothing more for me to do here, and I want to die.

They did not answer. If he wished to eat, he could not help but cooperate, and they all knew it, he most of all in the warm depths of his degraded capitulation. He had tried to starve himself once; they had not permitted it. They had their own lengths, how far they would go.

But they would never let *him* go.

His people, such as they were, had been—and even if they had been nothing, they had still been his—were all dead forever, passed beyond that second life into the only place he wanted now to be, the last fulfillment, the final step taken. So easy, with access to the right weapons, weapons nothing, the right *mindset*. Goad the wrong orderly, presto. But that was for dreary daydreams, he never in fact saw any orderlies, any nurses, anyone other than the increasingly sullen doctors and he had goaded them plenty already, they were unimpressed with his reasonings, his message and pity writ large; they wanted bodily fluids, they wanted to measure his eyeballs, they wanted him to flex his right arm twenty times and twenty times again, they wanted to see if he remained capable of a bowel movement, of a rise in temperature, of an erection. How human are you, they asked with their tests. How are you still like us?

Too much, he thought, and told them so.

"Why don't you just kill me?"

The doctor, young, thin; swift gloved brown hands, faintly cool pink palms. Large eyes that said nothing at all. "You know why."

Tears. He could still cry. "I want to die. Please just let me die."

Swabbing at his restraints, swiping lubricant beneath to keep the friable flesh intact. "It's not up to me." Making notes on the file, it was already *War and Peace,* what else was there to say? How long was this going to go on?

"Please," he said. "Let me go. Tell them to let me go."

Cold eyes, now. "Did you give your victims—pardon me, your *converts*—did you give them any choice? Did you *ask* them if they—"

"Yes! Yes, I did." Earnestly. "I asked them all, I never forced anybody. Once I explained to them how it was, that death is inevitable, they understood and they—"

"Let me explain something to *you.* You didn't bring anybody to a better life, you just killed them, all those people, you and that Salvation Army you organized, as if they weren't bad enough on their own."

And in his eyes, the question. The how.

Still, forever the unspoken how: when it was only why that mattered: how did you do it, how did you train them, how are you different? Weakness, calling to weakness, *made* for it, weak himself unto a loathing so pure it had gone for so long unrecognized that it became part of his body, his inner skin, did no one understand what it was to be *nothing*? "I did it for them," he said, and felt the truth of it, elemental as the taste itself; but how explain the helpless beauty of smell to the noseless and the blind?

Leaning down, now, and close, right in his face like they never did. "Who the hell do you think you are, anyway? Jesus? The Second Coming? If Jesus saw you he would puke. You killed people, and you ate them, and you knew what you were doing! All the time!"

And did he realize, that young doctor, did he begin to understand how the sudden fresh gust of his scent was in and of itself so incredible, so overwhelming, that those angry words were lost in it, contempt drowned delicious in the river of that smell, he was so *close*—

"God, *look* at you!" in new horror and disgust, actually leaping back, away, far away so his scent dwindled to a faint sweet ribbon, gone entirely when he left the room.

And left behind, abashed, his mouth weeping helpless drool, to turn his trembling head away.

To sink into nervous proto-dreams, thrashing against

the restraints to rejoin his people, whom he had tried to
save, empower by emptiness: his happy twice-dead people
in the painless landscape of Nox, a heaven of endless night
unfolding now before him in the space behind his eyes as
in the cubicles and offices beyond his room that day's con-
clusions, findings, results unto minutiae were entered into
list after list, as the lights above his twisting body glowed
continuous blue, a pitiless illumination for his helplessness
and grief, extinguished by immortality to the status of the
everlasting dead.

BEER RUN

GREGORY NICOLL

They were twenty-three minutes out of Shelter when they saw the first zom. Steve was rewinding Black Flag's *Damaged* in the tape deck when the staggering blueboy broke cover, wide-eyed and barefoot. He wanted to waste it with the Remington, but Rett told him to chill and steered their mini-truck straight into the zom.

The diesel engine grunted and rattled as it pushed the little VW harder. Its steel plow smacked their lumbering target and cleaved it with a *whump* like a bursting watermelon.

The sour-milk stink of putrid zomflesh overpowered the cool autumn pine scent in the air. The boys covered their noses as the wipers swept the windshield clear of entrails. They left the zom in a cloud of blue smoke, two halves writhing on the road.

Steve clicked the shotgun's safety back on. The breeze

from the truck's open window whipped his long hair around him like Medusa's snakes. "Damn," he said. "I need some beer."

Rett nodded. "Klon's Place has got it, dude." Leather creaked as he adjusted the position of the lever-action Marlin carbine in his shoulder holster. The big .44 was sawed off short as a pistol, like the one that ventilates Charles Bronson in Sergio Leone's *Once Upon a Time in the West*.

Steve rummaged in the tape case until he found *Let Them Eat Jelly Beans*. He slapped it in. Overdriven guitars roared.

"That's the Kennedys." Rett scowled. "The *Dead* Kennedys."

Steve switched it for Roky Erickson's *Casting the Runes*.

Rett adjusted his camo hunting cap and glanced down again at their custom fuel meter, its gauge big as a pie plate. A red wedge of tape marked the fail-safe point.

The needle was a cartridge's width from the edge of the tape when the truck rattled into the replica Bavarian village of Helen, Georgia. They passed its long-abandoned gas station, the sign still hawking Super Unleaded at $875 a gallon. Rett smiled. Good thing their VW diesel could burn veggie oil.

Now came the tricky part—running the gauntlet to Klon's.

It was Oktoberfest in the little mountain town. Worst time of year here. Decades earlier, legions of military retirees, aging German-Americans, and hophead UGA frat rats descended on Helen each fall for an annual barley pop binge. Now they spent their zomlife staggering in these streets, crowded as the trees in Unicoi State Park. An old oompah music tape kept pumping out the tune "In Heaven There Is No Beer." Klon's idea of humor.

Rett downshifted and drew his .44, thumbing the safety off as he cleared leather. Working the truck's stick *and* the Marlin hand cannon's lever was tricky—but the boy'd had practice.

Steve hung out the passenger window with the pump, leaving a trail of smoking shells and splattered Bavarian ghoul-ash. He paused twice to reload, once to fast-forward the Roky Erickson cassette past "I Walked with a Zombie."

They cleared town, reaching Klon's Place with the fuel needle just a razor's width from halfway to Now-We-Gotta-*Walk*-Home. The damn fools on the gate took forever lowering the drawbridge. It cost the boys two additional .44s and another shotgun shell, but they made it in okay.

Klon smiled, snapping his red suspenders against his great beer-barrel chest. "Good to see y'all again," he said, his voice smooth as pilsner. He admired their fortified vehicle, heavy on the covet. "Change your mind yet about selling me this truck?"

"Sooner sell you my dick," said Rett. "We came for beer."

Klon stroked his gray beard, nodded, and hooked his thumbs back under his suspenders. "Whatcha got to trade today?"

Steve pulled back the canvas tarp, revealing their cargo.

Klon couldn't suppress an appreciative whistle. "Let's talk."

They struck a deal for twelve cases of the big man's homebrew. Klon offered them plastic jugs—much lighter on the load—but they opted for bottles. "Easier to 'recycle,'" Rett explained. "They make great molotovs, fulla 'shine. Toss one on a zom and it's Pork Rind City."

Klon sweetened the deal with an old five-liter keg of Warsteiner. Its stamped expiration date had faded quietly into history some eighteen months ago, but what the hell— it was *German*.

They were loading for the road when Steve pointed at a big basket of cassettes in the corner. "Klon, how 'bout some tunes?"

"All right." The big man smiled. "Pick one."

Steve did the honors while Rett finished loading up. He rejected Jan & Dean's *Dead Man's Curve,* John Fogerty's *Eye of the Zombie,* four tapes by the Grateful Dead, two by the Dead Milkmen, and tossed away *The Best of Chevy Chase* when he found it contained the track "Generalissimo Francisco Franco Is Still Dead." He settled on a compilation called *British Invasion: Early Years*. Good-timey oldies: Hollies, Hermits. Safe stuff.

They rolled, the weight of their truck squeezing fresh zom juice under the drawbridge. The stink was lost in a cloud of diesel fumes and sulphurous gunsmoke. Hot brass jingled among the beer bottles as they shot their way out.

Halfway back to Shelter, Steve cracked open a brew and took a short sip. "I just remembered," he said, grinning, "something my brother used to tell me, back before this world went apeshit—'Steve, the only real essentials for a man to make it through this life are *beer* and *toilet paper*.'"

Rett shook his head, laughed. "Wonder what he'd say if he could see us now, makin' our living trading the one for the other?!"

Steve stuck in his new cassette. Smooth, moody bass notes and a gentle drumbeat eased from the speaker.

"Hey," said Rett, reaching for Steve's open brew, "isn't this that old song called 'She's Not There'?"

Steve reluctantly yielded the bottle. "I think so."

"But that's by the Zombies!"

The cassette spiralled from the truck's open window, its white plastic shell clicking along the blacktop. It shattered, scattering bonelike fragments, and spilling yards of glistening brown intestines.

PRAYER

DOUGLAS MORNINGSTAR AND MAXWELL HART

The minute I heard that familiar distant thunder, I left the house: working my way down the cement driveway until I reached a flat place in the shade, beside the highway that swerved drunkenly into the upper heights of the valley. There I lay, rigid, as the sound grew louder. Its powerful vibrations squeezed my guts until my mind screamed with crushing, mixed anguish and joy.

It was a feeling I knew all too well.

The first ones suddenly swept around the curve. Bearded, long-haired, and gracefully laid back on their gleaming bikes, they rode toward me: more and more of them, appearing around the bend in closely spaced twos and threes. Painfully, my stomach knotted with excitement. You lucky bastards, I thought to myself.

On and on they rolled, one of them a massive black leather giant: wild hair flying from beneath a faded blue handkerchief tied around his head, his huge chin pocked with stubble. He shot me a giant toothless grin, swerved toward me in mock threat before guiding the knucklehead back into his lane. I had been seen and acknowledged.

Drowning in the deafening roar of panheads and shovelheads, I concentrated on the parade of faces, drinking in all the varied emotions and mental states on display as they rolled past my adoring eyes. Some riding solo, some packing women. "Oh fuck, what women!" sobbed my aching heart and loins.

Twice, a smile was fired at me: one by a slender blond doll on a chromed Harley sled, the other by a brunette fox who tauntingly shook her conical jugs as she sped by. Both were riding behind wide-shouldered bikers whose pale, bloodshot eyes noted me with pity.

I soaked in the smiles like a grateful sponge, drowning in the pain.

Hungrily, almost worshipfully, I watched each bike as it passed across my field of vision, aware of the strength and vital life represented in the people riding those machines.

They would be out of these mountains before dark, traveling across the desert's vastness, where, perhaps, they would halt beside a spring-fed lake to dismount and stretch cramped muscles, to eat food cooked over an open fire, to get stoned on chilled wines and writhe in greedy, sweaty pleasure, draped only by the cool air beneath the stars. Because they were young and healthy, ripe with reckless confidence. Because they knew no evil or suffering.

Because they knew not what they had.

By morning they would ride again. Toward the cities, now splayed open before them like freshly gutted deer. They would take what they wanted. And then they would ride on. This was how they lived.

In the land of the dead . . .

But then the last rider came whipping fast around the bend, trying to close the gap between himself and the others. His startled gaze locked upon me, twisted into a pitying leer.

He flipped me the bird, as a righteous farewell.

And then he, too, was gone, leaving only the fading echoes of his thunderous machine: echoes slowly dying in the canyon's rock belly until, finally, silence erased all trace of their brief passing and I was alone.

But the pain remained.

My eyes traced over the reeking husk that had become my prison, as well as my tomb: the shattered, useless hips, in their blood-caked denim casings; the ruptured ribcage, hollowed out and filed to points where it scraped against the pavement. I looked at my legs, such as they were. They were cruel jokes on me, only vaguely attached.

And then, as always, I remembered the night that I crashed through the guard rail: one second of screaming agony, then my Panhead highsiding in the strobing head-light glare. Spinning through the air, like me.

While, up above, the worthless fuck who stole my life slammed on his brakes. His cheap piss-colored Toyota, fishtailing. From the center of my lane . . .

I closed my eyes, trying hard to swallow through my lifeless throat. I thought about the ones who had just gone by. And then, like so many times before, I began to pray.

"Please," I whispered through trembling, gray-green lips. *"You up there, or out there, or wherever you are. When you touch the ones who have to go, be decent about it, dammit! Snuff them quickly and clean! Don't leave them here like me!"*

But there was no answer. Just the echoing silence.

Many hours later, the cold moon rose; and, fearful of scavengers, I crawled back to the house.

CALCUTTA, LORD OF NERVES

POPPY Z. BRITE

I was born in a North Calcutta hospital in the heart of an Indian midnight just before the beginning of the monsoon season. The air hung heavy as wet velvet over the Hooghly River, offshoot of the holy Ganga, and the stumps of banyan trees on the Upper Chitpur Road were flecked with dots of phosphorus like the ghosts of flames. I was as dark as the new moon in the sky, and I cried very little. I feel as if I remember this, because this is the way it must have been.

My mother died in labor, and later that night the hospital burned to the ground. (I have no reason to connect the two incidents; then again, I have no reason not to. Perhaps a desire to live burned on in my mother's heart. Perhaps the flames were fanned by her hatred for me, the insignificant mewling infant that had killed her.) A nurse carried me out of the roaring husk of the building and laid me in my father's arms. He cradled me, numb with grief.

My father was American. He had come to Calcutta five years earlier, on business. There he had fallen in love with my mother and, like a man who will not pluck a flower from its garden, he could not bear to see her removed from the hot, lush, squalid city that had spawned her. It was part of her exotica. So my father stayed in Calcutta. Now his flower was gone. He pressed his thin chapped lips to the satin of my hair. I remember opening my eyes—they felt tight and shiny, parched by the flames—and looking up at the column of smoke that roiled into the sky, a night sky blasted cloudy pink like a sky full of blood and milk.

There would be no milk for me, only chemical-tasting drops of formula from a plastic nipple. The morgue was in the basement of the hospital and did not burn. My mother lay on a metal table, a hospital gown stiff with her dying sweat pulled up over her red-smeared crotch and thighs. Her eyes stared up through the blackened skeleton of the hospital, up to the milky bloody sky, and ash filtered down to mask her pupils.

My father and I left for America before the monsoon came. Without my mother Calcutta was a pestilential hellhole, a vast cremation grounds, or so my father thought. In America he could send me to school and movies, ball games and Boy Scouts, secure in the knowledge that someone else would take care of me or I would take care of myself. There were no *thuggees* to rob me and cut my throat, no *goondas* who would snatch me and sell my bones for fertilizer. There were no cows to infect the streets with their steaming sacred piss. My father could give me over to the comparative wholesomeness of American life, leaving himself free to sit in his darkened bedroom and drink whiskey until his long sensitive nose floated hazily in front of his face and the sabre edge of his grief began to dull. He was the sort of man who has only one love in his lifetime, and knows with the sick fervor of a fatalist that this love will be taken from him someday, and is hardly surprised when it happens.

When he was drunk he would talk about Calcutta. My little American mind rejected the place—I was in love with air-conditioning, hamburgers and pizza, the free and undiscriminating love that was lavished upon me every time I twisted the TV dial—but somewhere in my Indian heart I longed for it. When I turned eighteen and my father finally failed to wake up from one of his drunken stupors, I returned to the city of my bloody birth as soon as I had the plane fare in my hand.

Calcutta, you will say. What a place to have been when the dead began to walk.

And I reply, what better place to be? What better place than a city where five million people look as if they are already dead—might as well be dead—and another five million wish they were?

I have a friend named Devi, a prostitute who began her work at the age of fifteen from a tarpaper shack on Sudder Street. Sudder is the Bourbon Street of Calcutta, but there is far less of the carnival there, and no one wears a mask on Sudder Street because disguises are useless when shame is irrelevant. Devi works the big hotels now, selling American tourists or British expatriates or German businessmen a taste of exotic Bengal spice. She is gaunt and beautiful and hard as nails. Devi says the world is a whore, too, and Calcutta is the pussy of the world. The world squats and spreads its legs, and Calcutta is the dank sex you see revealed there, wet and fragrant with a thousand odors both delicious and foul. A source of lushest pleasure, a breeding ground for every conceivable disease.

The pussy of the world. It is all right with me. I like pussy, and I love my squalid city.

The dead like pussy too. If they are able to catch a woman and disable her enough so that she cannot resist, you will see the lucky ones burrowing in between her legs as happily as the most avid lover. They do not have to come up for air. I have seen them eat all the way up into the body cavity. The internal female organs seem to be a great delicacy, and why not? They are the caviar of the human body. It is a sobering thing to come across a woman sprawled in the gutter with her intestines sliding from the shredded ruin of her womb, but you do not react. You do not distract the dead from their repast. They are slow and stupid, but that is all the more reason for you to be smart and quick and quiet. They will do the same thing to a man—chew off the soft penis and scrotal sac like choice morsels of squid, leaving only a red raw hole. But you can sidle by while they are feeding and they will not notice you. I do not try to hide from them. I walk the streets and look; that is all I do anymore. I am fascinated. This is not horror, this is simply more of Calcutta.

First I would sleep late, through the sultry morning into the heat of the afternoon. I had a room in one of the decrepit marble palaces of the old city. Devi visited me here often, but on a typical morning I woke alone, clad only in twisted bedsheets and a luxurious patina of sweat. Sun came through the window and fell in bright bars across the floor. I felt safe in my second-story room as long as I kept the door locked. The dead were seldom able to navigate stairs, and they could not manage the sustained cooperative effort to break down a locked door. They were no threat to me. They fed upon those who had given up, those too traumatized to keep running: the senile, abandoned old, the catatonic young women who sat in gutters cradling babies that had died during the night. These were easy prey.

The walls of my room were painted a bright coral and the sills and door were aqua. The colors caught the sun and made the day seem cheerful despite the heat that shimmered outside. I went downstairs, crossed the empty courtyard with its dry marble fountain, and went out into the street. This area was barren in the heat, painfully bright, with parched weeds lining the road and an occasional smear of cow dung decorating the gutter. By nightfall both weeds and dung might be gone. Children collected cow shit and patted it into cakes held together with straw, which could be sold as fuel for cooking fires.

I headed toward Chowringhee Road, the broad main thoroughfare of the city. Halfway up my street, hunched under the awning of a mattress factory, I saw one of the catatonic young mothers. The dead had found her too. They had already taken the baby from her arms and eaten through the soft part at the top of the skull. Vacuous bloody faces rose and dipped. Curds of tender brain fell from slack mouths. The mother sat on the curb nearby, her arms cradling nothing. She wore a filthy green sari that was ripped across the chest. The woman's breasts protruded heavily, swollen with milk. When the dead finished with her baby they would start on her, and she would make no resistance. I had seen it before. I knew how the milk would spurt and then gush as they tore into her breasts. I knew how hungrily they would lap up the twin rivers of blood and milk.

Above their bobbing heads, the tin awning dripped long ropy strands of cotton. Cotton hung from the roof in dirty clumps, caught in the corners of the doorway like spiderweb. Someone's radio blared faintly in another part of the building, tuned to an English-language Christian broadcast. A gospel hymn assured Calcutta that its dead in Christ would rise. I moved on toward Chowringhee.

Most of the streets in the city are positively cluttered with buildings. Buildings are packed in cheek-by-jowl, helter-skelter, like books of different sizes jammed into a rickety bookcase. Buildings even sag over the street so that all you see overhead is a narrow strip of sky crisscrossed by miles of clotheslines. The flapping silks and cottons are very bright against the sodden, dirty sky. But there are certain vantage points where the city opens up and all at once you have a panoramic view of Calcutta. You see a long muddy hillside that has become home to a *bustee*, thousands and thousands of slum dwellings where tiny fires are tended through the night. The dead come often to these slums of tin and cardboard, but the people do not leave the *bustee*—where would they go? Or you see a wasteland of disused factories, empty warehouses, blackened smokestacks jutting into a rust-colored sky. Or a flash of the Hooghly River, steel-gray in its shroud of mist, spanned by the intricate girder-and-wirescape of the Howrah Bridge.

Just now I was walking opposite the river. The waterfront was not considered a safe place because of the danger from drowning victims. Thousands each year took the long plunge off the bridge, and thousands more simply waded into the water. It is easy to commit suicide at a riverfront because despair collects in the water vapor. This is part of the reason for the tangible cloud of despair that hangs over Calcutta along with its veil of humidity.

Now the suicides and the drowned street children were coming out of the river. At any moment the water might regurgitate one, and you would hear him scrabbling up the bank. If he had been in the water long enough he might tear himself to spongy gobbets on the stones and broken bricks that littered the waterfront; all that remained would be a trace of foul brown odor, like the smell of mud from the deep part of the river.

Police—especially the Sikhs, who are said to be more violent than Hindus—had been taking the dead up on the bridge to shoot them. Even from far away I could see spray-patterns of red on the drab girders. Alternately they set the dead alight with gasoline and threw them over the railing into the river. At night it was not uncommon to see several writhing shapes caught in the downstream current, the fiery symmetry of their heads and arms and legs making them into five-pointed human stars.

I stopped at a spice vendor's stand to buy a bunch of red chrysanthemums and a handful of saffron. The saffron I had him wrap in a twist of scarlet silk. "It is a beautiful day," I said to him in Bengali. He stared at me, half amused, half appalled. "A beautiful day for what?"

True Hindu faith calls upon the believer to view all things as equally sacred. There is nothing profane—no dirty dog picking through the ash bin at a cremation ground, no stinking gangrenous stump thrust into your face by a beggar who seems to hold you personally responsible for all his woes. These things are as sacred as feasting day at the holiest temple. But even for the most devout Hindus it has been difficult to see these walking dead as sacred. They are empty humans. That is the truly horrifying thing about them, more than their vacuous hunger for living flesh, more than the blood caked under their nails or the shreds of flesh caught between their teeth. They are soulless; there is nothing in their eyes; the sounds they make—their farts, their grunts and mewls of hunger—are purely reflexive. The Hindu, who has been taught to believe in the soul of everything, has a particular horror of these drained human vessels. But in Calcutta life goes on. The shops are still open. The confusion of traffic still inches its way up Chowringhee. No one sees any alternatives.

Soon I arrived at what was almost invariably my day's first stop. I would often walk twenty or thirty miles in a day—I had strong shoes and nothing to occupy my time except walking and looking. But I always began at the Kalighat, temple of the Goddess.

There are a million names for her, a million vivid descriptions: Kali the Terrible, Kali the Ferocious, skull-necklace, destroyer of men, eater of souls. But to me she was Mother Kali, the only one of the vast and colorful pantheon of Hindu gods that stirred my imagination and lifted my heart. She was the Destroyer, but all final refuge was found in her. She was the goddess of the age. She could bleed and burn and still rise again, very awake, beautifully terrible.

I ducked under the garlands of marigolds and strands of temple bells strung across the door, and I entered the temple of Kali. After the constant clamor of the street, the silence inside the temple was deafening. I fancied I could hear the small noises of my body echoing back to me from the ceiling far above. The sweet opium glaze of incense curled around my head. I approached the idol of Kali, the *jagrata*. Her gimlet eyes watched me as I came closer.

She was tall, gaunter and more brazenly naked than my friend Devi even at her best moments. Her breasts were tipped with blood—at least I always imagined them so— and her two sharp fangs and the long streamer of a tongue that uncurled from her open mouth were the color of blood too. Her hair whipped about her head and her eyes were wild, but the third crescent eye in the center of her forehead was merciful; it saw and accepted all. The necklace of skulls circled the graceful stem of her neck, adorned the sculpted hollow of her throat. Her four arms were so sinuous that if you looked away even for an instant, they seemed to sway. In her four hands she held a noose of rope, a skull-staff, a shining sword, and a gaping, very dead-looking severed head. A silver bowl sat at the foot of the statue just beneath the head, where the blood from the neck would drip. Sometimes this was filled with goat's or sheep's blood as an offering. The bowl was full today. In these times the blood might well be human, though there was no putrid smell to indicate it had come from one of the dead.

I laid my chrysanthemums and saffron at Kali's feet. Among the other offerings, mostly sweets and bundles of spice, I saw a few strange objects. A fingerbone. A shrivelled mushroom of flesh that turned out upon closer inspection to be an ear. These were offerings for special protection, mostly wrested from the dead. But who was to say that a few devotees had not lopped off their own ears or finger joints to coax a boon from Kali? Sometimes when I had forgotten to bring an offering, I cut my wrist with a razor blade and let a few drops of my blood fall at the idol's feet.

I heard a shout from outside and turned my head for a moment. When I looked back, the four arms seemed to have woven themselves into a new pattern, the long tongue seemed to loll farther from the scarlet mouth. And—this was a frequent fantasy of mine—the wide hips now seemed to tilt forward, affording me a glimpse of the sweet and terrible petalled cleft between the thighs of the goddess.

I smiled up at the lovely sly face. "If only I had a tongue as long as yours, Mother," I murmured, "I would kneel before you and lick the folds of your holy pussy until you screamed with joy." The toothy grin seemed to grow wider, more lascivious. I imagined much in the presence of Kali.

Outside in the temple yard I saw the source of the shout I had heard. There is a stone block upon which the animals brought to Kali, mostly baby goats, are beheaded by the priests. A gang of roughly dressed men had captured a dead girl and were bashing her head in on the sacrificial block. Their arms rose and fell, ropy muscles flexing. They clutched sharp stones and bits of brick in their scrawny hands. The girl's half-pulped head still lashed back and forth. The lower jaw still snapped, though the teeth and bone were splintered. Foul thin blood coursed down and mingled with the rich animal blood in the earth beneath the block. The girl was nude, filthy with her own gore and waste. The flaccid breasts hung as if sucked dry of meat. The belly was burst open with gases. One of the men thrust a stick into the ruined gouge between the girl's legs and leaned on it with all his weight.

Only in extensive stages of decay can the dead be told from the lepers. The dead are greater in number now, and even the lepers look human when compared to the dead. But that is only if you get close enough to look into the eyes. The faces in various stages of wet and dry rot, the raw ends of bones rubbing through skin like moldy cheese-cloth, the cancerous domes of the skulls are the same. After a certain point lepers could no longer stay alive begging in the streets, for most people would now flee in terror at the sight of a rotting face. As a result the lepers were dying, then coming back, and the two races mingled like some obscene parody of incest. Perhaps they actually could breed. The dead could obviously eat and digest, and seemed to excrete at random like everyone else in Calcutta, but I supposed no one knew whether they could ejaculate or conceive.

A stupid idea, really. A dead womb would rot to pieces around a fetus before it could come halfway to term; a dead scrotal sac would be far too cold a cradle for living seed. But no one seemed to know anything about the biology of the dead. The newspapers were hysterical, printing picture upon picture of random slaughter by dead and living alike. Radio stations had either gone off the air or were broadcasting endless religious exhortations that ran together in one long keening whine, the edges of Muslim, Hindu, Christian doctrine beginning to fray and blur.

No one in India could say for sure what made the dead walk. The latest theory I had heard was something about a genetically engineered microbe that had been designed to feed on plastic: a microbe that would save the world from its own waste. But the microbe had mutated and was now eating and "replicating" human cells, causing basic bodily functions to reactivate. It did not much matter whether this was true. Calcutta was a city relatively unsurprised to see its dead rise and walk and feed upon it. It had seen them doing so for a hundred years.

All the rest of the lengthening day I walked through the city. I saw no more dead except a cluster far away at the end of a blocked street, in the last rags of bloody light, fighting each other over the bloated carcass of a sacred cow.

My favorite place at sunset is by the river where I can see the Howrah Bridge. The Hooghly is painfully beautiful in the light of the setting sun. The last rays melt onto the water like hot *ghee,* turning the river from steel to khaki to nearly golden, a blazing ribbon of light. The bridge rises black and skeletal into the fading orange sky. Tonight an occasional skirl of bright flowers and still-glowing greasy embers floated by, the last earthly traces of bodies cremated farther up the river. Above the bridge were the burning *ghats* where families lined up to incinerate their dead and cast the ashes into the holy river. Cremation is done more efficiently these days, or at least more hurriedly. People can reconcile in their hearts their fear of strangers' dead, but they do not want to see their own dead rise.

I walked along the river for a while. The wind off the water carried the scent of burning meat. When I was well away from the bridge, I wandered back into the maze of narrow streets and alleyways that lead toward the docks in the far southern end of the city. People were already beginning to settle in for the night, though here a bedroom might mean your own packing crate or your own square of sidewalk. Fires glowed in nooks and corners. A warm breeze still blew off the river and sighed its way through the winding streets. It seemed very late now. As I made my way from corner to corner, through intermittent pools of light and much longer patches of darkness, I heard small bells jingling to the rhythm of my footsteps. The brass bells of rickshaw men, ringing to tell me they were there in case I wished for a ride. But I could see none of the men. The effect was eerie, as if I were walking alone down an empty nighttime street being serenaded by ghostly bells. The feeling soon passed. You are never truly alone in Calcutta.

A thin hand slid out of the darkness as I passed. Looking into the doorway it came from, I could barely make out five gaunt faces, five forms huddled against the night. I dropped several coins into the hand and it slid out of sight again. I am seldom begged from. I look neither rich nor poor, but I have a talent for making myself all but invisible. People look past me, sometimes right through me. I don't mind; I see more things that way. But when I am begged from I always give. With my handful of coins, all five of them might have a bowl of rice and lentils tomorrow.

A bowl of rice and lentils in the morning, a drink of water from a broken standpipe at night.

It seemed to me that the dead were among the best-fed citizens of Calcutta.

Now I crossed a series of narrow streets and was surprised to find myself coming up behind the Kalighat. The side streets are so haphazardly arranged that you are constantly finding yourself in places you had no idea you were even near. I had been to the Kalighat hundreds of times, but I had never approached it from this direction. The temple was dark and still. I had not been here at this hour before, did not even know whether the priests were still here or if one could enter so late. But as I walked closer I saw a little door standing open at the back. The entrance used by the priests, perhaps. Something flickered from within: a candle, a tiny mirror sewn on a robe, the smoldering end of a stick of incense.

I slipped around the side of the temple and stood at the door for a moment. A flight of stone steps led up into the darkness of the temple. The Kalighat at night, deserted, might have been an unpleasant prospect to some. The thought of facing the fierce idol alone in the gloom might have made some turn away from those steps. I began to climb them.

The smell reached me before I ascended halfway. To spend a day walking through Calcutta is to be assailed by thousands of odors both pleasant and foul: the savor of spices frying in *ghee*, the stink of shit and urine and garbage, the sick-sweet scent of the little white flowers called *mogra* that are sold in garlands and that make me think of the gardenia perfume American undertakers use to mask the smell of their corpses.

Almost everyone in Calcutta is scrupulously clean in person, even the very poor. They will leave their trash and their spit everywhere, but many of them wash their bodies twice a day. Still, everyone sweats under the sodden veil of heat, and at midday any public place will be redolent with the smell of human perspiration, a delicate tang like the mingled juices of lemons and onions. But lingering in the stairwell was an odor stronger and more foul than any I had encountered today. It was deep and brown and moist; it curled at the edges like a mushroom beginning to dry. It was the perfume of mortal corruption. It was the smell of rotting flesh.

Then I came up into the temple, and I saw them.

The large central room was lit only with candles that flickered in a restless draft, first this way, then that. In the dimness the worshippers looked no different from any other supplicants at the feet of Kali. But as my eyes grew accustomed to the candlelight, details resolved themselves. The withered hands, the ruined faces. The burst body cavities where ropy organs could be seen trailing down behind the cagework of ribs.

The offerings they had brought.

By day Kali grinned down upon an array of blossoms and sweetmeats lovingly arranged at the foot of her pedestal. The array spread there now seemed more suited to the goddess. I saw human heads balanced on raw stumps of necks, eyes turned up to crescents of silver-white. I saw gobbets of meat that might have been torn from a belly or a thigh. I saw severed hands like pale lotus flowers, the fingers like petals opening silently in the night.

Most of all, piled on every side of the altar, I saw bones. Bones picked so clean that they gleamed in the candlelight. Bones with smears of meat and long snotty runners of fat still attached. Skinny arm-bones, clubby leg-bones, the pretzel of a pelvis, the beadwork of a spine. The delicate bones of children. The crumbling ivory bones of the old. The bones of those who could not run.

These things the dead brought to their goddess. She had been their goddess all along, and they her acolytes.

Kali's smile was hungrier than ever. The tongue lolled

like a wet red streamer from the open mouth. The eyes were blazing black holes in the gaunt and terrible face. If she had stepped down from her pedestal and approached me now, if she had reached for me with those sinuous arms, I might not have been able to fall to my knees before her. I might have run. There are beauties too terrible to be borne.

Slowly the dead began to turn toward me. Their faces lifted and the rotting cavities of their nostrils caught my scent. Their eyes shone iridescent. Faint starry light shimmered in the empty spaces of their bodies. They were like cutouts in the fabric of reality, like conduits to a blank universe. The void where Kali ruled and the only comfort was in death.

They did not approach me. They stood holding their precious offerings and they looked at me—those of them that still had eyes—or they looked through me. At that moment I felt more than invisible. I felt empty enough to belong among these human shells.

A ripple seemed to pass through them. Then—in the uncertain candlelight, in the light that shimmered from the bodies of the dead—Kali did move.

The twitch of a finger, the deft turn of a wrist—at first it was so slight as to be nearly imperceptible. But then her lips split into an impossibly wide, toothy grin and the tip of her long tongue curled. She rotated her hips and swung her left leg high into the air. The foot that had trod on millions of corpses made a pointe as delicate as a prima ballerina's. The movement spread her sex wide open.

But it was not the petalled mandala-like cleft I had imagined kissing earlier. The pussy of the goddess was an enormous deep red hole that seemed to lead down to the center of the world. It was a gash in the universe, it was rimmed in blood and ash. Two of her four hands beckoned toward it, inviting me in. I could have thrust my head into it, then my shoulders. I could have crawled all the way into that wet crimson eternity, and kept crawling forever.

Then I did run. Before I had even decided to flee I found myself falling down the stone staircase, cracking my head and my knee on the risers. At the bottom I was up and running before I could register the pain. I told myself that I thought the dead would come after me. I do not know what I truly feared was at my back. At times I thought I was running not away from something, but toward it.

I ran all night. When my legs grew too tired to carry me I would board a bus. Once I crossed the bridge and found myself in Howrah, the even poorer suburb on the other side of the Hooghly. I stumbled through desolate streets for an hour or more before doubling back and crossing over into Calcutta again. Once I stopped to ask for a drink of water from a man who carried two cans of it slung on a long stick across his shoulders. He would not let me drink from his tin cup, but poured a little water into my cupped hands. In his face I saw the mingled pity and disgust with which one might look upon a drunk or a beggar. I was a well-dressed beggar, to be sure, but he saw the fear in my eyes.

In the last hour of the night I found myself wandering through a wasteland of factories and warehouses, of smokestacks and rusty corrugated tin gates, of broken windows. There seemed to be thousands of broken windows. After a while I realized I was on the Upper Chitpur Road. I walked for a while in the watery light that fills the sky before dawn. Eventually I left the road and staggered through the wasteland. Not until I saw its girders rising around me like the charred bones of a prehistoric animal did I realize I was in the ruins of the hospital where I had been born.

The hole of the basement had filled up with broken glass and crumbling metal, twenty years' worth of cinders and weeds, all washed innocent in the light of the breaking dawn. Where the building had stood there was only a vast depression in the ground, five or six feet deep. I slid down the shallow embankment, rolled, and came to rest in the ashes. They were infinitely soft; they cradled me. I felt as safe as an embryo. I let the sunrise bathe me. Perhaps I had climbed into the gory chasm between Kali's legs after all, and found my way out again.

Calcutta is cleansed each morning by the dawn. If only the sun rose a thousand times a day, the city would always be clean.

Ashes drifted over me, smudged my hands gray, flecked

my lips. I lay safe in the womb of my city, called by its poets Lord of Nerves, city of joy, the pussy of the world. I felt as if I lay among the dead. I was that safe from them: I knew their goddess, I shared their many homes. As the sun came up over the mud and glory of Calcutta, the sky was so full of smoky clouds and pale pink light that it seemed, to my eyes, to burn.

PART THREE

END GAMES

I WALK ALONE

ROBERTA LANNES

You're dead. Slow-rotting in the corner of our basement. I sit here and look at your mummy-wrapped body, your head emerging from the cellophane and graying pink bed-sheets like a dusty bee from a pale rose, and weep. I've been walking dead on the streets of Manhattan with nary an emotion for over a year. Now that I can feel, I would wish for joy or gladness, but at the moment I'll take sorrow. Any emotion at all.

I would have come down here sooner, but for the four months you've been locked up, hidden down here, my existence has gone from a zombie kind of hell to walking-dead splendor. If you'd been alive down here all of this time, you would have gone insane without your "things to do." That endless litany of exigencies; "needing to do this, having to do that." What a relief it's been to know you've just been fucking sitting still all this time and not have to hear about it.

Keeping you fresh like this was a good idea. One of the half-dead I've been hanging with, a gourmet chef from Balducci's, told me that it would preserve you, just in case you came back, sort of. If any of the ''usual'' types found you, they would have made off with you long ago. That's why I covered you with all that junk we had down here. Even with all the contempt I've found that I have for you, I still feel committed to you. To your best. To keeping you close. To an *us*. Love binds even in death.

There's so much to tell you. When you were last alive and we were still upstairs in number 9, you were scared to death to venture out, and thoroughly disgusted by my state of decay. That didn't bode well for the relationship. As I recall, I was too physically cold and emotionally unresponsive to fuck, and I'd lost my voluptuousness and copper-toned skin to the lean and pale. I didn't know then what I know now. I look good for being half-dead.

All the time and effort I put into keeping my California-girl appearance and radiant health before the scourge paid off. Yes. You thought it was vainglorious and a waste of time. Turns out, the way one ends up after death is determined by the lifestyle one led prior. The nutritionist, acupuncturist, herbalist, masseuse, personal trainer, de-toxing, infusions of BHT and other preservatives with my vitamin supplements, plus the hours getting facials, wraps, and moisturizing gave me the essential foundation for a healthy half-life. I'm not like the usuals with their graying skin, expressionless faces, stiff, ambling bulk, indiscriminately flesh-eating like crazed piranhas, their fingers and arms and ears falling off, groaning incoherently, lost in their pure instinctual being. I'm sort of an elite type.

I can hear you laughing, you bastard. You'd say it sounds snobbish and silly. But fuck it, you're lying there like a piece of beef Wellington, and I'm feeling damned lucky. I'm out there doing things. See, as a zombie, my blood runs like sap, everything is slowed down, except my thinking. Well, even if my mind is plodding, my awareness of it seems to be equally paced and nothing seems different.

The only things that come and go are my appetite, my compulsiveness, and my sex drive. My feelings died with me when I killed myself. Or so I thought. Enough stimulus, and the feelings respond. Unfortunately, uncontrollably so.

Agh, here comes the loneliness . . . agony for me sitting here looking at you. You useless fuck! Sorry, it's like this. One second I'm giddy, the next murderously mad. . . .

There are others like me. I found them two days after you died. I wandered over to SoHo one evening. It was during the spring thaw and the usuals were roaming the streets like cockroaches. I noticed a taxi on Houston, turning up Greene. The only vehicles still moving are driven by live ones, so I followed.

Up in a loft that had been left in mid-renovation, there was a party going on. I had dressed well and evidently looked as alive as I thought I did, because I was let in without question. There were thirty, forty people there, alive as you and I once were, or so I'd thought.

I was welcomed by a handsome couple. The Doctor, One-Eye, and his girlfriend, Rula.

"You're one of us, aren't you?" He stroked the patch over his missing eye.

"One of us?" My voice is more gravelly than it was before, but very sexy, I'm told.

"*Us*. The not-quite-wholly-dead, zombilina. Fucking purgatoryette time, dear. Dead, but a hell-of-a-lot better off than the stiffs on the street." He was smug. I didn't think I liked him. Rula hung on him like sweat.

"Do I look dead?" Maybe he was testing me. I'd fooled so many for so long—been chased as live meat by the usuals. I didn't even believe *he* was dead.

"Not so that it's obvious. But I can tell. Took good care of yourself before you went, am I right? Like the rest of us . . ." He gestured toward the crowd milling around tables of human delicacies.

"I tried." My appetite was returning.

"How'd you go, suicide? Drugs? You've got that fragile but angry look. And it's not local. You're not a New Yorker, are you?"

Without feelings then, I couldn't loathe him or get indignant at the pushy, ingratiating way he came on. But if I could, I would have.

"California-bred, transplanted for love. Died for it. And you . . . I'd guess uptown plastic surgeon, hooked on Xanex, who couldn't stand the thought of eating on, and disfiguring the former palette of his work and took his own life?"

He snarled, frowning. "Oooh, you're good. Done this long?" He turned on his heels and left without my answer. Having been a psychologist, I had an edge at determining the less discernible attributes of others. Too, I detected a distinct surge of emotions and got curious.

I stuffed myself with hors d'oeuvres, marveling at the taste of well-prepared human flesh, and gravitated over to the man of the evening, one Sammy Gagliano. He had six gorgeous women around him. He acknowledged me with a wink and a compliment. You'd be proud.

"A blonde! Get over here, beautiful. I need one more adoring girl for my entourage."

I told him, "I'm flattered."

"There isn't much beauty left in this fucking world, but what there is, I want around me, get it?" He grinned. He had a gold tooth. I took him for a drug dealer or a pimp. "So what's your name?"

"Katy. I live in the Village. Tenth Street and Sixth Avenue."

Everyone chuckled. Sammy stood up and reached out a hand. "Great joke. 'I *live* in the Village.' Well, Katy, welcome. Anybody who looks as good as you has to be part of this thing."

That's how it started. Into the wee hours of the morning we each told stories. I seemed to be the only one there without feelings and my humor was strained, but I told them about you, me. I said we met in California at a party. You were instantly impressed. I was married. Three months later you were sending me a ticket to come to New York as my marriage crumbled. I was sure to tell them the marriage was dead long before. It was passion and romance from the moment I got off the plane, until you ingratiated yourself into my life on the West Coast two months later.

I never asked you to come. You moving in, even though I objected, felt like rape. But I didn't tell them that. They wanted to hear the romantic drama. So I told them how, over the next six months, you used hysterical tantrums, suicide threats, and every romantic trick in the book to sway me. And it worked, you fucking pig!

In these bursts of anger, I can see what an utter, unredeemable psychopath you were. Why, when I recall the moments of sweetness, do I imagine you were sane?

I spared no detail in my tale when it came to your ultimatum that I move to Manhattan or we end the relationship, my moving here, and your subsequent emotional abandonment. Everyone "tsked" and shook their heads. I felt nothing. The end, when I explained how I woke up, realized I'd been fooled and found myself estranged in a bizarre and hostile city, then killed myself, garnered applause. It was mystifying.

"How is it you all seem to *feel* things? I haven't got an emotion. Not one." I looked around at them, stoically.

Rula sat pretzeled with Sammy, licking his ear and purring. He shivered. "Well, when you have a half-life full of maximum stimulation, your feelings get cranked. Maxing-out, it's good stuff."

"I miss my feelings. I think about how I would feel, but . . ." I shrugged.

"Hey, let's show Katy how we get off, huh?" Sammy gathered everyone together and we filed downstairs.

Oh, no. I'm weeping again. The pain, surging on me now like raging PMS, clenching my gut and bleeding me dry of tears. How I missed them. Like torture now, in the most ironic sense. But there they are. Damn.

If I thought New York was a war zone before this plague, I got to see guerrilla tactics up close that night. For them, a typical evening out "maxing" involves an abundance of activities. The women, as sexist as it seems, act as bait for the usuals, luring them places like the subway stations or the zoo in Central Park. There, expecting to have a bite of live flesh, they find themselves as subjects for "maxing."

Down in the subway, a hidden arsenal of baseball bats,

axes, clubs and knives aid in the restructuring of the usuals into disposable bits. The ultimate high comes when these elite types can get a dozen or more usuals down there and string them up like piñatas. At the zoo, the usuals are lured into cages where they are taken apart in spectacles Sammy likens to early Roman barbarism.

That night I watched it all without noticeable response. The next night was different. We went hunting. I'd wondered where they got the impeccably prepared human flesh at the party, and I found out. They search the living out, lure them with the most live-looking of the elite, by telling them of more secure housing or transportation out of the city. The captured "cunning and ruthless" ones are taken to Balducci's and slaughtered for food. You can't imagine what it's like to have someone who thinks that they are better than you—who are willing to throw you to the wolves first—in your power and watch them wither, humble and sniveling, into pot roast or tornadoes of flesh. I watched the whole process. My very first emotion was joy. Then disgust.

The live ones that Sammy's entourage can relate to, or intimidate, are invited to maintain their lives, protected by the elite, in exchange for their useful skills. They become the taxi drivers, subway engineers, beauticians, food preparers, waiters, maids, and the like. The third night out, I found a housekeeper for the apartment. She was so thankful to be spared, she ironed my sheets! The rush as I sensed her palpable fear was intoxicating.

Her name was Anisa, a Jamaican from Queens who was hiding in one of the best source hotels in the city, the Waldorf-Astoria. She didn't believe I was dead until I let her feel my pulse. She screamed for two full minutes, then fell to her knees to pray. We grew close, like friends, but I didn't tell her you were here. My eating habits and hygiene upset her enough, and she didn't want to be reminded that it's easy for me to take a life. I didn't want to lose her.

After the first month of maxing, like the others, I grew complacent with the resurgence of emotion, and then restless. I craved greater stimulation. Each of us, in turn, came up with new ways to max-out. One-Eye began performing surgical theater on the living who were destined for Balducci's, creating bizarre and sometimes wondrous creations in flesh as the patient howled and writhed on the table.

A former pimp named Smokey turned us onto "Splatters." We took the really fucked-up junkies who were too saturated with shit to eat and not skilled in anything useful and tossed them off the World Trade Center. Some of us got to heave, some receive on the ground. It was much more thrilling to throw them off as they pleaded and fought. Landings were simply messy and gruesome, unless they had last words or tried to drag their broken bodies away. Just a mild emotional jolt there, usually revulsion.

For two months, we tried other less stimulating games, but again we grew dysphoric. When those days of unease grew, I felt rages that ripped at my barely tethered soul, heartache that threatened to eat at my bones, gloom at my half-life condition, the killing, flesh consumption, head games, and endless struggle to keep up my appearance so that I was good enough to run with Sammy's crowd, that brought back the urge to snuff out the remaining life I had.

I recalled the utter anguish I knew when you told me time and time again how much you loved me, that everything you did, you did for us, yet how you stayed away all day and night only to crawl into bed exhausted and unwilling to share a word or scrap of affection. I replayed your hysterical fits of anger when you whined that I was so needy, that just my looking at you with my big sad eyes threw you into paroxysms of guilt and remorse for never being able to love me enough.

I believed you then. That it was all my fault. But now that I've had a year without emotions, most of it with you still alive and complaining that *I* was unavailable for *you,* and these last four months of soul-searching and emotional rescue, I can see what a fraud and master manipulator you were. My experience as a psychologist made me aware of such things in the lives of others, but in love I was blind, faithful to your vision. A warped and sick one. You coward. I've been released.

Damn, I'm crying again. Loss. I've never been tough enough with it.

Then it was my turn to find a maxing sport. I thought of those sex clubs you told me about from one of your seedier relationships. I couldn't remember any places, but as soon as I mentioned the idea to the others, some of them knew of live ones who had traded their lives for servitude in these dens of iniquity. Sammy kicked himself for not having thought of it sooner.

We piled into taxis and headed uptown. Twenty-sixth and Tenth Avenue. Close to the river. Lots of warehouses. As we walked from the corner, a summer drizzle was just starting up. I could smell the asphalt and the heat from the day rising up in the steam as the drizzle hit the street. And the stench of rotting flesh on bones that littered the entrances.

The twelve of us stood around outside this club like a bunch of kids caught out of school. I felt awkward, excited, *naughty*. There was nothing out front but a faded sign that read WHACKERS. The building was three stories tall. No windows. Just an imposing bulk of rusting sheet metal. We glanced over each other's shoulders casually at the odd clientele that seemed to bleed up from the cracks in the sidewalk. Two transvestites, looking like Laurel and Hardy in drag, ambled by. Then some old guys in ragged raincoats. A couple of butch biker babes. Four Upper East Side matrons, one I could swear was your friend Moira's mother. None of us moved as we got wet in the drizzle. We hadn't seen so many elite types in one place before besides us.

Sammy stepped away from us, eyeing a pretty slave girl, alive and not more than twenty years old, her face turned to the ground. She was leashed by a dog collar to a zombie master in an oxford-cloth shirt, polyester slacks, and heavy loafers just like the ones my seventh-grade math teacher wore. Sammy's gravelly voice cut through the quiet of the light rain.

"Whoa, she's what I want."

Her master turned and glared at him. "If I choose to auction her off for the night, you could never afford her." He sneered and pulled the young thing after him. Her coat flapped open in the breeze, exposing lots of living flesh and a smattering of black lace. I have to admit, she even made me hungry.

Sammy snorted. "Never underestimate the incomplete dead, man." We all nodded after him.

Rula yanked on One-Eye's sleeve, pouting. "I want to go in and have some fun. All I feel is bored."

One-Eye nodded. "Enough of this. Let's go on in."

We went in as one huddled mass. I looked up immediately. The ceiling was three stories tall in the gutted warehouse. Half of the wall that lined our way in was the bar, lit up like somebody's backyard barbecue at night. The patrons were drinking and talking, looking old and wrinkled; every facial flaw deeply etched, cast into shadows. Like dead people. A low fake-stone wall on the other side pointed us out onto a huge dance area. Centered there was a raised wooden platform, twenty feet square. Hanging ominously over that was a trapeze and gibbet. We hurried past some dancers as the loud rock music droned on and found ourselves in a circle of the fake stone.

I closed my eyes for a moment. The smells were unfamiliar; cheesy, rank, dusty, sweaty, oil-on-metal blended. The sounds of chains dragging, groaned conversations, and rubber hitting flesh made their way through the clamorous music. The ambience was one of desolation; stark and barren. I could feel it. I looked at the people, amazed at all the blank faces and empty eyes that looked back at me. Eyes of the living. I was awed. So many of us and so many live ones, all in one place and no one was feeding on the other.

Sammy pulled me further into the circle. There was a wooden frame there, where a naked Japanese woman stood chained by her ankles and wrists. Her black lover covered her body from our view as we moved closer. One-Eye was ahead of us. He turned back.

He shouted, "The guy's applying alligator clips to her nipples. This is serious S&M shit!"

Sammy swooned. "Maximum overload! I'm ready for this."

Rula leaned close and spoke into my ear. "I thought I'd seen everything, didn't you?" Her eyes were on the black man as he stepped away, the chain connecting the clips attached to his lover's nipples in his firm grasp.

"Not really." My eyes were riveted on the couple.

The black man yanked on the chain, twisting it, then pulled a rubber strap from his belt and began smacking her backside with it. I actually felt a shot of empathic pain.

Rula smiled wanly, leaning into me. "God, Katy, I'm feeling something. Something good."

Then I felt it, too. Sexual buzz. Sammy and the doctor were rubbing themselves against some of the girls like cats in heat. The black man began deep-kissing his woman. I was getting very turned on. *High.* I looked around, feeling anxious, sudden paranoia oozing from me like pus in a bad sore. Would anyone notice how naive I was? What now? Damn feelings. Things I can't control. Shit. Maximum stuff.

We found seats and watched the drama continue. There were more blank people with empty eyes, cold hearts, strumming each other, beating backsides, twisting, smacking and humiliating one another. Our group all came alive, our faces growing animated, reflecting the stirring within.

I noticed a troll-like woman beating a beautiful bare ass. When the man in her lap looked up, I recognized him as a regular on a television program I used to watch. The woman's mate stood by passively, his eye on me. He lumbered over.

"You want this?" He had an accent. Swedish. Norwegian. Exaggerated.

"Who, me?" I stared up at him, then past him to a huge mirrored ball suspended from the ceiling. Colors danced off of it like fireworks.

Sammy leaned over. "I do. Let me at the little bitch."

The guy lifted Sammy off of the bench. "She is the mistress. You want to get it, she give it to you. You don't touch her." He pointed to me. "I ask her, not you."

I cocked one eyebrow. "I don't want to be beaten." I shook my head.

"No, you give to live one. Gisella show you. This new for you, yes?"

I nodded. The guy was like a wall of meat with a shock

of white hair and small rat eyes. His voice was loud and deep, as if it came up from his bowels. He motioned for his partner to cut short her beating and join us.

She introduced herself. "I am Gisella, mistress of pain. You want to do this?" Her face reminded me of a gargoyle's and her accent was obviously fake. Now I wondered about his.

"Well, I don't know. . . ." Gisella began to turn away. "Yeah, I do. I want to try it." I tried to sound street-eager and worldly-wise. Me. The Vanilla Kid.

"Good." She groaned down at me. Grabbing her mate by the elbow, she shouted up to him.

"Take her to our room. Find her someone. Eric would be fine." She searched my eyes as if she could ascertain whether her choice was appropriate. "Yes, Eric."

The man reached out. "Come. I will take you to a bad boy who needs to be punished and disciplined. Follow me."

I stood. Gisella's gaze took in every pore of me as I turned to follow. She was licking her lips.

One-Eye stopped me as I went to pass him. "Katy, remember they are alive and we aren't aware of our strength. You could kill one. The rules, Katy, the rules."

"The rules?" I was in an emotional surge, unable to form a rational thought.

"Never take the life of anyone who might serve us or feed us. You could risk . . . well, there are stigmas attached. You know."

I did know. This was a tight group with scruples that worked. I was grateful to be a part of them and wouldn't want to lose them. God, no. And be alone again? Never.

I hurried after the master as he lumbered through the club. While we'd been watching the drama behind the wall, the room beyond had become crowded with old men in diapers with handcuffs and ankle manacles on, fat women in latex, *Rocky Horror*–type masters and mistresses, slimy-looking tax-consultant types in three-piece suits, their fists pumping under light wool worsted, and a whole gang of anorexic butch dykes whose tattoos gave their arms the appearance of being covered in black lace. The place now had the ambience of a chic Village club during a bad acid trip.

I could see the others in my group watching as I looked over my shoulder. My fear was growing the farther we got from the security of my friends.

We wended our way down a maze of hallways to a small room. It was occupied, so we turned to leave, but not before I saw the men in the dull neon lighting. Two guys in leather masks and G-strings were sodomizing a third man with the handle of a whip. The victim lay on his back with his knees up, on a concrete block. He made no sound, showed no sign of pain or pleasure, yet he quickly ejaculated over his belly at our arrival. The two perpetrators then argued between them over who was next.

I followed the master three doors down to another small room. Inside, three sweet, young, innocent-looking men stood against the wall smoking cigarettes and drinking. When we entered, the men fell to their knees and crawled to the master's boots and lowered their heads.

"Eric, stand." He was a third-year law-school dropout, bad-boy good-looking and alive. He began to grin when he saw who his mistress was, but the master frowned. "You will obey Mistress Katrina all evening. If she is not pleased, you will feed us, understand?"

Eric nodded nervously.

"You boys come with me." The man turned, walked out, and the other guys followed.

I pulled anxiously on a stray hair. "So, Eric, you come here often?" I stared at the floor, embarrassed.

"I live here, protected, so that I may serve you and others like you. You are . . . dead?"

"You're not sure?" I was flattered. Again.

"Sometimes not. So, how may I serve you, mistress?" He sounded mildly disinterested.

"Well, first of all, you could sound like you're into it. And take off those preppy clothes. Now!" An anger jolt. Appropriate for the moment. He was immediately chastised and eager to please. His clothes came off quickly and he stood before me.

He had a beautiful, youthful hardbody. Nothing sagging

or bloating or getting funny hairs on it like yours. He wore rings in his nipples and scrotum. They glittered in the single bare bulb light. He clasped his hands and bowed his head.

"I am yours, sweet mistress. I will submit to any pain or humiliation to serve you, gratify you."

I found a concrete seat and sat down. Behind me were whips and vinyl straps and restraining gear.

"I have to confess. I've never done this before." I was feeling awkward, inept. Not exactly feelings I missed.

He fell to my feet, kissing my red high heels. I grabbed him by the hair and lifted his head. His mouth was open just a bit and I found his lips very inviting. I began to kiss him, then pulled away.

"No. You must earn my kisses. Lay down here." I reached up and took some handcuffs, a bit of rope, and a whip as he reclined on the slab of cement beside me.

You would be screaming about now for me to shut up. You wouldn't want to hear a word about my sexual pleasure with anyone else but you. Ha. Pleasure with you . . . was fleeting. And not often. How many times can a woman watch a man lose his erection during lovemaking and finish almost every time with him jerking off, his eyes closed, his heart and mind closed, closeted in a fantasy where she is nowhere to be found? And be told it is all her fault. I needed to know it wasn't me. It wasn't me!

I found the anger and will to inflict pain on pretty Eric by thinking of you. I could have killed him if he hadn't begun to cry.

"Eric, what . . . what's happening?"

"Oh, Mistress Katrina, I am afraid you're strangling me. I deserve the pain. But I don't want to die." He wept, deeply. I took him up in my arms and held him. When the tears subsided, he told me how he'd held in his fear and anguish now for over a year, but he'd never been so close to dying.

"I must stop. I'm so turned on, I'm out of my mind. So angry, so intoxicated." I wiped his tears from his cheeks.

"I . . . I am turned on, also." He lifted his hips. His

cock was swollen. "But not here. It's not allowed. Only pain, no release."

"No sex, sex?"

He shook his head. I gave him our address and he met me there in the morning. He had to sneak out. It was so hot. God, I want to feel that right now. Too bad you couldn't perform. Maybe if I just take a look and see if it was all preserved . . .

Yes. Your broken middle-aged body and all its parts are intact. Funny, I would have thought I'd still want you. But I don't. Not like the others.

There have been others. Many. That's how I find myself here in the musty basement talking to you. So many. I'll go on.

That first night, Sammy ended up with Gisella while her mate, Wert, watched. Rula found two dykes, One-Eye got the slave girl, and Smokey took the Upper East Side matrons for the rides of their lives. So naturally we went back. Every night. They've all run together. I found a constant high. We all have.

And I crashed. One by one, we reached incredible ecstasy and maintained it, only to find ourselves growing more restless, anxious, surly, hungry. We tried to stay away for a few nights, try other maxing sports. It was no good.

Anisa told me she thought I was looking strung out. I heard her. We weren't just getting our feelings recharged, we were getting hooked. She told me back what I'd told her about you, your becoming a human doing instead of a human being. I remembered how you escaped your feelings of horrible shame and inadequacy in your "stuff." I've been escaping the existence I knew without feelings, then running from the feelings of pain and sorrow I get now that I'm emoting. I thought right then about quitting.

I couldn't stop. Nor could anyone else.

It was five days ago that we all hustled back to Whackers. It was auction night. We'd amassed a huge amount of "cash" over the weeks we'd been going to the club, buying drinks and flesh snacks and getting tickets good at auction as money.

Zelda, a three-hundred-pound Raggedy Ann look-alike

in leather, was the emcee. One by one, she announced willing victims and masters or mistresses for sale. Each of them stood on the platform and showed the crowd their bottoms or panties or genitals. I passed on a thirty-year-old computer nerd with a cute ass and the promise that he could take all of the spanking I might administer. I said no to a fiftyish banker type who wanted to be verbally humiliated. I balked on a couple that looked too mean to take orders. Then there was Tio.

Tio was a slight, beautiful Italian man. He danced off his lace panties from under his maid's costume to show all of us his pretty cock and buttocks. He flirted with the crowd, who began counting their tickets. Tio was willing to be a doormat, to lick and suck and pander to any orifice, to be beaten, humiliated, forced to degrade himself in extraordinary ways. He came with a key to the Dungeon. The response was huge.

Sammy saw me drooling, and knew that I would also want to save Tio from the hands of someone harsher and indifferent. He handed me his entire wad of tickets. Tio was mine.

For such a seasoned deviant, I was going to be a disappointment, I feared. Tio followed me obediently to one of the overstuffed sofas in the back of the room. Eric hurried over, excited for me.

"You have a key to the Dungeon! I've always wanted to go there. Mistress Katrina, you're lucky."

Suddenly, the thought of having the security of Eric along lessened my anxiety. "Come join us." I looked at Tio.

"Mistress, I will be a slave to you both. I will eat the cum from you after he has you. I will do anything for you." His accent was slight, charming.

I looked to Eric. "Is it all right to do whatever, the things we can't do here . . . in the Dungeon?"

Eric nodded. "It's in the basement, separate. Its own domain. I'll show you."

Remember the book on the Inquisition we looked at in that strange bookstore in San Francisco? This was a torture chamber to rival that. In the center of the room was a wrought-iron chandelier hanging loosely from the ceiling. On the walls were numerous hooks bearing every form of device I saw in that book as well as others I knew from the Tower of London tour. There were breast rippers, metal pears for any orifice, spiked necklaces and belts, cat's paws, a ladder-type rack, thumbscrews, whips, and gags. A long rack and pillory sat at one end of the room. An inquisitor's chair, scavenger's daughter, and iron maiden filled the main part of the dungeon. An open closet carried clothing, shelves with towels, bandages, and a spigot in the sink by the door dripped rusty water into a pail. With the room dimly lit like an intimate dinner party, I could barely find a place to sit until my eyes adjusted.

Eric knelt before me, stripped himself bare, and offered up a heretic's fork. "I deserve to wear this. I have blasphemed against the higher order."

"I don't know how it works." I grinned at Tio.

"I will show you, mistress." His hands shook as he placed the forked ends, one under Eric's chin, the other on his breastbone, then joined the metal notches on the collar securely behind Eric's head. The metal bar, from fork to fork, held Eric's head up at a sharp angle, stiffly.

"Can you speak?" I could see his eyes tearing up.

He garbled out a no, pulling me to him. He pushed my skirt up to my waist and took down my panties. With his head in the arched-back position, I had only to step over his face and find ecstasy.

Tio began touching my breasts as I took a step forward.

I was weakened by the orgasm and yet, with the level of addiction I had to the high, I couldn't stop. Tio crawled up onto the rack. Eric knelt beside it, whimpering in pain. I strapped Tio down and pulled a leather mask over his face until only his eyes and mouth were exposed. I rammed a gagball into his mouth, reeling with adrenaline and lust.

I cranked the ropes holding Tio tighter. He squealed around the metal ball. I grabbed two whips, one cat-o'-nine-tails, and a rectal pear. I set the whips down and greased up the metal orb. It slid too easily up Tio's ass. I kept turning the handle of the pear so that it could split into its four segments and fan out to stretch the walls of his rectum. I twisted until it no longer moved. Tio's eyes were wide with a pleasure I still didn't understand.

I began whipping Tio; the anger over your abandonment escalated my furor. I thought of how you made us a home here in New York, introduced me to all of your friends who quickly lost interest in me, went off to work, and never came back. I thought of what I'd given up back home. A husband, a good practice, my family and friends, and my house. For love. For the version you promised and never even got close to. Why? Why! I flogged Tio for the last two years I waited and believed I'd get loved back.

I got hotter and hotter, until I could no longer ignore the turgid product of my efforts on Tio. I climbed on top of him, impaled myself on his flesh, live, warm, pulsing inside of me. I grasped at his face mask, my mouth seeking his lips that were swollen around the ball. I bucked over him until I shouted into another climax.

I fell across his chest and lay my head at his chin. He seemed so quiet, still. I ripped out the gagball and put my lips to his. I noticed immediately how cold they were. Deathly cold.

Turning to Eric, I saw blood running down his chest from the fork in his breastbone. His eyes were huge. I moved off of Tio and undid the heretic's fork from around Eric's neck. He let his head fall, working his jaw.

I was shaking now. "He's dead, Eric. I killed him." Fear rose in my gut, claws extended.

Eric stood up, loosened the mask on Tio, and felt for a pulse. He shook his his head.

"Oh my God. What am I going to do? The others. They'll know. . . ."

Eric put his arm around me. "Mistress, we're in the Dungeon. It's all right. No one will know. Tio? He got what he wanted. He found heaven in your hands. Now you have to consume him."

"Eat him? Oh, then no one will find—"

"It's the last pleasure in this, his pleasure and yours. No one will know unless you tell them."

I thought of you. *Dead* dead. Soul in heaven. Forever, never to walk on this earth again. And I felt so sad. What if they knew about you, that I've been hoarding you all of this time?

"I can't. He's not prepared. I'm not a 'usual,' slathering over just any body." I slammed my fist on Tio's chest. "Damn you! Why did you have to die on me?!"

Eric took my shoulders in his hands and shook me. "Stop this. Be here with me. I want you to give me what you gave Tio. I've never witnessed such rapture. I am unworthy of anything less now. Give me death. Glorious death."

"What? How could you ask that? Can't you see how I feel?"

"If you don't, I'll tell them. Your friends." He got down on his knees, begging.

I broke down. I heaved sobs into a towel as I sat on the floor, so much built up from so many tiny sorrows over the year, flooding me. The loneliness, the angst, the regret. Simmering all this time, it erupted.

I lost track of time, but when the tears were fewer and quieter, I felt a hand on my head. My face and stomach hurt. I didn't want to deal with Eric's demand now. The hand lifted my face. It was Tio!

Tio, half-dead. A zombie masochist lover, doomed to forever take the punishment of others. For eternity. And I didn't care. All I knew was that Eric was gone and soon the others would know. Soon, once again, I would walk alone. All because I wanted to share some feelings with someone.

Damn, here come the tears.

And there you are, with sunken orbs not seeing, you with whom I wanted to walk always. You, whom I killed in the hopes we would both know the half-life, stay God-damned stone-cold dead in the corner. And some fucking Italian pervert gets a half-life on me!

In my heart that beats stronger, I feel your loss. A cruel injustice I can feel! The guilt, remorse, my misery. And you would tell me I asked for it. That I knew better, but I followed my impulse, anything to cure my despair. "Any act of desperation creates devastation in its wake," or something like that. I may be paying for taking your life, but I'll find a way to make it through. I've learned that I'm better than you made me think I was. So what if I walk alone . . .

I traded what remained of my soul for what I imagined would be sweet passion's return, a little emotional rescue. Some companionship in the name of love. Damn. But there is no love in this half-life. I have you now, you selfish asshole, and I won't find any more love here than I had before.

It's all over. The high life. I may not be able to get served at Balducci's anymore, or go to hot parties, but I'll find another way. Until then, I make do with you, you miserable fuck. Leftovers don't bother me.

UNDISCOVERED COUNTRIES

J. S. RUSSELL

The top of the skull was attached with velcro. Hodge shuddered slightly as Dr. Chari thrust two fingers beneath the scalp and tore back the dark skin and wiry hair.

"Come over here and look through the magnifier," Chari said.

Hodge walked the long way around and leaned over the body till his forehead brushed Chari's.

"See these striations within the sulci?" Chari asked.

"They look more like furrows," Hodge said. He adjusted the magnification and focus. "Jesus, they're goddamn trenches."

The brain was severely desiccated. The velcro seal was hardly air-tight, and dark blotches had formed across the pale grey surface of the cerebral cortex.

"What about the pattern?" Hodge asked.

"Non-specific so far as I can tell. You can see that

initially the striations followed the fissures of the sulci before branching off. Like starting a pathway at a natural clearing in a thicket.''

Hodge nodded. The furrows formed an intricate concentric design, which spiraled like a staircase through the meninges and down into the cerebrum. Chari had driven a plastic, surgical shim between the right and left hemispheres, neatly bisecting the corpus callosum.

''Now look at this,'' Chari said.

She snipped at a line of sutures that ran along the base of the cerebrum and slid a retractor underneath. She pried up a thin layer of tissue, then cut away another line of sutures and raised up the entire cerebrum just enough so that Hodge could get a good look.

''Jesus, Mary, and Joseph,'' he said. Chari allowed herself a smile.

The pustules hadn't been at all visible through the thick, vascular pia mater, but seen from beneath, it was clear that the cortex was rife with a thin layer of tiny purple lesions, growing like wild mushrooms.

Below that, the cerebellum and brainstem were positively *alive* with the bubbling pustules. They were slick and puffy and attached to the ridged brain surface like weeping sores. Chari prodded them with the flat edge of a scalpel and they gurgled slightly, roiling like overcooked, rancid oatmeal.

''Look here,'' Chari said.

She let the cerebrum slip back into place, and forcefully worked a syringe through the tough, fibrous dura and weblike arachnoid. She eased back the plunger until a viscous, mauve fluid spilled into the hypo, then withdrew the needle.

''Suhh . . . no, it can't . . .'' Hodge shook his head, but Chari was nodding.

''Cerebrospinal fluid,'' she said, and laughed nervously. ''And you ain't seen nothing yet.''

Chari handed the syringe to Hodge then walked over to the far wall.

''Girls,'' she said, flicking off the lights, ''you'd better hang on to your boyfriends.''

The fluorescent ceiling lamps had been the room's sole

source of illumination, but now a faint purple glow emanated from the syringe in Hodge's hand. The fluid was phosphorescent, and bright enough to cast Hodge's face in twisted, expressionistic shadows. But there was another light as well.

Hodge looked down at the body, saw the same violet glimmer spilling dimly from the opened skull. Hodge gasped as he watched the pulsating legions flicker like Christmas bulbs across the peeled-back cerebral cortex, fed by racing currents of the radiant fluid.

"I haven't the slightest idea why it does that," Chari said.

She turned the lights on again and walked back toward Hodge, who was still gaping at the exposed brain.

"And now for the big finish." Chari rooted through a tray of surgical instruments. "Where the hell is the . . . oh, screw it."

She leaned over and carefully but firmly grabbed the protruding edge of the shim between thumb and forefinger and, with a clean jerk, yanked it out of the brain.

Instantly, the corpse's eyes opened wide, the dilated pupils irising down to pinpoints and focusing on Chari.

The jaws mechanically opened and closed and a bloated, blackened tongue distended and flicked obscenely at the doctor. The stench of rotten meat wafted from its maw. It tried to lean forward, but Chari had disabled all motor function below the neck.

Hodge shrank away from the corpse, but Chari held her ground, watching the frantic gurgling of the purple lesions with something like awe.

She looked up at Hodge then, her face set in the widest smile he'd ever seen.

"I call him Mort," Chari said.

Hodge sighed deeply when he saw that his wife was watching the Zombie Channel again. She sat stiffly in a high-backed chair she'd dragged in from the dining room, swinging a cigarette back and forth between her lips and her ashtray in a regular, almost metronomic motion. Her head was tilted back against the top of the chair at an uncomfortable-looking angle, as if she was waiting for a shampoo.

Hodge came up behind her and planted a lifeless kiss on her forehead. Keiko was sweaty, and breathing hard. Her skin tasted of garlic and nicotine.

She didn't look up from the screen.

Three soldiers in Cermet body armor were circling around a gangrenous zombie in a ramshackle hut. Most of the action was Third World, these days, and the African footage consistently scored the highest ratings.

The perspective switched back and forth between cameras mounted in each soldier's helmet. A blinking digital readout in the corner of the screen marked time to the hundredth of a second. The rapid cross-cutting made Hodge slightly queasy, but Keiko didn't seem at all bothered.

The zombie was in bad shape; one eye was gone and a row of fractured, grey ribs poked out through its bloody chest. Hodge saw that the soldiers could finish it at anytime, but were dragging it out for the sake of a little drama.

"I don't like you watching this," Hodge said.

Keiko took a final drag on her cigarette, then snuffed it out and blew the smoke in Hodge's face.

Two of the soldiers had snared the zombie's arms in razor-wire lassos and pulled in opposite directions while the third, whose camera was active, circled slowly around them. Dark fluid spurted from the zombie's formerly bulging biceps as the wire dug through the mushy black flesh.

"I said—"

"Michael had an incident today."

"What?"

The circling soldier meticulously fired a couple of dozen rounds of tiny magnesium charges into the zombie's body. Each charge impacted with a sound like overripe fruit dropped from a great height. Keiko grabbed the remote and turned up the volume.

"What kind of incident? What happened?"

Keiko didn't answer. Hodge stepped directly in front of her, but her eyes never moved, as if she could see right through him to the big screen.

"Talk to me, goddammit."

Keiko stood up slightly, turned the chair ninety degrees to the left and sat back down. She turned on a second wall screen with the remote, then touched another button: each screen displayed the point of view from a different camera.

Half the room was now alive with video as the zombie began to smolder. Thin streams of smoke rose out of the tiny holes in its body as it started to jerk and spasm. The soldiers holding the creature closed the snares, severing the arms cleanly above the elbows. The zombie frantically flailed its stumps.

Hodge grabbed for the remote, but Keiko was too fast. She punched another button and a third screen, on the wall opposite to the second, lit up.

Three walls, three screens, three camera angles.

"His implant went haywire."

"Jesus Christ," Hodge exhaled.

The soldiers stepped back from the action. Camera one was in long shot, and camera two in medium, while the third held the creature's contorted face in brutal close-up.

Keiko punched the buttons, rearranging the images so that the close-up appeared on the largest, center screen. She was practically panting now, and dime-sized drops of sweat trickled down the side of her face.

Plumes of dark grey smoke billowed from the zombie.

"He was in class," she gasped, "when the corpse-men burst in. The teacher verified that he hadn't died, but they had to shoot him up and take him in."

"Procedure," Hodge said, nodding.

Keiko took an extra deep breath and held it.

The zombie threw back its head and then exploded. Dark grue spattered two of the lenses, spoiling the picture, but number three was a pro. He tracked the head as it detached from the torso, and kept it in frame as it hurtled through the air. Blood blossomed from the open mouth, and the remaining eye was blown out by the pressure.

Keiko exhaled with a throaty moan as the head ricocheted off the ceiling. All three screens went to close-up now, and slo-mo kicked in as the head spiraled down, cracking open on impact with the floor.

Keiko lit up another cigarette.

"They diagnosed the malfunction and put in a new implant. The doctor said it's a better model than what he had, and told me it was a lucky thing he happened to be in a roomful of witnesses, or . . ."

Hodge ran a hand through his thinning hair, and finally sat down on the futon. He stared vacantly at the one wall without a screen.

"Lucky," he said.

"Anyway, he's still in the hospital. They said he won't be conscious for another few hours, but they wouldn't let us see him, anyway. Not for twenty-four hours."

"Procedure. Why didn't you call me?"

"How do you know I didn't?"

The soldiers finished prying open the skull and fried the brain with electric prods. Hodge could now make out the characteristic furrows, though he had never noticed them before. He could even see some of the tiny lesions as they sizzled.

You had to know what to look for, he thought. Like the old lady and the young girl in the optical illusion. You only see one until someone points the other out to you. Then you can never *not* see it again.

"Let's fuck," Keiko said.

"This is crazy," Hodge said.

"That's what Mr. Hyde said to Dr. Jekyll," Chari quipped, but Hodge didn't laugh.

"We should at least bring in some security."

"Oh, yes. And let's have CNN cover it live, too."

Chari was stooped over Mort's open brain case, looking through the magnifier. Her gloved hands deftly manipulated the laser micro-scalpel. Hodge stood by as ad hoc scrub nurse, passing her the odd instrument and looking nervous.

"What if—"

"Look, Bill. I will stop if you want, but I thought we'd been through this. Mort's a quad, guaranteed, so there's no real danger. And seeing how we've already trounced over at least a dozen CDC regs, I don't see where one more really matters. Besides, what Phaedra Pharmaceutical doesn't know can't hurt them.''

''But *I* know, and *I'm* supposed to be responsible to them.''

''You're young. You'll find other work.''

Hodge still wasn't laughing, but he gave Chari the nod anyway. ''Middle-management lackey destroys world,'' he mumbled.

''Courageous administrator approves immortality project,'' Chari corrected. ''Besides, it's Frankenstein that everyone remembers, not his supervisor.''

''But everyone also thinks that Frankenstein is the monster.''

Chari didn't seem to find that amusing. She restored the last of the severed links in Mort's neural network and withdrew the laser. She then turned off the surgical lamp. Spreading tendrils of glowing mauve fluid were immediately visible as they raced through the brain.

''Better than barium,'' Chari said, marveling.

Within minutes a ridge of violet pustules, big as jujubes, had sprouted along the outer surface of the dura mater. Mort's entire brain expanded and contracted within the skull, the heavy folds of the gyri randomly inflating till the organ began bulging beyond the confines of its bony casing.

''Jesus, what the hell is happening?''

Chari shook her head. A number of the pustules had burst, spewing the thick, fluorescent fluid up in tiny purple geysers that stained Chari's lab coat.

''Make it stop, Ilona. Make it . . .''

The corpse's eyes shot open. Its jaw dropped and the creature started to moan, the swollen tongue mercifully muffling the monstrous sound. The small volume of air in its lungs was quickly expended, but its mouth hung open, the eyes still wide with terror as it tried to express its agony.

Its eyes were like capers floating in bloody milk. They darted left and right, settling finally on Hodge's astonished face.

Hodge didn't want to look, but he couldn't turn away. The creature had fixed on him as it continued its voiceless scream. With great effort the corpse managed to move its head and peered down at its decayed and useless body.

Mort looked back up at Hodge, its features twisted in desperate panic. Hodge saw its lips start to move, but just then the creature was racked by a series of spasms. A great spray of glowing liquid splooshed out from the open skull.

Chari said something but Hodge didn't hear it. His eyes were glued to the creature's shuddering lips.

Chari grabbed a shim from the table beside Hodge and brutally rammed it into Mort's brain.

The spasms ended and the eyes went dead, but the lips remained twisted in what Hodge believed could only be a curse.

When he finally turned to Chari, he saw she was back at her desk, frantically scribbling notes on a legal pad.

The man's sweaty, jaundiced face was in excruciating close-up on the screen. His eyes bulged out of their sockets, magnified and contained, it seemed, only by the thick lenses of his welfare-frame glasses. His eyebrows bobbed up and down like silverfish.

"For the Lord sayeth, 'If a man die, shall he live again?' And I say to you the answer is upon us, brethren, and the answer, most righteously, is yes. Yes, I say to you."

The camera pulled back a bit. A silent, robed choir stood behind the preacher, nodding vigorously at his every inflection.

"But man dieth and wasteth away: yea, man giveth up the ghost, and where is he? Where, you ask? Where? *Here,* is the answer.

"He discovereth deep things out of darkness, and bringeth out to light the shadow of death."

Hodge glanced away from the Right-to-Undeath preacher, and looked at his son. The only movement was the slight rise and fall of Mikey's chest facilitated by the respirator. Hodge eyed the cardiac monitor the way a nervous broker might eye the ticker on an October Monday.

An infection from the new implant caused the fever,

which had raged for a week. It was just one of those things. Antibiotics had no effect, and Mikey's brain activity was near zero. When the last tiny spike disappeared from his chart, they would be legally obliged to decapitate.

The voice drew his attention back to the screen.

"I will ransom them from the power of the grave; I will redeem them from death: O death, I will be thy plagues: O grave, I will be thy destruction."

Hodge remembered when his father had been in the hospital, with wires and machines hooked up every which way just like Mikey. Hodge had been in the room when the cardiac distress alarm went off.

He remembered how doctors and nurses came running from every direction, with crash carts and defibrillation paddles and grim determination. They had worked on his father for forty minutes before surrendering to the inevitable.

"I am he that liveth, and was dead; and behold, I am alive for evermore, Amen; and have the keys of hell and of death.

"To him that overcometh will I give to eat of the tree of life."

Hodge was on constant edge, waiting once again for the shrill peal of the alarm. He knew the reaction would be different now. No doctors and nurses, only armed guards and an emergency autopsy team.

It was too risky to permit anyone more than their one chance to live.

"He shall rule them with a rod of iron. I will not blot out his name out of the book of life."

Hodge was sobbing to himself. A nurse walked in the door, but turned quickly around when she saw him.

"Be thou faithful unto death, and I will give thee a crown of life."

The preacher's eyes, nose, and mouth completely filled the screen. A small piece of gristle dangled from between his yellowed front teeth.

"And *yes*. I said *yes*. I will. *Yes*."

•   •   •

"Mort's dead," Chari said.

Hodge tiredly looked up from his paperwork. "Yeah . . . ?"

Chari stood in the doorway hugging the jamb, one foot in, the other outside of Hodge's office.

"No, I mean he's really dead. Dead again. For good. Probably. I'm waiting on decapitation, just to be sure."

Hodge leaned back in his chair and gestured for Chari to come in and sit down, but she continued to slow-dance with the door frame.

"What happened?"

"I'm not sure. The virus didn't survive in the forebrain. It's funny, it seemed to be taking until I reactivated the neural network. Then, well, you saw."

Hodge flashed back on the look of horror on the corpse's reanimated face. He nodded.

"I'm thinking," Chari went on, "that it just got fried in the cortex. The electrical charge in the forebrain is slightly higher than in the brainstem. They're both so slight that we normally wouldn't worry about the difference, but to an organic substance that was growing there, it might be like walking along the third rail as somebody suddenly turns on the juice."

"What does it mean for the project?" Hodge asked.

Chari finally let go of the door and came into the office. She could hear the trace of desperate hope in his voice. She stood behind a leather armchair, stroking the headrest with the back of her hand and shaking her head.

"It's a big step back," she said with great deliberation. "The regeneration in brain tissue is only promulgated under the influence of the virus. Without successful regeneration of higher-level functions, I just don't see any means for maintaining control. I don't know, the gentech section has some new ideas. Maybe between us, we can make sense of things."

Hodge raised an eyebrow.

"Yeah," Chari said, "the report's written and filed. Don't worry, your lackey ass is covered."

They sat in silence for a while.

"You want to hear something stupid?" Chari asked.

''What?''

''I'd sort of come to like old Mort.'' Chari smiled demurely, but the look reeked of artifice.

''Never give them names,'' Hodge said.

''I know, I know. I've always done it, though. When I was a grad student, I used to name all those dopey lab rats. I'd end up all teary-eyed when it came time to fractionate them.''

Chari plucked an old styrofoam coffee cup off the armrest, and swirled the rancid dregs. ''You know, after rat brains have been centrifuged, they look exactly like that chocolate diet drink stuff. It's been the ruin of my figure.''

Chari put the cup down and headed back out of the office, stopping for a final turn with the jamb.

''I thought we had something there for a minute,'' she said. ''It's terribly unobjective, I know, but for a second or two after the reconnection I thought I saw a trace of, ummm, intelligence on Mort's face. Did you get any sense of that?''

Hodge was again staring down at his papers, but he saw in his mind the corpse's expression as it glanced down at itself. The terror in its eyes, the burgeoning plea on its lips.

''No,'' Hodge lied.

''Probably just a reflex,'' Chari said, and went out.

''Ilona . . .''

Chari ducked her head back into his office. Hodge forced himself to meet her gaze.

''Do you believe that there's dignity in death?''

Chari was about to say something smart, but caught herself. She thought about Hodge's son in the hospital, and all the possible responses, including the one she knew that Hodge wanted to hear. She settled on the truth.

''No,'' she said.

''Me either,'' Hodge said.

The barbed wire and cyclone fencing was really unnecessary at this point, but it seemed to make people in the area feel better, so they left it up.

The guard at the gate was pretty much a formality as

well, but his presence was still mandated by law. Although appearing to possess all the cunning instincts of a retired bank guard, he was always pleasant enough to Hodge. Hodge suspected the man welcomed any living visitors he could get.

Other than the guard and Hodge, the cemetery was deserted, both aboveground and below. Bright rectangles of thick, new sod stood out like hair-transplant plugs atop the graves, although a goodly number of the plots had yet to be reseeded.

The corpses that hadn't dug their own way out of the ground in the first few days had later been exhumed and torched during the long and ongoing cleanup process. Many of the headstones were charred, and a number had been broken or vandalized and not replaced. The cemetery hadn't been razed, however, though many had favored such a solution.

Hodge spent a great deal of time at the boneyard now, taking great comfort in the isolation and quietude. He had tried several times to get Keiko to accompany him or at least go on her own, believing it was what she needed. But she spent her days staring at the screens, bingeing on the endless loop of violent, final death.

It all made Hodge quite ill.

He never went directly to Mikey's plot. He preferred to walk slowly around the cemetery, stopping occasionally to read the chiseled inscriptions, still playing the game of finding the oldest grave.

Sometimes he didn't visit his son's grave at all. He just walked a slow circle around the yard—or sat in the grass and stared—and tried, most of all, not to cry.

Near the end, he had begged Chari to look at the boy. She was loath to get involved, but didn't know how to refuse.

"The organism," Hodge had entreated. "What if it were introduced into a living subject? Into Mikey?"

Chari was horrified but not surprised.

"No, Bill," she said. "You know that we aren't even close to that stage of the program. Human subjects are . . . Think of Mort."

Hodge did, but the memory no longer mattered. Mort had at least returned to life, and his son was about to die.

"For God's sake, Ilona. They're going to chop his head off. They're going to cut my son's head off."

Chari tried to reason with him, but it was impossible. She mollified him by agreeing to perform the spinal tap. "Exploratory," she told him.

Knowingly, she insisted that Hodge remain in the room as she drew the fluid. The boy never moved or made a sound as the thick needle penetrated his lower back.

With the sample still in her hand, Chari went over and closed the blinds. Hodge was stroking his son's feverish brow and didn't notice until she turned off the lights.

An ever-so-faint mauve glow shimmered slightly in Chari's shaking hand.

And he knew.

The autopsy team took the boy away within the hour.

Without even realizing it, Hodge found himself standing at the foot of Mikey's grave, not that the boy's body was actually buried below. The laws were very strict about that. They had merely buried some ashes, along with a photograph, and the boy's favorite stuffed animal: a purple-and-yellow cow that Mikey had unaccountably named Becky.

Few people even bothered with burial these days, but Hodge had insisted on it. He couldn't explain why at the time, but thought that perhaps he somehow knew how important it would be to him to have a grave to come to later.

Even in a world where death's undiscovered country held inconstant borders, there was an odd sort of peace to be found in such a place.

The day was almost gone. Clouds in the western sky radiated a majestic purple that sent a shudder through Hodge's body.

In the background, he heard the faint rattle of the guard's keyring, and knew the man was getting ready to lock the cemetery up for the night.

Hodge wasn't ready to go. He wasn't ready.

As night fell, Hodge cried, but no sound emerged as his bitter tears fell on an empty grave.

MOON TOWERS

BROOKS CARUTHERS

I

We have a new moon. It arrived only a few weeks after the dead began to walk again. It is young and swift, easily outrunning tired Diana in the evening, making a mockery of Apollo's chariot by day. The new moon is a rainbow matrix of pinlights on a small yellow sphere, a jewel-encrusted ball that cruises the heavens, rippling with color.

My beloved Viva dances in the new moon light. It washes her skin with a sickly, jaundiced hue. The pinlight colors glisten in her sweat. Her eyes shine with its rainbow waves. The new moles that cover her skin make her look like a wild, spotted animal. Her dance is precise, controlled. One moment she stands frozen, except for her arms which seem to rise toward the sky of their own volition. Then suddenly she is a whirling dervish, sweeping across the clearing in front of Tomkins's farmhouse. She stops again, but now her body undulates like an underwater plant.

Tomkins releases the cord binding his arm. "Beautiful." The hypodermic falls to the ground. "Beautiful. I can hear the music she dances to. The music of the moon." Doc and I nod. The flux of colors is like music, visual music, and watching Viva I imagine a sound like wind blowing through hollow trees and ancient canyons.

"We can hear it because we're tuned into it," says Doc. "The colors of the satellite are identical to the colors of the auras I photographed."

Photographing auras. I remember that. Click. I kiss Viva. Click. Pressed together. Click. Hands exploring genitals. Doc refocusing his camera. Click, click. I enter Viva. She pulls me deeper. Click. Our motions show as sensual blurs on the prints. Viva moans. I come. Click.

In the best prints, the best pictures, there is no me and no her. There is just this colored light, outlining a shape that may be us.

I met Doc and Viva in a pizza place called Vino's—until recently, the only place in Little Rock where you could get Bass Ale on tap. It was only two months before the dead arose. Vino's was downtown and it tended to be a magnet for art students, poets, musicians, and various other poseurs. I was sitting there with my friend Richard and we were checking out all the people dressed in black and making snide comments, speculating how many of them talked a good game to justify their dead-end jobs. When we realized we were describing ourselves, we drunkenly declared that we were the two biggest poseurs in the joint.

"Wish I'd seen that girl who pissed on stage last week for some performance art thing," said Richard.

"Pissing on stage? Hell, that's old hat," said I.

"Well yeah, but at least it takes more guts than the standing on one leg reading poetry kind of crap that we usually get around here. And besides"—he switched to his hick voice—"at least we'd have seen her damn *butt*."

"Hey Doc," said someone at the table next to us, "these guys are talking about your wife."

I turned and saw Tomkins. Scruffy beard and dirty-blond hair. I'd met him here several times before and he seemed nice enough. Always invited me out to his farmhouse to see some pictures. I always made excuses. He never looked too healthy, and right now he looked like a vegetarian that never studied nutrition.

Sitting with Tomkins was a grey-headed man in a short-sleeve button-down shirt. Doc. I stared dumbly at him while Richard said, "Oh wow! Did your wife really piss on stage?"

"Yes, she did."

I found my voice. "Why?"

"She was doing a piece called 'Euphemisms.' She constructed a story from a variety of sayings and clichés and then demonstrated what each saying meant while telling the story. At one point she had fifteen different expressions for pissing, so . . ."

We joined Doc at his table for a long conversation and several pitchers of beer. He said he was an art professor, but he never said where he taught. Our conversation drifted from industrial music to small press publications to strange videos, then Doc started talking about Kirilian photography and I said I thought that kind of bullshit went out with the seventies and just as things were beginning to heat up the most beautiful woman in the world came in and put an arm around Doc's shoulders.

"This is my wife, Viva."

She was at least ten years younger than Doc. Pale smooth white skin and peroxide punk hair. The laugh lines on her face gave her a look of perpetual, skeptical amusement. Her eyes were a blue so pale they seemed to be glowing. They transfixed me like an animal caught in car headlights. I distantly heard her voice say, "Invite your friend to dinner."

Friend? I looked around and realized Richard had left about fifteen minutes ago. Doc wrote something on a napkin. "Looks like I have to go now." He handed the napkin to me. "I'd like to talk to you some more. Why don't you come by our place tomorrow night. We do great chicken curry.''

I finally broke my gaze from Viva. "Sounds good.''

I scan the clearing. So far no dead have arrived. The initial hordes have dwindled. Their ashes surround the farmhouse. But we still we get a few. Tonight we're counting on them.

Tomkins contemplates his pistol. It's a vintage Colt .45 from the vintage gangster twenties. Another one of his toys.

Viva now stands in the middle of the clearing. Tomkins locks eyes with her. "It's time.''

"Wait,'' says Doc.

Tomkins rises from his chair. "I want to go now, before I come down. This way I'll meet Jim Carroll.'' He walks across the clearing to Viva, who waits with arms outstretched. He kneels before her and raises his pistol as an offering. She takes it and rests the muzzle on his forehead.

The vintage gun makes a vintage noise and Viva drops it next to Tomkins's body in the clearing. Tears streak an otherwise expressionless face.

Doc shakes his head. "Too soon. They may not go for him now.''

"Our society is obsessed with death because we try to deny it.'' Doc spooned curried chicken onto my plate. "I mean, we're used to eating dinner while watching death on the evening news, but would you be able to eat this with a real dead body lying on the floor over there?''

I took a big mouthful, chewed, swallowed, stared Doc right in the eye and said, "Hell yes.'' It wasn't so much that I disagreed with him. It was just his highfalutin' manner of spouting clichés.

Doc laughed and was suddenly a genial middle-aged man rather than a pretentious art professor.

We sat on the floor in a small apartment in the Hillcrest area and ate. The food was excellent; the atmosphere bohemian but clean. Books, paintings and large, moody photographs of nudes covered the apartment. The nudes wore

Viva's face and my eyes kept drifting between the photo and the lively, vital person sitting next to me. When I was in college, Doc and Viva would have been the coolest of the cool amongst the faculty and we'd have all aspired to be like them someday, but I haven't been in college for ten years now and I could see they were just another struggling couple trying to make the best of a meager salary.

Wine and conversation. I moved to the couch. Viva sat next to me. Then Doc excused himself to go do something.

"Do you like the photographs?" she asked.

"Yes. Are all of them yours?"

"All in this room, yes."

"Does it ever feel just a little bit funny, being surrounded by pictures of your body all the time?"

"I like my body. I like Doc's art. His pictures capture something of me that other photographers I've worked with can't. Some charge, some aspect of life . . ."

She leaned closer and closer as she talked, and then she kissed me. Our tongues touched. Click.

I jumped. Doc stood there with his camera. "Please continue. You may do anything you wish as long as I can stay to photograph it."

I almost ran. But Viva smiled at me and lightly stroked the hair behind my right ear. I stared at her pale blue eyes until I fell in.

Silence is broken by the rattling of pots and pans. Our dates have arrived. It's been an hour since Tomkins died. None of us has said a word. We're just sitting on the porch in our rocking chairs, Doc, Viva and I, swatting at insects and waiting for the dead and noticing that there are even more moles on our skin than there were yesterday.

But now the trip wires have been tripped. Doc switches on the headlights we pulled off of Tomkins's junk-car collection. The brights reveal six dead people crossing the clearing. They always seem to arrive in groups like that. As if they'd decided, "Hey, wanna go up to the Tomkins place and see what's cookin'?" Well, tonight's the lucky night for at least two of them.

"I like her," I say, pointing to a broken cheerleader who's obviously seen better days.

"Well, in that case I'll take her boyfriend over there," says Viva, pointing to a high school stud whose goofy grin is accentuated by the way his cheeks have split open.

We gun down the other four. Clean head shots. I'm amazed at how my marksmanship has improved. Lots of practice is the key. Practice twenty-four hours a day. Bang. Rest in peace.

Doc is checking his cameras. He wants to document all this. Don't know why he still bothers.

Young Stud and Cheerleader reach Tomkins's body and fall down to examine it. The three of us rise from our chairs and walk into the clearing.

I finally went to Tomkins's place to see his pictures. All of them were taken by Doc. In Tomkins Doc and Viva found what every artist desires: a rich fan. Tomkins's wealth was inherited, his parents dead. Doc and Viva were just one of his hobbies. Another was fixing up old cars—not antiques or sports cars or muscle cars—just a random series of autos from the sixties that appealed to Tomkins's aesthetic sense. This was his only profitable hobby, but all his earnings were now being eaten by his latest craze: heroin.

"Never met an Arkansas junkie before," I said to Tomkins.

"They're out there," said Tomkins. "Actually, I'd never met any either. That's why I took it up myself. Then I started meeting dozens of 'em."

All the best photographs were taken at Tomkins's farmhouse. Large prints filled the living room, the den, the halls and bedrooms:

Viva and I, entwined, Viva on top and leaning forward. Her whole body is a blur—the long exposure traces our frantic motions. I look like I'm screaming.

Viva and Doc. Doc is on top, back arched, face pointing toward the heavens, eyes closed. A green aura leaps from his head. Viva's aura is blue. Her eyes are open. She is looking directly at the camera with that sly smile of hers. I took that picture. She's smiling at me.

Viva and Tomkins. She stands, he kneels. He kisses her pubes. Her hands are on his shoulders. It's like they're in a trance. This is not a sex scene. It is a scene of worship.

We approach the dead teenage couple. They look up, see us, rise from Tomkins's corpse and stumble toward us. Doc tries to maneuver the woman back to Tomkins. She trips over the body and crawls toward Doc. He circles her, then reaches into Tomkins's abdominal cavity and pulls out some dripping tubes, which he offers to the dead woman. She tries to bite his arm.

"It's not going to work," says Viva. "Tomkins is old meat, cold meat. They want life; hot, wet meat."

"Then we'll have to give it to them," says Doc. He points his gun at me.

I spent more and more time at the farmhouse with Doc and Viva. I called in sick at work so often that I was fired. I didn't mind—that just gave me more time to spend with Viva.

One day Tomkins and Doc went shopping in Little Rock, leaving Viva and me alone together. For the first time we made love without the click of Doc's camera. We lay together and talked, surrounded by pictures of her body. It was still hard for me to believe that body was next to mine.

"I've always been something of an exhibitionist," she said. "Doc's camera understands why." She said that she didn't get along too well with other women, except for one she had an affair with several years ago—and even that eventually turned sour. "Other women call me a slut. But Doc put his finger on it. He said that I don't just have a sex drive . . . I have a *life* drive. Life pours out of me. If I don't show it, capture it, use it, it would go crazy on me, like a cancer."

"So you'll sleep with anyone." I realized how cold that sounded as soon as I said it. I bit my tongue. But she took it a different way, as if I was suffering from a hurt ego. I guess I was.

"No no no. Not anyone. There has to be a certain feeling, a certain vibe. It's what Doc captures with his pictures of auras. Doc has it. You have it. Tomkins has it in a weak sort of way. You're not the first person I've found with it, and, to be honest, you won't be last. But you are special."

"Then I'm lucky. I feel privileged to be with you." My rational mind was telling me that Viva was self-centered to a frightening degree. But my rational mind was helpless. I let her pour into me. Viva was full of herself, and I was full of her too.

I pointed to one of the stranger pictures, in which Viva straddled a man who seemed unaware of her existence. "Did he have that vibe?"

"No. He was dead." My body must have tensed. Viva sighed and rolled away from me. "It was Doc's idea. The idea repulsed me, but then I became fascinated by my own repulsion. I like to think of myself as fearless, you know? So I approached it as a performance, and I fucked that body in a sort of performance trance." Viva stared at the ceiling. She lifted her hands up, facing each other, as if gesturing for emphasis, and then she just held them steady, fingers twitching, as if electric arcs were passing from fingertip to fingertip. "I could feel my life drive pour into that dead man, filling him."

"You wake him up?"

She laughed. "No. Nothing happened. But I felt liberated afterwards. I mean, I know I'll die one of these days, but while I live, death just doesn't have a fucking *chance* against me!"

I thought of Viva with the dead cock inside her and mine began to shrivel. I was painfully aware of the fact that this was the first time we'd made love without a condom—Doc was very scrupulous about such things—and I felt this imaginary, cold death infection swimming up my urethra. Viva noticed. "What's the matter?"

"Hmmm. Looks like you've tuckered the ol' fella out." She smiled. "Men are so funny. You'd think their penises were some sort of alien organism grafted onto their bodies.''

''Don't you ever feel that way about your genitals?''

''No. It's *me*.'' She placed my hand on her womb. ''The center of my being is right *here*.'' And it was. I felt incredible heat in the palm of my hand. My penis ceased his retreat, snuck back toward her thighs, and began to probe actively.

Afterwards we slept and awoke to see Doc watching us. He had no camera. His face was expressionless. ''You need to watch this,'' he said. He switched on the television and left the room. Viva and I watched as a harried-looking anchorman explained how the world had changed overnight.

I hear only the sound of the stumbling dead, and their sad, gasping moans. I see only Doc's rifle. The hands that clutch it are almost colorless in the bright car lights. I smell the dead, all sickly-sweet. The black hole at the end of a rifle barrel is growing, opening up to swallow me.

The gunshot is thunderous. I still stand, feeling nothing. Doc looks surprised. A dark-red flower has exploded on his chest. He falls forward. Behind him stands Viva. She lowers her gun and smiles at me. ''Fresh meat. Hot meat.''

Young Stud and Cheerleader roll Doc over to feed on chest blossom. Viva approaches the male zombie and begins to tear off his clothes. ''This is a good one. And that woman was lovely once. Remember that when you take her.''

Tomkins's farmhouse was a good place to be when the world changed. After all, he'd originally set it up so he could withdraw from society whenever he wanted. Now that society consisted of hordes of hungry zombies, well . . .

Day in and day out we watched for more ravenous guests and sent them back to their graves. Nightly bonfires took care of the bodies.

I used to hate guns. I learned to sleep with one.

We must have always had a sick longing for apocalypse. Mixed with our nuclear nightmares was an odd sort of desire for a cleansing fire, a way to completely eliminate our old, dreary lives. It's kind of like when you wish for a nervous breakdown so you can, at least for awhile, give up and turn all your responsibilities over to doctors and nurses and relatives. It's a stupid, selfish desire. And yet . . .

The apocalypse has not been a cleansing fire, but it is beautiful. Our sunsets are rich, with theatrical clouds painted orange and blue, purple and red. It's Götterdämmerung and we are the dying gods. But nature still lives. There are no zombie fish or insects or bears or trees.

Viva and Doc and I still lived, and I was filled with Viva and death *was* impossible, we survived, we survived, we survived glowing with life, unstoppable life, crazy life. . . .

First we noticed what seemed like a swelling in the glands. Then our joints began to increase in size, just a little. I began to notice new moles on my body, and on Viva's.

Doc, in his endless theorizing, hit on a new idea. "Moles are benign tumors. I think that whatever brought the dead to life is affecting us as well. We're in danger. Soon the tumors may no longer be benign. Cancer will overtake us, wild cells will replace our tissue, and we will join the shambling dead."

Tomkins was the only one unaffected, and Doc had a theory for that as well. "The heroin keeps him closer to death, but it also keeps the crazy life in check, just as toxic drugs are used to keep cancer in check. When he runs out of junk, the crazy life will overtake him too."

"When I run out of junk," said Tomkins, "I'm going to place a bullet in my head."

Doc's idea of what was happening to us had no scientific justification at all, but then, neither did the walking dead. What mattered was what pleased Doc's sense of aesthetics. When he learned that Tomkins had only a few fixes left, he devised a plan that would give Tomkins a beautiful death, and possibly save the rest of us by bringing us closer to death. Much closer.

I was repulsed ... then fascinated by my repulsion. . . .

Viva rolls the Young Stud onto his back. Straddling him, she lowers one of Doc's intestines into the dead man's mouth. He snaps eagerly at the flesh tube. She eases herself onto his erection (food lust or just rigor mortis?).

Cheerleader's face is buried in Doc's abdomen. She slurps and sucks. It's easy for me to lower her panties and enter her from behind. She turns her head, looks at me, resumes chewing on Doc's heart, cradled in her hands. Her vagina is cool, and a black viscous fluid lubricates it.

Viva's man is happy. He moans a melody as he chews on his intestine. I think it's a song from a hot dog commercial. Viva smiles and leans over to kiss me. Her warm tongue forms a vivid contrast to the cool touch of the dead woman's cunt. An electric shock runs through me. As I come, I have a vision of my sperm coursing into the stagnant womb, toward the rotting ovaries, and sparking a different kind of life.

I pull out and watch Viva. She's rockin' and rollin' now, but the intestine is gone, and the dead man is trying to sit up; his hands rise; he grabs her shoulders. I grab the Colt .45 next to Tomkins's body and shoot. Young Stud's head explodes; his body spasms, and Viva gasps with pleasure.

The only sound is the smacking of the dead woman's lips. I run up to the porch for some lantern fuel and matches. When I return, Viva disengages herself from the headless corpse and kisses me again.

We are being watched. Doc's eyes have reopened. But he makes no attempt to rise. He doesn't even push away the dead woman feeding on his heart. I start pouring fuel on both of them.

"The chest," says Viva. "I was stupid. I shot him in the chest." She kneels above Doc and kisses the top of his head. Tears roll down her cheeks. "I'm sorry, my love. I didn't mean to put you through this." She shoots a bullet into his forehead, and his eyes cease tracking. This gets the attention of Cheerleader and she reaches an arm out for Viva. I toss a lit match and the dead woman quietly begins to burn, falling across Doc's body and setting it ablaze. For awhile she makes a quiet, whining sound, miffed at this new development.

Rather than form a funeral pyre, Viva and I walk amongst the bodies of the dead with the remaining fuel. Soon the clearing is a field of tiny fires.

We return to the farmhouse. Too tired to make love again, we collapse, naked, in each other's arms.

II

"No."

Viva's voice and a tugging sensation awaken me. "No." We'd slept nestled together, her back against my chest. Now her hands are trying to push me away— "No!"—and her back pulls hard on my chest. I hear a sound like a soft ripping and Viva grunts and I feel a burning, stinging pain all down the front of my body. I am bleeding. Viva is bleeding. It's the kind of bleeding you get from bad abrasions. She keeps pushing me away. I look down and see that the skin of her buttocks has grown into the flesh of my thighs.

"No!" She pulls and we rip again. The sides of my penis are attached to the inner surface of her thighs and I grab it and pull it away. The pain is white-hot, as if tiny pliers have nipped at all the places on my body where we'd touched.

Our lower legs are still lightly attached, but Viva kicks and thrashes, and with a final tearing we are separate. She begins to crawl away from me. I reach for her. "Viva?"

"Stay away from me!" She keeps crawling. All I can do is lie there. The blood cools on my skin. "I'm sorry," says Viva, "but just stay away."

She crawls out of the room and everything is turning red and I go away for a little while.

• • •

I come to alone. The pain is gone. I pour some water into Tomkins's old washbasin and sponge the old blood off my body. Already the rips have healed. Babysmooth tissue runs in strips down my chest and legs. I am fascinated by its softness. I stroke it with my fingertips. I scratch it with my nails. The scratching sends a warm tingle to my loins. I scratch harder. My penis stiffens. I scratch with one hand and masturbate with the other. When I am finished, my chest is bleeding again. I clean off the blood and put on clothes.

I notice that the moles that covered my body are gone. More of the soft skin has taken their place.

The farmhouse is empty. I should wait for Viva to return, but I don't think she will. I should stay here, where I'm safe, but I don't want to.

Viva left in the only car that would start. All the others had their batteries pulled. We've been charging them by day with a solar cell. I hook the strongest battery to the charger.

I eat outdoors. It's already midafternoon. No sign of the dead today. Trees, plants, insects, squirrels, birds—all are very much alive. They bustle and rustle and chirp and twitter. Life, everywhere life. Even the rocks seem to hum. I know Viva must still be alive, somewhere.

I find a Ford pickup that is more or less intact and place the battery in it and fill it with gas from the other cars, and load it up with all the supplies I can think of. I'm ready to go. The sun has just set. I should spend another night here. Fuck it. My need for Viva is immediate. My erection points me northwest.

A small country road takes me north. I drive for miles, and the only car I see is a wreck in the swamp. I drive by slowly. It's a new car, already covered with vines.

Something rustles inside the wreck. I speed up and leave it behind me.

Crickets and frogs charge the air with a sound like a massive sixty-cycle hum. My headlight beams form two cones of Brownian motion—moths and mosquitoes and dragonflies that quickly pepper my windshield with their guts. I use the wipers—a mistake. Now I can't see a damn thing.

No window-washing fluid. Fuck. I stop. Don't want to use my drinking water to clean the windshield. I find two warm beers in the back of the truck. Warm beer and an old t-shirt. That works pretty good. Beer and an ice scraper. That works better.

The bugs in the headlights come to sample the beer and my blood. I turn off the headlights.

Neither moon shines in the heavens. I scrape the windshield by feel and sound. Something splashes in the swamp. Then I hear a sound like reeds creaking and snapping. I stop and listen. Sixty-cycle insect hum.

I see a flash of light deep in the swamp. No, it's a steady round spot. Fading. There it is again, to the left.

Something lands with a wet thunk on my car hood. I leap in the truck, turn on the headlights and the dome light. It's a mouse. The head is gone. I start the truck, put it into reverse; the mouse and the beer and the t-shirt and the ice scraper slide off the hood. I shift to "drive" and head down the road, faster and faster. The road is long and straight. Seventy mph, eighty, ninety, and bugs cover the windshield again. The dome light illuminates the ripply details of their splotches.

Must have been an owl. That's it. An owl dropped its prey by accident. Slow down. Eighty. Seventy. Suddenly there's a car up ahead just parked in the middle of the road and I swerve and just miss it and I'm braking but still I feel a dull thud and a man in a lumberjack shirt and blue jeans with only half a face is pressed against my windshield, clutching for me, hands clawing on the glass goddamn! I send the truck into a skid and throw him off the hood.

The truck stops and I see the man with half a face struggling to his feet and I peel out and squash him and keep on driving, and now I see more dead on the side of the road; they're going my way, northwest, so I aim for them; help them along. Pedestrian. Fifty points. Little old lady bounces off the hood. One hundred points. Dead boy with a baseball cap snaps like a G.I. Joe doll—two hundred points!

There's my exit onto the I–440. Up the ramp and I see this woman and two men and I aim for the entire cluster and the woman screams; she's alive; I swerve too late and bodies hit the truck and I go right off the curve. For a moment we're flying and then we make a four point landing on the grassy embankment and the truck snaps and stops for good.

I sit and listen to the rhythmic ticks and pings of cooling metal. I am not in pain. I seem to be okay, but I don't want to move. All I can see is the woman's face in the headlights.

An unsteady beam of light shines through my side window. "You okay?"

I am fascinated by the moving shadows on the passenger seat. Finally I turn to look into the light. "Yeah."

"You saved my life."

"Uh."

"You surprised them. I ran. They didn't."

"Oh."

Her name is Toni. She was on the road after holing up in West Little Rock for a long time. "I just stayed in my apartment," she said, "except for supply runs. The only way I could tell who was living and who was dead is the live ones shot at me. I finally went stir-crazy and left. Just barely made it down here before running out of gas." She helped me out of the truck while talking, words like a nervous avalanche. Long black hair, stick thin, with a pretty, birdlike smile.

My truck has gas. Her car runs. It seems a simple enough basis for a partnership. We siphon away the truck's tank, pausing only long enough to deliver two head shots to the two crawling, broken, dead men when they finally reach us.

We walk for a mile. Suddenly I'm so tired I can't stand up. I lean on Toni. When we reach her car she fills the gas tank while I throw all my stuff into the front seat and then collapse in the back. Toni notices that I'm shaking. She digs a blanket out of the trunk, then gets in back and throws it over me. She shivers as well. We hold each other for awhile, under the blanket. We don't say anything. Her breathing finally slows down to the regular rhythm of sleep. I ride that rhythm. Away.

Someone is knocking insistently at the door. I pull Viva closer, hoping Doc will get it. He doesn't.

I force open my eyes to sunlight glare. The hands of a dead woman pound at the driver's-side window.

I shake the girl in the backseat with me. "Keys? Uh. Toni? Toni. Where are the keys?" She stirs and starts awake.

The car doesn't start. The dead woman pounds on the window. Toni pounds on the steering wheel. "Damn. I think we need to prime the carburetor."

"Huh?"

"I'll do it. You do something about her."

Another day, another damn day. I shoot the dead woman and Toni sprinkles the last few drops of gas on the air filter and I shoot two more dead and the car starts up and away we go.

"Where do you want to go?" asks Toni.

"Uh. Northwest." I jerk my thumb over my shoulder.

"I just came from there. Oh, what the hell. There's a few things I forgot to bring from my apartment." She does a U-turn in the grassy freeway divider, whipping around a sign that says DO NOT CROSS MEDIAN. "Yeee-hah," she says.

Ten minutes pass. A swerving pickup full of screaming, gun-shooting rednecks whips by us like something out of an old western. It's the only moving car we see. Little Rock is quiet and still. We exit the Interstate. A few walking dead stumble around shopping centers on Rodney Parham Road. There is no traffic, and no traffic lights.

•   •   •

Toni has a nice apartment. She must have made pretty good money.

"You've still got running water."

"Yeah," she says from the bathroom door. "That's all I got now, but I'm not looking a gift horse in the mouth or anything."

I sit on her sofa and stare at my hands. The webs between my fingers seem to have grown. I can still spread my fingers apart, but they're now connected at the middle knuckles.

Toni comes out of the bathroom wearing a nightgown. She tosses me a towel and a bathrobe. "These are both still clean."

The bathroom window faces the sun. I strip and discover that my legs are black with seed ticks. I scrub and scour my body. I'm covered with red welts. Where the ticks didn't get me, the mosquitoes and chiggers did.

All the flesh folds of my body have grown. My toes are webbed. The skin folds under my arms and ears are larger. The skin is smooth, like the new skin on my chest. Already the scratches I made yesterday morning have healed.

I leave the bathroom. Toni is asleep on the bed. I consider lying down next to her. Nah. I'm still tired. I don't want any kind of tension. I lie down on the

Cooking smells awaken me. I lie still and breathe them in for awhile.

I get up. Toni is warming up some stew. A can of sterno heats the pan. I didn't know people still had fondue sets.

She's laid out a perfect table with candlelight and wine. We eat and drink and she tells me how she used to cook for her boyfriend just once a week, not more than that, didn't want him to get too used to her cooking and all, but that one day a week she always found herself spending hours in the kitchen trying to come up with the perfect meal.

"What happened to your boyfriend?"

Silence. "The first time we went out looking for food

some guys cruised past us in a Trans-Am and shot him. I ran and hid. They kept calling for me to come out. 'C'mon. Bring out that hot wet pussy.' " Pause. "At least they shot him in the brain."

We lose our appetites and move to the couch with our wine glasses. I can't think of anything to say. She breaks the silence. "We could stay here for awhile longer. You want to? At least it's safe here. I don't know why I tried to leave." She sighs. "I guess that's like hiding in the past, though. It hasn't been long, but I miss it so much." I hear her voice shake. Tears on her face catch the candlelight. I reach out a tentative hand, place it on her shoulder.

She pours into my arms and I feel her pain more than I feel my own. I murmur comforting words. I try to think of what I have lost. I can't think of anything. I'm sure Viva is still alive, and I'll find her. But maybe I'm just kidding myself. She could easily be dead now. I should stay here with Toni. I should stay with what's real.

I stroke Toni's back. I kiss her cheek, then her lips. Our tongues tease each other. She kisses my ear like an electric shock. I lightly bite the nape of her neck. She runs her fingertips down my chest, opening my robe. "So smooth." She kisses my left nipple where the new flesh grows, and I'm shocked by the intensity. I hold her head there and she nips at it and I moan, it's a new feeling for me, like she's actually sucking at my teat and we slide off the couch onto the floor and our robes slide open and her skin is so hot and soft and I'm on top of her and her legs open and without any guidance my penis finds her vagina and sinks in.

Toni gasps. I slide out and in. She pulls me closer. Deeper now. Deeper. She moans. I twist my pelvis and she rises to meet it . . . and then she cries out and I feel a tug as I slide out and in and she cries out again and I respond with more passion thrusting in harder my god she's so wet and her cries are like screams and I come.

So wet. I slip out, and back away.

My penis is covered with blood. The carpet beneath us is stained. "Oh my god . . ."

Half-lidded eyes. "I'm sorry. Didn't think it was that time of month."

''I hurt you.''

''I got some irritation but . . .''

But her voice is very faint and blood is still coming out of her.

I stand and grab a napkin off the table. As I clean my pénis I notice that the glans is throbbing. I look more closely. The opening at the tip is flexing, opening much wider than I thought possible. When it opens, I can see tiny nested circles of teeth, like the mouth of a lamprey eel.

Toni doesn't move and blood still comes out of her.

I grab my clothes and run.

I drive through darkness punctuated by heat lightning. No thunder—all wind and snapshots of boiling clouds. Travelling west on Highway 10—didn't I take an exit back a ways? I'm not on 10. A sign ahead of me says PINNACLE MOUNTAIN STATE PARK. Okay. I follow the signs to the base of the hiking trail. I park and sit in the flickering dark. In my head I see Toni, blood flowing out of her. Lightning flash. Now I see Viva, dancing. I get an erection so strong it's all I can feel, like its pulling the life out of the rest of my body. Lightning flash. Toni, bleeding. No.

I'm shaking all over again, but I'm moving. What do I need? My guns. That's all. A flashlight. Flashlight and guns. A knife? A knife, flashlight and guns. A lighter would help. I try to scoop everything into a backpack. Not room for everything. Fuck it. Leave the rest behind.

I walk up the trail, with a circle of light from my flash bouncing before me. The trees sing in the wind. My footsteps crunch. Twigs snap. Pebbles bounce. Do all those sounds come from me? I stop.

I walk up the trail. I keep thinking about bears. The dead don't bother me but . . . bears, wolves, moving fast, very much alive. Big bears with large claws. I stop.

I walk up the trail and hear my own breath thundering in my ears. I hold my breath, and still there's a sound like gasping. I stop. The wind gets stronger and the rustling trees are very loud and that is all I hear. I shine my flashlight everywhere and see only tree trunks and rocky ground.

Trees. They can't get me in a tree. I climb the tallest I can find. A pine. My hands are all sticky. Little twigs brush against me, poking at my skin, my cheeks, my eyes. Something crawls over my hand. My flash reveals a clump of Daddy Longleg spiders. I climb above them and find a good perch, and sit. The wind sings loud and soft in the pine needles. Lightning plays games in the sky, silently. The tree sways back and forth. So soothing. Back and forth.

I wake up and grab the tree trunk just in time to catch myself. I cling to the trunk as if it were my mother for a long time.

I take off my coat and make a sling out of my belt and my shirt. I put the coat back on. The wind bites through the exposed skin on my upper chest, but in the rest of the coat I am warm and cozy and safe.

Grey light and warm rain. I'm soaked. The sound of the dripping branches is friendly, soothing. I hug my tree-mother closer, close my eyes again, happy just to breathe. The tree responds with a friendly crackly-crack and another breathing sound, ragged and uneven, well, hell, trees don't breathe like we do anyway.

Crackly-crack. Something pulls hard at my left foot.

The dead man wears a tweed jacket and narrow tie. He looks quite dapper, with many fashionable twig punctures on the grey skin of his face and neck and a tasteful accessory stick thrust into his left eyesocket. His mouth is wrapped around the toe of my boot. He must have been climbing for hours. All I have to do is kick, and back down he goes, bouncing off the branches like a pachinko ball. Snap! say the branches. Snap! say his bones.

I climb down to look at him. His shattered skeleton makes it possible for his body to twitch in all sorts of fascinating new directions. Bare muscles flex through open wounds. His good blue eye rolls in its socket to stare at me, but he's lost that natty little piece of wood that was in his empty eyesocket. I find another, larger stick and thrust it into the good eye. Vitneous humor and blood flowers. I push deeper, into the brain, stirring it into pudding. Slowly, like a dying spider, the twitching body stills.

I sit, leaning on the tree trunk, and watch the rain clean the corpse. Blood forms small red clouds and strings in the water on his face. The naked, broken bones are slowly cleansed to a delicate grey-white. Shades of grey. Except for the delicate pinks of muscles and ganglia, the dead man could be a black-and-white photograph.

A notion occurs to me, a notion that this man was alive, and I just killed him. They've all been alive. The dead don't walk again. I've been killing. I've been killing. I've been killing. Raping.

I can't get this notion out of my head. I sit in the rain and stare at the dead man. The rain washes him into a grainy illustration from a catalogue of atrocities.

I am at the top of Pinnacle Mountain. It's not really a mountain, just a bald knob of rock near the Arkansas River. It didn't take long to climb it in the daylight. When I started climbing I realized that I could still see my car in its parking place. I followed the simple trail and left most of the trees behind and climbed a sort of rock staircase.

Here at the top the peak splits in two, with a ridgelike peak to the north and a slightly higher, more rounded peak to the south. Between them is nothing but rocks and scrub brush and small, stunted trees.

The rain has stopped and the sun is out at last. I can see the Arkansas River, winding past bridges and a cluster of buildings that just might be Little Rock's downtown area. The last time I was here was about a year ago, during normal times. The scenic view looks just the same. The only difference is the quiet. A year ago I could hear distant trains and trucks all the time. Now all I hear is faint wind and the sound of insects.

Viva is around here somewhere. My cock knows this. It writhes restlessly in my pants, chewing impatiently on the cotton of my underwear. With nothing but rocks everywhere, I don't know where she could be hiding, but then hiding is something she's very good at. She once did a piece called "Tribute to Chris Burdon" where she hid in plain sight in the state capitol for three days. Doc had pictures of fat Arkansas congressmen, smiling and oblivious to Viva, who stood right behind them wearing an outrageous outfit that left her nipples exposed.

For some reason, I've decided that a fire would be a good idea, so I've spent the past few hours gathering kindling and firewood. There isn't much to be had up here. It took several expeditions off the main peak to gather my woodpile. I never once spotted Viva. She may be curled up like a snake between the rocks, stock-still—I might have passed her twenty times without seeing her. It's okay. I can wait.

The fire burns between two rocks at the very top of the mountain. It took a long time to get it going. I thought the wood might be too damp to catch, but at last the pine needles began to burn, and the twigs began to crackle, and finally the larger pieces of wood gave themselves up to oxidation.

My clothes are sticky and uncomfortable, all bunched up and itchy. I take them off. The front of my underwear has numerous tiny holes chewed in it. I inspect my penis and pull a thread out from between the teeth.

All my tick scars, mosquito and chigger bites are gone. The skin around my lower legs is smooth and hairless. It has a strange consistency to it, almost like a thick, rubbery putty. I can leave thumbprints in the skin, which slowly fade. But when I slice it with the knife, it bleeds. The cuts don't hurt. My penis wets its mouth. It's all I can do to keep from flaying my skin off for the pleasure of it. But I'd rather let Viva do that.

It's another beautiful sunset. All I've had to eat is some peanut butter. My head floats as I watch the sun fade like a great orange explosion on the horizon.

•   •   •

Dark. The two moons and the stars and the light of my fire are all I have. No radio towers. No city glow. No lights by the river.

I squat, staring at my fire. I think I've been here for a very long time. My clothes are dry now, but I haven't put them back on yet.

Waves of color run across the pinprick lights of the New Moon. I stand and watch it. Something about those color changes. They give me the same feeling I get listening to a melancholy string quartet. I reach up a hand to the New Moon. I want . . . I don't know. My eyelashes are wet.

"You feel it, too?" I jump. Viva stands nude on the other side of the fire. Her skin has also changed. Her sweat has a strange, sweetish smell. She is webbed and beautiful.

I step around the fire toward her. "Where have you been?"

She steps in the same direction, keeping the fire between us. "Hiding. Watching you."

We chase each other, counter-clockwise. "I came here looking for you. Why did you hide?"

"I was hoping you would leave."

"You know I wouldn't."

"I know. But you scared me. When we were almost fused together—I wasn't ready for that. But now . . ."

I stop. She stops and says, "What we did acted as a catalyst, opening our bodies to the change that brought the dead to life. It's like hyper-life. I'm so full of life I could explode. I need you, now—"

I hold my arms out to her, over the fire. My fingers drink in the heat. I should run. What happened to Toni—

I can't leave. Eye to eye. Her eyes are the same pale blue I originally fell into. Viva raises her hands to mine. Magnetism pulls us together. Our hands catch fire with tiny, multicolored flames that run up and down our arms. Closer. Closer. Our hands touch. . . .

We fall together over the fire and all the lights of the New Moon burn up and down our bodies like electrical shocks and Viva's legs open and I plunge into her and somehow we're still standing and we scratch each other and moan and . . .

Pain. We scream in unison. Pain, like a sharp stab to the gut. I look down. Two long teeth, as slender as snake fangs, have sprung from the corners of Viva's cunt, piercing my cock and holding it in place. My cock thrashes within her, biting. Our blood hisses as it dribbles into the fire.

"Goddamn. Goddamn you!" Viva whispers. "I'll rip it off if it doesn't stop."

"If you rip it off," I whisper back, "there'll be nothing to stop it, and it'll burrow deeper and deeper inside of you."

No. She pushes at me, but we've already begun to meld. Her breasts flow into my chest and our stomachs merge. The pain flows in waves and between each wave is a warm tingling. The fire still burns below us, but it has no effect on our new putty flesh. The moon flames have gone out.

We breathe together, in and out. Then we hear ragged breathing, and the scuffling of rocks. "Oh shit!" says Viva.

The dead climb up the rocks from all sides. Most are on their hands and knees, crawling and broken after falling on the steep rocks over and over.

We sway and then move, an awkward four-legged animal with very short legs. Our arms are still free. With my head over Viva's left shoulder, and her head over mine, we can see in all directions. (My left ear flows into hers.) We scuttle for our guns. The rocks thrill our feet with cuts.

We find a way to squat so that Viva can pick up her rifle. We move to my backpack and I retrieve a pistol. Viva's rifle cracks and the butt kicks into my shoulder. I fire into the forehead of a sweet little old lady with meat dangling in strips from her dentures.

We slowly circle, counter-clockwise.

Oh no! Viva whispers. We turn and I see a dead man stumble toward us with his pants down around his ankles. Amazing that he could climb up here like that. *I didn't mean to* thinks Viva. There's a bloody hole where his penis would have been. *I didn't know and he screamed and I didn't stop* and the man falls at my feet and bites into my ankle. Strong teeth sink into the thick putty-flesh and Viva and I gasp together with pleasure. The pain of our union subsides.

I feel more teeth on Viva's knee. A woman in a torn business suit chews and sucks at the kneecap.

Viva and I stop moving and abandon ourselves to the pleasure. I hold her soft back, my hands sinking into her. She runs her fingernails up and down my spine. The businesswoman and Viva's lover cease chewing. They suck on us, quietly, happy as newborns at the tit. I see through Viva's eyes that the skin of her knee is flowing over the dead woman's face.

Two more zombies reach us, bite in, and relax as our drug pours into them, easing the pain of their new life. We are what they've been seeking all along.

Day and night and day and night. Our flesh has completely absorbed the bodies of the businesswoman and Viva's lover and the other first-comers. They dissolve within us, and we grow. Flesh stretches down from our buttocks until it reaches the ground and blossoms out, taking our weight off our legs. We stretch upward as well. Our heads have merged into the top of a spire. We spiral as we grow, watching the landscape spin slowly around us night and day and night and day.

I remember Viva's past as a possessor. She remembers my past as one who was possessed. She panicked briefly during our final melding, as our heads fused. "It's only me. It's only me." Her resistance snapped off abruptly. *It's only we*.

The dead make their pilgrimage up Pinnacle Mountain, and we feed on them and grow. Our flesh base now covers much of the taller peak. We tower above the peak—a flesh tower.

Toni's body recently joined us. This made us happy. We soothed her and digested her.

Every night the pinprick lights of the New Moon are clearer to us. It *is* music, calling to us. We struggle to make it manifest. Slowly, parts of our spire develop thin drumlike membranes. When the moon passes over us, we let the membranes vibrate in the wind. We flex the membranes and sing the moon's song.

Recently we've begun to notice the songs of other towers. They also sing the song of the New Moon, but with their own patterns, voices, variations. We hear them from farther and farther away, from all over the planet.

Together we form a chorus, an orchestra of moon towers.

Together we reach for the matrix of pinpointed lights.

We will absorb all humanity, both the living and the dead.

Together we reach for the sky.

PASSION PLAY

NANCY HOLDER

It was a chilly May morning, and Cardinal Schonbrun's knees cracked as he took his seat beside Father Meyer in the Passionsspielhaus. Father Meyer heard the noise very clearly; he was acutely aware of every sound, smell, and sight around him: of the splinters in the planks of the large, open-air stage before them, the smell of dew, the dampness of his palms. The murmurs of anticipation of the assembling crowd, and those of speculation—and derision— when his own people, scattered among the thousands, caught sight of him. He was aware that he looked like a prisoner, wedged between his friend Hans Ahrenkiel, the bishop of Munich, and his nemesis, the cardinal. He was aware that his life as a priest would be over that day.

The cardinal scowled at Father Meyer and said, "Is it true what I've just heard?"

Father Meyer licked his lips. How had he hoped to keep it a secret? "That depends upon what it is, Eminence."

"Did you give absolution to the *wandelnder Leichnam* this morning?"

Though his heart sank—someone had betrayed him—Father Meyer regarded the cardinal steadily. "*Ja.* Does that surprise you?"

Cardinal Schonbrun made a shocked noise. On Father Meyer's left, the bishop shook his head mournfully.

"Did it partake of the Holy Eucharist?"

The cardinal was a much younger man than Father Meyer could ever remember being. Blond and blue-eyed, vigorous and vital. Filled with New Ideas for the New Church. The kind of man Rome wanted to lead her flocks into the twenty-first century.

The kind of man Father Meyer, gray and aged, was not.

Father Meyer raised his chin. "The Church has always offered her mercy to the condemned. *Ja,* I did it."

The cardinal's face mottled with anger. He opened his mouth, glanced at the swelling audience, and spoke in a harsh, tense whisper. "Think what you've done, man! Polluted the body of Christ. You've made a mockery of the Sacraments, of your own vows—"

Father Meyer spread open his hands. "All I know, Your Eminence, is that Oberammergau, my village and that of my ancestors . . . that this village made a vow to God. And that now, three hundred and eighty years later, we're shamming that vow with what we are doing today."

Bishop Ahrenkiel touched Father Meyer's arm. They had sat in the rectory together, drinking ancient Benedictine brandy and discussing the New Ideas. In companionable silence, they'd listened to Father Meyer's collections of Gregorian chants, gone through scrapbooks of Passion Plays through the centuries. Father Meyer had hoped that Bishop Ahrenkiel, at least, would understand. But he, alas, was a New Bishop.

"I thought we'd gone through all that, Johannes," he said now, for the obvious benefit of the cardinal. "These are not living creatures. They have no souls. The Vatican has spoken on the matter, and—"

"The Vatican is wrong." Father Meyer turned anguished eyes toward the young cardinal. "Everyone is wrong. Your Eminence, I've spent time among these *Leichname*. I—I feel they are my ministry. They aren't merely corpses, as science would have us believe. I hear their hearts, though they cannot speak. They seek the Father, as we all do. They hope for love, and mercy, and justice."

"Father Meyer," the cardinal began, but at that moment, the single voice of the Prologue, a man dressed in a simple white robe with a band of gold around his forehead, called them to order:

"Bend low, bend low. . . ."

Those same words had rung through the Passion Meadow for centuries, as once again the Bavarian village of Oberammergau renewed its covenant with God: the townspeople would perform a play glorifying the suffering and resurrection of Christ—the Passion—if the Lord would spare them from the ravages of the Plague. In 1633, it had worked: no more fevers that shook the body; no more pustules that burst and ran; no more deaths. After the vow, grace.

Oberammergau was not unique in this bargaining; in the 1600's, many villages, towns, and cities promised to put on Passion Plays in return for survival. But in all the world, Oberammergau was the only village that still honored its pledge. The villagers pointed to this fidelity as the reason the town had also been spared the horrors of the more recent plague, the one that turned men and women, even tiny babies, into hellish monsters—the walking dead, rotting, slathering, mindless. What terror had run throughout the world.

Now, of course, the zombies were contained, and could even be controlled—as they would be today, on the Passion stage. Such a gift from God, such a miracle.

And as through the centuries, people from all over the world came to see God's miracles. Nearly half a million souls flocked to Oberammergau in the course of each decade's one hundred summer performances. But this year, the numbers were doubling—tripling—because of the introduction of the new element—a Newer way to glorify the agony and suffering of Our Lord Jesus Christ.

"Death from the sinner I release," sang the Prologue figure. And the crowd stirred—in eagerness, Father Meyer thought bitterly, at what was to come. But if his plan worked, they would leave this place with their bloodlust unsated.

"Sir," Father Meyer began, but a stalwart hausfrau behind him tapped him on the shoulder and said, "Hsst!"

The Prologue soloist sang on. It was Anton Veck, whom Father Meyer knew well. Anton had been an altar boy, was still busy in the parish church of St. Peter and St. Paul in a thousand helpful little ways. *Anton, Anton,* he thought, *was it you who told them?* Anton had been there. And he had not approved.

And, most damning of all, he was a cousin of Kaspar Mueller.

With a sigh, Father Meyer bowed his head and pulled his rosary from his pocket. He would not watch the play, though he, like every other Oberammergauer, counted his life not in years but in how many Passion Plays he had either performed in or seen. At sixty-five, this was his sixth cycle.

And though until this year, he had held the position of second-in-command on the Council of Six and Twelve, the committee that oversaw every aspect of the play, including the most important one: choosing the actors who were to play out the Passion of Christ.

He'd known the rules: they had to be Oberammergauers, or to have lived among the native-born for at least twenty years. In the case of the women, they had to be virgins, and young—cast-off restrictions reimposed during the cycle of the zombie plague, in the hope of pleasing God more fully.

He'd known the rules: the most prominent families must be represented.

And he hadn't disregarded the rules. He'd simply answered to a higher law; and that was why, after today, he knew he would be defrocked. No matter. He would continue in the work without the blessing of his Church.

Without the blessing. His throat tightened. Thumb and forefinger slipped over the worn wooden beads of the rosary his father had carved for him. "Put that away," the cardinal whispered angrily. Rosaries were not appreciated in the New Church.

Father Meyer covered the rosary with both his hands. His lips moved as he mentally counted the beads. Carved with love, in rosette shapes to honor the Virgin. It was a beautiful thing, and should be in a museum. Like the Old Church, he thought, with Her compassion and Her love.

His thoughts drifted back to the choosing of the roles. It had been a foregone conclusion, at least to the others, that Kaspar Mueller would play Christ. He had done so for three cycles, and no family in Oberammergau was more prominent, nor more powerful, than his. But to play Christ for a fourth Play? Thirty years older than when he began? Father Meyer had pointed out, correctly enough, that women over the age of thirty-five weren't even allowed in the play. Should a sixty-three-year-old man portray a man almost half his age?

"That doesn't matter. It's his spiritual qualities that matter most," Adolph Mueller, who was on the Council—and another of Kaspar's cousins—had asserted.

But the fact of his health remained. He was older, frailer. The part of Christ was grueling—each Passion Play lasted eight hours, with only a break for lunch; and then there was the matter of hanging on the Cross—

—and then there was the matter of Kaspar's falling from his front porch and breaking his ribs.

Father Meyer had assumed that would end the discussion; they would have to choose another, younger man. But Kaspar let it be known he wouldn't hear of it, wouldn't share the stage with anyone else. Nor would he allow his understudy to take over the role.

The priest was concerned, and let that fact be known to the Council. And in deference to his office, the discussion continued. But Father Meyer should have realized the weakness of his position; the Muellers were one of the founding families of Oberammergau, and they owned the largest hotel, two restaurants, and four taverns. They also donated generously each year to the village's State Wood-carving School. Father Meyer's family hadn't arrived until near the end of the nineteenth century. To most Oberammergauers, the Meyers were little better than interlopers. And of what benefit would it be to please the parish priest over the largest employer in town?

Yet finally, after much deliberation, Kaspar announced he would allow the placement of a double of himself upon the Cross during the crucifixion scene: one of the zombies, the *wandelndere Leichname*—changing corpses, as they were called in German—changed yet again, to look like him.

"Think of it," Adolph Mueller had exhorted the Council. "At last we can depict the true Passion of Christ. We can drive nails through its palms, and pierce its—"

"Father, really, you must watch or people will talk," Cardinal Schonbrun said as he stood.

Father Meyer shook himself. The sun was high in the sky. The stage was empty, the curtains closed. It was the lunch interval. Four hours had passed.

It was time. He called upon the Virgin for courage.

"People already talk, Eminence," he said. "The talk hasn't stopped since I stepped down from the Council."

"Which is why we're here," the cardinal cut in, gesturing to the bishop and the many priests assembled around them. "To prove that the Church approves of these proceedings, even if you do not."

Bishop Ahrenkiel put his arm around Father Meyer. "Come. Let's go have some sausage and a beer. The cardinal would surely not object?"

Father Meyer's heart jumped in his chest. Now was the moment. *Goodbye*, his soul whispered to Holy Mother Church. *Forgive me*. "I—I'm not hungry," he stammered, his fear showing. "If I may be excused to go to my house for the interval?"

The cardinal regarded him. "I think not. I think you should eat with us, Father."

He forced himself not to panic. "But I'm not feeling—"

"*Nein*. You must come with us, Father Meyer."

Father Meyer sagged. The cardinal must have guessed his plan to slip backstage and free the ten *Leichname* the village had purchased. Why had he dreamed it would be possible? He was a fool. A cursed old fool.

"Father Meyer?" Cardinal Schonbrun pressed, gesturing for him to walk beside him.

Father Meyer forced back tears. Perhaps he could find another way. He could not believe that in four hours they would actually crucify the pitiful thing.

"It's done in movies and things all the time," Bishop Ahrenkiel murmured as Father Meyer plodded slightly behind the cardinal. "It has been approved by the various humane organizations, the unions, the—"

"Don't speak to me." Father Meyer turned his head away from his old friend.

"But, Johannes—"

"Don't."

They sat in the crowded rooms of the Mueller Hotel, among the tourists, who were titillated by the presence of live zombies in their midst. Though long ago the contagion had been stopped, still people held the old fears.

Maria Mueller, Kaspar's daughter, brought the priests large mugs of beer, and plates of pork ribs and sauerkraut. Though in her forties, she curtsied daintily to the bishop and the cardinal, but pointedly turned her back on Father Meyer. No one in the village had spoken to him since he'd resigned from the Council.

"It goes well, does it not?" she asked the churchmen. "Are you enjoying it?"

"I never cease to wonder at the Play," Bishop Ahrenkiel told her. "Everyone must be so proud."

She frowned. "This is our holy obligation, Your Excellence. We don't do it out of pride."

Father Meyer pursed his lips. One of the Lord's own creatures would be made to suffer horribly this afternoon, for another's sin of pride.

They had told him the zombies had no nerve endings.

Father Meyer sat hunched in his seat with tears running

down his cheeks. He clutched his rosary while he watched the creature writhe in agony as they stretched open its palm and slammed the nail through.

"The movements are being directed with a remote-control device, Johannes," the bishop reminded him, with a hint of pride in his voice. "It really doesn't feel anything. It's only made to look that way."

The other palm. The sound of the hammer on the nail echoed against the baffles on the walls. Blood spurted in the air and streamed over the end of the cross and onto the stage.

Chang, whang whang whang!

The creature struggled. Its mouth opened, closed, opened.

The hausfrau behind them moaned.

"Do you see?" Cardinal Schonbrun said to Father Meyer. "This reminds everyone of the suffering of Our Lord. It brings them nearer to God. I've never felt such emotion during a Passion Play. The scourging . . . that was excellent, Bishop Ahrenkiel, was it not?"

The bishop grunted, neither assent nor dissent.

Father Meyer brought his rosary to his heart as they hoisted the cross upward. The zombie swayed, then fell forward, pinioned in place by the spikes in its hands and feet. Blood flowed in rivulets from the crown of thorns, some into its mouth. The blue contact lenses gleamed as its—*his*—eyes gazed toward heaven. Such monumental pain. Father Meyer doubled his fists, feeling upon his own flesh the whip marks, the holes in his hands, the thorns digging into his scalp.

Unable to suppress a sob, he remembered what he had done that morning.

Dawn had been hours away. In the high Alps, in his beloved, unheated church, it was freezing.

He looked at the unmoving figure in the darkened confessional, closed the curtain, and rested his hand against the side of the booth. The swell of an ancient chant, *Rorate cacli,* masked the thundering of his heart. He inhaled the bittersweet odor of incense and gazed at the crucifix above the altar, at the gentle face carved five, six hundred years before by one of the Oberammergau faithful. The wounds, as fresh and red as at Calvary; the agony, the love.

"Most wondrous Savior," Father Meyer whispered, "if I'm doing wrong, forgive me. Please understand, Oh Lord, that I believe this to be a child of Thine, and if it—if he— is not, and I do pollute Thy body, as the Church charges . . . if I offend Thee, I am heartily sorry."

He stepped into his side of the confessional and drew the curtain. He sat, took a deep breath, and, crossing himself, began.

"Bless me, Father, for I have sinned. It has been . . ." He hesitated. Who could say how long it had been, for the one who sat in silence on the other side of the screen?

". . . it has been some time since my last confession. These are my sins." He swallowed hard and thought for a moment. How to proceed? It had been so clear last night, when he'd resolved to do this. So obviously a divine inspiration. But now, now when he was doing it, really risking it, he felt alone, untried.

But thus had Our Savior felt, he thought, and was comforted in his fear.

"I have had . . . thoughts, Father. I have had thoughts that were other than those Our Lord would have us think. I have wished for things. . . ."

He leaned his damp forehead against the screen. Such monumental pride, to speak for another! To dare to dream what was in another's heart. A heart that didn't even beat, not really. A mind that didn't think.

Nein, he didn't believe that.

"Listen," he whispered to the silhouette he could see through the screen. "I absolve you and forgive you of any sinful thought or deed, in the Name of the Father, and the Son, and the Holy Ghost, amen." He squinted through the crosshatches. "Do you understand? Go in peace. God has forgiven—"

"Father," came a voice, and Father Meyer started violently. It had spoken! Praise be to God! He knew, he had always believed, he had prayed—

"It's Anton," the voice went on, and he realized it was the Veck boy, standing just outside the curtain. "The cardinal and the bishop are at my cousin's hotel. They're asking for you.''

Father Meyer looked now at the figure on the cross. The figure he had dared to forgive. The stage was set for the climax of the Play, the Passion and suffering of the Lord. The three crosses had been raised—on the other two, the actors playing the Thieves hung supported by belts beneath their loincloths, as Kaspar Mueller would have been. The Holy Women in their veils and robes clasped their hands and wept. The Roman Centurion stood to one side, pondering. The players gazed up at the *wandelnder Leichnam,* nailed to Kaspar Mueller's cross while the old man hid behind a pile of rocks, which would be used later in the Resurrection scene. They spoke to the zombie, and it was Kaspar who answered, in his quavering, old man's voice.

Behind the cross, Kaspar cried out, *"Eil, Eil, lama sabachtani!"* and Pharisees reviled him for calling out to the prophet Elias.

And the figure on the cross, pale and slight, panted and looked up, then down. *Reanimated corpse,* Father Meyer's head insisted.

His heart replied, *An innocent man, doomed to suffer like this ten times.* For each zombie was to be used for ten performances: they had devised ways to fill the holes in its—*his*—hands with wax, to stitch up and conceal the wound in its side. Ten times they would do this to it. For the glory of God.

And the glory of Oberammergau.

The soldier offered the sponge of vinegar to the creature when Kaspar Mueller cried out, "I thirst." And it tasted the bile. Father Meyer was certain of it.

"Mother, behold thy son," Kaspar Mueller gasped.

The zombie looked down at Krista Veck.

Father Meyer gripped his rosary. He could not let this continue. His holy office required he speak the truth of God as he knew it. As long as he was a priest, he was compelled to act on behalf of the Shepherd's lambs—

"It is over," said Kaspar. The ribcage of the zombie

worked furiously. "Into Thy hands I commend my spirit." Its head drooped forward.

"Ah," murmured the Cardinal.

A low, ominous rumbling filled the theater. It was the time in the Play for the earthquake and the rending of the Temple. The crosses jittered on the stage. The zombie's palms began to bleed again.

"It is God's hand on us!" cried the actor who played Enan.

Blood streamed from its side and hands. Its—his— head bobbed. Father Meyer could abide no more. He rose to his feet and cried, "*Ja!* It is!"

"Father!" the Cardinal said, grabbing his hand.

Father Meyer shook him off and crawled over him. He ran down the stairs to the front of the stage. Before anyone could stop him, he leaped onto it and grabbed the wrist of the startled Centurion.

"You cannot do this! As a priest of God, I order you to stop!"

"What? What?" Kaspar demanded, appearing from behind the rocks. He was dressed as the risen Christ, in pure white robes.

"Blasphemer!" Father Meyer shouted at him. He thrust himself away from the Centurion, pushed Maria Veck and the other Holy Women out of his way and scrabbled onto the rocks. "Help me get him down! For the love of God, help me!"

"Get down from there!" The cardinal's voice rang over the rising voices of the crowd and the actors. "Get Father Meyer off the stage."

"Father, please." Rudi Mangasser, the Centurion, grasped Father Meyer's ankle. The priest yanked his leg free.

"For God's sake, Rudi! I baptized you. Help me!" Father Meyer pulled at the spike in the middle of the *Leichnam's* palm. It was hammered in all the way to the bone; blood pooled around it, smearing Father Meyer's fingers.

"Help me. Help me." He stared at the audience, which had leapt to its feet. Angry faces. Looks of horror. Some were backing away, others rushing forward. Others were crying.

"He is a being! We cannot do this!" He reached across the limp body and yanked off the crown of thorns, bringing skin with it.

A sudden, piercing chorus of screams erupted from the onlookers. Startled, Father Meyer froze and looked at them. Fingers pointed toward the stage—at him, he supposed. He dug his fingers into the zombie's palm, straining to pull out the nail.

The head slowly lifted. Who had the remote-control device? Father Meyer wondered vaguely. But the screams grew louder. People turned to run from the theater. The cardinal and the bishop crossed themselves and sank to their knees.

The head wobbled. Father Meyer took hold of it beneath the jaw to support it. The flesh was hot.

Hot—

The head turned. It was covered with large, red sores from which pus flowed like blood.

"The Pest!" someone shrieked. "It has the Plague!"

Shaking, Father Meyer stared into the sightless eyes. New sores exploded over the zombie's body even as Father Meyer watched. They ruptured in a jagged line along the wound in its side; they traveled over its chest, its stomach.

The heavens filled with a rumbling. The earth—not just the stage—began to shake.

"It's a trick!" someone shouted. "The priest has the control box!"

There were cries of outrage now. Maria Veck tore off her veil and shook her fist at Father Meyer while Rudi Mangasser scrambled onto the rocks and pulled him down.

"*Idiot!*" Rudi shouted, slapping Father Meyer across the face as they both fell to the stage floor. "What are you doing, you crazy old man?"

"I? I?" Father Meyer pushed Rudi aside and knelt in front of the zombie. He made the sign of the cross and folded his hands. Two red sores bubbled from his own palms.

Stigmata. But stigmata of a different sort. Of the New

Church. And a New sickness, he supposed, which would cripple the world, as the Old sickness had four hundred years before.

He burst into tears and opened his arms. "The covenant is broken. God has spoken through one of His children, to tell us of His great displeasure."

His wounds dripped onto the boards. "A changing corpse? My beloved, my brethren, we are all changing corpses! All!"

"Get him off the stage!" Cardinal Schonbrun shouted again.

"No, don't touch me! I have it already!" Father Meyer warned, but he knew it was too late.

Then, as one being, the throng roared and flew at him. A hundred hands grabbed him, hitting, punching, crushing. They kicked his shins and aching knees. Someone slammed a fist into his side. A woman he had never seen before wrapped her fingers around his clerical collar and choked him, choked hard until he couldn't breathe, couldn't see.

Then the face of the woman swelled with boils. He watched, horrified, as they burst and a thick, oozing pus ran down her face.

"She's got it, too!" shouted a man beside her.

She grabbed her face and wailed. Sores rose on the backs of her hands, exploded, splattering the man's face; and everywhere the infection touched him, pustules rose, crusted, split. The man fell to his knees, shrieking.

The contagion engulfed the crowd like a flood of forty days and forty nights. Cries of terror shattered Father Meyer's ears. The sky pounded with thunder, the hoofbeats of four horsemen; timbers and scenery fractured and crashed. The stage split open, and the ground beneath it, and people screamed and flailed wildly as they tumbled into the pit. All, all tore asunder.

A jag of lightning slammed into the cross on the stage, igniting it at the base, bonfire-hot. Hellfire-hot. The zombie opened its mouth once, twice. Its head lolled to the side, and its sightless gaze moved, moved.

It fixed on Father Meyer. Seemed to look at him . . .

yes! Froze there, staring at the priest of the old Church, the old Love.

Behold thy son. Behold him.

Father Meyer raised his hand and blessed him. The zombie bowed its head. The flames engulfed it, and it was gone!

"He did this to us!" Cardinal Schonbrun cried, and three men grabbed Father Meyer, pulling at him, beating him, weeping with rage.

Father Meyer stared at the fire as his arms were wrenched from their sockets, as blows and burning splinters rained down on his head. New sores erupted, burst, ran over his other wounds. No pain could be worse; no agony—

No; no pain could surpass that in his heart.

No fear could be greater than the fear in his soul.

He raised his gaze to heaven. "Father, forgive us," he whispered, with the last breath of his body. "We didn't know. We really didn't."

BRIGHT LIGHTS, BIG ZOMBIE

DOUGLAS E. WINTER

*"When I started using dynamite, I believed in many
things. . . . Finally, I believe only in dynamite."*
—*Sergio Leone*, Giu la testa

IT'S SIX A.M.
DO YOU KNOW
WHERE YOUR BRAINS ARE?

You are not the kind of zombie who would be at a place
like this at this time of the morning. You are not a
zombie at all; not yet. But here you are, and you cannot
say that the videotape is entirely unfamiliar, although it is
a copy of a copy and the details are fuzzy. You are at an
after hours club near SoHo watching a frantic young gentleman named Bob as the grooved and swiftly spinning point
of a power drill chews its way through the left side of his

skull. The film is known alternatively as *City of the Living Dead* and *The Gates of Hell,* and you're not certain whether this version is missing anything or not. All might come clear if you could actually hear the soundtrack. Then again, it might not. The one the other night was in Swedish or Danish or Dutch, and a small voice inside you insists that this epidemic lack of clarity is a result of too much of this stuff already. The night has turned on that imperceptible pivot where two A.M. changes to six A.M. Somewhere back there you could have cut your losses, but you rode past that moment on a comet trail of bulletblown heads and gobbled intestines and now you are trying to hang onto the rush. Your brain at this moment is somewhere else, spread in grey-smeared stains on the pavement or coughed up in bright patterns against a concrete wall. There is a hole at the top of your skull wider than the path that could be corkscrewed by a power drill, and it hungers to be filled. It needs to be fed. It needs more blood.

THE DEPARTMENT
OF VICTUAL
FALSIFICATION

Morning arrives on schedule. You sleepwalk through the subway stations from Canal Street to Union Square, then switch to the Number 6 Local on the Lexington Avenue Line. You come up from the Thirty-third Street exit blinking. Waiting for a light at Thirty-second, you scope the headline of the *Daily News*: STILL DEAD. There is a blurred photograph of something that looks vaguely like a hospital room. You think about those four unmoving bodies, locked somewhere inside the Center for Disease Control in Atlanta. You think about your mother. You think about Miranda. But the light has changed. You're late for work again and you've worn out the line about the delays at the checkpoints. There is no time for new lies.

Your boss, Tony Kettle, runs the Department of Victual Falsification like a pocket calculator, and lately your twos and twos have not added up to fours. If Kettledrum had his way, you would have been subtracted from the staff long ago, but the magazine has been shorthanded since Black Wednesday and sooner or later you manage to get your work done. And let's face it, you know splatter films better than almost anyone left alive.

The offices of the magazine cover a single floor. Once there were several journals published here, from sci-fi to soft porn to professional wrestling. Now there is only the magazine, a subtenant called Engel Enterprises, and quiet desperation. You navigate the water-stained carpet to the Department of Victual Falsification. Directly across the hall is Tony's office, and you stagger past with the hope that he's not there.

"Good morning, gorehounds," you say as you enter the department. There are six desks, but only three of them are occupied. Brooks is reading the back of his cigarette package: Camel Lights. Elaine shakes her head and puts her blue pencil through line after line of typescript. Stan, who has been bowdlerizing an old Jess Franco retrospective for weeks, shuffles a stack of stills and whistles an Oingo Boingo tune. J. Peter and Olivia are dead.

What once was your desk is now a prop stand for a mad maze of paper. An autographed photo of David Warbeck is pinned to the wall, and looks out over old issues of *Film Comment, Video Watchdog, Ecco, Eyeball,* the *Daily News.* Here are the curled and coffee-stained manuscripts, and there the rows of reference volumes, from *Gray's Anatomy* to Hardy's *Encyclopedia of Horror Film.* Somewhere in the shuffle are two lonely pages of printout, the copy you managed to eke out yesterday from the press kit for John Woo's latest bullet ballet, smuggled through Customs between the pages of a Bible.

Atop it all is a pink message slip with today's date: Ruggero Deodato called. Don't forget about tonight. "And hey," Brooks says, finally lighting up a cigarette. "We had another visit from the Brain Police." You are given a look that is meant to be serious and significant.

You have spent the last five years of your life presenting images of horror, full color and in closeup, to a readership—perhaps you should say viewership—of what you suspected were mostly lonely, adolescent and alienated males who loved these kinds of films. The bloodier the better. Special effects—the tearing of latex flesh, the splash of stage crimson, the eating of rubber entrails—were the magazine's focus, and in better days, after a particularly vivid drunk that followed a screening of the latest *Night of the Living Dead* ripoff, you and J. Peter and Tony came to call yourself the Department of Victual Falsification.

That was then, and this is now. The dead came back, not for a night, but for forever. Your mother. Black Wednesday. Miranda. Cannibals in the streets. The bonfires in Union Square. Law and order. Congressional hearings. Peace, complete with special ID cards and checkpoints and military censors.

You remember, just before the Gulf War, reading newspaper articles about high school students who paged through magazines that were to be sent to the troops in Saudi Arabia, coloring over bras and bare chests, skirts that were too short, cigarettes caught up in dangling hands. You thought that this was supremely funny. Now each month you do something much the same. The magazine publishes the latest additions to the lists, recounts the seizures from the shelves of the warehouses and rental stores. At first the banished titles were the inevitable ones, the old Xs and the newer NC-17s and, of course, anything to do with the living dead. In recent months the lists have expanded into the Rs and a few of the PG-13s.

You are detectives of the dying commodity called horror, and there are fewer places where the magazine is sold, and fewer things that you can say, and fewer photos for you to run and, of course, there are fewer people left alive, fewer still who care.

THE FUTILITY
OF FICTION

You see yourself as the kind of zombie who would appreciate a quiet night at home with a good book. You watch tv instead. Tonight there is the Local News, followed by the National News, and then, of course, the game shows begin and will continue on until the Local News, followed by the National News, and then, of course, the game shows again. There are 106 other channels on your television set, but all of them are awash in a sea of speckled grey and have been for nearly a year.

The path that awaits you is clear. You reach into the back of your bookcase, behind the wall of unread Literary Guild Alternate Selections, to slip out tonight's first videotape, a pristine copy, recorded on TDK Pro High Grade at SP, of the Japanese LaserDisc of Ruggero Deodato's *Cannibal Holocaust*. You waited months for your dealer to get this one, and now you wait patiently for the first real moment of truth, that glimpse of the tribesmen as they tear off and eat the flesh of their prey. Although you tell yourself that this is what you want, that this is really what you want, this is not what you get. There is a cornfield on your forty-inch television monitor. It is late summer, nearly the harvest, and there in the tall stalks is Miranda, walking with racehorse grace in her bleached jeans and turtleneck sweater, hair in golden braids and face shining with the sun.

You turn your back on the monitor and you listen. For some time after Miranda died, you knocked on the door of the apartment before you entered. You would turn the key slowly in the lock and then pause here in the living room in the hope that you would hear her in the bedroom, that she had returned, that she was waiting for you, that none of this had happened, that none of this was real.

The video plays on. "How could you explain what a movie is?" A voice calls to you from the screen: "They're all dead, aren't they?" You look back and the cannibals at last are feasting. You watch, and you wish. Nothing seems to be what you want to do until you consider horror. A random sampling of the titles hidden at the back of the bookcase induces a delicious expectancy: *Anthropophagus*. *Eaten Alive*. *Trap Them and Kill Them*. Little wonder that the Gore Commission should have found so many of these films so wanting. The covers of the video boxes are themselves a kind of foreplay, wet and bright with colors, most of them red. *Make Them Die Slowly.* Here the label reads: "Banned in 31 countries." Make that 32. You know so much about these motion pictures, about the stories that they have to tell. You feel that if only they had given you the camera back then in the eighties, back when such things could be, you could have given shape to this uncertain passion that nightly inhabits your gut.

You have always wanted to make films. Getting the job at the magazine was only the first step toward cinematic celebrity. You never stopped thinking of yourself as a writer and director of horror films, biding his time in the Department of Victual Falsification. But between the job and the life there wasn't much time for the screenplays or even the short experimental films. That first, and only, Christmas, Miranda had given you the videocamera. For a few weeks afterward, you would shoot Miranda as she walked around the apartment, Miranda with shampoo in her hair, Miranda and the new kitten, Miranda at the stove, Miranda at the fireplace, Miranda and Miranda and Miranda. Then, what with the zombies and everything, life started getting more interesting and complicated. You worked for the magazine and you had once met George A. Romero and you had your collection of videos, so chic now that the lists were out and the tapes were gone from the rental shelves. People were happy to meet you and to invite you to their parties. Then things got worse, and then came Black Wednesday and the bodies in the streets and the soldiers and the fires in Union Square.

You pull your videocamera from its hiding place beneath the floorboards of the closet and set it up on its tripod. You have no blank videotape, of course. You take the cassette from the VCR and push it into the camera. You decide to start immediately with the film you have in mind. You aim the camera at the far wall of the apartment, bare and white. The autofocus blurs, then holds. Through the viewfinder you see exactly what you want. You press the start button. You tape nothing.

A TOMB WITH A VIEW

You dream about the Still Dead. You sneak down the corridors of the Center for Disease Control. Nobody can see you. A door with a plaque reading *C'est La Mort* opens into the Department of Victual Falsification. Miranda is spreadeagled across the top of your desk, her wrists and ankles bound with strips of celluloid, the censored seconds from the first reel of Deodato's *Inferno in diretta*. Around her in white hospital beds, like the four points on a compass, are the Still Dead. You approach and discover that she isn't moving. You touch her. She is cold. Quiet. One of them. Still dead. But then she opens her eyes and looks at you. You make a sound like a scream but it is the telephone ringing. The receiver is hot and wet in your hand.

"I'm sick." You expect the caller to be Elaine or, worse yet, the Kettledrum himself. *Ta-dum, ta-dee, ta . . .*

"I knew that from the day I met you." The voice is unmistakable. In his prime he made the covers of *New York* and *Interview* and *Spy*. Now no one cares; but you never know, perhaps they will again. Sunlight is in your eyes. The clock says ten. You listen to Jay's latest proposition. A duplication center somewhere in the Bronx. Edit onto one-inch tape, copies to VHS. Sales in back rooms, some bars, the private clubs, on the street. Money to be made. Fame. And most important, screen credits. "Your name in lights."

In this new world there is no longer a place for dreams. Yet you have no doubt that he can do these things. It is the catch that troubles you, but only for a moment. You know you can be had. Jay says *ciao* and he's gone.

You're not dressed and out of the apartment until eleven. The uptown train pulls away just as you make the platform. Clutched beneath your elbow, the *Daily News* is screaming: BRIDGE BLOWN. This time it was the George Washington. You wonder whether the dead are being kept out, or the living kept in. Now if you want to get to New Jersey, you swim. The Still Dead are buried on page five.

No new developments: "Still Dead." The CDC will issue another statement on Sunday. Billy Graham will lead a candlelight prayer vigil. The President has expressed cautious optimism.

It's eleven-thirty when you reach Park Avenue South, eleven-forty by the time you get a cup of coffee and an elevator. Kettledrum is waiting, and he holds his glasses in his hand. A bad sign. You consider saying something. An excuse, an apology. Just offering a smile. It is all a joke. The glasses start to twirl. You know you are in trouble.

Tony does not waste words. The magazine has had visitors again. The military censor took a hard look at the new issue and found not one, but two, discussions of the contents of listed videos in your article on Umberto Lenzi.

"What about the First Amendment?" Tony looks at you. You look at Tony. Tony is the first to laugh. You decide to nod your head and join in when you see the photo in Tony's hands. Black and white and red all over. It's Miranda. Her legs are spread wide, left hand fondling the rope of raw intestine that dangles provocatively between them, dripping wet blots of blood onto the headless body on the floor. You look again and it is not Miranda. Of course not. It is some actress from a splatter film, and this is a publicity photo. A still. Still life.

LES YEUX
SANS VISAGE

You met her in one of those midwestern towns where the sunsets were gold and not impaled by tall buildings. You had gone from NYU Film School to waiting for jobs to waiting tables at the Salvador Deli, and when the magazine asked, you answered. Soon after you had written the expected fanboy froth about Troma and Incarnate and the rest of the local scene, you were sent into the heartland to write the set report on the latest annual installment in the film life of a hockey-masked hooligan. At night you would stand around for hours while thirty-year-olds trying to act like teenagers were taped up with rubber tubes that would, for the few seconds of a take, spout out a mixture of Karo Syrup and melted chocolate that looked something like blood. In the mornings you would sleep and then, in the afternoons, write a few pandering paragraphs of the usual nonsense before taking a walk around the town, the reporter from the big city, and stop by the Rexall and the Kroger and the Payless Shoe Store and on the third day, after boredom had set in soundly, you found her in a place called Kenny's. You remember that she was drinking a Nehi, leaning easily against a wall, one bluejeaned leg crossed over the other. She was wearing black Keds. Her eyes were closed and she was listening to a song on the jukebox, something by Public Image Limited, the two of them so out of place there in Hicksville that you thought you had walked into a dream. You wanted to shoot her, just to shoot her right then and there, and you wished that you had a camera. You told her she should be in movies, and of course this is what she wanted to hear.

Within the week she had moved in with you. She talked about the day your movie would go into production. All your plans were aimed at Hollywood. She wanted to live in the Malibu and you wished to join the film life of El Lay. You watched videocassettes of Lang and Franju, Bava and Pasolini, and bullshitted her with beginning film theory until you both had enough to drink and then you went to bed. It wasn't long before you decided you would marry her.

You returned to New York with the question of what Miranda was going to do. She had talked about college, talked about modeling, talked about children. She wasn't sure what she wanted to do. People were always telling Miranda that she should be in movies. At dinners you would talk about directors and their actress wives: Bardot and Vadim, Russell and Roeg, Rossellini and Lynch. About how only you could direct her. About how only you could show the world Miranda. And then, of course, she died.

STILL DEAD

No one is kind. Their jobs are on the line. You have been inclined of late to underestimate the value of the dollar. Now you wonder what you would do if the magazine were gone.

You wander down the hall to the archives and browse through back issues. That first appearance of the magazine, way back in 1979, wore Godzilla on the cover and promised a photo preview of *Alien*. It seems like a century ago. No one in this country had heard of Deodato or Lenzi or Fulci; certainly no one cared. You flip through the years, and the bright-blooded covers, and you wonder at everything that has changed.

Later you find an empty office and make the call. You take a deep breath and dial the number of Jay's loft. You don't recognize the voice at the other end. "Tell him I'll do it." The voice asks you to identify yourself. "Tell him that Dario Argento called, and that he'll do it." The voice says that she has no idea what you are talking about, but that if you would leave your number, Jay would call right back. You hang up the phone and wonder whether it could have been traced. In your mind are images of men in blue suits with badges.

You escape the building without incident. It is a cold, snowy morning. Fall or winter. Miranda died in October. They called it Black Wednesday, but the day was bright and clear. There were leaves on the ground the morning she died, a blanket of green and gold that turned wet and red by noon and then grey with ash by night. It was mid-afternoon before the National Guardsmen had secured the apartment building. It was two weeks until the barricades were complete and the city was safe again. Each morning you would awaken to the smell of Miranda on your pillow, and then the other smell, the smell of the corpses burning in the midnight heaps at Union Square.

You slip into a bar near Penn Station. On the large-screen TV is a repeat of the Morning News. The daily CDC press conference is uninformative. As is that from Central Command. Protests continue outside the White House. The bartender rolls his eyes and says, "Fucking hippies." No one trusts a man who will not wear a flag on his lapel or tie a yellow ribbon to the antenna of his car. You nod and drink your beer.

It's late when you leave the bar, your footsteps uncertain, the sidewalk slick with ice. You haven't seen a taxi in months. Ahead is a checkpoint and you brush your pockets, trying to remember if you're holding. You imagine a patdown, the sound of a gloved hand on a plastic case. A copy of Fulci's *Zombie* in your coat could get you six months, maybe a year with the right judge; don't even think about the contents of your apartment. You're next at the gate. The soldier shines a flashlight into your eyes and you say, "Jack Valenti." No smile. "Forty-fifth President of the United States." He doesn't appreciate the joke, just waves you through, and you can't help but feel that you have escaped something.

At your apartment you discover an envelope with the logo of Jay's former employer, a comic book company, stuck beneath the door. Inside there is a note: *Soon.*

CANNIBALS, QUESTI, AND GUINEA PIGS

Your interest in film doesn't normally take you beyond the racks marked Horror and Suspense, but at the moment there seems to be a shortage of inventory in both departments. This morning you are standing on the second floor of RKO Video on Broadway, where a patron is complaining to the cashier about the quality of her copy of *Pretty Woman*. You are looking for something, anything, with the word "dead" in its title. Nothing is to be found. You start looking instead for the word "living."

He walks past you, blood-brown Armani coat flapping like wounded wings. "Mister . . ."

"Fulci," you say, slipping a copy of *Heaven Can Wait* from the shelf in front of you.

He nods and smiles and follows you back to the checkout counter. The woman there looks like she would rather be at the dentist's. It could be a mistake to rent this tape and leave some sort of record of where you were and when. You excuse your way to the front of the line and announce in a loud but tempered voice that·you would like to special order *Faces of Death,* all three installments, and by the time that the kid has hold of you, pulling you back, people are talking and the woman at the counter has a telephone in her hand.

You run for the doorway and the lights suddenly are bright. A security guard looms in front of you; he doesn't like what he sees. You toss him the video and his hands react. A perfect catch. You feel the kid pushing and you look back over your shoulder as you reach the exit. You are laughing a little too hard.

Outside you take opposite sides of Broadway, and when you watch the kid wander into an alley off Fifty-seventh, you step in after him and try on a smile.

"Got it, dude." Now he is smiling, too. "All yours. Uncut *Django Kill.* From Argentina. *Se habla? No más, mi muchacho. Inglés,* my man, with subtitles."

"How much?"

"Hundred dollar."

"Get lost."

"Pure stuff. Uncut. Got the scalping scene."

"Right. Twenty-five."

"I ain't giving the stuff away."

"I can't do more than fifty."

"It's a steal. Fifty. You're robbing me."

You can't believe you're doing this. Finally you follow the kid farther down the alley. "I want a look."

"Shit," he says. "Who do you think you are, Siskel and Ebert? This is a steal, man. I'm telling you it's good."

You give him the fifty and then there is nothing to do but hustle it back to your apartment and give it a try. The tape is unmarked but for a torn handwritten label that reads GIULIO QUESTI. You want to believe that this means something. Images of dust and blood and molten gold are burning in your mind. You watch a few seconds of noise, and then a faded color spectrum appears. Finally you see a picture, so grainy that you need to squint. It's not *Django Kill,* oh no, not at all. You *think* you can see something happening, something with a Japanese girl tied to a dingy bed, and there is a man in a samurai helmet standing over her, the lights turned blue and a longhandled knife that dips down into her torso and comes up wet. He cuts away her right hand, throws blood onto the walls. You seem to think that this video is called *Guinea Pig*. There is no story to it, just the girl kidnapped, bound, and slowly cut into pieces. Finally the psycho eats her eyeballs. You want to feel something, do something, say something, but it's only eleven-thirty in the morning and everyone else in the world is dead or has a job.

NO CULTURE

Over coffee and toast you read the *Daily News*. Miami is gone, carpet-bombed back into swampland. The President is regretful but unshaken in his resolve. Food riots in Boston and Providence. A news team in Palm Springs got footage of what looks like a zombied Tom Cruise, his buttocks chewed away but otherwise intact. And there is another entry in the Still Dead. This makes five of them. Five who have died only once. Five who have not returned. They wait in that white room at the CDC, and the whole world waits for them.

At dawn you woke like a man accustomed to the hour, your vision clear and in focus. You are committed to the task that awaits you. You wanted to call Jay again, maybe tell him you see the storyboards, you see frame by frame, you see and see and see.

It is Saturday and your apartment is a dungeon from which you must escape. You decide to go to the movies. The only remaining theatres are in Times Square, but the Times Square you remember is gone. A Holiday Inn has supplanted the Pussycat empire on Broadway. What was the Peppermint Lounge is now Tower 45. You pass the Marriott Marquis and walk onto Forty-second Street. The UDC has done its work so very well. Ghosts of grindhouses past fade in and out like distant television signals. The

Adonis, the XXXtasy Video Center, Peepland: all gone. Even the Funny Store has vanished beneath the weight of another office tower. Progress is our most important product, and progress has taken them, one by one.

The new theatres on Forty-second Street are sedate and shadowless waiting rooms, places of pleasant dreams, not nightmares. The first is showing Disney cartoons, the next *Jesus of Nazareth*. You wonder what they will do about Lazarus. There is no choice but the third one, which does not admit children. You are hopeful, but there is no doubting the fear.

With two cans of beer hidden in your coat, you move away from the ticket booth and find a seat in the middle of the theater. The lights dim. An animated usherette tells you not to smoke and to use the trash receptacles as you exit. The following preview has been approved for all audiences by the Motion Picture Association of America. *The Absent-Minded Professor*. Your knees are shaky. You sip at the first beer. You stand and walk back up the aisle. This will not work.

Finally the previews are at an end. You sneak another drink of beer and take a seat on the aisle, just in case. The following motion picture has been rated PG–13 by the Motion Picture Association of America. This is a London Film Production. There is a clock tower, Big Ben; the time is eleven. The music is so very strange, plucking strings, a zither. The film is called *The Third Man*. Written by Graham Greene. Directed by Carol Reed. It is set in Vienna, after the Second World War. Some man named Holly Martins, a writer, comes to visit his friend Harry Lime, but Harry Lime is dead. There is no color. The faces look out at you in black-and-white. Nothing is happening. The actors are just talking and talking, walking and walking.

You clutch at the armrests and wait for the next surge to hit you. It comes just as you begin to understand. Harry Lime is back from the dead. He was never dead, not really. It was a joke of some kind. "We should have dug deeper than a grave." As the audience murmurs, you stand up, knowing that Harry Lime is alive, yes alive, even to the very end, when the bullets find him. You think about the squibs that could explode from beneath his clothing, sending clots of blood across the grey walls of the sewers, and you hear yourself groan with the knowledge of what is missing, what is gone, what was never there.

People are turning in their seats to look at you. They are saying *Sit down*! and *What does he want*? An usher in a suit is hurrying down the aisle. At least he is in color. Another usher is coming from the other side. You move along the row of seats, bumping knees and outstretched hands. The beer falls onto the carpet, another unseen stain. You do not resist as one of the ushers takes your arm.

In the lobby you see nothing but the poster for the film, and then the night waiting outside. There, in black-and-white, is the knowledge of the way that we have chosen to be entertained, like a book read once too often, leaving a trail of images and emotions so familiar that there is nothing left to see or feel. You know the future, and it is now; it always will be now.

BLOOD AND SYMPATHY

Later you return to the scene of your crimes. You wonder at the silence, whether it is absolute or only the hour. There are no signs that the magazine has been closed down. Still you feel strange stepping out of the elevator and into an unlit corridor. That the hour is past midnight doesn't help.

Tony's door is closed and dark. There's a light on in the Department of Victual Falsification. Elaine is at her desk. She looks up when you come in, but she does not seem surprised. You tell her that you've come to get your things. "Don't bother," she tells you. Then: "I've been waiting here all day for you." Waiting for what? "You could have called." That is when you notice that your desk is clear. The photo on the wall looks down on nothing. You don't need to look to know that the drawers are empty.

"We had more trouble here this morning," Elaine says. "A search warrant." Now you realize that she is holding a pistol in her left hand. "Tony says it's over. Done. Finished.'' The pistol looks like it might be loaded. ''What do you think?''

You want to tell her the truth. Instead you say: ''I think it's only just begun.''

She's smiling. The pistol is back in her purse. ''I thought you might want these.'' Four plastic cases. ''My secret stash.''

You hold up the first of the videos, factory fresh and labeled: *Revenge of the Dead*. It is Pupi Avati's *Zeder*. You deep-breathe and feel your nostrils go like ice.

''Elaine.'' She raises her eyebrows. Now you are committed. In the elevator, you ask her where she wants to go.

''How about your place?''

You walk and walk and at Fifth Avenue, just past the Flatiron Building, Elaine takes your hand and leads you into a Chinese carryout, where she orders dim sum for you both. From the restaurant you walk toward Union Square. Each step takes you closer to your apartment, to the place where Miranda lived. Where Miranda died. This was your neighborhood. That boarded-up storefront was your grocer, the next your video store. Now the vista has gone upside down, and nothing will ever be the same.

''Best bonfire in the city,'' Elaine says, pointing to Union Square. A trio of National Guardsmen in urban camouflage huddle with their cigarettes. They watch over a graveyard of concrete and ash, circled with rolls of barbed wire. The fragrance reminds you of the mornings after Black Wednesday, when you woke to the smell of the corpses burning, the perfumed ghost of Miranda sleeping beside you. It seems a lifetime ago, but still you can see her sleeping, the flicker of flames across the face that wasn't there.

Soon Elaine is lying next to you in that same room, her dark hair a shadow on the pillow. The only light is from the small bedside television. After *Zeder* you watch the uncut *Apocalypse Domani*, and after that she opens your shirt, her hand against your chest. You watch the tv screen go blank, then grey, and in the moments before you try, but fail, to make love, she says: ''When there are no more films, we'll have to make our own.''

SOMETIMES
A VOGUE
NATION

You wake up with a severed head on your chest. Its lips are moving but you can't hear the words. After a few seconds you realize that the head isn't talking, it is chewing. A hand rises into view, clutching a fistful of entrails. The clock on the VCR blinks a continuous 12:00. That would be noon, judging by the sunlight that zigzags through the blinds. The last thing you remember was that Elaine was sleeping while you watched the final moments of Deodato's *L'ultima cannibali*. The tribesmen had split Mei Mei Lay open from groin to breastbone, dug out her organs, and sewn her back up for cooking. You have the feeling that you may have missed something good.

You remove the little television from your chest just as Doctor Butcher begins to rev up his band saw. The shot is static, almost matter-of-fact. The stage blood, when it comes, is orangish, surreal. You would have given the scene depth, momentum; not simply shock, but true anguish. There is a note on the nightstand, a few lines in black ink; you read it and smile a thank-you to Elaine. You are on your second cup of coffee and the final moments of *Doctor Butcher, M.D.* when the telephone rings. It's Joe D'Amato. He wants to take you sightseeing, probably tonight or tomorrow, sometime after ten. He'll call again. You tell him you'll be waiting.

Then you hit the streets, in search of a sandwich and today's *Daily News*. You wonder what Jay will do for lighting and whether you will need your tripod. At your favorite Greek diner you order chicken salad and more coffee. When you spread the newspaper across the counter, you learn that the first of the Still Dead, a thirty-three-year-old black male from suburban Chicago, otherwise unidentified, came back last night and was trepanned with a surgical power saw. Life is still imitating art. Doctor Butcher would have been proud.

Across a few more streets and down an alley is the backdoor to Forbidden Planet. You keep your head down, feel like you look guilty, and shove your hands deep into your pockets. Money talks and bullshit walks. You need an extra battery for your camera, and maybe somebody at the Planet will be selling.

"Got what you want," someone says, though it's hard to hear over the noise of a boom box, an incessant orgy of doom thrash metal. The kids lean into the walls and don't look at you. They wear their biker jackets, black t-shirts, and jeans like uniforms.

"Say man." A skinheaded nymphet in torn fishnets twists down the volume, raises her pastewhite face to you. "You know where we could get some stuff?"

"Stuff?" You want to keep walking, get this over with as quickly as you can. Who knows who might be watching.

"You know." Her eyes, black circles scored at their far corners with silver, dart around, mock fugitive. She sucks at her cigarette, blows back smoke and the word of the hour. "Some good G-O-R-E?"

"No can do." Your hands seem caught in your pockets. These are your readers. Your public. They sent you letters, sometimes. But you never thought of them when you wrote, not really. You thought about something else, something—

"Like *New York Ripper*?"

"No." But you can't walk away. You are—

"*Eaten Alive,* maybe? *Man from Deep River*? Some cannibal—"

"Listen, I—"

"I do," she says, and for the first time she is alive, truly alive. She bites at her purple lips, finally works up a smile. "Like we know where we can score something but we don't got the dollars. You wanna go in with us, maybe?"

You look at them, and they look back at you, expectant; a line of lost moviegoers, waiting for what you can show them. You tell yourself that you are not this desperate. You are looking for a battery. That's all. At last you shrug and start to walk away. She turns the music back up, and now that rotten Johnny Lydon is ranting away:

This is what you want
This is what you get
This is what you want
This is what you get. ...

You feel them pulling at you, pulling you back. But it's not them, not really. You want so desperately to see. You came here in search of something, something you thought you wanted, but now you aren't sure. You wonder if you ever were sure. You want to give in to it, let it take you away again to that place where you never need to be sure.

Whether you want to or not, you think about Miranda. You try to remember the way she was before Black Wednesday, before the night she died, before the dead came back and the apartment walls went red with blood. And before everything was whitewashed back into this thing they call reality.

THE NIGHT
SHIFTS

You are hungry and you are thirsty; you need to see something, but you're not sure what. Nothing hidden on your bookshelf is enough anymore.

You walk down into SoHo, past all the empty restaurants and art galleries, a showplace of spraypaint and shattered glass. When you cross Prince Street, a walkie-talkie crackles at you from the darkness. A cough and clipped voices. Soldiers are on the street corners. All of the city seems armed and ready. Like the morning after Black Wednesday.

At first you could not believe that Miranda was dead. Now you find it hard to believe that she was ever really alive. That you were married. Shared wine and loud music and laughter. That there ever was anything but this.

You decided long ago not to think about that day. It was months after the first reports came in from the Pennsylvania countryside. About the dead that came back to life.

The dead that walked. The dead that ate the living. You had your doubts about the stories, even when it was Dan Rather who told them. After all, this was the stuff of horror movies.

Before it happened you had never thought about Miranda's death. You were too young, too happy, to think about it. You spent no time in anticipation of it because death was something that would not happen, could not happen, at least until you yourself were old and tired and ready.

Helicopters flutter overhead. Their searchlights bite holes in the darkness. At Houston you find a market that is still open, buy a carton of beer, and head back to the apartment.

"Do you love her?" your mother had asked that first, and last, time the two of you visited. You didn't know what to say. Of course you loved her. You had married her, hadn't you?

You thought you would faint when you came home that night, in those long lost moments of shadow and flame. Miranda had been beautiful. That was the way you wanted to remember her. Like in the photographs her parents had sent, now on the mantle of the apartment, taken when she was younger than you had ever known her.

You could have given her life eternal through the lens of your camera. Video. Film. Pictures. You could have loved her forever. How could you explain the feeling of being misplaced, of always standing to one side of the world, of watching the world as if it existed only when recorded and replayed on tape, and wondering if this was how everyone felt. You always believed that other people could see more directly, could actually see and understand the world through their own eyes, and didn't worry quite so much about why. You could see it only through a lens, through what you could record and edit and assemble into a tangible, meaningful whole, locked safely and securely within the four walls of a picture. Then, and only then, could you see and understand . . . and yes, love.

You drink more than one beer on your trek back to the apartment, and once there you drink more than one more. You slip another video into the deck. Deodato again. *Camp-*

ing del terrore, although for once you prefer the English title: *Body Count.* More beer and another video, and then another and another, and after a time the images blur and bleed into a single color.

Sooner or later the telephone rings. It is time.

GONE

The barricades are back up at the major intersections, and the city has become very small. Your head is hollow, cracked and scooped out like an oyster on the half shell. You followed the flicker of red video across the television screen in pursuit of some kind of answer. Then the tapes ran out; as you watched the last line of credits, superimposed on a staggering horde of zombies as they crossed the Brooklyn Bridge, you suddenly saw yourself in hideous closeup, gapemouthed in worship before a forty-inch altar of flickering light.

You caught the telephone on the second ring. Through the noise and a distant sound that sooner or later you realized was gunfire, you heard that it was Jay, that he wanted you to meet him at Patchin Place. This is not a test. Your presence, and your videocamera, are required. You told him you'd be there in minutes, and now you're there, camera in hand, and you can feel it about to happen.

The alleyway is awash in the yellow spray of flares and flashlights. Elaine stands in the shadows, her pistol pointed into the night sky; at her side is some black guy with a shotgun. Jay is watchful; waiting, waiting. Finally he looks at you.

"Do it," he says, and then gestures grandly to the others. "Lights." Shadows twist over a gas generator; a ratcheting, a cough, and a spray of white cuts the alley into an urban dreamscape, the stuff of Lang and Reed.

"Something's happening, uptown and down. . . ." He wears a joker's grin, a shotgun in his black-gloved hand. "Could be Black Wednesday all over again." You hear a shout, footsteps racing on wet concrete. He shrugs and nods into the darkness. "Someone has to shoot the picture." His hand busses your shoulder. "So do it," he says again. "Sound," he announces; and, as he walks away, "Speed." Then you're alone, with your finger on the trigger.

Through the viewfinder you see the world, your world, the world made flesh on the grey-silver screen. Mad shadows chase one of Jay's nerdy protégés into view, and he dances before you, arms in flight, and mugs breathlessly for the camera. Finally he leans in at you and cries: "They're heeeeer!"

Then he is gone, and your world is the world of the dead. The first one is an oldtimer, workshirt and spotted trousers, shuffling around the corner in vague pursuit. The left side of his face is gone; eaten. You can see the teeth marks as you smashzoom in on him. From somewhere to your left comes the bullroar of the black guy's shotgun. The top of the oldtimer's head lifts away. You watch him fall and see your take replayed endlessly on the monitors of an editing bay. Perfect. Picture perfect. He collapses to the sidewalk in an unceremonious and uncinematic heap.

You slide the camera over the corpse and up the wall, where the shadow of the next one spiderwebs nicely into p.o.v. "Got him," you hear Elaine call. This one is a kid, your random Puerto Rican street punk, and he looks fairly fresh. You hit him with a medium closeup just in time to catch the jagged line of bulletholes that Elaine punches into his chest. Craters erupt—grey skin, blood and squirming maggots—and you zoom into one then out just in time to catch the headshot as the black guy steps in stage right, swings his shotgun up and lets both barrels go. The body cartwheels back, out of the light, and you've lost it to the black beyond.

"Take . . . it . . . easy." Jay sounds anxious and upset. "Not . . . so . . . fast." But there are sirens in the distance and the sound, you think, of radios and marching feet. White noise and distant voices. Order is about to be restored. You don't have much time.

You peek over the viewfinder and there is another shadow climbing the wall. Elaine is twisting a speedloader from her belt. Shell casings ping-pong down the alley. You look in again and see shadow turn to skin. It's a woman.

Tall. Long blond hair. Pale skin. As you squint and let the focus go, ready for a soft fade-in, you hear her footsteps stumble forward. Your finger finds the autofocus as you let the lens sweep the pavement slowly to her feet. Black Keds. Then up. Bleached jeans. Slowly. White blouse, half-unbuttoned, a tiny pearl necklace at her throat, and pale, pale skin. Slowly up to her face. Her beautiful face. A small clicking sound is coming from your throat. The picture shivers once, twice, then dims. Finally you hear your voice: "Mir-an-da!"

You pull the shot away from her and left. Elaine kneels, stiffarms the handgun. You hear sounds like belches and swing your eyes, the camera, back. Miranda's left forearm angles impossibly, then breaks, strands of flesh stretching, then snapping, hand clutching at empty air as it spins and floats away. You see the shot in slow motion, a mad Peckinpah pirouette, suddenly shattered in midturn as the force of a shotgun blast kicks out her legs. You fall to your knees with her, losing your balance, nearly dropping the camera; still you hold onto the shot. You have her now. She can't escape you. You feel the urge for a closeup, but you cannot risk moving from the medium shot as Miranda rears back into frame. Another roar, and the top of her right shoulder explodes. A great brown geyser of blood erupts, grey flesh and bone graffiti the alley wall.

Somehow she stands, keeps walking. Her head jerks to the right as the black guy chunks in another round; the shotgun kicks again, a miss that showers a grey snow of brick and dust. You swing the camera down then up from her bulletblown knees in time to catch Elaine's next volley, three shots that spit through Miranda's chest and neck and crease her cheek. Her mouth opens wide in response. You don't know if it is a laugh or a scream.

Still she is coming, past the black guy, past Elaine, who looks at you with angry fear. They can't fire now, not back at you and Jay and the rest of the crew. Your shot is steady, sure, a reverse zoom that frames her just so, the alley seeming to widen behind her as she approaches. Now your back is against the wall and the lens is open wide; she walks on and gives you your closeup. She is yours, all yours.

A flash of movement cuts the picture; the camera is nearly lost from your arms as she skitters backward. Then you see the muzzle and hardwood butt of the shotgun, and Jay's gloved right hand as he hits her again, and you hold the shot as she falls and you're down on the ground with her, the camera looking up across her body into a night sky punctured by distant stars. You can see her tongue through the open left side of her face. One of her eyes is blinking, out of control; the other one is gone. You know she has never been more beautiful than now. She is yours, and will be yours forever.

You watch as Jay joins you at her side. He lowers the shotgun; the barrel slides along her stomach, her chest, her neck, to the tip of her chin. Finally its hot and smoking mouth kisses hers. And as you hold her in lingering close-up, he shoves the barrel down. You hear the crack of teeth and bone and then the shotgun kicks and there is a shriek and you are caught in a warm wet rain that washes over the lens until you can see nothing, nothing, nothing at all but red.

You hear laughter and you know that it is your own. You can no longer see, but you can run, and you drop the camera, hear the shatter of glass and plastic, the whir of the eject as you grab at the tape and you run, you run and run into the darkness, into the night until at last you can see a distant light, and you run in its direction. You hold on to your tape and run.

Finally you see the sanitation trucks lined before you on this side of Union Square. You watch as body bags are carried out by men in gasmasks and white camouflaged parkas, and dumped onto the fire, sending smoke, and the smell, over you. No matter how far you run, the smell will follow you. It recalls you to another morning. You arrived home from the magazine after drinking most of the night; Miranda had called just before midnight, wondering where you were. When you arrived, the apartment was steeped in this same aroma. The soldiers stood warming themselves around the flames. Miranda was gone. You could count the bullet holes across the lobby, the stairway, and the walls of the apartment itself; you could count the bodies sprawled in the streets, fuel for the flames. You had seen it all before; you had seen it all, but you had never believed in it. It wasn't real; it could never be real. But it was. The films, the videos, were just the coming attractions, a sneak preview of the epic now playing around the clock in the world outside.

You approach the last of the trucks. A sanitation worker hefts another body bag from its wide belly, drops the heavy plastic cocoon unceremoniously to the pavement.

"Dead." This is what you say to him, although you meant to say something more.

"What was your first clue?" He turns and walks toward the Square. The fire rages high, a false dawn. The workers, and the soldiers who guard them, look at the flames, and not at you.

You get down on your knees and tear open the body bag. The smell of the corpse envelops you. When you touch it your hands find something soft and wet. The first bite sticks in your throat and when you try to swallow, you almost gag.

You will have to go very slowly.

You will have to forget most everything you have ever learned.

for *Steve Bissette*

ABOUT THE EDITORS

John Skipp and Craig Spector are the editors of both *Books of the Dead*. They also write books, music, essays, and films; live life to the fullest; and await the Millennium. They like Ren & Stimpy, the Thrill Kill Kult, Toy Matinee, and their girlfriends . . . not precisely in that order.

They hope for the best and prepare for the worst.

They currently reside in L.A.